A COLD
CREEK NOEL

BY
RAEANNE THAYNE

MILLS
&BOON

First published in Great Britain 2013
by Mills & Boon, an imprint of Harlequin (UK) Limited,
Eton House, 18-24 Paradise Road, Richmond, Surrey TW9 1SR

© RaeAnne Thayne 2012

ISBN: 978 0 263 90164 1

23-1213

Harlequin (UK) policy is to use papers that are natural, renewable and recyclable products and made from wood grown in sustainable forests. The logging and manufacturing processes conform to the legal environmental regulations of the country of origin.

Printed and bound in Spain
by Blackprint CPI, Barcelona

RaeAnne Thayne finds inspiration in the beautiful northern Utah mountains, where she lives with her husband and three children. Her books have won numerous honors, including RITA® Award nominations from Romance Writers of America and a Career Achievement Award from *RT Book Reviews*. RaeAnne loves to hear from readers and can be contacted through her website, www.raeannethayne.com.

To Tennis and Kjersten Watkins, with love.
We can't wait to see what life has in store
for the two of you!

Chapter One

"Come on, Luke. Come on, buddy. Hang in there."

Her wipers beat back the sleet and snow as Caidy Bowman drove through the streets of Pine Gulch, Idaho, on a stormy December afternoon. Only a few inches had fallen but the roads were still dangerous, slick as spit. For only a moment, she risked lifting one hand off the steering wheel of her truck and patting the furry shape whimpering on the seat beside her.

"We're almost there. We'll get you fixed up, I swear it. Just hang on, bud. A few more minutes. That's all."

The young border collie looked at her with a trust she didn't deserve in his black eyes and she frowned, her guilt as bitter and salty as the solution the snowplows had put down on the roads.

Luke's injuries were *her* fault. She should have been watching him. She knew the half-grown pup had a curious streak a mile wide—and a tendency not to listen to her when he had an itch to investigate something.

She was working on that obedience issue and they had made good strides the past few weeks, but one moment of inattention could be disastrous, as the past hour had amply demonstrated. She didn't know if it was arrogance on her part, thinking her training of him was enough, or just irresponsibility. Either way, she should have kept him far away from Festus's pen. The bull was ornery as a rattlesnake on a hot skillet and didn't take kindly to curious young border collies nosing around his turf.

Alerted by Luke's barking and then the bull's angry snort, she had raced to old Festus's pen just in time to watch Luke jig the wrong way and the bull stomp down hard on his haunches with a sickening crunch of bone.

Her hands tightened on the steering wheel and she cursed under her breath as the last light before the vet's office turned yellow when she was still too far away to gun through it. She was almost tempted to keep going. Even if she were nabbed for running a red light by Pine Gulch's finest, she could probably talk her way out of a ticket, considering her brother was the police chief and would certainly understand this was an emergency. If she were pulled over, though, it would mean an inevitable delay and she just didn't have time for that.

The light finally changed and she took off fast, the back tires fishtailing on the icy road. She would just have to trust the salt bags she carried for traction in the bed of the pickup would do the job. Even the four-wheel drive of the truck was useless against black ice.

Finally, she reached the small square building that held the Pine Gulch Veterinary Clinic and pulled the pickup to the side doors where she knew it was only a short transfer inside to the treatment area.

She briefly considered carrying him in by herself, but it had taken the careful efforts of both her and her brother Ridge to slide a blanket under Luke and lift him into the seat of her pickup. They could bring out the stretcher and cart, she decided.

She rubbed Luke's white neck. "I'm going to go get some help, okay? You just hold tight."

He made a small whimper of pain and she bit down hard on her lip as her insides clenched with fear. She loved the little guy, even if he was nosy as a crow and even smarter, which was probably why his stubbornness was such a frustration.

He trusted her to take care of him and she refused to let him die.

She hurried to the front door, barely noticing the wind-driven sleet that gouged at her even under her Stetson.

Warm air washed over her when she opened the door, familiar with the scent of animals and antiseptic mixed in a stomach-churning sort of way with new paint.

"Hey, Caidy." A woman in green scrubs rushed to the door. "You made good time from the River Bow."

"Hi, Joni. I may have broken a few traffic laws, but this is an emergency."

"After you called, I warned Ben you were on your way and what the situation was. He's been getting ready for you. I'll let him know you've arrived."

Caidy waited, feeling the weight of each second ticking away. The new vet had only been in town a few weeks and already he had made changes to the clinic. Maybe she was just being contrary, but she had liked things better when Doc Harris ran the place. The whole reception area looked different. The cheerful yellow walls had been painted over with a boring white and the weathered, comfortable, old eighties-era couch and chairs were gone, replaced by modern benches covered in a slate vinyl that probably deflected anything a veterinarian's patients could leak on it. A display of Christmas gifts appropriate for pets, including a massive stocking filled to the top with toys and a giant rawhide bone that looked as if it came from a dinosaur, hung in one corner.

Most significant, the reception area used to sit out in the open but it was now stuck behind a solid half wall topped with a glass partition.

It made sense to modernize from an efficiency point of view, but she had found the comfortably worn look of the office before more appealing.

Not that she cared about any of that right now, with Luke lying out in her truck, cold and hurt and probably afraid.

She shifted impatiently. Where was the man? Trimming his blasted nails? Only a few moments had passed but every second delay was too much. Just when she was about call out to Joni to see what was taking so long, the door into the treatment area opened and the new vet appeared.

"Where's the dog?" he asked abruptly, and she had only a vague impression of a frowning dark-haired man in blue scrubs.

"Still out in my truck."

He narrowed his gaze. "Why? I can't treat him out there."

She wanted to take that giant rawhide bone out of that stocking and bean him with it. "Yes, I'm aware of that," she said, fighting down her frustration. "I didn't want to move him. I'm afraid something might be broken."

"I thought he was gored."

She wasn't sure what, exactly, she had said in that frantic call to let Joni know she was on her way.

"He did end up on the business end of a bull at some point. I'm not sure if that was before or after that bull stepped on him."

His mouth tightened. "A young dog has no business running wild in the same vicinity as a dangerous bull."

His criticism stung far too close to her own guilt for comfort. "We're a working ranch at the River Bow, Dr. Caldwell. Accidents like this can happen."

"They shouldn't," he snapped before turning around and heading back through the treatment area. She followed him, heartily wishing for Doc Harris right now. The grizzled old vet had taken care of every dog she had ever owned, from her very first border collie and best friend, Sadie, whom she still had.

Doc Harris was her friend and mentor. If he had been here, he would have wrapped her in a warm hug that smelled of liniment and cherry Life Savers and promised her everything would be all right.

Dr. Ben Caldwell was nothing like Dr. Harris. He was abrasive and arrogant and she already heartily disliked him.

His eyes narrowed with surprise and displeasure when he saw she had followed him from the waiting room to the clinic area.

"This way is quicker," she explained. "I'm parked by the side door. I thought it would be easier to transport him on the stretcher from there."

He didn't say anything, only charged through the side door she indicated. She trotted after him, wondering how the Pine Gulch animal kingdom would get along without the kindness and compassion Dr. Harris had been renowned for.

Without waiting for her, he opened the door of the truck. As she watched, it was as if a different man had suddenly taken over. His harsh, set features seemed to ease and even the stiff set of his shoulders relaxed.

"Hello there," he crooned from the open vehicle door to the dog. "You've got yourself into a mess, haven't you?"

Even through his pain, Luke responded to the gentle-sounding stranger by trying hard to wag his tail. There was no room for both of them on the passenger side, so she went around to the driver's side and opened that door, intent on helping to lift the dog from there. By the time she made it that short distance, Dr. Caldwell had already slipped a transfer sheet under the dog and was gripping the edges.

His hands were big, she noticed, with a little light area of skin where a wedding ring once had been.

She knew a little about him from the gossip around town. It was hard to miss it when he was currently staying at the Cold Creek Inn—owned and operated by her sister-in-law Laura, married to Caidy's brother Taft.

Though Laura usually didn't gossip about her guests, over dinner last week her other brother, Trace—who made it his business as police chief to find out about everyone moving into Pine Gulch—had interrogated her so skillfully, Laura probably didn't realize what she had revealed.

From that conversation, Caidy had learned Ben Caldwell had two children, a girl and a boy, ages nine and five, respectively, and he had been a widower for two years.

Why on earth he had suddenly pulled up stakes to settle in a quiet town like Pine Gulch was a mystery to everyone. In her experience, people who came to this little corner of Idaho in the shadow of the Tetons were either looking for something or running away.

None of that was her business, she reminded herself. The only thing she cared about was the way he treated her dogs. Judging by how carefully he moved his hands over Luke's injuries, he appeared competent and even kind, at least to animals—something she generally considered a far more important character indicator than how a man treated other people.

"Okay, Luke. Just lie still, there's a good boy." He spoke in a low, calm voice. "We're going to move you now. Easy. Easy."

He handed the stretcher across the cab to her and then reached for the transfer sheet. "I'm going to lift him slightly and then you can slide the board under him. Slowly. Yes. That's it."

She had plenty of experience transferring injured animals. Years of experience. It bothered her to be treated as if she didn't know the first thing about this kind of emergency care, but now didn't seem the time to correct him.

Together they carried the stretcher into the emergency treatment room and set the dog gingerly down on the exam table.

She didn't like the pain in Luke's eyes. It reminded her a lot of how Lucky, her brother Taft's little beagle cross, had looked right after the car accident that had nearly killed him.

Now Lucky was happy as a pig in clover, she reminded herself. He lived with Taft and Laura and their two children at Taft's house near the mouth of Cold

Creek Canyon and thought he ruled the universe. If Lucky could survive his brush with death, she couldn't see any reason for Luke to do otherwise.

"That's a nasty puncture wound. At least an inch or two deep. I'm surprised it's not deeper."

That could be because she had managed to pull Luke to safety before Festus could finish taking his bad mood out on a helpless dog.

"What about the leg? Can you save it?"

"I'm going to have to x-ray before I can answer that. How far are you prepared to go for his care?"

It took her a moment to realize what he was asking in his blunt way. A difficult part of life as a vet was the knowledge that, although a vet might have the power to treat an animal successfully, sometimes the owner's ability—or willingness, for that matter—to pay was the ultimate decision maker.

"Whatever is necessary," she answered stiffly. "I don't care about the cost. Just do what you have to do."

He nodded, his attention still on her dog, and she wanted to think his hard expression thawed slightly, like a tiny crackle of ice on the edge of a much deeper lake.

"Regardless of what the X-ray shows, his treatment is going to take a few hours. You can go. Leave your number with Joni and I'll have her call you when I know more."

"No. I'll wait."

That surprise in his blue eyes annoyed the heck out of her. Did he think she would just abandon her dog here with a stranger for a couple of hours while she went off to have her hair done?

"Your choice."

"I can help you back here. I've…had some training

and I often helped Doc Harris. I actually worked here when I was a teenager."

If her life had gone a little more according to plan, *she* might have been the one taking over Doc Harris's clinic, though she hoped she wouldn't be as surly and unlikable as this new veterinarian.

"That won't be necessary." Dr. Caldwell dismissed all her hopes and dreams and volunteer work at the clinic as if they meant nothing. "Joni and I can handle it. If you insist on waiting, you can go ahead and have a seat in the waiting room."

What a jerk. She could push the matter. She *was* paying for the treatment here, after all. If she wanted to stay with her dog, there was nothing Dr. Ben No-Bedside-Manner Caldwell could do about it. But she didn't want to waste time and possibly jeopardize Luke's treatment.

"Fine," she muttered. She turned and pushed through the doors into the waiting room, seething with frustration.

After quickly sending a message to Ridge updating him on the situation and reminding her brother he would have to pick his daughter, Destry, up from the bus stop, she plopped onto one of the uncomfortable gray benches and grabbed a magazine off the side table.

She was leafing through it, barely even registering the headlines in her worry over her dog, when the bells on the door chimed and a little boy of about five burst through, followed a little more slowly by an older girl.

"Daaad! We're here!"

"Hush." A round, cheerful-looking woman who looked to be in her early sixties followed more slowly. "You know better than that, young man. Your father might be in the middle of a procedure."

"Can I go back and find him?" the girl asked.

"Because Joni isn't out here either, they must both be busy. He won't want to be bothered. You two sit down here and I'll go back to let him know we're here."

"I could go," the girl said a little sulkily, but she plopped onto the bench across from Caidy. Like father, like daughter, she thought. This was obviously the new vet's family, and his daughter, at least, seemed to share more than blue eyes with her father.

"Sit down," the girl ordered her brother. The boy didn't quite stick his tongue out at his sister, but it was a close one. Instead, he ignored her—probably a much worse insult, if Caidy remembered her own childhood with three pesky brothers—and wandered over to stand directly in front of Caidy.

The little boy had a widow's peak in his brown hair and huge dark-lashed blue eyes. A Caldwell trait, apparently.

"Hi." He beamed at her. "I'm Jack Caldwell. My sister's name is Ava. Who are you?"

"My name is Caidy," she answered.

"My dad's a dog doctor."

"Not just dogs," the girl corrected. "He's also a cat doctor. And sometimes even horses and cows."

"I know," Caidy answered. "That's why I'm here."

"Is your dog sick?" Jack asked her.

"In a way. He was hurt on our ranch. Your dad is working on him now."

"He's really good," the girl said with obvious pride. "I bet your dog will be just fine."

"I hope so."

"Our dog was hit by a car once and my dad fixed him and now he's all better," Jack said. "Well, except he only has three legs. His name is Tri. My dad says it's 'cause he always tries hard, even though he only has three legs."

Despite her worry, she managed a smile, more than a little charmed by the boy—and by the idea of the taciturn veterinarian showing any hint of sweetness.

"Tri means three," Ava informed her in a haughty sort of tone. "You know, like a *tri*cycle has three wheels."

"Good to know."

Before the children could say anything else, the older woman came back through the door leading out of the treatment room, her features set in a rueful smile.

"Looks like we're on our own for dinner, kids. Your dad is busy fixing an injured dog and he's going to be a while. We'll just go catch some dinner and then head back to the hotel for homework and bed."

"You're staying at the Cold Creek Inn, aren't you?" Caidy asked.

The other woman looked a bit wary as she nodded. "I'm sorry. Have we met?"

"I'm Caidy Bowman. My sister-in-law Laura runs the inn."

"You're Chief Bowman's sister?" There was a definite warmth in the woman's voice now, Caidy noticed wryly. Her charmer of a brother often had that effect on those of the female persuasion, no matter their age.

"I am. Both Chief Bowmans." With one brother who was the police chief and the other who headed up the fire department, not much exciting happened in town without someone in her family being in the thick of it.

"How nice to meet you. I'm Anne Michaels. I'm Dr. Caldwell's housekeeper. Or I will be when he finally gets into his house. With the maids at the inn cleaning our rooms for us, there's not much for me to do in that department. Right now I'm just the nanny, I suppose."

"Oh?"

The woman apparently didn't need any more encouragement than that simple syllable. "Dr. Caldwell is building a house on Cold Creek Road. He was supposed to close on it last week, but the contractor ran into some problems and here we are, still staying at the inn. Which is lovely, don't get me wrong, but it's still a hotel. After three weeks, all of us are a little tired of it. And now it looks like we'll be there until after the New Year. Christmas in a hotel. Can you imagine such a thing?"

Maybe that explained the man's grouchiness. She felt a little pang of sympathy, then she remembered how he had basically shoved her out of the treatment area. No, he was probably born with that temperament. He and Festus would get along just fine.

"It must be very frustrating for all of you."

"You don't know the half of it. Two children in a hotel, even a couple of rooms, for all those weeks is just too much. They need space to run. All children do. Why, in San Jose, the children had a huge backyard, complete with a pool and a swing set that rivaled the equipment at the nearest park."

"Is that where you're from, then? California?"

Anne Michaels nodded and Caidy thought she saw a note of wistfulness in the woman's eyes that didn't bode well for the chances of Dr. Caldwell's housekeeper-slash-nanny sticking around in Pine Gulch.

Anne watched the children, who were paying them no heed as they played a game on an electronic device Ava had pulled out of her backpack.

"Yes. I'm from California, born and bred. Not Dr. Caldwell. He's from back East. Chicago way. But he left everything without a backward look to head west for veterinary school at UC-Davis and that's where he met the late Mrs. Caldwell. They hired me to help out around the house when she was pregnant with little Jack there and I've been with them ever since. Those poor children needed me more than ever after their mother died. Dr. Caldwell too. That was a terrible time, I tell you."

"I'm sure."

"When he decided to move here to Idaho, he gave me the option of leaving his employment with a glowing recommendation, but I just couldn't do it. I love those children, you know?"

Caidy could relate. She loved her niece Destry as fiercely as if the girl were her own. Stepping in to help raise her after her mother walked out on Ridge and their daughter had created a powerful bond between them as unshakable as the Tetons.

"I'm sure you do."

Anne Michaels gave a rueful shake of her head. "Look at me, going on to a perfect stranger. Staying at that hotel all these weeks is making me batty!"

"Perhaps you could find a temporary rental situation until the house is finished," she suggested.

"That's what I wanted to do but Ben doesn't think we can find anyone willing to rent us a place for only a few weeks, especially over the holidays."

Caidy thought of the foreman's cottage, empty for the past six months since the young married couple Ridge had hired to help around the ranch had moved on to take a job at a Texas ranch.

It was furnished with three bedrooms and would probably fit the Caldwells' needs perfectly, but she was hesitant to mention it. She didn't like the man. Why on earth would she want him living only a quarter mile away?

"I could ask around for you if you'd like. We have a few vacation rentals in town that might be available. At least it might give you a little breathing space over the holidays until the house is finished."

"How kind you are!" Mrs. Michaels exclaimed.

A fine guilt pinched at her. If she were truly kind, she would immediately offer the foreman's cottage.

"Everyone here in Pine Gulch has been so nice and welcoming to us," the woman went on.

"I hope you feel at home here."

Again that wistfulness drifted across the woman's features like an autumn leaf tossed by the breeze, but she blinked it away. "I'm guessing the dog Dr. Caldwell is working on back there is yours, then."

Caidy nodded. "He had a run-in with a bull. When you pit a forty-pound dog against a ton of beef, the bull usually wins."

She should be back there with him. Darn it. If she were better at handling confrontations, she would have told Dr. Arrogant that she wasn't going anywhere. Instead, she was sitting out here fretting.

"He's a wonderful veterinarian, my dear. I'm sure your pet will be better before you know it."

The border collies at the River Bow Ranch weren't exactly pets—they were a vital part of the workload. Except for Sadie, anyway, who was too old to work the cattle anymore. She didn't bother to correct the woman, nor did she express any of her own doubts about the new veterinarian's competence.

"I'm hungry, Mrs. Michaels. When are we going to eat?" Bored with the game apparently, Jack had wandered back to them.

"I think your father is going to be busy for a while yet. Why don't you and Ava and I go find something? Perhaps dinner at the café tonight would be fun and we can pick something up for your father for later."

"Can I have one of the sweet rolls?" he asked, his eyes lighting up as if it were already Christmas morning.

The housekeeper laughed. "We'll have to see about that. I'd say the café's business in sweet rolls has tripled since we came to town, thanks to you alone."

"They are delish," Caidy agreed, smiling at the very cute boy.

Mrs. Michaels rose to her feet with a creak and a pop of some joint. "It was lovely to meet you, Caidy Bowman."

"I'm happy to meet you too. And I'll keep my eye out for a suitable vacation rental."

"You'll need to take that up with Dr. Caldwell, but thank you."

The woman seemed to be efficient, Caidy thought as she watched her herd the children out the door.

The reception room seemed even more bleak and colorless after the trio left. Though it was just past six, the night was already dark on this, one of the shortest days of the year. Caidy fidgeted, leafing aimlessly through her magazine for a few moments longer, then finally closed it with a rustle of pages and tossed it back onto the pile.

Darn it. That was her dog back there. She couldn't sit out here doing nothing. At the very least she deserved to know what was going on. She gathered her courage, took a deep breath and pushed through the door.

Chapter Two

Ben made the last stitch to close the incision on the puncture wound, his head throbbing and his shoulders tight from the long day that had started with an emergency call to treat an ailing horse at four in the morning.

He would have loved a nice evening with his kids and then a few hours of zone-out time watching basketball on the hotel television set. Even if he had to turn the sound low so he didn't wake up Jack, the idea sounded heavenly.

The past week had been a rough one, busy and demanding. This was what he wanted, he reminded himself. Even though the workload was heavy, he finally had the chance to build his own practice, to forge new relationships and become part of a community.

"There. That should do it for now."

"What a mess. After seeing how close that puncture

wound was to the liver, I can't believe he survived," Joni said.

He didn't want to admit to his assistant—who, after three weeks, still seemed to approve of the job he was doing—that the dog's condition was still touch and go.

"I think he's going to make it," she went on, ever the optimist. "Unlike that poor Newfoundland earlier."

All his frustration of earlier in the afternoon came surging back as he began dressing the wound. A tragedy, that was. The beautiful dog had jumped out of the back of a moving pickup truck and been hit by the car driving behind it.

That dog hadn't been as lucky as Luke here. Her injuries were just too severe and she had died on this very treatment table.

What had really pissed him off had been the attitude of the owner, more concerned at the loss of all the money he had invested in the animal than in the loss of life.

"Neither accident would have happened if not for irresponsible owners."

Joni, busy cleaning up the inevitable mess he always left behind during a surgery, looked a little surprised at his vehemence.

"I agree when it comes to Artie Palmer. He's an idiot who should have his privileges to own any animals revoked. But not Caidy Bowman. She's the last one I would call an irresponsible owner. She trains dogs and horses at the River Bow. Nobody around here does a better job."

"She didn't train this one very well, did she, if he was running wild and tangled with a bull?"

"Apparently not."

He turned at the new voice and found the dog's

owner standing in the doorway from the reception area, her lovely features taut. He swore under his breath. He meant what he said, but he supposed it didn't need to be said to *her*.

"I thought I suggested you wait in the other room."

"A suggestion? Is that what you city vets call that?" She shrugged. "I'm not particularly good at doing as I'm told, Dr. Caldwell."

Sometime during the process of caring for her dog, Ben had come to the uncomfortable realization that he had acted like a jerk to her. He never insisted owners wait outside the treatment room unless he thought they might have weak stomachs. So why had he changed policy for Caidy Bowman?

Something about her made him a little nervous. He couldn't quite put a finger on it, but it might have something to do with those impossibly green eyes and the sweet little tilt to her mouth.

"We just finished. I was about to call you back."

"I'm glad I finally disregarded your strongly worded *suggestion,* then. May I?"

He gestured agreement and she approached the table, where the dog was still working off the effects of the anesthesia.

"There's my brave boy. Oh, Luke." She smoothed a hand over the dog's head. The dog's eyes opened slightly then closed again and his breathing slowed, as if he could rest comfortably now, knowing she was near.

"It will probably take another half hour or so for the rest of the anesthesia to wear off and then we'll have to keep him here, at least overnight."

"Will someone stay with him?"

At his practice in San Jose, he and a technician would alternate stopping in every few hours through the night when they had very ill dogs staying at the clinic, but he hadn't had time yet to get fully staffed.

He nodded, watching his plans for a nice steak dinner and a basketball game in the hotel room go up in smoke. He had become pretty used to the cot in his office lately. Whatever would he do without Mrs. Michaels?

"Someone will be here with him. Don't worry about that."

A look of surprise flickered in her eyes. He couldn't figure out why for a moment, until he realized she was reacting to his soft tone. He really must have been a jackass to her.

"I'm sorry about…earlier." Apologies didn't come easily. He could probably thank his stiff, humorless grandfather for that, but this one seemed necessary. "About not letting you come in during the treatment, I mean. I should have. And about what I said just now. I'm usually not so…harsh. It's been a particularly hard day and I'm afraid I may have been taking it out on you."

She blinked a little but concealed her emotions behind an impassive look. For some reason, that made him feel even more like an idiot, a sensation he didn't like at all.

"You were able to save his leg. I thought for sure you would have to amputate."

"He wouldn't be much use as a ranch dog, then, would he?"

Her look was as cool as the December night. "Probably not. Isn't it a good thing that's not the only thing that matters to me?"

So she wasn't like his previous client, who hadn't cared about his injured dog—only dollars and cents.

"I was able to pin the leg for now, but there's no guarantee it will heal properly. We still might have to take it. He was lucky, if you want the truth. Insanely lucky. I don't know how he made it through a run-in with a bull in one piece. His injuries could have been much worse."

"What about where he was gored?"

"The bull missed all vital organs. The puncture wound is only a couple inches deep. I guess the bull wasn't that serious."

"You would think otherwise if you had been there. He definitely was seeing red. After I pulled the dog out, he rammed the fence so hard he knocked one of the poles out of its foundation."

She pulled the dog out? Crazy woman, to mess with a bull on a rampage. What was she thinking?

"Looks like he's coming around," he said, not about to enter that particular fray.

The dog whimpered and Caidy Bowman leaned down, her dark hair almost a match to the dog's coat. "Hey there. You're in a fix now, aren't you, Luke-my-boy. You'll be all right. I know it hurts now and you're confused and scared but Dr. Caldwell fixed you up and before you know it you'll be running around the ranch with King and Sadie and all the others."

Though he had paperwork to complete, he couldn't seem to wrench himself away. He stood watching her interact with the dog and winced to himself at how quickly he had misjudged her. By the gentleness of her tone and the comforting way she smoothed a hand over his fur, it was obvious the woman cared about her animal and was not inexperienced with injuries.

Next time maybe he wouldn't be quick to make surly comments when he was having a miserable day.

She smelled delicious, like vanilla splashed on wild-flowers. The scent of her drifted to him, a bright counterpoint to the sometimes unpleasant smells of a busy veterinary clinic.

It was an unsettling discovery. He didn't want to notice anything about her. Not the sweet way she smelled or the elegant curve of her neck or how, when she tucked her hair behind her ear, she unveiled a tiny beauty mark just below the lobe...

He caught the direction of his thoughts and shut them down, appalled at himself. He forced himself to move away and block the sound of her low voice crooning to the dog.

He had almost forgotten about his technician until she came out of the employee changing room, shoving her arms through the sleeves of her parka. "Do you mind if I go? I'm sorry. It's just past six-thirty and I'm supposed to be at my Bible study Christmas party in half an hour and I still have to run home and pick up my cookies for the swap."

"No. Get out of here. I'm sorry I kept you late."

"Wasn't your fault."

"Blame my curious dog," Caidy said with an apologetic smile that didn't mask the concern in her eyes.

Joni shrugged. "Accidents happen, especially on a ranch."

Ben felt another twist of guilt. She was right. Even the most careful pet owner couldn't prevent everything.

"Thanks, Ben. You both have a good night," Joni said.

"I'll walk you out," he said.

She rolled her eyes—this was an argument they had been having since he arrived. His clinic in San Jose hadn't been in the best part of the city and he would always make sure the women who worked for him made it safely to their cars in the parking lot.

It was probably an old-fashioned habit, but when he had been in vet school, a fellow student and friend had been assaulted on the way to her car after a late-night class and had ended up dropping out of school.

The cold air outside the clinic blew a little bit of energy into him. The snow of earlier had slowed to just a few flurries. The few houses around his clinic blinked their cheerful holiday lights and he regretted again that he hadn't strung a few strands in the window of the clinic.

Joni's SUV was covered in snow and he helped her brush it off.

"Thank you, Dr. Caldwell," Joni said with a smile. "You're the only employer I've ever had who scrapes my windows."

"I don't know what I'd do without you right now," he said truthfully. "I just don't want you getting into an accident on the way home."

"Thanks. Have a good night. Call me if you need me to spell you during the night."

He nodded and waved her off, then returned to the office invigorated from the cold air. He pulled open the door and caught the incongruous notes of a soft melody.

Caidy was humming, he realized. He paused to listen and it took just a moment for him to recognize the tune as "Greensleeves." He was afraid to move, not wanting to intrude on the moment. The notes seemed to seep through him, sweet and pure and somehow peaceful amid the harsh lights and complicated equipment of the clinic.

Judging by her humming, he would guess Caidy Bowman had a lovely voice.

He didn't think he had made a sound, but she somehow sensed him anyway. She looked up and a delicate pink flush washed over her cheeks. "Sorry. You must think I'm ridiculous, humming to a dog. He started to get agitated and…it seemed to calm him."

No surprise there. The melody had done the same to *him*. "Looks like he's sleeping again. I can take things from here if you need to go."

She looked uncertain. "I could stay. My brother and niece can handle chores tonight for the rest of my animals."

"We've got this covered. Don't worry. He'll be well taken care of, Ms. Bowman."

"Just Caidy. Please. No one calls me Ms. anything."

"Caidy, then."

"Is someone coming to relieve you?"

"I'm not fully staffed yet and Joni has her party tonight and then her husband and kids to get back to. No big deal. I have a cot in my office. I should be fine. When we have overnight emergency cases, I make do there."

He had again succeeded in surprising her, he saw.

"What about your children?" she asked.

"They'll be fine with Mrs. Michaels. It's only for a night."

"I… Thank you."

"You'll have a hefty bill for overnight care," he warned.

"I expected it. I worked here a decade ago and know how much things used to cost—and I've seen those charges go up in the years since." She paused. "I hate to leave him."

"He'll be fine. Don't worry. Come on. I'll walk you out."

"Is that a service you provide for every female who comes through your office?"

Close enough. "I need to lock up anyway."

She gathered her coat and shrugged into it, and then he led her back the way he had just come. The moon was filtering through the clouds, painting lovely patterns of pale light on the new snow.

Caidy Bowman drove a well-used late-model pickup truck with a king cab that was covered in mud. Bales of hay were stacked two high in the back.

"Be careful. The roads are likely to be slick after the snows of earlier."

"I've been driving these roads since before I turned sixteen. I can handle a little snow."

"I'm sure you can. I just don't want you to be the next one in need of stitching."

"Not much chance of that, but thank you for your concern. And for all you've done today. I'm sorry you won't see much of your children."

"The clinic is closed tomorrow. I can spend the whole day with them. I suppose we'll have to go look for a temporary furnished house somewhere or I'm going to have a mutiny on my hands from Mrs. Michaels, which would be a nightmare."

She opened her mouth, then closed it again, and he had the distinct impression she was waging some internal debate. Her gaze shifted to the door they had just exited through and back to him, then she drew in a breath.

"We have an empty foreman's cottage on the River Bow where you could stay."

The words spilled out of her, almost as if she had been trying to hold them back. He barely noticed, stunned by the offer.

"It's nothing fancy but it's fully furnished," she went on quickly. "It does only have three bedrooms, but if you took one and Mrs. Michaels took the other, the children could share."

"Whoa. Hold on. How do you know Mrs. Michaels? And who told you we might be looking for a place?"

"We met in the waiting room earlier. I knew you were staying at the inn because my sister-in-law Laura runs it."

If not for that moment of sweetness when he had found her humming a soothing song to her dog, he would have had a tough time believing the warm and welcoming innkeeper could be any relation to this prickly woman.

"Anyway, your housekeeper mentioned you might be looking for a place. I, uh, immediately thought of the foreman's cottage on our ranch. Nobody's using it right now, though I do try to stop in once a week or so to keep the dust down. Like I said, it's not much."

"We could manage. Are you certain?"

"I'll have to ask my brother first. Though all four of us share ownership of the ranch, Ridge is really the one in charge. I don't think he'll say no, though. Why would he?"

He didn't understand this woman. He had been extraordinarily rude to her, yet she was offering to help solve all his domestic problems in one fell swoop.

"I'm astonished, Ms. Bowman. Er, Caidy. Why would you make such an offer to a complete stranger?"

"You saved my dog," she said simply. "Besides that, I liked Mrs. Michaels and I gather she's had enough of hotel living. And how will St. Nick find your children in a hotel, as lovely as the Cold Creek Inn might be these days? They should have a proper house for the holidays, where they can play."

"I agree. That was the plan all along, but circumstances haven't exactly cooperated."

He had planned to spend the entire next day looking around for somewhere that better met their needs. He never expected the answer would fall right in his lap. A less cynical man might even call it a Christmas miracle.

"I still have to talk to Ridge. I can let you know his answer in the morning when I come to check on Luke."

"Thank you."

She gave him a hesitant smile just as the moonlight shifted. The light combined with her smile managed to transform her features from pretty to extraordinarily beautiful.

"Good night. Thank you again for your hard work."

"You're welcome."

He watched her drive away, her headlights cutting through the darkness. When he had agreed to buy James Harris's practice, he had been seeking a quiet, easy community to raise his family, a place where they could settle in and become part of things.

Pine Gulch had already provided a few more surprises than he expected—and he suddenly suspected Caidy Bowman might be one more.

Chapter Three

"You say the new vet only needs a place to stay for a few weeks?"

Caidy nodded at her oldest brother, who stood at the sink loading his and Destry's supper dishes into the dishwasher. "That's my understanding. He's building a new house on Cold Creek Road. I'm guessing it's in that new development near Taft's place. Apparently, it was supposed to be finished before he took the job, but it's behind schedule. Now it won't be ready until after Christmas."

"That's a nice area. Heck of a view. I imagine his house is probably a good sight better than our foreman's cottage."

"They're at the inn now. I got the impression the children and the housekeeper might be going a little stir-crazy there."

Ridge straightened and gave her a look she recognized well. It was his patented *What were you thinking?* look. He was ten years older than she was and she loved him dearly. He had stepped in after their parents died and had raised her for the last few years of high school and she would never be able to repay him for being her rock, even when his own marriage was faltering. He was tough and hard on the outside and sweet as could be underneath all the layers.

He still drove her crazy sometimes.

"You ever stop to think that Laura might not be too thrilled if you go around finding other lodging arrangements for her paying guests?"

"I called her already and she was cool with it. I know it's lost business, but all I had to do was paint the mental picture of Alex and Maya cooped up in a couple of hotel rooms for weeks on end—including through Christmas—and she had complete sympathy for Dr. Caldwell and his housekeeper. She thought it was a great idea."

She didn't bother telling her brother that Taft's wife had also dropped a couple of matchmaking hints a mile wide about how gorgeous the new vet was. He was kind to animals and he loved his kids. What more did she need? Laura had implied.

Ridge didn't need to know that. Much as she loved both of her sisters-in-law and considered Laura and Becca perfect for each respective twin, she didn't need her brothers joining in and trying to look around for prospective partners for her. The very idea of what they might come up with gave her chills.

After one of his long, thoughtful pauses, Ridge finally nodded. "Can't see any harm in Dr. Caldwell and his family moving in for a few weeks. The house is only sitting there empty. I can run the tractor down the lane to make sure it's cleared up for them. It might need the cobwebs swept and a little airing out."

"I'll take care of everything tomorrow after I check on Luke."

So it was settled, then. She had to fight the urge to give a giant, cartoon-style gulp. What had she just gotten herself into? She didn't want the man here.

Okay, he had been a little less like a jackass toward the end of her visit to the clinic with Luke, but that didn't mean she was obligated to invite him to move in down the road, for Pete's sake.

She still wasn't quite sure what had motivated her offer. Maybe that little spark of compassion in his blue eyes when he had tended to Luke with that surprising gentleness. Or maybe it was simply that she couldn't resist his cute son's charm.

Whatever the reason, they would only be there a few weeks. She likely wouldn't even see the man, especially as it appeared he spent most of his time at the veterinary clinic. And she could be comfortable knowing she had done her good deed for the day. Wasn't Christmas the perfect time for a little welcoming generosity?

"What did you think of his doctoring?" Ridge asked.

She thought of Luke and his carefully bandaged injuries. "He's not Doc Harris but I suppose he'll do."

Ridge chuckled. "You'll never think anybody is as good as Doc Harris. The two of you have taken care of a lot of animals together."

She had loved working at the vet clinic when she was in high school. It was just about the only thing that had kept her going after her parents died, those quiet moments when she would be holding a sick or injured animal and feeling some measure of peace.

"He's a good man. Dr. Caldwell has some pretty big boots to fill," she answered.

"From rumors I've been hearing around town, he's doing a good job of it so far."

She didn't want to talk about the veterinarian anymore. It was bad enough she couldn't seem to think about anything else since she had left the clinic.

"What were you saying to Destry after I started clearing the dishes? I heard something about the wagon," Caidy said.

He glanced through the open doorway into the dining room, where Destry was bent over the table working on a homework assignment about holiday traditions in Europe.

"Des asked me if she could invite Gabi and a couple of their other friends over for a wagon ride Sunday night. She suggested caroling to the neighbors."

She never should have shared with Destry her memories of doing that very thing with their parents when she and the boys were young. "What did you tell her?"

He didn't answer, but he didn't need to. She could tell by his expression that he had given in. Ridge might be a hard man when it came to their cattle and the ranch, but when it came to his daughter he was soft as new taffy.

"You're a good father, Ridge."

"She loves Christmas," he finally said. "What can I do?"

The rest of them weren't quite as fond of the holidays as Des but they put on a good show for her sake. Since their parents' murders just a few days before Christmas eleven years ago, the holidays seemed to dredge up difficult emotions.

Becca and Laura had worked some kind of sparkly holiday magic over Trace and Taft. This year the twins seemed to be more into the spirit of Christmas than she'd ever seen them. They had both volunteered to cut trees for everyone. They had even gone a little overboard, cutting a few extras for neighbors and friends.

She and Ridge didn't share their enthusiasm, though they both went through the motions every year. Caidy even had all her Christmas presents wrapped and the actual holiday was still more than a week away. No more last-minute panics for her this year.

"What time are they coming?"

"I told her to make arrangements for about seven. I figured we would be done with Sunday dinner by then."

Though Taft and Trace both lived closer to town, her brothers usually brought their families out to the ranch every week. With the hectic pace of their lives protecting and serving the good people of Pine Gulch, it was sometimes the only chance she had to see them all week.

"I'll throw some cookies in just before they get here so they can have something warm in their little bellies before they go. And I'll make hot chocolate for the ride, of course."

"Thanks. Destry will appreciate that, I'm sure." He finished wiping down the countertop and set the cloth on the sink's edge. "You won't consider coming with us?"

By his solemn expression, she knew he was aware just what he asked of her. "I don't think so."

"You would really send me off on my own with five or six giggly girls?"

"You can take one of the dogs with you," she offered with a grin.

He made a face but quickly grew serious again. "It's been eleven years, Caidy. Taft and Trace have moved on and both have families. Of all of us, you deserve to do the same. I wish you could find a little Christmas joy again."

"I find plenty of joy the rest of the year. Just not so much in December."

His mouth tightened, his eyes darkening with familiar sadness. Each of them had struggled in different ways after their parents' deaths. Ridge had become more stoic and controlled, Taft had gone a little crazy dating all the wild women at the tavern in town and Trace had become a dedicated lawman.

And she was still hiding away here at the River Bow.

"You need to move on," her brother said. "Maybe it's time you think about trying school again."

"Maybe." She gave a noncommittal answer, too tired to fight with him right now after the ordeal of Luke's injury and the hours spent in the waiting room of the veterinary clinic. "Hey, thanks again for letting the vet stay in the foreman's cottage. It shouldn't be longer than a few weeks."

Ridge wasn't fooled for a moment. He knew she was trying to change the subject. For once he didn't try to call her on it.

"Just think. For a few weeks anyway we'll have our own veterinarian-in-residence. With your menagerie, that should come in pretty handy."

She made a face. Given her unwilling reaction to the man, she would rather not have need of his professional services again anytime soon.

A good four inches of snow fell during the night. It clung to the trees and bowed down the branches, turning the town into an enchanting winter wonderland, especially with the craggy mountains looming in the distance.

Added to the few inches that had fallen the previous evening, that should be plenty for Destry to have a great time with her friends on the sleigh ride the next night, Caidy thought as she drove through the quiet stillness of the unplowed roads on her way to the clinic the next morning.

It wasn't yet seven. She hadn't slept well, her dreams a troubled, tangled mess. With worry for Luke uppermost in her mind, she had risen early and finished her chores. Ridge could take care of breakfast for him and Destry when he finished his own chores. Saturday morning pancakes were his specialty.

Even with her restless sleep, she could appreciate the beauty of the morning. Colorful Christmas trees gleamed in the windows of a few houses, and she liked to imagine the children there rushing to plug in the lights the moment they woke up so they could enjoy the display before the sun was fully up.

When she reached Dr. Caldwell's office, she wasn't particularly surprised to see the parking lot hadn't been plowed yet. Like many of the small businesses in Pine Gulch, he probably paid a service to take care of that for him and the plows hadn't made it here yet.

With four-wheel drive and high clearance, her truck had no problem navigating through the snow. Mindful of helping the plow work around her vehicle, she parked at the edge of the lot, next to a snow-covered Range Rover she assumed must belong to Ben.

As she headed for the building, she worried she might be waking him after a long night of watching over Luke. The sidewalks had been cleared, though. Unless he paid someone else to take care of that chore, she guessed Ben had taken care of the shoveling himself.

She wasn't surprised to find the front door locked. When Doc Harris was here, she never had to bother with the front door; she could use the side entrance she had used the night before.

Likely that's where she would find Ben Caldwell. She trudged through the snow, enjoying the brisk cold and the scent of snowy pine. A couple hard raps on the door elicited no response. She checked the door and the knob turned easily in her hand.

After a quick internal debate, she turned the knob and stepped inside. She opened her mouth to call out a greeting but the words vanished somewhere in the vicinity of her tongue—along with any remaining air in her lungs—at the sight of the new veterinarian coming out of the locker room wearing only jeans and toweling off his wet hair.

That dramatic cartoon gulp sounded in her head again. Wow. Double wow. With ice cream on top.

His chest was broad and well-defined with solid muscle and a little line of hair arrowed down to disappear in the waistband of his Levi's, where he hadn't yet fastened the top button.

Awareness bloomed inside her, as bright and vivid as the always unexpected crocuses that popped up through the snow along the fenceline of the River Bow every spring.

Her toes tingled and her heartbeat kicked up a notch and she wanted to stand here for the next few years and just stare.

He continued toweling his hair, oblivious to her, biceps flexing with the motion, and she completely forgot about the reason she had come. Suddenly he dropped the towel and saw her standing there.

His pupils widened and for a long moment, he returned her stare. Tension seethed between them, writhing and alive. Her insides trembled and every thought in her head seemed scrambled and incoherent.

Finally he cleared his throat. "Oh. Hi. I didn't hear you come in."

"Sorry." Her voice sounded raspy and she quickly cleared it, mortified that he had caught her gaping at him like Destry and her friends at a Justin Bieber concert. "I knocked and was just checking the door and it opened and…there you were."

Could she sound any more stupid? Good grief. She wanted to slink away through the door and bury her face in a pile of snow somewhere. Anybody might think she'd never seen a gorgeous, half-naked man before.

"I just… I can go and come back, uh, later."

"Why?" He grabbed a clean scrub top and she couldn't seem to look away as he pulled it over that delicious chest, her gaze fixed on the disappearance of that little strip of hair trailing down his abdomen.

Despite his towel job, his hair was still wet and sticking up in spikes. He made an effort to smooth it down but only ended up making it look more tousled and sexy.

She wanted to gulp again, feeling very much like some ridiculous maiden aunt.

Which she was.

"I shouldn't have come so early. I was just…concerned about how you made it through the night."

He shrugged, though she thought she noticed a little spark of *something* in the depths of his blue eyes. "Not too badly. Luke slept most of the night. I imagine he's going to be ready for a walk around the yard soon."

That must have been why he had cleared away the snow around the sidewalk. She had wondered why that had been a priority, especially because he had told her the clinic would be closed that day.

She fought the little burst of warmth in her chest. *Get a grip,* she told herself. She wasn't interested in some prickly veterinarian who jumped to conclusions and made snap judgments about people before he knew the facts.

Even if he did have a flat stomach she wanted to trail her fingers along…

She blushed and looked away. Her dog. That's why she was here—to check on Luke. Not to engage in completely inappropriate fantasies about a man who would be living just a stone's throw away from her.

"I can take him out if you're sure he's up to it."

"We made one trip out in the night. He seemed to handle it okay. Let's try again."

She headed to the crate where Luke lay. As if sensing her presence, his eyes opened and he tried to wag his tail, which just about broke her heart. "Shhh. Easy. Easy. There's my boy. How's my favorite guy?"

The dog's black tail flapped again on the soft blankets inside the crate. He tried to scramble up, then subsided again with a whimper.

"He's due for pain meds again. I was planning to try to slip a pill in some peanut butter."

She unlatched the door of the crate and reached in to rub his chin. "I hope you didn't keep Dr. Caldwell up all night."

"Not too bad." Ben hadn't shaved yet and the dark shadow along his jawline gave him a rugged, rather disreputable air. He probably wouldn't appreciate her pointing that out—and he *definitely* wouldn't be interested in knowing about her unwilling attraction to him.

"We had a few rough moments." He paused, giving her a careful look. "To tell the truth, I wasn't completely convinced he would make it through the night. He's a tough little guy."

"It helps to have a good vet," she said. Even Doc Harris wouldn't have stayed all night. It was a hard admission, but honesty compelled her to face it. As much as she loved the old veterinarian, she had noticed he sometimes had a bit of a cavalier attitude about the seriousness of some cases.

Apparently that wasn't the case with Dr. Caldwell.

"Sometimes all the veterinarian skills in the world aren't enough. I guess you would know that, as an animal lover."

That was her big worry right now with Sadie. Her old border collie, the very first dog who had been only hers, was thirteen. In border collie terms, that was ancient. As much as she loved her, Caidy knew she wouldn't be around forever.

"Luke seems alert now. That's a good sign, isn't it?"

He joined her in petting the dog. Their fingers accidentally touched and she didn't miss the way he quickly lifted his hands. "You can call him Lucky Luke."

"My brother and his family already have a dog named Lucky Lou," she said with a smile. "He survived being hit by a car."

"Your brother?"

She rolled her eyes. "No, but there was a time plenty of the scorned women of Pine Gulch would have gladly tried to run him down. No, Lou. He was a stray, a little corgi-beagle mix who used to wander around our ranch. I was trying to lure him in so I could find his owner, but he was pretty skittish. Then one afternoon he didn't move fast enough and some speeder hit him. He's doing great now and is extremely spoiled by Taft's kids."

Stepchildren, actually, but Maya and Alex had quickly been absorbed into the Bowman clan.

"Well, you can add this one to your collection of lucky pups."

"When can I take him home?"

"Maybe later today, as long as he remains stable."

"That would be great. Thank you for everything."

He shrugged. "It's my job."

She owed him now. It was an uncomfortable realization—she didn't like being beholden to anyone, especially not very attractive veterinarians.

In this case, she could even the playing field a little bit. "I talked to Ridge last night. He says you and your family are more than welcome to move into the foreman's cottage until your house is finished."

"Did he?" he asked, his expression pleased and more than a little relieved. "That would make the holidays much more comfortable all the way around."

"You may want to come out to the ranch and take a look at the place before you agree. We've kept it up well, but it could probably use a remodel one of these days."

"Three bedrooms, you said?"

"Yes. And Ridge suggested we work something out with rent in trade for vet services, if you're agreeable. I'll still probably owe you my firstborn but maybe not my second."

He smiled—not a huge smile but a genuine one. Her stomach flip-flopped again and she remembered that moment when she had walked into the clinic and found him half-dressed.

What in heaven's name had come over her? She did

not react to men this way. She just didn't. Oh, she dated once in a while. She wasn't a complete hermit, contrary to what her brothers teased her about. She enjoyed the occasional dinner or movie out, but she usually worked hard to keep things casual and fun. The few times a guy had tried to push for more, she had felt panicky and pressured and had done her best to discourage him.

She couldn't remember having such an instant and powerful reaction to a man, this immediate curl of desire. She certainly wasn't used to this jittery, off-balance feeling, as if she were teetering in the loft door of the barn, gearing up to jump into the big pile of hay below.

Ridiculous. She wasn't even sure she *liked* Ben Caldwell yet. She certainly wasn't ready to jump into any pile of hay with him, literally or figuratively.

"I'm sure it's fine," he answered. "If it has three bedrooms and a halfway decent kitchen for Mrs. Michaels, I don't care about much else."

She drew in a breath and subtly shifted to ease her shoulder away from his. "For all you know, it might be a hovel. You would be surprised at the living conditions some ranchers force on their workers."

"I would like to think you wouldn't have suggested it if you didn't think it would work for my family."

"That's trusting of you. You don't know anything about me. For all you know, maybe I make it a habit of bilking unsuspecting newcomers out of their rent money."

"Since we're talking about trading veterinary services for rent, that's not an issue, is it? But if you insist, I guess I could stop by your ranch later this morning after Joni comes in to relieve me. She's coming in around ten."

"That should work. I should have just enough time to

rush back there and hide all the mousetraps and roach motels."

This time he laughed outright, as she had intended. It was a full, rich sound that shimmied down her spine as if he'd pressed his lips there.

This was a gigantic mistake. Why had she ever opened her big, stupid mouth about the foreman's cottage in the first place? The last thing she needed on the ranch right now was a gorgeous man with a sexy chest and a delicious laugh.

"Should I help you take Luke outside before I go?"

He seemed to know she was doing her best to change the subject. "No. I can handle it."

She nodded. "I'll see you in a bit, okay?" she said, rubbing the dog's head again. "You need to stay here just a little longer and then you can come home."

Luke whined as if he knew she were going to leave. It was tough but she shut the crate door again.

"You know he'll probably never be a working dog now. I set the bones as well as I could, but he'll never be fast enough or strong enough to do what he used to."

"We're not so cruel that we'll make him sing for his supper, Dr. Caldwell. We'll still find a place for him on the River Bow, whether he can work the cattle or not. We have plenty of other animals who live on in comfortable retirement."

"I'm glad to hear that," he answered.

She firmly ignored his disreputable smile and the jumping nerves it set off in her stomach.

"Thanks again for everything. I guess I'll see you later."

She headed to the door, but to her dismay, he beat her to it and held it open, leaving her no choice but to brush past him on her way out. She ignored the little shiver of awareness, just as she had ignored all the others.

She could do this, she told herself. It would only be for a few weeks and she likely would see far more of his housekeeper and children than she would Ben, especially if he consistently maintained these sorts of hours.

Chapter Four

"But I *like* staying at the hotel. We have Alex and Maya to play with there and someone makes breakfast for us every day. It's kind of like Eloise at the Plaza."

Ben swallowed a laugh, certain his bristly nine-year-old daughter wouldn't appreciate it. If there was one thing Ava hated worse than eating her brussels sprouts, it was being the object of someone else's amusement.

Still, as lovely as the twenty-four room Cold Creek Inn was, the place was nothing like the grand hotel in New York City portrayed in the series of books Ava adored.

"It has been fun," he conceded, "but wouldn't you like to have a little more room to play?"

"In the middle of nowhere with a bunch of cows and horses? No. Not really."

He sighed, not unfamiliar with Ava's condescending attitude. He knew just where it came from—her maternal grandparents.

Ava wasn't thrilled to be separated from his late wife's parents. She loved the Marshalls and tried to spend as much time as she could with them. For the past two years, since Brooke's death, Robert and Janet had filled Ava's head with subtle digs and sly innuendo in an ongoing campaign to undermine her relationship with her father.

The Marshalls wanted nothing more than to take over guardianship of the children any way they could.

He blamed himself for the most part. Right after Brooke's death, he had been too lost and grief-stricken to see the fissures they were carving in his relationship with his children. The first time he figured it out had been about six months ago. After an overnight stay, Jack had refused to give him a hug.

It had taken several days and much prodding on his part, but the boy had finally tearfully confessed that Grandmother Marshall told him he killed dogs and cats nobody wanted—a completely unfair accusation because he was working at a no-kill shelter at the time.

He had done his best to keep distance between them after that, but the Marshalls were insidious in their efforts to drive a wedge between them and had even gone to court seeking regular visitation with their grandchildren.

He knew he couldn't keep them away forever, but he had decided his first priority must be strengthening the bond between him and his children, and eventually he had decided his only option was to resettle elsewhere to make the interactions between them more difficult.

"It's only for a few weeks, until our house is finished," he said now to Ava. "Haven't you missed Mrs. Michaels's delicious dinners?"

"I have," Jack opined from his booster seat next to his sister. "I looove the way she makes mac and cheese."

Ben's mouth watered as he thought of the caramelized onions she scattered across her gooey macaroni and cheese.

"If we move into this new place, that will be the first thing I ask her to make," he promised Jack and was rewarded with a huge grin.

"It hasn't been bad going for dinner at the diner or having stuff from the microwave in the hotel room," Ava insisted. "I haven't minded one single bit."

He sighed. Her constant contrariness was beginning to grate on every nerve.

"What about Christmas? Do you really want to spend Christmas Eve in the hotel, where we don't even have our own tree in our rooms?"

She didn't immediately answer and he could see her trying to come up with something to combat that. Before she could, he pursued his advantage. "Let's just check it out. If we all hate it, we can stay at the hotel through the holidays. With any luck, our new house will be done by early January."

"Will I have to ride the bus to school for the last week of school before Christmas vacation?"

He hadn't thought that far ahead. He supposed he should have considered the logistics before considering this option. "You can if you want to. Or we can try to arrange our schedules so I can take you to school on my way to the clinic."

"I wouldn't want to ride a bus. It's probably totally gross."

That was another lovely gift from his late wife's parents, thank you very little. Janet Marshall had done her best to turn his daughter into a paranoid germaphobe.

"You can always use hand sanitizer." This had become his common refrain, used to combat her objections for everything from eating in a public restaurant to sitting on Santa's lap at the mall.

She sniffed but didn't have a response for that. Much to his relief, she let the subject go and subsided into one of her aggrieved silences. He had a feeling Ava was going to drive him crazy before she made it to the other side of puberty.

A few moments later, he pulled into a side road with a log arch over it that said River Bow Ranch. Pines and aspens lined the drive. Though it was well plowed, he was still grateful for his four-wheel drive as he headed up a slight hill toward the main log ranch house he could see sprawling in the distance.

Not far from the house, the drive forked. About a city block down it, he saw a smaller clapboard home with two small eaves above a wide front porch.

He couldn't help thinking it looked like something off of one of the Christmas cards the clinic had received, a charming little house nestled in the snow-topped pines, with split rail fencing on the pastures that lined the road leading up to it.

"Can we ride the horses while we're here?" Jack asked, gazing with excitement at a group of about six or seven that stood in the snow eating a few bales of alfalfa that looked as though they had recently been dropped into the pasture.

"Probably not. We're only renting a house, not the whole ranch."

Ava looked out the window at the horses too, and he didn't miss the sudden light in her eyes. She loved horses, just like most nine-year-old girls.

But even the presence of some beautiful horseflesh

wasn't enough. "You said we were only looking at it and if we didn't like it, we didn't have to stay," she said in an accusatory tone.

Oh, she made him tired sometimes.

"Yes. That's what I said."

"I like it," Jack offered with his unassailable kindergarten logic. "They have dogs and horses and cows."

A couple of collies that looked very much like the one currently resting in his clinic watched them from the front porch of the main house as he pulled into the circular drive in front.

Before he could figure out what to do next, the door opened and Caidy Bowman trotted down the porch steps, pulling on a parka. She must have been watching for them, he thought. The long driveway would certainly give advance notice of anybody approaching.

She wore her dark hair in a braid down her back, topped with a tan Stetson. She looked rather sweet and uncomplicated, but somehow he knew the reality of Caidy Bowman was more tangled than her deceptively simple appearance would indicate.

He opened his door and climbed out as she approached his vehicle.

"The house is just there." She gestured toward the small farmhouse in the trees. "Why don't you drive closer so you don't have to walk through the snow? Ridge plowed it out with the tractor this morning so you shouldn't have any trouble. I'll just meet you there."

"Why?" He went around the vehicle and opened the passenger door. "Get in. We can ride together."

For some reason she looked reluctant at that idea, but after a weird little pause, she finally came to where he was standing and jumped up into the vehicle. He closed the door behind her before she could change her mind.

The first thing he noticed after he was once more behind the wheel was the scent of her filling the interior. Though it was a cold and overcast December day, his car suddenly smelled of vanilla and rain-washed wildflowers on a mountain meadow somewhere.

He was aware of a completely inappropriate desire to inhale that scent deep inside him, to sit here in his car with his children in the backseat and just savor the sweetness.

Get a grip, Caldwell, he told himself. So she smelled good. He could walk into any perfume counter in town and probably get the same little kick in his gut.

Still, he was suddenly fiercely glad his house would be finished in only a few weeks. Much longer than that and he was afraid he would develop a serious thing for this prickly woman who smelled like a wild garden.

"Welcome to the River Bow Ranch."

He almost thanked her before he realized she was looking in the backseat and talking to his children. She wore a genuine smile, probably the first one he had seen on her, and she looked like a bright, beautiful ray of sunshine on an overcast day.

"Can I ride one of your horses sometime?"

"Jack," Ben chided, but Caidy only laughed.

"I think that can probably be arranged. We've got several that are very gentle for children. My favorite is Old Pete. He's about the nicest horse you could ever meet."

Jack beamed at her, his sunny, adorable self. "I bet I can ride a horse good. I have boots and everything."

"You're such a dork. Just because you have boots doesn't make you a cowboy," Ava said with an impatient snort.

"What about you, Ava? Do you like horses?"

In the rearview mirror, he didn't miss his daughter's eagerness but she quickly concealed it. He wondered sometimes if she was afraid to hope for things she wanted anymore because none of their prayers and wishes had been enough to keep Brooke alive.

"I guess," she said, picking at the sleeve of her parka.

"You've come to the right place, then. I bet my niece Destry would love to take you out for a ride."

Ava's eyes widened. "Destry from my school? She's your niece?"

Caidy smiled. "I guess so. There aren't too many Destrys in this neck of the woods. You've met her?"

Ava nodded. "She's a couple years older than me but on my very first day, Mrs. Dalton, the principal, had her show me around. She was supernice to me and she still says hi to me and stuff when she sees me at school."

"I'm very glad to hear that. She better be nice. If she's not, you let me know and I'll give her a talking-to until her ears fall off."

Jack laughed at the image. Ava looked as if she wanted to join him but she had become very good at hiding her amusement these days. Instead, she looked out the window again.

"Here we are," Caidy said when he pulled up front of the house. "I turned up the heat earlier when I came down to clean a little. It should be nice and cozy for you."

How much work had she done for them? He hoped it wasn't much, even as he wondered why she was making this effort for them when he wasn't at all sure she really wanted them there.

"So all the rattraps are gone?" he asked.

"Rats?" Ava asked in a horrified voice.

"There are no rats," Caidy assured her quickly. "We

have too many cats here at the River Bow. Your father was making a joke. Weren't you?"

Was he? It had been quite a while since he had found much to joke about. Somehow Caidy Bowman brought out a long-forgotten side of him. "Yes, Ava. I was teasing."

Judging by his daughter's expression, she seemed to find that notion just as unsettling as the idea of giant rodents in her bed.

"Shall we go inside so you can see for yourself?" Caidy said.

"I want to see the rats!" Jack said.

"There are no rats," Ben assured everybody again as Caidy pushed open the front door. It wasn't locked, he noticed—something very different from his security-conscious world in California.

The scent of pine washed over them the moment they stepped inside.

"Look!" Jack exclaimed. "A Christmas tree! A real live one of our very own!"

Sure enough, in the corner was a rather scraggly pine tree as tall as he was, covered in multicolored Christmas lights.

He gazed at it, stunned at the sight and quite certain the tree hadn't been there a few hours earlier. She had said the house was empty, so somehow in the past few hours Caidy Bowman must have dragged this tree in, set it in the stand and strung the Christmas lights.

She had done this for them. He didn't know what to say. Somewhere inside him another little chunk of ice seemed to fall away.

"You didn't need to do that," he said, a little more gruffly than he intended.

"It was no big deal," she answered. In the warmth

of the room he thought he saw a tinge of color on her cheeks. "My brothers went a little crazy in the Christmas tree department. We cut our own in the mountains above the ranch after Thanksgiving, and this year they cut a few extras to give to people who might need them. This one was leftover."

"What about the lights?"

"We had some extras lying around. I'm afraid this one is a little on the scrawny side, but paper garland and some ornaments will fix that right up. I bet your dad and Mrs. Michaels can help you make some," she told Ava and Jack. As he might have expected, Jack looked excited about the idea but Ava merely shrugged.

He wouldn't know the first thing about making ornaments for a Christmas tree. Brooke had always taken care of the holiday decorating and his housekeeper had stepped in after her death.

"Come on. I'll give you the grand tour. It's not much, as you can see. Just this room, the kitchen and dining room and the bedrooms upstairs."

She was too modest. This room alone was already half again as big as one of the hotel rooms. The living room was comfortably furnished with a burgundy plaid sofa and a couple of leather recliners, and the television set was an older model but quite large.

One side wall was dominated by a small river rock fireplace with a mantel made of rough-hewn lumber. The fireplace was empty but someone—probably Caidy—had stacked several armloads of wood in a bin next to it. He could easily imagine how cozy the place would be with a fire in the hearth, the lights flickering on the tree and a basketball game on the television set. He wouldn't even have to worry about turning the volume down so he didn't wake Jack. It was an appealing thought.

"Through here is the kitchen and dining area," she said.

The appliances looked a little out-of-date but perfectly adequate. The refrigerator even had an ice maker, something he had missed in the hotel. Ice from a bucket wasn't quite the same for some reason.

"There's a half bath and a laundry room through those doors. It's pretty basic. Do you want to see the upstairs?"

He nodded and followed her up, trying not to notice the way her jeans hugged her curves. "We've got a king bed in one room, a queen in the second bedroom and bunk beds in that one on the left. The children won't mind sharing, will they?"

"I want to see!" Jack exclaimed and raced into the room she indicated. Ava followed more slowly, but even she looked curious about the accommodations, he saw.

The whole place smelled like vanilla and pine, fresh and clean, and he didn't miss the vacuum tracks in the carpet. She really must have hurried over to make it ready for them.

"There's a small bathroom off the master and another one in the hall between the other bedrooms. That's it. Not much to it. Do you think it will work?"

"I like it!" Jack declared. "But only if I get the top bunk."

"What do you think, Ava?"

She shrugged. "It's okay. I still like the hotel better but it would be fun to live by Destry and ride the bus with her and stuff. And *I* get the top bunk. I'm older."

"We can work that out," Ben said. "I guess it's more or less unanimous. It should be great. Comfortable and spacious and not that far from the clinic. I appreciate the offer."

She smiled but he thought it looked a little strained. "Great. You can move in anytime. Today if you want. All you need are your suitcases."

The idea of a little breathing space was vastly appealing. "In that case, we can go back to the inn and pack our things and be back later this afternoon. Mrs. Michaels will be thrilled."

"That should work."

"Can we decorate the tree tonight?" Jack asked eagerly.

He tousled his son's hair, deeply grateful for this cheerful child who gave his love unconditionally. "Yeah. We can probably do that. We'll pick up some art supplies while we're in town too."

Even Ava looked mildly excited about that as they headed back outside.

"Oh, for goodness' sake," Caidy said suddenly. "What are you doing all the way down here, you crazy dog? Just want to make a few new friends, do you?"

She spoke to an ancient-looking collie, with a gray muzzle and tired eyes, that was sitting at the bottom of the porch steps. Caidy knelt down, heedless of the snow, and petted the dog. "This is Sadie. She's just about my best friend in the world."

Ava smiled at the dog. "Hi, Sadie."

Jack, however, hovered behind Ben. His son was nervous about any dog bigger than a Pekingese.

"She's really old. Thirteen. I got her when I was just a teenager. We've been through a lot, Sadie and me."

"Sadie and Caidy. That rhymes," Ava said unexpectedly, earning a giggle from Jack.

"I know, right? My brothers used to call the dog and

I would think they wanted me. Or they would call me and Sadie would come running. It was all very confusing but we're used to it now after all these years. I didn't name her, though—the rancher my parents got her from had already given her a name. By then she was already used to it so we decided not to change it."

He saw a hint of sadness in her eyes and wondered at the source of it as she hugged the dog. "Do you know, she was a Christmas present the year I turned fourteen? That's not much older than you, Ava."

His daughter looked thrilled that someone would think she was anywhere close to the advanced age of fourteen instead of nine and he suddenly knew Caidy had said it on purpose.

"For months I'd been begging and begging for a dog of my own," she went on. "We always had ranch dogs but my brothers took over working with them. I wanted one I could train myself. I was so excited that morning when I found her under the tree. She was so adorable with a big red bow around her neck."

He pictured it clearly, a teenage Caidy and a cute little border collie puppy with curious ears and a wagging tail. He could certainly relate to the story. When he had been a boy, he had begged for a dog every year from about the time he turned eight. Every year, he had hoped and prayed he would find a puppy under the tree and every year had been another disappointment.

He held the door open. "Ava, you can sit in the middle next to Jack so we can make room for Sadie."

"Oh, no. That's not necessary. She's probably wet and stinky. We can walk. It's not that far."

"If there's one thing we don't mind in this family, it's wet stinky dogs, isn't that right? Just wait until we bring Tri out here to romp in the snowdrifts."

Both children giggled, even Ava, which filled him with a great sense of accomplishment.

He turned his attention away from his children to find Caidy watching him, her hand still on her dog's scruff and an arrested expression in her eyes. He felt a return of that tensile connection of earlier, when he had walked out of the shower room to find her standing in the hallway.

The moment stretched between them and he couldn't seem to look away, vaguely aware of Jack and Ava climbing into the SUV with their usual bickering.

Finally she cleared her throat. "Thanks anyway, but I'm not quite ready to go. I just need to dust out the two spare bedrooms."

This wasn't going to work. He didn't want this sudden attraction. He didn't want to feel this heat in his gut again, the sizzle of his blood.

He thought about telling her he had changed his mind, but how ridiculous would that sound? *I can't stay here because I'm afraid I'll do something stupid if I'm in the same general vicinity of you.*

Anyway, now that he had seen the charming little house, he really didn't want to go back to the cramped quarters of the inn. He would just have to work hard to stay out of her way. How tough could that be?

"The place looked fine. We can dust," he said. "You don't have to do that."

"We Bowmans are a proud lot. Though we might not be in the landlord business as a regular thing, I'm not about to let you stay in a dirty place."

He decided not to argue. "I'll check on Luke while we're in town. If I feel like he is stable enough to be here, I'll pick him up and bring him out with us when we come back."

She smiled her gratitude and he felt that inexorable tug toward her again. "Thank you! We would love that, wouldn't we, Sadie?"

The dog nudged her hand and seemed to smile in agreement.

"Luke is her great-grandson," she explained to the children. "So I guess I'll see you all later. I'm glad the house will work for you."

Space-wise, the house was perfect. Neighbor-wise, he wasn't so sure.

After he loaded up the kids and started down the gravel drive, he glanced in the rearview mirror. Caidy Bowman was lifting her face to the pale winter sun peeking between clouds, one hand on the dog's grizzled head.

For some ridiculous reason, a lump rose in his throat at the sight and he had a hard time looking away.

Chapter Five

For the next few hours, Caidy couldn't shake a tangled mix of dread and anticipation. Offering Ben and his family a place to stay over the holidays had been a friendly, neighborly gesture. She was grateful those cute kids would be able to have the fun of sneaking downstairs Christmas morning to see their presents under their very own tree and that Mrs. Michaels could cook a proper dinner for them instead of something out of the microwave.

Even so, she had the strangest feeling that life on the ranch was about to change, maybe irrevocably.

It was only for a few weeks, she told herself as she finished mucking out the stalls with Destry while Sadie plopped on her belly in the warm straw and watched them. She could handle anything for a few weeks. Still, the strange, restless mood dogged her heels like the collies in a thunderstorm as she went through her Saturday chores.

"You ladies need a hand in here?"

Destry beamed at her father, thrilled when he called her a lady. She was, Caidy thought. Her little girl was growing up—nearly eleven now and going to middle school the next year. She didn't know what she would do then.

"Since we've got your muscles here, why don't you bring us a couple new straw bales? I'd like to put some fresh down for the foaling mares."

"Will do. Des, come give your old man a hand."

The two of them took off, laughing together about something Destry said in answer, and Caidy again felt that unaccountable depression seep over her.

Her brother didn't really need her help anymore with Destry. She had been happy to offer it when the girl was young and Ridge had been alone and struggling. *More* than happy, really. Relieved, more like, to have something useful to do with her time, something she thought she could handle.

Destry was almost a young woman now and Ridge was an excellent father who could probably handle things here just fine by himself.

She leaned her cheek on the handle of the shovel and watched Sadie snoring away. They didn't need her. Nobody did. She sighed heavily just as Ridge came back alone with a bale on each shoulder.

"That sounds serious. What's wrong? Having second thoughts about the new vet and his family moving in?"

And third and fourth. She shrugged, picked up a pitchfork and started spreading the straw around. "What's to have second thoughts about? He needed a place to stay for a few weeks and we have an empty, furnished house just sitting there."

"Destry will enjoy having other children around the ranch, especially for Christmas."

"Where is she?"

He grabbed the other pitchfork to help her. "She got distracted by the new barn kittens. She's up in the loft giving them a little attention."

Her niece loved animals every bit as much as Caidy had at her age. Maybe she would be a veterinarian someday. "I'm afraid we're not very good company for her this time of year, are we? Things will be better in January."

Ridge gave her a long look. "You remember how much Mom loved Christmas. She would hate thinking you would let her and Dad's deaths ruin the holidays forever."

"I know." It wasn't a new argument between them and right now she wasn't in the mood, not with this melancholy sidling through her. "Don't make it sound like I'm the only one. You hate Christmas too."

"Yeah, well, I think it's time we both moved forward with our lives. Taft and Trace both have."

You weren't there, she wanted to cry out. None of her brothers were. She had been the one hiding under that shelf in the pantry, listening to her mother's dying gasps and knowing there wasn't a damn thing she could do about it.

You weren't there and you weren't responsible.

She couldn't say the words to him. She never could. Instead she spread a little more straw in an area that already had plenty.

"I think it's time you went back to school."

She didn't need this again, today, of all days, when

she felt so oddly as if she were teetering on the brink of some major life shift.

"I'm twenty-seven years old, Ridge. I think my school days are past me."

Her brother's handsome features twisted into a scowl. "They don't have to be. Plenty of people finish college when they're a little older than the traditional student. Sometimes it takes a person a few years to figure out what they want out of life."

"Have I figured that out yet?" she muttered.

"You won't while you're stuck here. I should never have let you come home after your first year of college. I should have made you stick it out. Believe me, I've regretted it bitterly, more than I can say. The truth is, after Melinda walked out, I needed you here to help me with Destry. I was lost and floundering, trying to run the ranch and take care of her too."

He pulled his gloves off and shoved them in his back pocket, then tugged at an earlobe. These words weren't easy for him, she knew. Of all her brothers, Ridge was the most stoic, hiding his emotions and his thoughts behind the hard steel it took to run a ranch like the River Bow.

"The truth is, I chose the easy path instead of the right one," he said, regret in his eyes.

"You didn't choose anything. I did. I wanted to come home. I would have dropped out regardless of whether you needed me here."

"Not if I hadn't made it so easy for you to find a soft place to land back home."

She wasn't sure if her brothers blamed her for the murders of her parents. She had always been afraid to ask and none of them had ever talked about it.

How could they not blame her on some level? Neither she nor her parents were even supposed to have been home that night. That was the reason an art burglary had turned into a surprise home invasion robbery and then a double murder when her father had tried to stop the thieves.

Caidy would have died with them if her mother hadn't shoved her into the pantry and ordered her to hide.

Sometimes she felt as if she had been hiding ever since.

"*You* should be the new veterinarian in town, not some new guy from the coast," Ridge went on, his voice fierce. "It's been eating at me ever since this Caldwell showed up. Becoming a vet was all you ever wanted. I know Doc Harris had once hoped you would follow in his footsteps. I can't help thinking how, if things had gone differently, you could have taken over his practice when he retired."

He managed to hit exactly on the reason for her restlessness. The straw rustled under her feet as she shifted her boots, releasing its earthy scent. Ben Caldwell was living her dream now. It was hard to admit, especially when she knew she had absolutely no right to be upset.

"I made my choices, Ridge. I don't regret them. Not for a moment."

"You need a life of your own. A home, a family. You never even date."

"Maybe I'll just run off with the new veterinarian. Then where would you be?"

As soon as the words escaped, she heartily wished she had kept her big mouth shut. Again. What could possibly have possessed her to say such a thing? Ridge lifted an eyebrow and gave her a long, searching look, and she had to hope the heat she could feel in her cheeks wasn't as bright red as it felt.

"I would be happy for you as long as he's a good man who treats you well," Ridge said quietly. For some unaccountable reason, her heart ached sharply. Before she could come up with a response, Destry clambered down the loft ladder. "They're here! I just saw a couple of cars driving up."

The heat in her cheeks spread down her neck and over her shoulders. "Great," she managed to say, trying for a cheerful voice.

"Do you think they'll have Luke with them?"

"I guess we'll find out."

The three of them walked out of the barn into the cold, overcast afternoon just as one SUV pulled up, followed closely by another one. Neither vehicle took the fork in the driveway that led to the foreman's house. They headed toward the main house, pulling into the circular driveway.

Ben climbed out as she, Ridge and Destry approached the vehicles. Her stomach did that ridiculous little jumpy thing again. She had forgotten in the past few hours just how gorgeous the man was. The memory she had been trying without success to forget flooded back into her head in excruciating detail—of walking into the clinic that morning and finding him wet and hard-muscled as he came out of the shower.

She thought of what she had said to her brother. *Maybe I'll just run off with the new veterinarian, and then where would you be?*

The bigger question was, where would *she* be? She could easily see herself making a fool over this man and she had to do her very best to make sure that didn't happen, especially when she couldn't logically find a way to avoid him, when she trained dogs for a living and he was the town's only veterinarian.

He waved at them all and held a hand out to Ridge. "Hi. You must be Caidy's brother."

"Right. I'm Ridge Bowman. This is my daughter, Destry. I guess you know our Caidy. Nice to meet you. Welcome to the River Bow."

"Thank you."

The two of them shook hands and then, much to the girl's astonished delight, Ben shook hands with Destry too. She grinned at him, braids flying under her cowboy hat as she turned the handshake into a vigorous exercise.

Ben gave Caidy a friendly sort of smile—much warmer than any he'd given her so far. Her cheeks flamed and she didn't miss Ridge's careful look at the two of them. Drat her big mouth. She should never have said what she did earlier in the barn. Knowing her brother, now he was never going to let her forget it.

"I really appreciate you opening the house for us like this."

Ridge shrugged. "Why not? It's empty. With apologies to my sister-in-law, children ought to be in a house at Christmastime if they can."

"A little breathing room will certainly make the holidays more comfortable for all of us," he answered. "I've got someone else back here who's anxious to be on the River Bow."

He headed to the back of the SUV and reached to open the hatch.

"You really think Luke is ready to be home?" she asked.

"He should be. He was moving on his own and seemed far more comfortable this afternoon than earlier. He's a fighter, this one. You'll still have to keep a sharp eye on him, but there's no reason he can't be home for that. It'll save you a little on the clinic bill."

All of them converged on the rear of the vehicle. Sure enough, Luke was resting in a travel crate. When he saw her, he whimpered and whined. Ben unlatched the door and the dog's nails scrabbled on the plastic floor of the crate as he tried to stand.

"Easy," Ben said, and his calm voice did the trick. Luke subsided again.

"Hey, Lukey. Hey, buddy." Destry rubbed her cheek against the dog's and scratched under his ears. "You poor thing. Look at that big bandage."

"Hi, Destry. I'm sorry your dog got hurt."

Destry smiled into the backseat, where both Ava and Jack were watching the proceedings with interest.

"Me too. But he's not really my dog. He's one of my aunt Caidy's. I like cats most of all."

"I like cats too," Ava said.

"Not me," Jack answered cheerfully. "I like dogs. This is our dog. His name is Tri."

The dog yipped in answer to his name and Caidy had to smile at the adorable little thing, some kind of chihuahua.

"Can he walk?" Ridge was asking as he studied the injured dog in the crate.

Ben nodded. "He can, but it won't be comfortable for him for a while now. Probably better if we let him take it easy. Do you mind helping me carry him inside?"

"No problem," Ridge said. The two of them carried the crate with Luke inside. Caidy wondered if she should stay with the children or take them inside. Before she could make a decision, Mrs. Michaels joined them from the other vehicle. "You probably want to go help settle your dog, don't you?"

"Yes," she said quickly. "Why don't you all come inside?"

"I think we'll be better off staying put. I'm sure Dr. Caldwell won't be long and the children are anxious to start settling into the house."

She followed the low murmur of men's voices and found them in the kitchen, setting the crate down in the small area she had arranged earlier, in hopes for this very moment.

"Caidy likes to keep her patients right here in the kitchen," Ridge was saying. "This way her bedroom, right down the hall, is close enough to keep an eye on them."

"It's close to the back door for easy trips outside. That's the important thing," she said.

"This works. I like the enclosure," he said. Years ago, she had purchased a small baby play yard that worked well when she was treating an animal whose physical activity needed to be limited.

"Come on out," Ben coaxed the dog. Luke didn't seem to want to move but with their encouragement and Dr. Caldwell helping him along, he rose slowly and hobbled out of the crate, then headed immediately for the soft bed of old blankets she had fashioned in the enclosure.

"What sort of special instructions do I need?"

"Our biggest fear right now is infection. We need to keep the injuries as clean as possible, especially that puncture wound from the bull."

"You don't have to worry about anything," Ridge said. "Caidy's an expert. She used to work at the clinic with Dr. Harris."

"So I hear."

"She should have become a veterinarian," Ridge went on. "It's all she ever wanted to do."

Apparently blabbermouth syndrome ran in the family.

"Is that right?" Ben said, giving her a curious look. She could tell he was wondering why she hadn't pursued her dreams. What was so wrong about a person's life changing direction?

"Yes. I also wanted to be a ballerina when I was eight. And a famous movie star when I was eleven."

And a singer. She decided not to mention she had once wanted to sing professionally. That was another dream she had pushed aside.

"I suppose you're anxious to move into the house. The key is inside on the kitchen table. All the information, like the phone number to the house and the address, are on a paper I've also left for you there."

"Thanks."

One thing she had never anticipated doing with her life was being a landlord to an entirely too sexy veterinarian. Yet here she was. "Call if you have any problems or can't figure out any of the appliances."

"I'm sure we'll be fine. Make sure you let me know if you have any problems with Luke. Here. Let me leave my cell number."

He pulled a business card out of the inside pocket of his coat and left it on the kitchen counter. "If he starts to run a fever or has any other unusual symptoms that concern you, I want you to call me. Day or night."

She doubted she ever would. Even after all her years of working with Doc Harris, she hadn't felt comfortable calling the old veterinarian in the middle of the night.

"Thank you," she answered.

"I'd better head out. The kids are anxious to start decorating their tree."

"Oh. That reminds me. Destry and I dug through our old Christmas things earlier and found a few things we're not using. You're welcome to them."

She picked up the box off the kitchen table and handed it to him. He looked a little disconcerted but then smiled.

"Thank you. I'm sure Mrs. Michaels and the children will find great use for them."

"Not you?"

"I'm sure I'll be roped into helping, like it or not." He looked more resigned than truly reluctant.

"If you'd like, I can carry it out for you while you two get the crate."

"That would be great. Thanks." He smiled at her and she felt those ridiculous flutters again.

"He seems nice," Ridge said after they had loaded the crate and the ornaments and stood on the porch watching the two SUVs head back down the driveway toward the foreman's house.

She thought of how abrupt and harsh he had been the evening before at the clinic. *Nice* wouldn't have been the word she used to describe Ben Caldwell then, but now she was beginning to wonder.

"I guess," she answered in what she hoped was a noncommittal voice.

Ridge gave her a sidelong look. "You might want to think about showing a little more enthusiasm if you plan to run off with the man. At least to him. Occasionally a guy needs a little encouragement."

She rolled her eyes but quickly hurried into the house before Ridge could notice the blush she felt heating her cheeks. She suddenly had a very strong feeling she would have to work hard at being casual and uninterested in order to keep Ridge—and probably the rest of the Bowmans—from trying to do a little matchmaking for Christmas.

A woman's body was a mysterious thing, full of secret hollows and soft, delectable curves.

He was in heaven, warm, sweetly scented heaven. Ben trailed his fingers over the woman in his arms, his hands exploring all those hidden delights. He wanted to stay here forever with his face buried in skin that smelled sweetly of vanilla and rain-washed wildflowers and his hands finding new and exciting terrain to discover.

His body was rock-hard and he pressed against her heat, tangling his fingers in acres of dark, silky hair. She smiled at him out of that sinfully delicious mouth that sent his imagination into overdrive, and her green eyes were bright as springtime. He groaned, his hunger at fever pitch, and kissed her.

Her mouth was as warm and welcoming as the rest of her and when she danced her tongue along his, he groaned and gripped her hands, kissing her with all the pent-up need aching inside him.

"Yes. Kiss me," she murmured in that lilting, musical voice. "Just like that, Ben. Don't stop. Please, don't stop."

All he could think about was burying himself inside. He shifted and prepared to do just that, his body taut and ready, when a phone trilled close to his ear.

He froze…and woke up from the first sexy dream he'd had in ages.

He could still see Caidy Bowman, tangled around him, her body soft and warm, but when he blinked she disappeared.

The phone trilled again and a quick glance at the alarm read 3:00 a.m. Nobody called at this hour unless it was an emergency. He grabbed for it, ignoring the lingering arousal of his body that had no chance in hell of being satisfied by an actual female right now.

"Hello?" he growled.

"I shouldn't have called. I'm sorry." Hearing Caidy Bowman's voice in his ear after he had just heard her in his dreams, pleading with him for more, was so disorienting that for a moment he couldn't process the shift.

"Hello? Are you there?" she asked. The urgency and, yes, fright in her voice pushed away the last clinging tendrils of his sultry dream.

"I'm here. Sorry." He swung his legs over the side of the bed and reached for the jeans he'd left there the night before. "What's wrong? Luke?"

"Yes. He's not… Something's wrong. I wouldn't have called you, except…I don't think it's good. He's struggling to breathe. I thought it might be an infection, but I haven't seen any signs of a fever or anything. I lifted both dressings and they looked clean."

He growled and flipped on the bedside light, then scrubbed at his face to rub the last tendrils of that blasted dream away.

"Give me five minutes."

"Is there something I can do so you don't have to come up here?"

"Probably not. Five minutes."

As he threw on a T-shirt and his jacket, a hundred possibilities raced through his head, very few of them leading to a good outcome. He quickly scribbled a note for Mrs. Michaels and stuck it on her door, though by now she was used to him dashing out in the middle of the night.

Snow lightly gleamed in his headlights as he drove up to the ranch house. He saw lights in the kitchen and pulled as close as he could to the side door on the circular driveway, then hurried up the snow-covered walkway, his emergency kit in his hand.

He didn't even have to rap softly on the door before she yanked it open, her hair tangled around her face and her eyes huge with worry.

"Thank you for coming so quickly. I didn't want to call you but I didn't know what else to do."

He had a strong feeling that wasn't an easy admission for her to make. She struck him as a woman who didn't like relying on others.

Yes. Kiss me. Just like that, Ben. Don't stop. Please, don't stop.

He pushed away the memory of that completely inappropriate dream and did his best not to notice her faded T-shirt or the yoga pants she wore that stretched over every curve, to focus instead on the issue at hand.

"It's fine. I'm here now. Let's see what we have going on."

The dog was clearly in distress, his respiratory rate fast and his breathing labored. His gums and lips were blue and Ben quickly pulled out his emergency oxygen mask and fit it over the dog's mouth and nose.

"It's gotten worse, just in the few minutes since I called you. I don't know what to do."

He ran his hand over the dog's chest and knew instantly what the problem was. He could hear the rattle of air inside the chest cavity with each ragged breath. He bit out an oath.

"What is it?"

"Traumatic pneumothorax. He has air trapped in his chest cavity. We're going to have to get it out. I have a couple of options here. I can take him into the clinic and do an X-ray first, or I can go with my instincts. I can feel the problem. I can try to extract the air with a needle and syringe, which will help his breathing. It's your choice."

She paused for just a moment, then nodded. "I trust you. If you think you can do it here, go ahead."

Her faith in him was humbling, especially given the cold way he had treated her the day before. He fished in his bag for the supplies he would need, then knelt down beside the dog again.

"What can I do?" she asked.

"Try to calm him as best you can and keep him still."

The next few moments were a blur. He was aware of her speaking softly, of her strong, capable hands at his side as she held the dog as firmly as possible. For the most part, he entered that peculiar zone he found whenever he was in the middle of a complicated procedure. He listened with his stethoscope until he could isolate the pneumothorax. The rest was quick and efficient: cleaning the area, inserting the needle in just the right spot, extracting the air with a gurgle, then listening again with the stethoscope to the dog's breath sounds.

This was one of those treatments that was almost instantly effective. Miraculous, even. One moment the dog was frantically struggling to breathe, the next his airway was free and clear and his respiratory rate slowed, his wild trembling with it.

In just moments, he was moving air just as he should through his lungs and had calmed considerably. Satisfied, Ben took the emergency oxygen mask off Luke and returned the syringe to its packaging to be discarded back at the clinic.

"That's it?" Caidy's eyes looked stunned.

"Should be. We're still going to want to watch him closely. If you'd like, I can take him back for another night at the clinic just to be safe."

"No. I... That was *amazing!*"

She was gazing at him as if he had just hung the moon and stars and Jupiter too. He had a funny little ache in his chest, and another inappropriate bit of that crazy dream flashed through his head.

"Thank you. Thank you so much. I was worried sick."

"I'm glad I was close enough to help."

"I'm sorry I had to wake you, though."

So was he. Or he told himself he was anyway. If she hadn't, he probably would have a great deal more of his unruly subconscious to be embarrassed about. "No problem. It was worth it."

"Is there anything else I need to be concerned about?"

"I don't think so. We cleared his lungs. If he has any more breathing trouble, we're going to want to x-ray to see if something else is going on. If you don't mind, I'd like to stick around a little longer to make sure he remains stable."

"Can I get you something? Coffee probably isn't a good idea at three-thirty in the morning if you want to catch a few hours of sleep when we're done here, but we have tea or hot cocoa."

"Cocoa would be good."

He didn't want to think about how comfortable, almost intimate, it was to sit here in this quiet kitchen while the snow fluttered softly against the window and the big log house creaked and settled around them. Only a few moments later, she returned with a couple of mugs of hot chocolate.

"It's from a mix. I thought that would be faster."

"Mix is fine," he answered. "It's all I'm used to anyway."

He took a sip and almost sighed with delight at the rich mix of chocolate and raspberry. "That's not any old mix."

She smiled. "No. I buy from a gourmet food store in Jackson Hole. It's imported from France."

He sipped again, letting the sensuous flavors mix on his tongue. Worth an interrupted night's sleep, just for a little of that divine hot chocolate.

She sat across the table from him and he couldn't help noticing how the loose neckline of her shirt gaped a little with each breath.

"So how is the house working out?"

"Fine, so far. But then, I haven't even had one full night's sleep in it." And what little sleep he *had* enjoyed had been tormented by futile dreams of something he couldn't have.

"I'm sorry again about that, especially considering you had to stay the night with Luke last night."

He shrugged. "Don't be sorry. I didn't mean that. It's just part of my life, something I'm very used to. I often get emergency calls."

Even without the work-related sleep disruptions, his sleep was frequently restless. "The house works well. The kids are happy to have a little more room and Mrs. Michaels is over the moon to have a kitchen again. She made her famous macaroni and cheese for dinner. You'll have to try it sometime. It's as much a gourmet treat as your hot chocolate. I have to admit, I've missed her cooking."

"You must feel very lucky that she was willing to come with you from California."

"Lucky doesn't begin to describe the half of it. I would be completely lost without her. Since Brooke—my wife—died, Anne has kept us all going."

"Of all the places you could have bought a practice, why did you pick Pine Gulch?" She seemed genuinely interested and he leaned back in his chair, sipping at his drink, enjoying the quiet conversation more than he probably should.

"Doc Harris and I have known each other since before I graduated from veterinary school. We met at a conference and had kept up an email correspondence. When he told me he was retiring and wanted to sell his practice, it seemed the perfect opportunity. I had...reasons for wanting to leave California."

She didn't press him, though he could see the curiosity in her eyes. He wanted to tell her. He wasn't sure why—perhaps the quiet peace of the kitchen or the way she had looked at him with such admiration after the thoracentesis. Or maybe just because he hadn't talked about it with anyone, not even Mrs. Michaels.

"My wife has been gone for two years now and I think the kids and I both needed a new start, you know? Away from all the old patterns and relationships. The familiar can sometimes carry its own burdens."

"I can understand that. I've had plenty of moments when I just want to pick up and start over."

What would she want to run from? he wondered. He had a feeling there was far more beneath the surface of Caidy Bowman than a beautiful cowgirl who loved animals and her family.

"So you just packed everybody up and headed to the mountains of Idaho?"

"Something like that."

She sipped at her hot cocoa and they lapsed into silence broken only by the dog's breathing, comfortable and easy now, he was gratified to see. She had a little dab of chocolate on her upper lip and he wondered what she would do if he reached across the table and licked it off.

"Is it rude and intrusive for me to ask about your wife?"

That was one way to squelch his inappropriate desire. He shifted in a chair that suddenly felt as hard and unforgiving as a cold block of cement.

"She…died in a car accident after slipping into a diabetes-related coma while she was behind the wheel."

He didn't add the rest, about the unborn child he hadn't wanted who had died along with her, about how angry he had been with her for the weeks leading up to her death, furious that she would put him in such an untenable position after they had both decided to stop once Jack was born, when doctors warned of the grave risks of a third pregnancy.

He hated himself for the way he had reacted. The temper he had inherited from his grandfather, the one he worked constantly to overcome, had slipped its leash and he had been hateful and mean and had even taken to sleeping in the guest room after she told him she was pregnant, just days after they had decided he would have a vasectomy.

Caidy gave him a sympathetic look, which he definitely did not deserve. "Diabetes. How tragic. She must have been young."

"Thirty."

Her mouth twisted. "I'm sorry. Really sorry."

Yes. Tragic. Something that never should have happened. He blamed himself—and so did Brooke's parents, which was the reason they were trying to poison Ava and Jack against him.

"You must miss her terribly. I can understand why you wanted to make a new start away from the memories."

He did miss her. He had adored her when they first married, until the rather willful, spoiled part of her he had overlooked as part of her charm when they were dating began to show itself in difficult ways.

Brooke had selfishly believed she was stronger than her diabetes. She didn't deserve to have it, thus she shouldn't have to worry about taking care of herself. She was cavalier to the point of recklessness about checking her levels and taking her insulin.

She had been a loving mother, he would never say otherwise, even if he sometimes wondered how a loving mother could risk her own health when she already had so much simply because she wanted more.

"What about you?" he asked to change the subject. "Ever been married?"

She was in midsip with her hot cocoa and coughed a little. "Me? No. I date here and there but…nothing serious. The dating pool around Pine Gulch is a little shallow. I've known most of the unmarried men around here my whole life."

You haven't known me.

The dangerous thought whispered through his mind and seemed to move right in. No. He definitely didn't want to go there. She was a beautiful woman and he was very attracted to her—he only needed to remember that dream if he needed proof—but he would never do anything about that attraction but sneak those tantalizing glimpses at her and wonder.

He had his children to consider and a new practice

he was trying to build. He could see no room for a complicated woman like Caidy Bowman in that picture anywhere.

Why did she hide herself away here in a small town like Pine Gulch? Why hadn't she become a veterinarian? He had the same strange thought of earlier in the day when he had seen her standing on the River Bow porch with her brother and her niece. She was lonely. He had no idea why he thought so, but he was suddenly certain of it.

"So why not dip your feet in other waters? It's a big world. You could always try internet dating."

"Wow. You're a veterinarian *and* a relationship coach. Who would have guessed? It seems an odd combination, but, okay."

He laughed gruffly, only because that was absolutely *not* his usual modus operandi. Usually he was completely oblivious to the interpersonal dramas and entanglements of other people, except when it came to their relationships with their pets.

"That's me. I'll fix up your dog and your broken heart, all for one low fee. And I offer monthly installment plans."

She smiled, the right side of her mouth just a bit higher than the left to create a sweetly pleasing imbalance. The quiet, companionable silence wrapped around them like the trailing tendrils of a woolen scarf.

He wanted to kiss her.

The hunger for a taste—just one little sampling—of chocolate and raspberry and soft, warm woman was intense and bewitching. He needed to get out of there. Now, before he did something completely insane like try to turn his midnight fantasies into reality and received a well-earned slap for it.

The dog snuffled softly and that was the excuse he needed to leave her side and return to the cozy little warren she had created for Luke.

Unfortunately, she followed right behind as he crouched down to check the dog's breathing with his stethoscope.

"How does he sound?"

"Good. Breathing is normal now. I think we solved the problem."

"Thank you again, for everything. I'm not sure Doc Harris could have done the job as well."

Her words seeped inside him. He was inordinately pleased by the compliment. "You're very welcome."

"I hope I don't need to call you in the middle of the night again."

"Please don't hesitate. I'm just down the lane now."

She smiled. "Ridge said it would be like having our own veterinarian-in-residence. Just to put your mind at ease, I promise not to take advantage."

Please. Take advantage all you want. He cleared his throat. "For what it's worth, I think the guys around here are crazy. Even if you did grow up with them."

He wasn't quite sure why he said the words. He was no more a player than he was a relationship coach, for heaven's sake. She flashed him a startled look, her eyes wide and her mouth slightly parted.

He might have left things at that, safe and uncomplicated, except her eyes suddenly shifted to his mouth and he didn't miss the flare of heat in her gaze.

He swore under his breath, already regretting what he seemed to have no power to resist, and then he reached for her.

Chapter Six

As his mouth settled over hers, warm and firm and tasting of cocoa, Caidy couldn't quite believe this was happening.

She was being kissed by the sexy new veterinarian just a day after thinking him rude and abrasive. For a long moment, she was shocked into immobility, then heat began to seep through her frozen stupor. Oh. Oh, yes!

How long had it been since she had enjoyed a kiss and wanted more? She was astounded to realize she couldn't remember. As his lips played over hers, she shifted her neck slightly for a better angle.

She splayed her fingers against his chest—that strong, muscled chest she had seen firsthand just that morning—and his heat soaked into her skin, even through the cotton of his shirt.

Her insides seemed to give a collective shiver. Mmm.

This was exactly what two people ought to be doing at 3:00 a.m. on a snowy December day.

He made a low sound in his throat that danced down her spine and she felt the hard strength of his arms slide around her, pulling her closer. In this moment, nothing else seemed to matter but Ben Caldwell and the wondrous sensations fluttering through her.

This was crazy. Some tiny voice of self-preservation seemed to whisper through her. What was she doing? She had no business kissing someone she barely knew and wasn't even sure if she liked yet. If she kept this up, he was going to think she kissed every guy who happened to smile at her.

Though it took every last ounce of strength, she managed to slide away from all that delicious heat and moved a few inches away from him, trying desperately to catch her breath.

The distance she created between them seemed to drag Ben back to his senses. He stared at her, his eyes as dazed as she felt. "That was wrong. I don't know what I was thinking. Your dog is a patient and…I shouldn't have…."

She might have been offended by the dismay in his voice if not for the arousal in his eyes and the way he couldn't seem to catch his breath. Because she was having the same sort of reaction—dismay mixed with lingering arousal and a sudden deep yearning—she couldn't very well complain.

His hair was a little rumpled and he had the evening shadow of a beard and all she could think was *yum*.

She cleared her throat, compelled to say something in the strained moment. "Relax, Dr. Caldwell. You didn't do anything wrong, as far as I can see. I didn't exactly push you out the door, did I?"

He ran a hand through his hair. "No. No, I guess you didn't."

"It's late and we're both tired and not quite thinking straight. I'm sure that's all this was."

A muscle flexed in his jaw. He looked as if he would like to argue with her, but after a moment he only nodded. "I'm sure you're right."

"No harm done. We'll both just forget the past five minutes ever happened and go back to our regularly scheduled lives."

"Great idea."

His ready agreement sent a hard kernel of regret to lodge somewhere in her sternum. For a moment, she had felt almost normal, just like any other woman. Someone who could flirt and smile and attract the interest of a sexy male.

He wanted to forget it ever happened, whereas she was quite certain she would never be able to erase these few moments from her memory.

"I should, uh, go."

"Yes." *Or you could stay and kiss me for a few more hours.*

"Call me if anything changes with the dog."

She drew in a breath. "I hope we're past the worst of it. But I will."

That last was a lie. She had absolutely no intention of calling him again in the middle of the night. She would drive Luke to the vet in Idaho Falls before she would drag Ben Caldwell out here again anytime soon.

"Good night."

She nodded, not trusting herself to reply, just wishing he would go already. He gave her a long, searching look before he shrugged back into his ranch coat and left through the side door.

A blast of cold air curled into the room from that brief moment he had opened the door. Chilled by more than just the winter night, she shivered as it sidled under her T-shirt.

What in heaven's name just happened here?

She wrapped her arms around herself. She had *known* he would be trouble. Somehow she had known. She never should have suggested he move into the foreman's house. If she had only used her brain, she might have predicted she would do something stupid around him, like develop a very awkward and embarrassing crush.

She spent most of her days here on the ranch, surrounded by her brothers and his few ranchhands, most of whom were either fresh-faced kids just out of high school or grizzled veterans who either were already married or held absolutely no appeal to her.

The ranch was safe. It had always been her haven from the hardness of the world. Now she had messed that up by inviting a tempting man to set up temporary residence smack in the middle of her comfort zone.

The man certainly knew how to kiss. She couldn't deny that. She pressed a hand to her stomach, which still seemed to be jumping with nerves. The last time she had been kissed so thoroughly and deliciously had been...well, never.

She sighed. It wouldn't happen again. Neither of them wanted this. She had only to remember the stunned dismay in Ben's eyes in that moment when he had come to his senses. He was likely still grieving for his wife, taken from him far too soon. And she...well, she had told herself she wasn't interested in a relationship, that she was content here helping Ridge with Destry and training her dogs and the occasional horse.

For the first time in a long time, she was beginning to wonder what else might be out in the big, scary world, waiting for her.

"I think he's feeling better, don't you?"

Caidy glanced up from the dough she was kneading to see her niece sitting cross-legged beside Luke's blanket. The dog's head was in her lap and he was gazing up at the girl with adoration.

"Yes. I think so. He seems much happier than he was even a few hours ago."

"I'm glad. I really thought he was a goner when I saw old Festus go after him."

Guilt socked her in the gut again. If she had kept a closer eye on Luke, he wouldn't be lying there with those bandages and she wouldn't be so beholden to Ben Caldwell.

"I hope that's a good reminder to you about how dangerous the bulls can be. That could just as easily have been you. I don't ever want you to take a chance with Festus or any of the bulls. They're usually placid guys most of the time, even Festus, but you never know."

"I know. I know. You and Dad have told me that like a thousand times. I'm not a little kid anymore, Aunt Caidy. I'm smart enough to know to keep my distance."

"Good. The ranch can be a dangerous place. You can't ever let your guard down. Even one of the cows could trample you if you lost your footing."

"It's a miracle I ever survived to be eleven years old, isn't it?"

Caidy made a face. "Smarty. You can't blame your dad and me for worrying about you. We just want you to be safe."

And happy, she added silently. She wanted to think

her presence here at the ranch had contributed in that department. If Ridge had been left on his own after Melinda left, forced to employ a string of nannies and babysitters, she wasn't sure Destry would have come through childhood with the same cheerful personality.

"What's going to happen to Luke? You can't train him to be a real cow dog now, can you?"

Even without his injuries, she suspected Luke would always be nervous around the cattle. How could she blame him, especially when she could relate, in a sense? Not to fearing cattle. She had no problem with the big animals. Her fears were a little closer to home. This time of year, her heartbeat always kicked up a bit when the doorbell rang, even when they were expecting company.

The memory of that fateful night was as much a part of her as the sprinkle of freckles on her nose and the tiny scar she had at the outside edge of her left eyebrow from an unfortunate encounter with the business end of a pitchfork when she was eight.

"I'm not really sure yet about Luke," she finally answered Destry as she formed a small ball of dough and set it into the prepared pan. "I'm guessing from this point on, he'll just be a pet."

"Here at the River Bow?"

"Sure. Why not?" They had plenty of dogs and didn't really need another one that was just a pet. Sadie, too old to work, sort of filled that role, but she supposed they would make room for one more.

"Good," Destry said, cuddling the dog close. "It's not his fault he got hurt. Not really. He was only being curious. It doesn't seem fair to get rid of him for an accident."

Destry was a sweet girl, compassionate and loving. Maybe too compassionate sometimes. Caidy smiled, remembering the previous Christmas when she had claimed she didn't want any presents that year. Instead she only wanted cash.

They all learned later she and some of her schoolmates were being scammed out of money and belongings...by none other than Gabi, the youngest sister of Trace's new wife.

She hadn't been part of their family then, of course. She had only been a troubled, lost young girl abandoned by her heartless witch of a mother and trying to find her way.

Trace had given both Becca and Gabi the loving family they all deserved—and Gabi and Destry had moved on and become best friends. That wasn't always a good thing. Trouble seemed to find the two of them like a pack of bloodhounds on the scent.

With the dog sleeping soundly now, Destry carefully set his head back down on the blankets, then rose and wandered over to the work island. "Need help rolling out the dough?"

"Sure. I'm doing cloverleaf rolls for dinner this afternoon. You remember, you roll three small balls and stick them together. Wash your hands first."

Destry complied quickly and the two of them worked together in mostly silence for a few moments. Caidy savored these small moments with her niece, who was growing up far too quickly.

She loved making dinner for her family on Sundays, when everyone gathered together to laugh and talk and catch up. Having all these new children—Alex, Maya, Gabi—only made family time together more fun.

She would never be a gourmet chef, but she enjoyed creating meals her family enjoyed. Warm rolls slathered in her homemade jam were her specialty. She still used the recipe her mother had taught her in this very kitchen when she was about Destry's age.

Her life was pretty darn good, she thought as she worked the elastic dough in a kitchen that was warm and comfortable and already smelled delicious from the roast beef that was cooking. She had family and friends, a couple of jobs she enjoyed, a home she loved, a dog who was on the mend.

She didn't need Ben Caldwell blowing into her world, bringing that sweet, rare smile and those stunning kisses, making her feel as if something vital was missing.

"Can I turn on the radio?" Destry asked after a few more minutes.

"Sure. Something we can dance to," she said, pushing away thoughts of Ben with a smile. A moment later, the kitchen filled with music—upbeat Christmas songs. Not really what she had in mind, but what could she do?

Destry was singing "Winter Wonderland" at the top of her lungs and jigging from side to side when the door opened and Ridge came in, stomping snow off his boots.

"It's coming down pretty hard out there. You might be in for a chilly sleigh ride, kiddo."

Destry grinned. "Snow is perfect. What could be more fun? Aunt Caidy already said she would make some of her good hot cocoa and we're going to mix up dough for oatmeal raisin cookies so we can put them in the oven right before we go. That way they'll still be hot on the wagon."

"Sounds like you've got it all figured out."

"It's going to be *great!* Thanks so much for agreeing to take us. You're awesome, Dad."

"You're welcome, kid."

He smiled at his daughter for a moment then turned

to Caidy. She noticed with no small degree of apprehension the deceptively casual expression on her brother's rugged features. "Hey, how would you feel if we added a few more at dinner?"

It wasn't a completely unusual request. Ridge had a habit of inviting in strays. She took care of the four-legged kind, and he often focused on the human variety.

"Shouldn't be a problem. It's a big roast and I can always throw in a few more potatoes and add more carrots. Who did you invite?"

He shrugged. "Just the new vet and his kids."

Just the new vet? The man she happened to have tangled lips with in this very kitchen twelve hours earlier? The very man she was trying to shove out of her brain. She opened her mouth to answer but nothing came out except an embarrassing sort of squeak.

"He was out shoveling when I cleared the drive with the tractor and we started chatting. I mentioned dinner and then the sleigh ride after and asked if they would like to join us."

She suddenly wanted to take the ball of dough in her hand and fling it at her brother. How could he do this to her? She had warned him not to get any ideas in his head about matchmaking, yet here he was doing exactly that.

She supposed she shouldn't be so surprised. All three of her brothers seemed to think their mission in life was to set her up with some big, gorgeous cowboy. Ben wasn't exactly a cowboy, but he had the big and gorgeous parts down.

How was she supposed to sit across the dinner table from the man when all she could remember was the silky slide of his tongue against hers, the hardness of those muscles against her, his sexy, ragged breathing as he tasted her mouth?

"You don't mind, do you?"

She would have laughed if she suddenly wasn't feeling queasy.

"No. Why should I mind?" she muttered, while in her head she went through about a dozen reasons. Starting and ending with that kiss.

"That's what I figured. You and Becca and Laura are always making way too much food. Inviting the vet and his family for dinner seemed like a nice way to welcome them to the ranch. And I figured his kids might get a charge out of going with us on the sleigh ride later."

Of all her three brothers, Ridge was the most taciturn. His failed marriage and the burden of responsibility that came with running the family ranch while the twins pursued other interests made him seem hard sometimes, but he also showed these flashes of kindness that tugged at her heart.

"I'm sure they will. It's bound to be something new and exciting for a couple of kids from California. They probably don't have much snow where they're from."

"Awesome!" Destry exclaimed. "I hope they're good singers."

Right. Singing and Ben Caldwell. Two things she should avoid at all costs thrown right in her face. This should prove to be a very interesting evening.

Chapter Seven

"Do you think Alex and Maya will be there?"

"It's a good bet, kid," Ben told his son as the three of them walked down the plowed lane through the gentle snowfall toward the ranch house. The snow muted all sounds, even the low gurgle of the creek, on the other side of the trees that formed an oxbow around the ranch.

The cold air smelled of hay and pine and woodsmoke. He breathed deeply, thinking it had been far too long since he had taken time to just savor his surroundings. The River Bow was unexpectedly serene, with the mix of aspens and pine and the mountains soaring to the east.

"I hope Gabi is there," Ava said, looking more enthusiastic about the outing than she had about anything in a long time. "She's superfunny."

"I'm sure she will be. Ridge said their whole family was coming for dinner and she's part of the family."

He and his kids, however, were *not*. They were only temporary guests and he probably had no business dragging his children to their family dinner, especially after the events of the night before.

He should have said no. Ridge Bowman took him by surprise with the invitation while they were out clearing snow and he had been so caught off guard, he hadn't known quite how to reply.

The kids would enjoy it. He had known that from the get-go. He was fairly sure he wouldn't. He didn't mind socializing. Brooke had loved to throw parties and some part of him had missed that since her death. But this party was obviously a family thing and he hated to impose.

If that wasn't enough, he also wasn't ready to face a certain woman yet—Caidy Bowman, of the soft curves and the silky hair and the warm mouth that tasted like cocoa and heaven.

That kiss, coming on the heels of his vivid, sexy dream about her, left him aching and restless. He hadn't slept at all after he left her house. He had tossed and turned and punched his pillow until he had finally gotten up at 6:00 a.m., before the children, and started shoveling snow to burn away some of this edgy hunger. Mother Nature had dumped quite a bit of snow throughout the day, so he had plenty of chances to work it off.

That kiss. He had wanted to drown in it, just yank her against him and tease and taste and explore until they were both shaking with need. Somehow he knew she would respond just as he had dreamed, with soft, eager enthusiasm.

How did a guy engage in casual chitchat with a woman after he had kissed her like that without wanting to do it all over again?

Despite the December chill, he unzipped his coat. He probably couldn't do much about his overheated imagination, but the rest of him didn't need to simmer.

A couple of dogs came up to greet them as they approached the house and Jack eased behind him. Though his son saw plenty of strange dogs at the clinic, he was often apprehensive around animals he didn't know. A large, untrained mastiff had cornered him once at the clinic a few years earlier, intent only on friendliness, but Jack had been justifiably frightened by the encounter and wary ever since.

"They won't hurt you, Jack. See, both of their tails are wagging. They just want to say hi."

"I don't want to," Jack said, hiding even further behind him.

"You don't have to, then. Ava, can you carry the bag with Mrs. Michaels's salad and toffee while I give your brother a lift?"

She grabbed the bag away from him and hurried ahead while he scooped up his son and set him on his shoulders for the last hundred yards of the walk, much to Jack's delight. It wouldn't be long before the boy grew too large for this but for now they both enjoyed it, even with his son's snowy boots hitting his chest.

In the gathering dusk, the log ranch house was lit up with icicle lights that dripped from the eaves and around the porch. People on the coast would pay serious money for the chance to spend Christmas here at a picturesque cattle ranch in the oxbow of a world-class fly-fishing creek.

Several unfamiliar vehicles were parked in the circular driveway in front of the ranch house and that awkwardness returned. If not for his children's anticipation, he probably would have turned on his heels and headed back to the cottage.

Ava reached the porch before they did and skipped up the stairs to ring the doorbell. As Ben and Jack reached the steps a woman he didn't know with dark hair and a winsome smile answered. "You must be the new veterinarian. Ridge mentioned you and your family were joining us. Hi. I'm Becca Bowman, married to Trace. Come in out of the snow."

He walked inside and went to work divesting the children of their abundance of outerwear: coats, gloves, hats, scarves and boots. Becca gathered them all up and set them inside a large closet under the curving log staircase.

"Are you Gabi's mom?" Ava asked, sitting on the bottom step to slip out of her boots.

"I'm her big sister actually. It's a long story. But I guess in every way that matters, I'm her mother."

An intriguing story. He wondered at the details but decided they weren't important. Becca had obviously stepped up to raise her sister and he couldn't help but find that admirable.

"Where is Gabi?" Ava asked eagerly.

"She and Destry are around somewhere. They'll be so excited to see you. They've been waiting impatiently for you to get here for the past hour."

Ava beamed with an enthusiasm that had been missing for far too long. Maybe staying here at the ranch near a friend for a few weeks would be good for her. Maybe it would finally help her resign herself to their move to Idaho, to the distance now between her and her grandparents.

"Last I saw them, they were playing a video game in the den. Straight down that hall and to the left."

Ava took off, with Jack close on her heels. He thought about calling them back but decided to let them figure things out. Kids usually did a much better job of that than adults.

"I think dinner is nearly ready," Becca said to him. "Come on into the great room and I'm sure one of the boys can hook you up with something to drink."

She led him into a huge room dominated by a massive angled wall of windows and the big Christmas tree he had seen glimmering from outside as they approached. Where was Caidy? he wondered, then was embarrassed at himself for looking for her straight away.

Her brother Ridge headed over immediately with a cold beer. "Hey, Doc Caldwell. Glad you could make it."

At least one of them was. "Thanks."

"Have you met my brothers?" Ridge asked.

"I know Chief Bowman. Fire Chief Bowman," he corrected. He could only imagine how confusing that must be for the town, to have a fire chief and police chief who were not only brothers but identical twins.

"You've deserted us at the inn, I understand," Taft Bowman said.

He winced. The only thing that bothered him worse than being obligated to Caidy was knowing he had checked out prematurely from the Cold Creek Inn. "Sorry. We were bursting at the seams there."

"Oh, no worries about that. Laura's already booked your rooms through the holiday. She had to turn away several guests in the past few weeks and ended up contacting some of them who wanted to be on standby. They were thrilled at the last-minute cancellation."

He had expected the immensely popular inn would do just fine without his business. "That's a relief."

"She's been saying for a week how she thought your

kids needed to be in a real house for the holidays. She was thrilled when Caidy talked to her about having you stay here. As soon as she hung up the phone, she said she couldn't believe she'd never thought of the fore-man's cottage out here."

"I'm already missing those delicious breakfasts at the inn," he said. That was true enough, though Mrs. Michaels was also an excellent cook and had taken great delight just that morning in preparing pancakes from scratch and her famous fluffy scrambled eggs.

In his three weeks of staying at the Cold Creek Inn, Laura Bowman had struck him as an extraordinarily kind woman. The whole family, really, had welcomed him and his children to town with warm generosity.

"The guy over there on his cell phone is my husband, Trace," Becca said. "He's the police chief and is lucky enough to be off duty tonight, though his deputies often forget that."

The man in question waved and smiled a greeting but continued on the phone. Ben suddenly remembered the toffee and pulled out the tin. "Where would you like me to put this?"

"You didn't have to fix anything," Becca scolded.

"I didn't have anything to do with it," he admitted. "My housekeeper did all the heavy lifting. She sends her apologies, by the way. She would have come but she needed to take a call from her daughter. She's expecting her first grandchild and the separation has been difficult."

He felt more than a little guilty about that. Anne had come with them to Idaho willingly enough but he knew she missed her daughter, especially during this exciting, nerve-racking time of impending birth. They communicated via videoconferencing often, but it wasn't the same as face-to-face interaction.

"Let's just set it on the table here. Wow. I've got to taste some first. I love toffee."

"Ooh, send some this way," Taft said, so Becca passed the tin of candy around to all the brothers.

"She also made a salad. Greek pasta."

"That sounds delicious too. I'll take it in to see where Caidy wants it."

"I can do that." His words—and anticipation to see her again—came out of nowhere. "I should probably check in on my patient while I'm here anyway."

"Okay. Sure. Just through the hall and around the corner."

He remembered. He had a feeling every detail of the Bowman kitchen would be etched in his memory for a very long time.

When he entered, his gaze immediately went to Caidy, and the restlessness that had dogged him all day seemed to ease. She stood at the stove with her hair tucked into a loose ponytail, wearing an apron over jeans and a crisp white shirt.

She looked pretty and fresh, and something soft and warm seemed to unfurl inside him.

She must have sensed his presence, though it was obvious she was spinning a dozen different plates. She glanced around and he saw her cheeks turn pink, though he wasn't certain if it was from the heat of the stove or the memory of the kiss they had shared in this very room.

"Oh. Hi. You're here."

"Yes. I've brought a salad. Greek pasta. My house-keeper made it, actually. And toffee. I brought toffee too."

Good grief. Could he sound any more like an idiot?

"That's great. Thank you. The salad can go on the buffet in the dining room. I don't imagine the toffee will last long with my brothers around."

"They were already working on it," he said.

"Oh, man. I love toffee. They know it, too, but do you think they're going to save me any? Highly doubtful. It's going to be gone before I get a taste."

"I'll have Mrs. Michaels make more for you," he offered, his voice gruff.

She smiled. "That's sweet of you. Or I could just arm wrestle my brothers for the last piece."

"Right." He cleared his throat. "Uh, I'll just take this into the dining room."

This was stupid. Why couldn't he talk to her? Yes, she was a beautiful, desirable woman who had moaned in his arms just a few hours earlier, but that didn't mean he couldn't carry on a semi-intelligent conversation with her.

Determined to do just that, after he had taken the salad into the dining room he returned to the kitchen instead of seeking the safety of the great room with the rest of the Bowmans.

Caidy looked surprised to see him again so soon.

"I wanted to check on Luke," he explained.

"He seems to be feeling better. I moved him into my room so he has a chance to rest during all the commotion of dinner."

"You mind if I take a look at him?"

She glanced up, surprise in her eyes. "Really? You don't have to do that. Ridge didn't invite you to dinner to get free vet care out of the deal."

Why *had* Ridge invited him? He had been wonder-

ing that all afternoon. "I'm here. I might as well see
how he's progressing."

"Can I take over stirring the gravy so you can show
Ben to your room?"

For the first time, he noticed Laura Bowman, who
had been standing on the other side of the kitchen slicing olives.

"Thank you. It should be done in just a few minutes."

Caidy washed her hands, then tucked a loose strand
of hair behind her ear, nibbling her lip between her teeth
just enough to remind him of how that lip had tasted between his own teeth and sent blood pooling in his groin.

She led the way down the hall to a door just off the
kitchen and he heard a little bark from inside the room
just before she pushed open the door.

He had a vague impression of, not so much fussi-
ness, as feminine softness. A lavender-and-brown quilt
and a flurry of pillows covered a queen-size bed, and
lace curtains spilled from the windows. His gaze was
drawn to a lovely oil painting of horses grazing in a
flower-strewn field that looked as if it could be somewhere on the River Bow. It hung on the wall at the foot
of the bed, the first thing she must see upon awakening
and drifting off to sleep.

He shouldn't be so interested in where she slept—
or what she might dream about—he ordered himself,
and he quickly shifted attention to the dog. The border
collie was lying beside the bed near the window, in the
same enclosure he had rested in while in the kitchen.

When he saw Caidy, Luke wagged his tail and tried
to get up but she bent over and rested a comforting
hand on his head. He immediately subsided as if she
had tranquilized him.

"Look who's here. It's our friend Dr. Caldwell. Aren't you glad to see him?"

Because he had spent two hours operating on the dog and shoved a needle into his lungs a few hours earlier, Ben highly doubted he ranked very high on the animal's list of favorite humans, but he wasn't going to argue with her.

"No more breathing trouble?"

"No. He slept like a rock the rest of the night and has been sleeping most of the day."

"That's the best thing for him."

"That's what I figured. I've been keeping his pain medication on a consistent schedule. Ridge has been helping me carry him outside for his business."

He stepped over the enclosure and knelt inside so he could run his hand over the dog. Though he focused on his patient, some part of him was aware the whole time of her watching him intently.

Did she feel the tug and pull between them, or was it completely one-sided?

He didn't think so. She had definitely kissed him back. He vividly relived the sweetness of her mouth softening under his, the little catch in her breathing, the way her pulse had raced beneath his fingers. His gut ached at the memory, especially at the knowledge that a memory and those wild dreams were all he was likely to have from her.

"I think he's healing very nicely. I would think in a day or two you can let him have full mobility again. Bring him into the office around the middle of the week and I can check the stitches. I'm happy to see he's doing so well."

"You didn't think he would survive, did you?"

"No," he said honestly. "I'm always happy when I'm proved wrong."

"You've really gone above and beyond in caring for him. Coming out in the middle of the night and everything. I…want you to know I appreciate it. Very much."

He shrugged. "It's my job. I wouldn't be very good at it if I didn't care about my patients, would I?"

She opened her mouth as if to say something else but then closed it again. Awkwardness sagged between them, heavy and clumsy, and he suddenly knew she was remembering the kiss too.

He sighed. "Look, I need to apologize about last night. It was…unprofessional and should never have happened."

She gazed at him out of those impossibly green eyes without blinking and he wondered what the hell she might be thinking.

"I don't want you to think I'm in the habit of that."

"Of what?"

He felt stupid for bringing it up but didn't know how else to move past this morning-after sort of discomfort. Better to face it head-on, he figured. "You know what. I came over to help you with your dog. I shouldn't have kissed you. It was unprofessional and shouldn't have happened."

Unexpectedly, she gave a strained-sounding laugh. "Maybe you ought to think about adding that to your list of services, Dr. Caldwell. Believe me, if word got out what a good kisser you are, every woman in Pine Gulch who even *thought* about owning a cat or dog would be lining up at the adoption day at the animal shelter just for the perk of being able to lock lips with the sexy new veterinarian."

He could feel himself flush. She was making fun of

him, but he supposed he deserved it. "I was only try-ing to tell you there's no reason to worry it will hap-pen again. It was late and I was tired and not really myself. I never would have even *thought* about kissing you otherwise."

"Oh, well. That explains it perfectly, then."

He had the vague feeling he had hurt her feelings somehow, which absolutely hadn't been his intention. He suddenly remembered how much he had hated the dating scene, trying to wade through all those nuances and layers of meaning.

"Good to know your weaknesses," she went on. "Next time I need veterinary care in the middle of the night for one of my animals, I'll be sure to call the vet over in Idaho Falls. We certainly wouldn't want a re-peat of that hideous experience."

"I think we can both agree it wasn't hideous. Far from it." He muttered the last bit under his breath but she caught it anyway. Her pupils flared and her gaze dipped to his mouth again. His abdominal muscles con-tracted and he felt that awareness seethe and curl be-tween them again, like the currents of Cold Creek.

"Just unfortunate," she murmured.

"Give me a break here, Caidy. What do you want me to say?"

"Nothing. We both agreed to forget it happened."

"That's a little easier said than done," he admitted.

"Isn't everything?"

"True enough."

"It's no big deal, Ben. We kissed. So what? I enjoyed it, and you enjoyed it. We both agree it shouldn't hap-pen again. Let's just move on, okay?"

As easy as that? Somehow he didn't think so, but he wasn't about to argue.

"I should get back to the kitchen. Thank you for taking the time to check on Luke."

"No problem," he said. He followed her out of the room, wishing more than anything that circumstances could be different, that he could be the sort of man a woman like Caidy Bowman needed.

Chapter Eight

Insufferable man!

When they left her bedroom, Ben headed into the great room with the others while Caidy, unsettled and annoyed, returned to the kitchen to finish the preparations for dinner.

How could he reduce what had been one of the single most exhilarating moments of her life to a terrible mistake teeming with awkwardness?

Yes, the kiss shouldn't have happened. They both accepted it. He didn't have to act as if the two of them had committed some horrible crime and should beat themselves up with guilt about it for the rest of their lives.

It was late and I was tired and not really myself. I never would have even thought *about kissing you otherwise.*

That removed any doubt in her mind that he was attracted to her. He had kissed her because he was tired and because she was there. The humiliation of that was almost more than she could bear, especially given the enthusiastic way she had responded to him and the silly fantasies she had been spinning all day.

"Is something wrong? Are you ready for us to start taking dishes out to the dining room?" Becca asked.

With a jolt, Caidy realized she had been staring without moving at the roast she had taken out of the oven. She frowned, frustrated at herself and at Ben, and did her best to drag her attention away from her pout.

"Yes. That would be great, thank you. Everything should be just about ready to go. I ought to let the roast sit for another few minutes, but by the time we get everything else on the table, it will be ready to carve."

Becca and Laura picked up covered bowls and took them out to the table, chattering as they went about their respective plans for Christmas Eve. Caidy smiled as she listened to them. She loved both of her sisters-in-law deeply. Having sisters had turned out to be far more wonderful than she ever imagined. The best part about them was that each was perfect for her respective Bowman brother.

Becca, with that hidden vulnerability and her flashes of clever humor, brought out the very best in Trace. Since she and Gabi had come into his life the previous Christmas, Caidy had seen a soft gentleness in Trace that had been missing since their parents were murdered.

Laura Pendleton was exactly the woman Caidy had always wanted for Taft to soothe the wildness in him. Taft and Laura had once been deeply in love until their engagement abruptly and mysteriously ended just days before their wedding.

Seeing them together, reunited after all these years,

filled her with delight. She especially loved seeing Taft shed his carefree player image and step up to be a caring father to Laura's two children, energetic Alex and the adorable Maya.

She wasn't jealous of the joy her brothers had found—she was happy for them all. Maybe she grew a little wistful when she watched those sweet little moments between two people who loved each other deeply, but she did her best not to think about them.

Still chattering, both Laura and Becca came back into the kitchen to grab the salads they had each prepared out of the refrigerator. At least the Sunday dinners had become much easier since her brothers married. She used to fix the whole shebang on her own, but now the two women and often Gabi pitched in and contributed their own salads or desserts.

She didn't know how much longer this Sunday dinner tradition could continue. She wouldn't blame Taft and Trace for wanting to spend their free time with their own nuclear families. For now, everyone seemed content to continue gathering each week when they could.

"So the new veterinarian is gorgeous. Why didn't anybody tell me?" Becca said, putting the rolls Caidy had removed from the second oven into a basket.

"I don't know," Laura answered. "Maybe we figured since you're married to Trace Bowman, who is only second in all-around gorgeousness to his twin brother, you really didn't need to know about the cute new vet."

Caidy felt another of those little pangs of envy at Becca's sudden cat-who-ate-the-canary smile.

"True," she answered. "But you should have warned me before I opened the door to find this yummy man on the doorstep—and added to the yum factor, the very adorable little boy on his shoulders."

Caidy didn't say anything as she carved the roast beef. This was usually Ridge's job, for some reason, but she didn't want to call him in from entertaining said veterinarian out in the other room.

"What about you, Caidy?" Becca said. "You're the only available one here. Don't you think he's gorgeous? Something about those big blue eyes and those long, long lashes…"

She had a sudden vivid memory of those eyes closing as he kissed her the night before, of his mouth teasing and licking at hers, of the heat and strength of his arms around her and how she had wanted to lean into that broad chest and stay right there.

Her knees suddenly felt a little on the weak side and she narrowly avoided slicing off her thumb.

"Sure," she said. "Too bad he's got the personality of a honey badger."

She didn't miss the surprised looks both women gave her. Laura's mouth opened and Becca's eyebrows just about crept up to her hairline, probably because Caidy rarely spoke poorly about anyone. Every time she started to vent about someone when they weren't present, her mother's injunction about not saying something behind a person's back you wouldn't say to his face would ring in her ears.

She wouldn't have said anything if she wasn't burning with humiliation about that kiss he obviously regretted.

Laura was the first to speak. "That's odd you would say that. I found him very nice while he was staying at the inn. Half of my front desk staff was head over heels in love with him from the start."

After that kiss, she was very much afraid it wouldn't take more than a slight jostle for her to join them. She couldn't remember ever being this drawn to a man—the fact that she was so attracted to a man who basically found her a nuisance was just too humiliating.

"I'm not surprised," she finally said, hoping they would attribute the color she could feel soaking her cheeks to the overwarm kitchen and her exertions fixing the meal. "Do you want to know what I think about Ben Caldwell? I think he's a rude, arrogant, opinionated jerk. Some women are drawn to that kind of man. Don't ask me why."

"Don't forget, he's also often inconveniently in the wrong place at the wrong time."

At the sudden deep voice, she and both of her sisters-in-law gave a collective gasp and turned to the doorway. Every single molecule inside her wanted to cringe at the sight of Ben standing there, watching the three of them, his face void of expression.

"My son spilled a glass of water," he explained. "I came in looking for a towel to clean it up. Unless you think that's too rude of a request."

Becca reached almost blindly into the drawer where Caidy kept the dish towels, pulled one out and handed it to him.

"Thanks," he answered, then left without another word. Caidy wanted to bury her face in the gravy.

"Wow. I guess the two of you haven't exactly hit it off," Becca said.

Caidy thought of that sizzling kiss, apparently mostly one-sided. "You could say that," she answered.

Her mother would have yanked her earlobe and sent her to her bedroom for being so unconscionably rude to a guest in their home. She couldn't face him again. How could she sit at the table beside him after what he had heard her say? The worst of it was, none of it was true. She was just being petty and small, embarrassed that she was so fiercely attracted to a man who regretted ever touching her.

How could she figure out a way to stay here in the kitchen all evening?

She let out a heavy breath. She was going to have to find a way to apologize to him, but how on earth could she manage that without giving him some kind of explanation? She couldn't tell him the truth. That would only add another layer of mortification onto her humiliation.

"Um, I think I'll just take these rolls out," Becca said into the sudden painful silence.

After she hurried out of the kitchen, Laura placed a hand on Caidy's arm. "Okay, what was that about? Did something happen between the two of you?"

Her dear friend had known her for many years—long before her parents were killed, when everything in her world changed. She didn't want to tell her. She didn't want to talk to *anyone*—she just wanted to hide out in her room with Luke. He, at least, was one male she didn't feel awkward and stupid around.

She sighed. "I called him to come over last night. One of those frantic, middle-of-the-night emergencies. Luke was having trouble breathing and I was upset and didn't know what else to do. He… Before he left, he… We kissed. It was…great. Really great. But today he told me what a mistake it was. He acted like it was this horrible experience that we should both pretend never happened. I guess I was more hurt than I realized by his reaction. I lashed out, which wasn't fair. I don't believe any of those things. Well, I did at first. He was quite rude to me after Luke's accident and treated me like it was my fault. I guess it was, in some ways, but he really twisted the knife. He's been... We've been fine since then, except just now in my room."

Laura was silent for a moment, apparently digesting that barrage of information. Finally she spoke with that calm common sense Caidy loved about her.

"I've had the chance over the past few weeks while he's been staying at the inn to talk with Mrs. Michaels," she said. "She's told me a few things about Ben's situation. More than she probably should have, probably. Take it easy on the man, okay? He's been through a rough few years. His wife's death was horrible apparently."

"He told me she died of complications from diabetes."

"Did he also tell you she was pregnant at the time?"

"No. Oh, no."

Laura nodded. "Apparently she went into a diabetic coma while she was driving and crashed into a tree. Their baby died along with her. It was a miracle Ava and Jack weren't in the car too. They were with their grandparents."

Those poor children. And poor Ben. If she felt bad before about what she had said, now she felt about a zillion times worse.

"According to Mrs. Michaels, his late wife's parents blame him for their daughter and grandchild's death and have done all they can to drive Ava and Jack away from him. That's the main reason he came here, I believe. To put some distance between them and try salvaging his family."

She paused and squeezed Caidy's arm. "I think he could really use a friend."

She had never considered herself a petty person before but she was beginning to discover otherwise. So what if the man regretted kissing her? So her pride was bruised. She tried to be a good person most of the time. Couldn't she look past that and be that friend Laura was talking about?

"Thanks for telling me. I'll…figure out a way to apologize. But not right now, okay? Right now I have a dozen people to feed."

Laura hugged her. "I know you will. Apologize, I mean. You're a good person, Caidy. Someone I'm pleased to call my sister. I just have one more question and it's an important one. I want you to think long and hard before you answer me."

She felt more than a little trepidation. "What's that?"

"Besides being arrogant and rude, how is our Dr. Caldwell in the kissing department?"

Despite everything, she gave a strained laugh. "Let me put it this way. Luke wasn't the only one having trouble breathing last night."

Laura grinned at her, which gave her a little burst of courage. Enough, at least, that she could draw in a deep breath, pick up the platter with the roast beef slices and head out into the other room with squared shoulders to face what just might be the most embarrassing meal of her life.

Dinner wasn't quite the ordeal she had feared.

By the time she reached the table, the only seat left was at the opposite end of the table from Ben, between Ridge at the head and Destry. Good. She needed a little space from Ben while she tried to figure out how she could possibly face the man after making a complete idiot of herself over him, again and again.

He was deep in conversation with her brothers and Becca when she sat down, and he didn't look in her direction, much to her relief. After Ridge said grace, blessing the food and welcoming their guests to the ranch, various conversations flowed around her. Caidy moved her food around in silence, for the most part, until Destry, Gabi and Ava enlisted her opinion about how old she was when she started wearing makeup.

She didn't wear much now unless she was dressing up for something. "I think I was about thirteen or fourteen before I wore anything but lip gloss. You've got a few years to go, girls."

"I'm ready now," Gabi declared.

"Me too," Destry chimed in.

"My grandma let me keep some eye makeup and lip stuff at her house when we lived in California," Ava said. "I could only put it on while I was there or when we went shopping or out to lunch. I had to wash it off before I left so my dad didn't freak, which was totally stupid."

Destry looked slightly appalled at the idea of keeping makeup—or anything else—from her father. "I could never do that!"

"My grandma said it was okay."

In the mode of adults sticking together, Caidy gave the three girls a mild look. "Here's a pretty good rule— if you can't wear it, taste it or say it in front of your dad, you probably shouldn't wear it, taste it or say it when he's not there."

"Agreed." Ridge interjected into the conversation. "You hear that, Des?"

The three girls giggled and started talking about something from school, leaving Caidy's mind to follow the conversation between the twins and Ben at the other end of the table.

"So, Dr. Caldwell, how are you finding Pine Gulch?" Trace was asking.

"Ben. Please, call me Ben. We're enjoying living here so far. The town seems to be filled with very kind people. For the most part anyway."

He didn't look in her direction when he spoke but she cringed anyway, certain his pointed barb was aimed at her.

"It's the *least part* you have to worry about," Taft said with a wink. "I could name a few people in town whose bad side you want to stay far clear of. I'm sure Trace knows a few more on the law enforcement side. We've got our share of bad customers."

"I'm sure you do," Ben murmured. "Rude, arrogant jerks."

"You better believe it," Taft said.

Becca quickly cleared her throat. "Uh, can you pass the potatoes?" she asked Ben.

"Sure, if there are any left." He picked up the bowl Caidy always served the mashed potatoes in, the flower-lined earthenware that had always been one of her mother's favorites.

For the first time since she sat down, he looked in her direction, though his gaze was focused somewhere above her head. "Everything is really delicious," he said. "Isn't that right, Ava? Jack?"

"Supergood," Jack said. He had a smudge of gravy on his cheek and looked absolutely adorable. "Can I have another roll? Ooh, with jam! I *love* strawberries."

Ben grabbed one of her cloverleaf rolls and spread some of her jam on it. When he handed it to his son, Jack gobbled it in three bites, smearing red along with the gravy. Ben shook his head, picked up his napkin and dabbed at the mess on Jack's face. She watched out of the corner of her gaze as those big hands that had held her close attended to his child, and something soft and warm unfurled inside her chest.

He looked up at just that moment and caught her watching. Their gazes held for one long, charged moment while the conversation flowed around them. Then Ridge asked him another question and he looked away, breaking the connection.

He and his children fit in well with the family. Taft's stepson, Alex, and Jack seemed like two peas in a proverbial pod, with Maya attending closely to their every word, and Gabi and Des had been quick to absorb Ava into their circle.

This was only temporary, she reminded herself. After the holidays, he would take his cute kids and his friendly housekeeper and move into the big house he was building. In a matter of days, he would be just a peripheral figure in her world. He wouldn't even be that if she didn't need to take one of the dogs for the occasional visit to the veterinarian.

She should be relieved about that, she told herself. Not glum.

"I love that painting over the fireplace," Ben said into a temporary lull of the conversation. "I see the artist's last name is Bowman. Any relation?"

The rest of the table fell silent—even the children. Nobody seemed willing to jump in to answer him except Ridge.

"Yes," her oldest brother finally said. "She is a relation. She was our mother."

Ben glanced around the table, obviously picking up on the sudden shift in mood.

"I'll admit, I don't know much about art, but I find that piece striking. I don't know if it's the horses in the foreground or the mountains or the fluttery curtains in the window of the old cabin but every time I look away for a few moments, something draws me back. That's real talent."

Her heart warmed a little at his praise of their mother's talent. "She was brilliant," Caidy murmured.

He looked at her and she saw an unexpected compassion in his eyes. Seeing it made her feel even more guilty. She didn't deserve compassion from him, not after her mean words.

"Several of her paintings were stolen eleven years ago," Trace said. "Since then, we've done our best to recover what we can. We've had investigators tracking some of them down. This one was located about three years ago in a gallery in the Sonoma area of California."

"It was always Caidy's favorite," Ridge put in. "Finding it again was something of a miracle."

This shifted all attention to her again and she squirmed. Did anybody besides Laura and Becca pick up the tension in the room? She doubted it. Her brothers usually were oblivious to social currents and the kids were too busy eating and talking and having fun. Just as they should be.

To her relief, Laura—sweet, wonderful Laura— stepped up to deflect attention. "So, Dr. Caldwell, you and your children are coming along on the sleigh ride after dinner, aren't you?"

"Sleigh ride!" Jack exclaimed and he and Alex, best buddies now, did a cute little high-five maneuver.

Ben watched them ruefully. "I don't know. I kind of feel like we've intruded enough on your family."

"Oh, you have to come," Destry exclaimed.

"Yes!" Gabi joined her. "It's going to be awesome!

We're going to sing Christmas carols and have hot chocolate and everything. Oh, please, come with us!"

If things weren't so funky between them right now, she would have told him he was fighting a losing battle. One man simply couldn't fight the combined efforts of the Bowmans and their progeny, adopted or otherwise.

"We're not going far," Ridge promised. "Only a couple miles up the canyon. Probably shouldn't take more than an hour."

"Resistance is futile," Taft said with a grin. "You might as well give in gracefully."

Ben laughed. "In that case, sure. Okay."

The kids shrieked with excitement. Caidy wished she could share even a tiny smidgen of their enthusiasm. The only bright spot for her in the whole thing was that Ben's presence probably eliminated the need for her to go along. Ridge couldn't claim they didn't have enough adults now. She would just offer an excuse to stay at the house and let the rest of them have all the Christmas fun.

She was still going to have to figure out a way to apologize to the man, but at this point she would take any reprieve she could find, however temporary.

Chapter Nine

After dinner had been cleared, the girls' other friends began arriving. Caidy threw in the trays of cookies she and Destry had readied, her brothers headed out to hitch up the big draft horses to the hay wagon and everyone else began donning winter gear. After the cookies came out, Caidy walked through the house gathering all the blankets she could find.

As she headed down the stairs with an armload of blankets, she saw through the big windows that the snow had eased and was only falling now in slow, puffy flakes. Moonlight had peeked behind the storm clouds, turning everything a pearlescent midnight-blue.

It was stunning enough from here. She could only imagine how beautiful it would be to ride through the night on the wagon, with the cold air in her face and the sound of children's laughter swirling through the night.

She was almost sorry she wasn't going with them. Almost.

She continued down the stairs, doing her best to avoid making eye contact with Ben, who was helping Jack into his boots.

"Sleigh ride. Sleigh ride. Sleigh ride," Maya chanted, wiggling her hips that were bundled up along with the rest of her in a very cute pink snowsuit with splashy orange flowers.

Caidy couldn't help laughing. "You're going to have a wonderful time, little bug," she said, kissing Maya's nose. She loved all of the children in her family but sweet, vulnerable Maya held a special place in her heart.

"You come," Maya said, reaching for her hand.

"Oh, honey. I'm not going. I'll be here when you get back."

"What do you mean, you're not going? You have to come," Ridge said sternly. "Where's your coat?"

"In the closet. Where it's staying. I figured somebody needs to stay here. Keep the home fire burning and all that."

"Don't worry about that," Becca said from underneath Trace's arm. "I've got that covered."

For the first time, Caidy realized her sister-in-law wasn't wearing a coat either.

"Why aren't *you* going?" Ridge asked, looking even more disgruntled.

"I'm planning to sit this one out. I have court tomorrow and some work to do before then. And, to be honest, I'm not sure being bounced around on a hay wagon right now would be the best thing for, well, for the baby."

For a moment everyone stared at her. Even the girls who had come for Gabi's little sleigh ride party stopped their giggly chatter.

"Baby? You're having a baby?" Laura exclaimed.

Becca nodded and Trace hugged her more tightly, then kissed the top of her head, clearly a proud papa.

"When?" Caidy asked, thrilled for both of them.

"June," Gabi declared proudly. "I've been *dying* to tell everyone! I kept my mouth shut, see, Trace? You said I couldn't. Ha!"

Her brother laughed and grabbed his wife's sister with his free arm, pulling her into their shared embrace. "You did good, kid. We were going to tell everyone at dinner but the right moment never quite came."

"There's never a *wrong* moment for that kind of great news," Ridge said. "Congratulations. Another Bowman. Just what the world needs."

The next few moments were spent with hugs and kisses and good wishes all the way around. Even Ben shook both of their hands and kissed Becca's cheek, though he had just met her that afternoon.

She suddenly remembered with a pang that he had lost a child when his wife died. Was this spontaneous celebration of impending parenthood difficult for him? If it was, he didn't show it by his manner.

Now Maya's chant changed to "baby, baby, baby," but she didn't lose the hip wiggle. Caidy hugged her too. "It's wonderful news, isn't it? You'll have a new cousin."

"I like cousins," Maya said.

"Me too, bug."

When Caidy finally worked her way around the crowd, she hugged Becca. "I can't wait to be an aunt again. I'm thrilled for both of you."

Becca hugged her back. "Thank you, my dear."

"All the more reason I should stay here and keep you company, just in case you need anything."

Becca gave her a knowing look. "You're the soul of

helpfulness, Caidy. Either that, or you're trying to avoid a certain rude, arrogant veterinarian."

She cringed at the reminder. "Well, there is that."

"Sorry, hon. I'd like to help you out but I think Ridge probably needs your help corralling all those kids. Besides that, I don't think it's a good idea to keep avoiding him."

"Am I that obvious?" she asked ruefully.

"A little bit. Probably Laura and I were the only ones who picked up on it. And maybe Ben."

Caidy blew out a breath. Drat. Becca was right. Ridge probably *did* need her help. "I hate being a coward," she murmured.

"It's only a sleigh ride. An hour out of your life. You can handle that. You've been through much worse."

"I don't want to leave you."

"I could use a little quiet, if you want the truth. Go, Caidy."

"As exciting as this news is, we need to get this show on the road," Ridge declared, as if on cue. "Let's load up."

The girls squealed loudly. Maya covered her ears with her mittened hands, wearing a look of alarm.

Caidy gave her a reassuring smile. "Don't worry about those silly girls. They just want to go have fun."

"Me too. You come."

She sighed, resigned to her fate. "Yes, Queen Maya."

The girl gave her sweet giggle as Caidy grabbed her coat out of the closet and quickly found mittens and a quite fancy chapeau handmade by Emery Kendall Cavazos that she had won in the gift exchange a few weeks earlier at the Friends of the Library Christmas party.

"Hurry up, Caid," Taft said. "We don't have all night.

The sooner we go, the sooner we can get it over with and come back to watch the basketball game. Come on, Maya."

"I stay with Auntie," the girl said and Caidy's heart melted, as it frequently did around her.

"I've got her," she told her brother.

"Are you sure?"

"Yes. We're coming. I'm almost ready."

Taft left and she quickly finished shoving on boots, grabbed Maya's hand and hurried out to the hay wagon.

The horses stamped and blew in the cold air, which smelled of woodsmoke and snow. What a beautiful night. Perfect for a sleigh ride. Well, not officially a sleigh ride because the wagon had wheels, not runners, but she didn't think any of them would quibble.

Ridge had lined the wagon with straw bales. To her dismay, everyone else was settling as they approached the wagon and the only free space left for her and Maya was near the back of the wagon—right next to Ben. Had her brothers colluded to arrange that? She wouldn't put it past them.

Right now, Ben was more likely to throw her over the side than cooperate with any Bowman matchmaking efforts, but her brothers had no way of knowing that— unless Laura or Becca had spilled to their husbands.

"Auntie, up," Maya said.

How was she going to manage this? Maya wasn't heavy but Caidy didn't think she could climb the ladder with her in her arms and she wasn't sure Maya could negotiate them on her own. "If you want to lift her up, I can help her the rest of the way," Ben said, obviously noticing her predicament.

Caidy scooped Maya into her arms and held her up for him. Their arms brushed as he easily tugged the girl the rest of the way. Did he feel the sparks between them, or was it just her imagination? Caidy climbed the ladder and stood for a moment, wishing she could squeeze up front with Ridge. Unfortunately, he already had Alex and Jack riding shotgun.

"Sit down, Caidy, or you're going to fall over when Ridge takes off," Taft ordered. Heaven save her from brothers who didn't think she had a brain in her head.

Left with no choice, she sat on the same bale as Ben—who looked rugged and masculine in a fleece-lined heavy ranch coat the color of dust. At least Maya sat between them, providing some buffer.

Ridge turned around to make sure all his passengers were settled and then clicked to the big horses. They took off down the driveway, accompanied by the jangle of bells on the harnesses.

"Go, horsies! Jingle bells, jingle bells!" Maya exclaimed and Caidy smiled at her. When she lifted her gaze, she found Ben smiling down at the girl too. Her heart stuttered a little at the gentleness on his expression. She had called him rude and arrogant, yet here he was treating Maya, with her beautiful smile and Down syndrome features, with breathtaking sweetness.

She had to say something. Now was the perfect time. She clenched her fingers into her palms inside her mittens and turned to him. "Look, I...I'm sorry about earlier. What I said. It wasn't true. Not any of it. I was just being stupid."

"What?" he yelled, leaning down to hear over the rushing wind and the eight laughing girls.

"I said I'm sorry." She spoke more loudly but at that moment all the girls started actually singing "Jingle Bells" in time with the chiming bells from the horses.

"What?" He leaned his head closer to hers, over

Maya's head, and she didn't know what else to do but lean in and speak in his ear, though she felt completely ridiculous. She wanted to tell him to just forget the whole thing. She had come this far, though. She might as well finish the thing.

Up close, he smelled delicious. She couldn't help noticing that outdoorsy soap she had noticed when they were kissing....

She dragged her mind away from that and focused on the apology she should be making. "I said I was sorry," she said in his ear. "For what I said in the kitchen to my sisters-in-law, I mean. They were teasing me, uh, about you...and I was being completely stupid. I'm sorry you overheard. I didn't mean it."

He turned his head until his face was only inches from hers. "Any of it?"

"Well, you are pretty arrogant," she answered tartly.

To her surprise, he laughed at that and the low, sexy timbre of it shivered down her spine and spread out her shoulders to her fingertips.

"I can be," he answered.

"Sing!" Maya commanded as the girls broke into "Rudolph the Red-Nosed Reindeer."

She laughed and picked the girl onto her lap, grateful for her small, warm weight and the distraction she provided from this very inconvenient attraction she didn't know what to do about to a man who was sending her more mixed signals than a broken traffic light.

She was taken further off guard when Ben began to sing along with Maya and the girls in a very pleasing tenor. He even sang all the extra lines about lightbulbs and reindeers playing Monopoly.

She had to turn away, focusing instead on the homes

they passed, their holiday lights glittering in the pale moonlight.

This wasn't such a bad way to spend an evening, she decided. Even with the caroling, she was surrounded by family she loved, by beautiful scenery, by the serenity of a winter night. She was happy she had come, she realized with some shock.

The girls broke into "Silent Night" after that, changing up the lighthearted mood a little, and she hummed softly under her breath while Maya mangled the words but did her best to follow along. In the middle of the first "Sleep in heavenly peace" injunction, Ben leaned down once more.

"Why aren't you singing?" His low voice tickled her ear and gave her chills underneath the layers of wool.

She shrugged, unable to answer him. She wasn't sure she could tell him at all and she certainly couldn't tell him on a jangly, noisy sleigh ride surrounded by family and Destry's friends.

"Seriously," he pressed, leaning away when the song ended and they could converse a little more easily. "Do you have some ideological or religious objection to Christmas songs I should know about?"

She shook her head. "No. I just…don't sing."

"Don't listen to her," Taft said. She must have spoken louder than she intended if her brother could overhear from the row of hay bales ahead of them.

"Caidy has a beautiful voice," he went on. "She used to sing solos in the school and church choir. Once she even sang the national anthem by herself at a high school football game."

Goodness. She barely remembered that. How did Taft? He had been a wildlands firefighter when she was in high school, traveling across the West with an elite smoke-jumper squad, but she now recalled he had been home visiting Laura and had come to hear her sing at that football game.

He was the only one of her brothers who had been able to make it. Ridge had still been feuding with their father and had been living on a ranch in Montana and Trace had been deployed in the Middle East.

She suddenly remembered how freaked she had been as she walked out to take the microphone and had seen the huge hometown crowd gathered there, just about everybody she knew. Despite all her hours of practice with her voice teacher and the choir director, panic had spurted through her and she completely forgot the opening words—until she looked up in the stands and saw her mother and father beaming at her and Taft and Laura giving her an encouraging wave. A steady calm had washed over her like water from the irrigation canals, washing away all the panic, and she had sung beautifully. Probably the best performance of her life.

Just a few months later, her parents were dead because of her and all the songs inside her had died with them.

"I don't sing *anymore*," she said, hoping that would be the end of it. She didn't want to answer the question. It was nobody's business but her own—certainly not Ben Caldwell's.

He gave her a long look. The wagon jolted over a rut in the road and his shoulder bumped hers. She could have eased far enough away that they wouldn't touch but she didn't. Instead, she rested her cheek on Maya's hair, humming along with "O Little Town of Bethlehem" and gazing up at the few stars revealed through the wispy clouds as she waited for the ride to be over.

* * *

He sensed a story here.

Something was up with the Bowmans when it came to Christmas. He noticed that while Laura and the children were singing merrily away, Caidy's brothers seemed as reluctant as she to join in. The police chief and fire chief would occasionally sing a few lines and Caidy hummed here and there, but none of them could be called enthusiastic participants in this little sing-along.

At random moments over the evening he had picked up a pensive, almost sad mood threading through their family.

He thought of that beautiful work of art in the dining room, the vibrant colors and the intense passion behind it, and then the way all the Bowmans shut down as if somebody had yanked a window screen closed when he had asked about the artist.

Their mother. What happened to her? And the father was obviously gone too. He was intensely curious but didn't know how to ask.

The three-quarter moon peeked behind a cloud, and in the pale moonlight she was almost breathtakingly lovely, with those delicate features and that soft, very kissable mouth.

That kiss hadn't been far from his mind all day, probably because he still didn't quite understand what had happened. He wasn't the kind of man to steal a kiss from a beautiful woman, especially not at the spur of the moment like that. But he hadn't been able to resist her. She had looked so sweet and lovely there in her kitchen, worry for her ailing dog still a shadow in her eyes.

Holding her in his arms, he had desired her, of course, but had also been aware of something else tangled with the hunger, a completely unexpected tenderness. He sensed she used her prickly edges as a defense against the world, keeping away potential threats before they could get too close.

He remembered her cutting words to her brothers' wives and that awkward moment when he had walked into the kitchen just in time to hear her call him arrogant and rude.

Why hadn't he just slipped out of the kitchen again without any of the women suspecting he might have overheard? He should have. It would have been the polite thing to do, but some demon had prompted him to push her, to let her know he wasn't about to be dismissed so easily.

She had apologized for it, said she hadn't meant any of her words. So why had she said them?

He made her nervous. He had observed at dinner that she was warm and friendly to everyone else, but she basically ignored him and had been abrupt in their few interactions. It was an odd position in which to find himself and he wasn't sure how he felt about it—just as he didn't know how to deal with his own conflicted reaction to her.

One moment he wanted to retreat into his safe world as a widower and single father. The next, she forcibly reminded him that underneath those roles, he was still a man.

Brooke had been gone for two years. He would always grieve for his wife, for the good times they had shared and the children she had loved and raised so well. He had become, if not complacent in his grief, at least comfortable with it. This move to Idaho seemed to have shaken everything. When he agreed to take the job, he intended to create a new life for the children, away from influences he considered harmful. He never expected to find himself so drawn to a lovely woman with secrets and sadness in her eyes.

Through the rest of the sleigh ride, though he tried to focus on the scenery and the enjoyment his children were having, he couldn't seem to stop watching Caidy. She was amazing, actually, keeping her attention focused on entertaining the very cute niece on her lap and making sure none of the gaggle of preadolescent girls suddenly fell out of the wagon. She managed all of those tasks with deft skill.

She obviously loved children and she was very good with them. Why didn't she have a husband and a wagon-load of children herself?

None of his business, he reminded himself. Her dog was his patient and he was currently a temporary tenant at her ranch, but that was the extent of their relationship. He would be foolish to go looking for more. That didn't stop him from being intensely aware of her as the wagon jostled his shoulder against hers every time Ridge hit a rut.

"Brrr. I'm cold," Maya said, snuggling deeper into Caidy's lap.

"So am I," she answered. "But look. Ridge is taking us home now."

Ben looked around. Sure enough, her brother had perfect timing. Just as the enthusiasm began to wane and the children started to complain of the cold, Ben realized the big, beautiful draft horses were trudging under the sign announcing the entrance to the River Bow Ranch.

"No more horsies?" Maya asked.

"Not today, little bug." Taft held his arms out and his

stepdaughter lunged into them. "We'll come back and go for another ride sometime soon, though, I promise."

"She's a huge fan of our horses," Caidy said with a fond smile for the girl. "Especially the big ones for some odd reason."

Instead of heading toward the ranch house, Caidy's brother turned the horses down the little lane that led to the house he was renting. The wagon pulled up in front.

"Look at that. Curb service for you," Caidy said. She finally met his gaze with a tentative smile. He was aware of an unsettling urge to stand here in the cold, staring into those striking green eyes for an hour or two. He managed a brief smile in return, then turned his attention to climbing out of the wagon and gathering his kids.

"Let's go. Jack, Ava."

"I don't want to get off! Why does everyone else get to keep riding?" Jack had that tremor in his voice that signaled an impending five-year-old tantrum.

"Only for another minute or two," Ridge promised. "We're just heading back to the house and then the ride will be done. The horses are tired and need their beds."

"So do you, kiddo," Ben said. "Come on."

To Ben's relief, Jack complied, jumping down into his arms. Ava clearly wanted to stay with the other girls but she finally waved to them all. "See you tomorrow on the bus," she said to Destry.

"Great. I'll bring that book we were talking about."

"Okay. Don't forget."

Ava waved again and jumped down without his help.

"Thanks for letting us tag along," he said to the wagon in general, though he meant his words for Caidy. "Ava and Jack had a blast."

"What about you?" she asked.

He didn't know her well enough yet to interpret her moods. All he knew was that she looked remarkably pretty in the moonlight, with her eyes sparkling and her cheeks—and the very tip of her nose—rosy.

"I enjoyed it," he answered. He was a little surprised to realize it was true. He hadn't found all that many things enjoyable since his wife died. Who would have expected he would enjoy a hayride with a bunch of giggly girls and Caidy and her forbidding brothers, who would probably have thrown him off the wagon if they had known about that late-night kiss—and about how very much he wanted to repeat the experience?

"I especially enjoyed the peppermint hot cocoa."

She looked pleased. "I'm glad. Peppermint is my favorite too."

"Good night."

He waved and carried Jack into the foreman's cottage, wondering what the hell he was going to do about Caidy Bowman. She was an intriguing mystery, a jumble full of prickles and sweetness, vinegar and sugar, and he was far more fascinated by her than he had any right to be.

Chapter Ten

After the sleigh ride, Caidy made it a point for the next few days to stay as far as possible from the foreman's house. She had no reason to visit. Why would she? Ben and the children and Mrs. Michaels were perfectly settled and didn't need help with anything.

If she stood at her bedroom window, looking out at the night and the sparkling lights nestled among the trees, well, that was her own business. She told herself she was only enjoying the peace and serenity of these quiet December nights, but that didn't completely explain away the restlessness that seemed to ache inside her.

It certainly had nothing to do with a certain dark-haired man and the jittery butterflies he sent dancing around inside her.

She couldn't hope to avoid him forever, though. On Wednesday, less than a week before Christmas, she woke from tangled dreams with an odd sense of trepidation.

The vague sense of unease dogged her heels like a blurred shadow as she headed out to the barn with a still-sleepy Destry to feed and water the horses and take care of the rest of their chores.

She couldn't figure it out until they finished in the barn and headed back to the welcoming warmth of the house for breakfast before the school bus came. When they walked into the kitchen, they were greeted by a happy bark from the crate she had returned to the corner and she suddenly remembered.

This was the day she had to take Luke back to the veterinarian to have his wound checked and his stitches removed. She stopped stock-still in the kitchen, trepidation pressing down on her. Drat. She couldn't avoid the man forever, she supposed. A few more days would be nice, though. Was it too late to make an appointment with the vet in Idaho Falls?

"What's wrong?" Destry asked. "Your face looks funny. Did you see a mouse?"

She raised an eyebrow. "In my kitchen? Are you kidding me? I better not. No. I just remembered something…unpleasant."

"Reverend Johnson said in Sunday school that the best way to get rid of bad thoughts is to replace them by thinking about something good."

The girl measured dry oatmeal into her bowl and reached for the teakettle Caidy always turned on before they headed out to the barn. "I've been trying to do that whenever I think about my mom," she said casually.

Thoughts of Ben flew out the window as she stared at her niece. Destry *never* talked about her mother. In recent memory, Caidy could only recall a handful of times when Melinda's name even came up. Destry was so sweet and even-tempered, and Ridge was such an attentive father, she had just assumed the girl had adjusted to losing her mother, but she supposed no child ever completely recovered from that loss, whether she was three at the time or sixteen.

"Does that happen often?" she asked carefully. She didn't want to cut off the line of dialogue if Destry wanted to open up. "Thinking about your mother, I mean?"

Destry shrugged and added an extra spoonful of brown sugar to her oatmeal. Caidy decided to let it slide for once. "Not really. I can hardly remember her, you know? But I still wonder about her, especially at Christmas. I don't even know if she's dead or alive. Gabi at least knows her mom is alive—she's just being a big jerk."

Jerk was a kind word for the mother of both Gabi and Becca. She was a first-class bitch, selfish and irresponsible, who had given both of her daughters childhoods filled with uncertainty and turmoil.

"Have you asked your dad about…your mother?"

"No. He doesn't like to talk about her much." Destry paused, a spoonful of steaming oatmeal halfway between the bowl and her mouth. "I really don't remember much about her. I was so little when she left. She wasn't very nice, was she?"

Another kind phrase. Melinda showed up in a thesaurus as the antonym to nice. She had fooled them all in the beginning, especially Ridge. She had seemed sweet and rather needy and hopelessly in love with him, but time—or perhaps her own natural temperament—had showed a different side of her. By the time she finally left River Bow, just about all of them had been relieved to see her go.

"She was...troubled." Caidy picked through her words with caution. "I don't think she had a very happy life when she was your age. Sometimes those bad things in the past can make it tough for a person to see all the good things they have now. I'm afraid that was your mother's problem."

Destry appeared to ponder that as she took another spoonful of oatmeal. "It stinks, doesn't it?" she said quietly after a long moment. "I don't think I could ever leave my kid, no matter what."

Her heart ached for this girl and for inexplicable truths. "Neither could I. And yes, you're right. It does stink. She made some poor choices. Unfortunately, you've had to suffer for those. But you need to look at the good things you have. Your dad didn't go anywhere. He loves you more than anything and he's been here the whole time showing you that. I'm here and the twins and now their families. You have lots and lots of people who love you, Des. If your mom couldn't see how wonderful you are, that's her problem—not yours. Don't ever forget that."

"I know. I remember. Most of the time anyway."

Caidy leaned over and hugged her niece. Des rested her head on her shoulder for just a moment before she returned to her breakfast with her usual equanimity.

Caidy wasn't the girl's mother, but she thought she was doing a pretty good job as a surrogate. Worlds better than Melinda would have done, if Caidy did say so herself.

After Destry finished breakfast and helped her clean up the dishes, Caidy had just enough time to spare to run her the quarter mile from the house to the bus stop.

"Ava and Jack aren't here," her niece fretted. "Do you think they forgot what time the bus comes? Maybe we should have picked them up."

"I'm sure Mrs. Michaels knows what time the bus comes," she answered. "They've been here the past few days in plenty of time, haven't they? Maybe they just caught a ride with their father today."

"Maybe," Destry said, though she still looked worried.

Caidy could have given Des a ride into town this morning on her way to the vet, she realized. She hadn't even thought about that until right now—just as the school bus lumbered over the hill and stopped in front of them with a screech of air brakes.

After Destry climbed on the bus and Caidy waved her off, she hurried back to the house and carried the dog crate out to the ranch's Suburban, then returned for the dog, who was moving around much more comfortably these days.

"Luke, buddy, you're not making things easy on me. If not for you, I could pretend the man doesn't exist."

The dog tilted his head and gazed at her with an expression that looked almost apologetic. She laughed a little and hooked up his leash before leading him carefully out to the Suburban, where she lifted him carefully into the crate.

Maybe Ridge could take him into the vet for her.

The fleeting thought was far too tempting. As much as she wanted to ask him for the favor, she knew she couldn't. This was all part of her ongoing effort to prove to herself she wasn't a complete coward.

For a brief instant as she slid behind the wheel, a random image flitted through her memory—cowering under that shelf in the pantry, gazing at the ribbon of light streaming in under the door and listening to the squelchy sounds of her mother's breathing.

She pushed away the memories.

Oh, how she loathed Christmas.

She was in a lousy mood when she pulled up in front of the vet clinic, a combination of her worry over Destry missing her mother and missing her *own* mother, not to mention her reluctance to walk inside that building and face Ben again after all the awkwardness between them.

This was ridiculous. She frowned at herself. She was tough enough to go on roundup every year to get their cattle from the high mountain grazing allotment. She helped Ridge with branding and with breaking new horses and even with castrating steers.

Surely she was tough enough to endure a fifteen-minute checkup with the veterinarian, no matter how sexy the dratted man was.

With that resolve firmly in mind, she moved around to the back of the Suburban with Luke's leash. Border collies were ferociously smart, though, and he clearly was even more reluctant than she to go inside the building. He fought the leash, wriggling his head this way and that and trying to scramble as far back as he could into the crate.

She imagined this building represented discomfort and fear to him. She could completely understand that, but that didn't change the fact that he would have to suck it up and go inside anyway.

If she did, he did.

"Come on, Luke. Easy now. There's a boy. Come on."

"Problem?"

Her heart kicked up a beat at the familiar voice. She turned with an air of trepidation and there he was in all his gorgeousness. A flood of heat washed over her, seeping into all the cold corners.

"You've got a reluctant patient here." *And his reluctant person.*

"A common problem in my line of work. I saw you from the window and thought it might be something like that."

"I didn't want to yank him out for fear of hurting something."

He gestured to the crate. "May I?"

"Of course."

She moved out of the way and he stepped forward, leaning down to the opening of the crate. She tried not to notice the way the morning sunshine gleamed in his dark hair or the breadth of those shoulders under his blue scrubs.

She was beginning to find it extremely unfair that the only man to rev her engine in, well, ever, was somebody who was obviously not interested in a relationship. At least with her.

"Hey there, Luke. How's my bud?" He spoke in a low, calm voice that sent shivers down her spine. If he ever turned that voice on *her,* she would turn into a quivery mass of hormones.

"You want to come inside? There's a good boy. Come on. Yeah. Nothing to worry about here."

As she watched, Luke surrendered to the spell of that gentle voice and stood docile while Ben hooked on the leash and carefully lifted the dog down to the snowy ground.

"He's moving well. That's a good sign."

Luke promptly lifted a leg against the tire of the Suburban, just in case any other creatures around wondered to whom it might belong. Ben didn't seem fazed.

No doubt that also was a natural occurrence in his line of work.

After Luke finished, Ben led them to the side door she had used so many times when she worked for Doc Harris. "Let's just head straight to the exam room. I had a break between patients this morning and I'm all ready for you. We can take care of the paperwork afterward."

He closed the door and she immediately wondered how such an ordinary act could completely deplete all available oxygen. Being alone with him in this enclosed space left her breathless, off balance and painfully aware of him.

She sank into a chair while he started his exam of the dog. The whole time she tried to ignore that low, calming voice and his easy, comfortable manner with the animal, focusing instead on her mental to-do list before Christmas Eve, which was in less than a week.

"Everything looks good," Ben finally said. "He's progressing much more quickly than I expected."

"Great news. Thank you."

"If it's all right with you, I'd like to leave the stitches in for a few more days. I'll try to stop by over the holidays to remove them."

"I don't want you to go to so much trouble. I can probably remove them. I've done it before."

He raised an eyebrow. "You *have* had experience at this."

She shrugged. "Most everybody who grows up on a ranch gets basic veterinary experience. It's part of the life. I took it a little further when I worked with Doc Harris, that's all."

"If you ever want another job, I could use an experienced tech."

Oh, wouldn't that be a disaster? She couldn't think

straight around the man. She could only imagine what sort of mess she could create trying to help him in a professional capacity.

"I'll keep that in mind."

"Actually, I do need a favor. Advice, really. You know just about everybody in town, don't you?"

"Most of them. We've had some new people move in lately but I'm sure I'll get around to meeting them."

"Do you know any after-school babysitters?"

"Is something wrong with Mrs. Michaels?" she asked, concerned all over again about the children not making it to the bus stop that morning.

His sigh was heavy. "No. Not with her, but she has a married daughter in California who just had a baby."

"Oh, that's great. I remember you mentioned her daughter was expecting."

"She wasn't due for another month, but apparently she went into premature labor yesterday and had the baby this morning. The baby is in the newborn ICU. Anne wants to be there, which I completely get. She's trying to make arrangements to fly out today so she can be there when her daughter comes home from the hospital, and then she plans to stay through the holidays."

"Understandable."

"I know. I do understand, believe me. It just makes *my* life a little more complicated right now, at least temporarily. The children can always come here after school. I don't mind having them. But according to Ava, hanging out at the clinic is 'totally boring.' Plus Jack can usually find trouble wherever he goes, a skill that sometimes can be a little inconvenient at a clinic filled with ailing animals."

"I can see where that might pose a problem."

"I need to find someone for this Saturday at least.

We have clinic appointments all day because of our shortened holiday hours next week and I don't feel right about sticking them here for ten hours."

Against her will, she felt a pang of sympathy for the man. It couldn't have been easy, moving to Pine Gulch where he didn't know anyone. He and his children had left behind any kind of support network, all trace of the familiar. Starting over in a new community would be tough on anyone, especially a single father also trying to keep a demanding business operating.

"This is easily fixed, Ben," she said impulsively. "Ava and Jack can come to the ranch house after school and hang out with me and Destry. It will be great fun."

He looked faintly embarrassed. "That wasn't a hint, I swear. I honestly never even thought about asking you. Because you know everyone in town and all, I thought you might be aware of someone who might be willing to help out this time of year."

"I do know a few people who do childcare. I can certainly give you some names, if that's your preference. But I promise, having them come to the ranch after school would be no big deal. Destry would love the company and I might even put them to work with chores. They can ride the bus home with Destry the rest of the week, just like they would if Mrs. Michaels were there. Saturday's no problem either. Des and I are making Christmas cookies and can always use a couple more hands."

He shifted. "I don't want to bother you. I'm sure you're busy with Christmas."

"Who isn't? Don't worry about it, Ben. If I thought it would be too much of a bother, I wouldn't have offered."

"I don't know."

He was plainly reluctant to accept the help. Stubborn

man. Did he think she was going to attach strings to her offer? One kiss per hour of childcare?

Tempting. Definitely tempting...

"I was only trying to help. I thought it would be a convenient solution to your problem with the side benefit of helping me keep Destry entertained in the big crazy lead-up to Christmas Eve, but it won't hurt my feelings if you prefer to make other arrangements. You can think about it and let me know."

"I don't need to think about it. You're right. It is the perfect solution." He was quiet, his hands petting Luke's fur. Lucky dog.

"It's tough for me to accept help," he finally said, surprising her with his raw honesty. "Tougher, probably, to accept help from *you*, with things so...complicated between us."

"Complicated. Is that what you call it?" Apparently she wasn't the only one in tumult over this attraction that simmered between them.

"What word would you use?"

Tense. Sparkly. Exhilarating. She couldn't use any of those words, despite the truth of them.

"Complicated works, I guess. But this, at least, is relatively easy when you think about it. I like your kids, Ben. I don't mind having them around. Jack has a hilarious sense of humor and I'm sure he'll talk my ear off with knock-knock jokes. Ava is a little tougher nut to crack, I'll admit, but I'm looking forward to the challenge."

"She's struggling right now. I guess that's obvious."

"The move?"

"She's angry about that. About everything. My former in-laws did a number on her. They blame me for Brooke's death and have spent the past two years trying to shove a wedge between Ava and me. Both kids, really, but Jack is still too young to pay them much attention."

"Do they have any real reason to blame you?" she asked.

"They think they do. Brooke had type 1 diabetes and nearly died having Jack. The doctors told us not to try again. She was determined to have a third child despite the danger. She could be like that. If she wanted something, she couldn't see any reason why she couldn't have it. I wasn't about to risk a pregnancy. We took double precautions—or at least I thought I did. I intended to make things permanent, but the day I was scheduled for the big snip, she told me she was pregnant."

"Oh, no."

He raked a hand through his hair with a grimace. "Why am I compelled to spill all this to you?"

She chose her words with Ben as carefully as she had with Destry earlier, sensing if she said the wrong thing to him this fragile connection between them would fray. "I would like to think we can be friends, even if things between us are…complicated."

He gave a rough laugh. "Friends. All right. I guess I don't have enough of those around."

She sensed that wasn't an admission he was comfortable with either. "You will. Give it time. You just moved in. It takes time to build that kind of trust."

"Even with my friends back in California, I never felt right about talking about this. It sounds terrible of me. Disloyal or something. I loved my wife but…some part of me is so damn angry at her. She got pregnant on purpose. I guess that's obvious. She stopped taking birth control pills and sabotaged the condoms. She thought she knew better than the doctors and me."

What kind of mother risked her life, her future with a husband who loved her and children who needed her, simply because she wanted something she didn't have? Caidy couldn't conceive of it.

"I loved her but she could be stubborn and spoiled when she wanted her way. She wouldn't consider terminating the pregnancy despite the dangers," Ben went on. Now that he had started with the story, she sensed he wanted to tell her all of it. "For several months, things were going well. We thought anyway. Then when she was six months along, her glucose levels started jumping all over the place. As best we can figure out, it must have spiked that afternoon and she passed out."

His hands curled in Luke's fur. "She was behind the wheel at the time and drove off an overpass. She and the baby both died instantly."

"Oh, Ben. I'm so sorry." She wanted to touch him, offer some sort of comfort, but she was afraid to move. What would he do if she wrapped her fingers around his? Friends did that sort of thing, right? Even complicated friends?

"Her parents never forgave me." He spoke before she could move. "They thought it was all my fault she got pregnant in the first place. If only I'd stayed away from her, et cetera, et cetera. I can't really blame them."

She stared. "I can. That's completely ridiculous. Are they nuts? You were married, for heaven's sake. What were you supposed to do? It's not like you were two teenagers having a quickie in the backseat of your car."

He gave a rough, surprised-sounding laugh, and she was aware of a tiny bubble of happiness inside her that she could make him laugh despite the grim story.

"You're right. They are a little nuts." He laughed again and some of the tension in his shoulders started to ease. "No, a *lot* nuts. That's the real reason I moved here. Ava was becoming just like my mother-in-law. A little carbon copy, right down to the tight-mouthed expressions and the censorious comments. I won't let that happen. I'm her father and I'm not about to let them feed her lies and distortions until she hates me."

"Is the move working the way you hoped?"

"I think it's too soon to tell. She's still pretty upset at moving away from them. They can give her things I can't. That's a tough thing for a father to stomach."

This time she acted on the impulse to touch him and rested a hand on his bare forearm, just below the short sleeve of the scrub shirt. His skin was warm, the muscle hard beneath her fingers.

"They can't give either Ava or Jack the most important thing. Your love. That's what they're going to remember the rest of their lives. When they see how much you have loved them and sacrificed for them, it won't matter what lies their grandparents try to feed them."

"Thank you for that." He smiled at her, his eyes crinkling a little at the corners, and she wanted to stand in this little office basking in the glow forever.

Why, again, hadn't she wanted to bring Luke to the vet? She couldn't imagine anywhere she would rather be right now.

"I mean it about the kids, Ben." Though it took a great deal of effort, she managed to slide her hand away. "Destry and I would love to have the children hang out with us for a few days. And if you need help between Christmas and New Year's, we'll be happy to keep an eye on them."

The conviction in her voice seemed to assuage the last of his concerns. "If you're sure, that would be great. Thank you. You've lifted a huge weight off my mind."

"No problem." She smiled to seal the deal. His gaze flickered to her mouth and stayed there as if he couldn't look away. He was thinking of their kiss. She was certain of it. Awareness fluttered through her, low and enticing. When his gaze lifted to hers, she knew she wasn't imagining the sudden hunger there.

She swallowed, her face suddenly hot. She wanted him to kiss her again, just wrap his arms around her and press her back against the wall for the next hour or two.

Not the time or the place. He was working and had other patients he needed to see. Besides that, though he might be forging this tentative friendship with her, she had a feeling the rest of it was just too tangled for either of them right now.

"I'll, um, see you later," she mumbled. "Thanks for… everything."

"You're very welcome." His low voice thrummed over her nerves. She did her best to ignore it as she grabbed the end of Luke's leash and escaped.

Chapter Eleven

Two nights later, Ben pulled off the main road onto the drive into the River Bow, wishing he could hang a left at the junction, climb into his bed at the cottage and sleep for the next two or three days.

His shoulders were tight with exhaustion, his eyes gritty and aching. When he finally found time to sleep, just past midnight, he had only been under for a few minutes when he received an emergency call to help a dog that had been hit by a car on one of the ranch roads. He had ended up packing his sleepy kids—poor things—into the backseat of the SUV and taking them inside his office to sleep while he attended to the dog.

He really needed Mrs. Michaels—or someone like her. At least the kids had fallen quickly back to sleep. He considered that a great blessing. Even after he packed them back to the ranch and into their beds, they had again fallen asleep easily.

He had envied them that as he tossed and turned, energized by the case and the successful outcome. Before he knew it, the alarm was going off and he had stumbled out of bed to face a packed schedule of people rushing to take their animals into the vet before the clinic went on its brief holiday hiatus.

So far, he hadn't seen any slowdown in business after taking over from Dr. Harris. Another blessing there. Although he was grateful for the business and glad that the people of Pine Gulch had decided to continue bringing their animals to him, right now he was too tired to savor his relief.

As he pulled up to the River Bow ranch house, Christmas lights gleamed against the winter night and the darker silhouettes of the mountains in the distance and the pines and aspens of the foreground. Warm light spilled out the windows into the snow and that big Christmas tree twinkled with color.

The place offered a cheery welcome against the chilly night. He couldn't help thinking about his grandparents' home in Lake Forest. In sheer square footage, Caldwell House was probably three times as big as the River Bow, but instead of warmth and hominess, he remembered his childhood home as being sterile and unfriendly to a young boy, all sharp angles, dark wood and uncomfortable furniture.

His grandparents hadn't wanted him. He had known that from the beginning when their daughter, his mother, had dropped him and his sister off before running off with her latest hard-living boyfriend.

She hadn't come back, of course. Even at age eight, he had somehow known she wouldn't. Now he knew she had died of a drug overdose just months after dropping him and Susie with her parents, but for years he had watched and waited for a mother who would never return.

Oh, his grandparents had done their duty. They had given him and Susie a roof over their head, nutritious meals, an excellent education. But he and his sister had never been allowed to forget they came from a selfish, irresponsible woman who had chosen drugs over her own children.

He had his own family now. Children he loved more than anything. He would never treat them as unwanted burdens.

Eager to pick them up now, he pulled up in front of the River Bow. The night was clear and cold, with a brilliant spill of stars gleaming above the mountains. Inside the door, he could hear laughter and a television show, along with a couple of well-mannered barks.

The door opened just seconds after he rang the bell. His stomach rumbled instantly as the spicy, doughy smells wafting outside immediately transported him to his favorite pizzeria in college.

"Hi, Dad!" Jack let go of the doorknob just an instant before launching himself toward Ben. With a laugh, he held his arms out and Jack did his traditional move of spider-walking up his legs before Ben flipped him upside down, then scooped him up into his arms.

He always found it one of life's tiny miracles that his exhaustion could seep away for a while when he was reunited with his kids at the end of the day, even if Ava was in a cranky mood.

"How was your day, bud?"

"Great! I got to help feed the horses and play with some kittens. And guess what? I don't have to go back to school until next year."

"That's right. Last day of school and now it's Christmas vacation."

"And Santa Claus comes in *three days!*"

He had so dang much to do before then, Ben didn't even want to think about it. "I can't wait," he lied.

As he spoke, Ben became aware of what Jack would have called a disturbance in the Force. Some kind of shift in air currents or spinning and whirling of the ions in the air or something, he wasn't sure, but he sensed Caidy's approach even before she came into view.

"Hi! I thought I heard a doorbell."

She was wearing a white apron and had a bit of flour on her cheek, just a little dusting against her heat-flushed skin.

"Sorry I'm a little later than I told you I would be on the phone," he answered, fighting the urge to step forward and blow away the flour.

"No problem. We've been having fun, haven't we, Jack?"

"Yep. We're making pizza and I got to put some cheese on."

His stomach growled again and he realized he hadn't had time for lunch. "It smells great. Really great."

Jack grabbed one of his hands in both of his. "Can we stay and have some? Please, Dad!"

He glanced at Caidy, embarrassed that his son would offer invitations to someone else's meal. "I don't think so. I'm sure we've bothered the Bowmans long enough. We'll find something back at our place."

Exactly what, he wasn't quite sure. Maybe they would run into town to grab fast food, though right now loading up into the vehicle again and heading to the business district was the last thing he felt like doing. Maybe there was a pizza restaurant he hadn't discovered yet—because that smell was enticing.

"Of course you'll stay!" Caidy exclaimed. "I was planning on it."

"You're doing us enough favors by letting the kids come hang out with you. I don't expect you to feed us too."

She narrowed her gaze at him. "I just spent an hour making enough pizza dough to feed the whole town of Pine Gulch. You can stay a few minutes and eat a slice or two, can't you?"

He should make an excuse and leave. This house was just too appealing—and Caidy was even more so. But he didn't have plans for dinner. If they ate here, that was one less decision he would have to make. Besides, pizza on a cold winter night seemed perfect.

They could stay for a while, just long enough to eat, he decided. Then he and his children would head for home. "If you're sure, that would be great. It really does smell delicious."

"I'm going to be a lousy hostess and ask you to hang your own coat up because my hands are covered in flour, then come on back to the kitchen."

Without waiting for an answer, she turned around and walked back down the hall, Jack scampering after her. After a pause, Ben shrugged out of his ranch coat and hung it alongside Jack's and Ava's coats on the rack in the corner.

He expected to see a crowd of children when he walked into the kitchen but Caidy was alone. She tucked a strand of hair behind her ear, leaving another little smudge of flour, and gave him a bright smile that seemed to push off another shackle of his fatigue.

"The kids are just getting ready to watch a Christ-

mas show in the other room. You're more than welcome
to join them while I finish throwing things together in
here."

He should. A wise man would take the escape she
was handing him, but he didn't feel right about leaving
her alone to do all the work. "Is there anything I can
help you do in here?"

Surprise flickered in her eyes, then she smiled again.
"You're a brave man, Ben Caldwell. Sure. I've got a
cheese pizza cooking now to satisfy the restless natives.
Give me a minute to toss out another pie and then you
can put the toppings on."

He washed his hands, listening to the familiar
opening strands of a holiday television special he had
watched when *he* was a kid in the big rec room of
Caldwell House. He found something rather comforting about the continuity of it, his own children enjoying the same things that had once given him pleasure.

"Would you like a drink or something? We don't
keep much in the house but I can probably rustle up
a beer."

"What are you having?"

"I like root beer with my pizza. It's always been kind
of a family tradition and I apparently haven't grown out
of it. Silly, isn't it?"

"I think it's nice. Root beer sounds good, but I can
wait until the pizza is done."

She smiled as her hands expertly continued tossing
the dough into shape. "What about you? Any traditions
in the Caldwell family kitchen?"

"Other than thoroughly enjoying whatever Mrs. Michaels fixes us, no. Not really."

"What about when you were a kid?"

Traditions? No, not unless she might count formal

family dinners with little conversation and a serious dearth of kindness. "Not really. I didn't come from a particularly close family."

"No brothers or sisters?"

"A sister. She's several years younger than I am. We've lost touch over the years."

Susan had rebelled against their grandparents by following in their mother's footsteps, burying her misery in drugs and alcohol. Last he heard, she was in her third stint at rehab to avoid a prison sentence.

"I can't imagine losing touch with my brothers." Sympathy turned Caidy's eyes an intense green. "They're my best friends. Laura and Becca are like sisters to me now too."

"You Bowmans seem a united front against the world."

"I guess so. It hasn't always been that way, but it's the now that counts, right?"

"Yes. You're very lucky."

She opened her mouth to speak, then appeared to think better of it. "I think this should be ready now."

With a twist of her wrist, she deftly tossed the dough onto a pizza peel sprinkled with cornmeal and crimped the edges before handing the whole peel to him with a flourish.

"Here you go. All yours."

"Uh." He stared helplessly at the naked pizza dough, not quite sure what she expected of him.

"You haven't done this before, have you?"

He gave a rough laugh. "No. But I can tell you by heart the phone number of about half a dozen great pizza places in California."

She shook her head and stepped closer to him, stirring the air with the scent of wildflowers, and suddenly he forgot all about being hungry for pizza. Now he was just hungry for her.

"Okay, I'll walk you through it this time. Next time you come over for Friday night pizza, though, you're on your own."

Next time. Whoever would have guessed those two words could hold so much promise? He knew darn well he shouldn't feel this little kick of anticipation for something so nebulous and uncertain as a next time.

Better to just enjoy *this* moment. As she said, it was *now* that mattered. In a few weeks, he and his children would be moving away and Caidy Bowman and this wild attraction to her would be conveniently distant from him.

For now, she was here beside him, her skin unbelievably soft-looking and her hair teasing him with the scent of flowers and springtime.

"Okay, first thing you do is spoon a little sauce on. I like to use the bowl of the big spoon to spread it to the edge of the dough. That's it. Good."

He supposed it was fairly ridiculous to feel the same sense of pride in spreading sauce on a pizza dough as he had the first time he helped deliver a difficult foal.

"Now sprinkle as much cheese as you usually like. Perfect. I see you like it gooey."

She smiled at him and he suddenly wanted to toss the unfinished pizza to the floor, press her up against that counter and kiss her until they were both breathing hard.

"Okay, now put your toppings on. I was planning a pepperoni and olive for the next one but you can be creative. Whatever you think the kids might like."

"Pepperoni and olive sounds good." He cleared away the ragged edge to his voice. "My kids always like that."

She didn't appear to notice. "The third one can be a little more sophisticated. By then, Destry and her friends—and Ridge, when he's home—have had their fill."

Who made three homemade pizzas on a Friday night? Caidy Bowman apparently.

She was a woman of more layers than a supreme pizza and he was enjoying the process of uncovering each one.

"Now your toppings. Don't skimp on the olives."

He picked up a stack of pepperoni and dealt them like cards on poker night, then tossed handfuls of olives to the edge of the crust. This was going to be the best damn Friday night pizza she had ever had, he vowed.

"Okay, now another layer of cheese and then a bit of fresh Parmesan on the top. Oh, that looks delicious."

"Thank you."

"If the vet thing ever gets old, you can always get a job at the pizza place in town."

He laughed. "A backup plan is always helpful. Good to know I can still feed my kids."

She smiled back at him and he knew he didn't imagine it when her gaze flickered to his mouth and stayed there long enough to send heat pulsing through him. The moment stretched between them, heady and intoxicating, and he again wanted to kiss her, but she stepped away before he could act on the urge.

"I guess this one is ready."

"Now what?"

"Now I take the cheese pizza out, then we call in the locusts and watch it disappear."

He watched while she did just that, shoving a second pizza peel under the cooked pizza on a stone in the oven and deftly working the dough onto the peel before pulling the whole thing back out.

The cheese bubbled exactly the way he loved and the crust was golden perfection.

"Des!" she called. "The first pizza's ready. Can you pause the show and bring everybody in here?"

The herd of children galloped in a moment later, a few more than he expected. Ava was deep in conversation with Destry and Gabi while Jack was chattering away with Caidy's nephew, Alex, and niece Maya.

"Hi." Maya grinned at him in her adorable way and he couldn't help smiling back.

"Hi there."

"Did I mention I was babysitting Maya and Alex for a few hours tonight? Taft and Laura had some last-minute Christmas things to take care of. Laura's mom usually helps them out but she had a party tonight so I offered. I figured, what's a few more? And when Gabi heard Ava was coming over, of course she had to come too."

Now he understood why she was making so many pizzas.

Six kids. How did she handle it? He was overwhelmed most of the time with his own two, but Caidy seemed to juggle everything with ease. After transferring the other pizza from the peel to the stone in the oven, she poured drinks for the younger children, handed plates to the older girls and passed out napkins to everyone.

"Better grab a slice fast or it's going to be gone," she advised him. He snagged one of the few remaining pieces and a glass of frothy root beer and took a place at the kitchen table next to Jack.

All the children seemed ramped up for the holidays

but Caidy managed to keep them distracted by asking about the show they were watching, about their school parties that day, about what they wanted Santa to bring them.

He was too busy savoring the pizza to contribute much to the conversation but after the first blissful moments, he decided he had to try. "This is really delicious. I grew up in Chicago so I know pizza. The sauce is perfect."

"Thank you." She probably meant her pleased smile to be friendly and warm but he was completely seduced by it, by her, by this warm kitchen that seemed such a haven against the harsh, cold world outside.

"What about the third one? What's your pleasure?"

He could come up with several answers to that, none of them appropriate to voice with six children gathered around the table. "I don't really care. What's your favorite?"

"I like barbecue chicken. The kids generally tolerate it in moderation, so that only leaves more for me."

"I didn't realize you were such a devious woman, Caidy Bowman."

"I have my moments."

She smiled at him and he was struck by how lovely she was, with her dark hair escaping the ponytail and her cheeks flushed from the warmth of the stove.

He was in deep trouble here, he thought. He didn't know what to do about this attraction to her. He was hanging on with both hands to keep from falling hard for her, and each time he spent time with her, he slid down a few more inches.

"Do you know my dog?" Maya asked him earnestly. "His name is Lucky."

Grateful for the diversion, he shifted his gaze from

Caidy to her very adorable stepniece. "I don't think I've met Lucky yet. That's a very nice name for a dog."

"He *is* nice," Maya declared. "He licks my nose. It tickles."

"We have a dog named Tri," Jack announced.

"My dog's name is Grunt," Gabi said. "Trace says he's ugly but I think he's the most beautiful dog in the world."

"Lucky's beautiful too," Alex said. "He has super-long ears."

"Tri only has three legs," Jack said, as if that little fact trumped everything else.

"Cool!" Gabi said. "How does he get around?"

"He hops," Ava, who usually only barely tolerated the dog, piped in. "It's really kind of cute. He walks on his front two and then hops on the one back leg he's got. It takes *forever* to go on a walk with him, but I don't mind. Maya, you drank all your root beer. Do you want some more?"

Maya nodded and Ben smiled at his daughter as she poured a small amount of soda for the girl. All the children treated Maya with sweet consideration and it touched him, especially coming from Ava. Though she could be self-absorbed sometimes, like most children, she had these moments of kindness that heartened him.

"Here's pizza number two!" Caidy sang out to cheers from the children. While they had been talking about dogs, he had missed her pulling his pepperoni-and-olive creation out of the oven. Now she set it on the middle of the table and expertly sliced it. As before, the children each grabbed a slice. He nabbed a small one but noticed Caidy didn't take one.

"Want me to save you a piece? You'd better move fast."

She sat down on the one remaining chair at the table, which happened to be on his other side. "I'm saving my appetite for the barbecue chicken."

"It's all delicious. Especially this one, if I do say so myself." He gave a modest shrug.

"You're a pro." She smiled and he felt that connection between them tug a little harder.

"I love pizza. It's my favorite," Maya declared.

"Me too!" Alex said. "I could eat pizza every single day."

"It's my triple favorite," Jack, not to be outdone, announced. "I could eat it every day and every night."

Ava rolled her eyes. "You're such a dork."

The kids appeared to be done after finishing most of the second pizza.

"Can we go finish the show now?" Destry asked.

Caidy glanced at him. "As long as Dr. Caldwell doesn't mind sticking around a little longer."

He should leave. This kitchen—and the soft, beautiful woman in it—were just too appealing. A little fuel had helped push away some of the exhaustion, but he still worried his defenses were slipping around Caidy.

However, that barbecue chicken pizza currently baking was filling the kitchen with delicious, smoky smells. She had gone to all the effort to make it. He might as well stay to taste it.

"How much time is left on the show?" he asked.

"I don't know. Not that much, I'm sure," Destry said, rather artfully, he thought.

Caidy looked doubtful but she didn't argue with her niece.

"We can stay awhile more," he finally said. "If it goes on too much longer, we might have to leave before the show ends."

Despite the warning, his ruling was met with cheers from all the children.

"Thanks, Dad," Ava said, gifting him with one of her rare smiles. "We're having too much fun to go yet."

"I love this show," Jack said. "It's *hilarious*."

A new word in kindergarten apparently. He smiled, feeling rather heroic to give his children something they wanted. As soon as all the kids hurried out to start the show again, he realized his mistake. He was alone again with Caidy, surrounded by delicious smells and this dangerous connection shivering between them.

She rose quickly, ostensibly to check on the pizza, but he sensed she was also aware of it. As she slid the third pizza onto the peel and then out of the oven, he racked his brain to come up with a topic of polite conversation.

He could only come up with one. "What happened to your parents?"

The words came out more bluntly than he intended. Apparently, they startled her too. She nearly dropped the paddle, pizza and all, but recovered enough to carry it with both hands to the table, where she set it down between them.

"Wow. That was out of the blue."

He was an idiot who had no business being let out around anything with less than four feet. Or three, in Tri's case.

"It's none of my business. You don't have to tell me. I've been wondering, that's all. Sorry."

She sighed as she picked up the pizza slicer and jerked it across the pie. "What have you heard?"

"Nothing. Only what you've said, which isn't much. I've gathered it was something tragic. A car accident?"

She didn't answer for a moment, busy with slicing

the pizza and lifting a piece to a plate for him and then for herself. He was very sorry he had said anything, especially when it obviously caused her so much sadness.

"It wasn't a car accident," she finally said. "Sometimes I wish it were something as straightforward as that. It might have been easier."

He took a bite of his pizza. The robust flavors melted on his tongue but he hardly noticed them as he waited for her to continue.

She took a small bite of hers and then a sip of the root beer before she spoke again. "It wasn't any kind of accident," she said. "They were murdered."

He hadn't expected that one, not here in quiet Pine Gulch. He stared at the tightness of her mouth that could be so lush and delicious. "Murdered? Seriously?"

She nodded. "I know. It still doesn't seem real to me either. It's been eleven years now and I don't know if any of us has ever really gotten over it."

"You must have been just a girl."

"Sixteen." She spoke the word softly and he felt a pang of regret for a girl who had lost her father and mother at such a tender age.

"Was it someone they knew?"

"We don't know who killed them. That's one of the toughest aspects of the whole thing. It's still unsolved. We do know it was two men. One dark-haired, one blond, in their late twenties."

Her mouth tightened more and she sipped at her root beer. He wanted to kick himself for bringing up this obviously painful topic.

"They were both strangers to Pine Gulch," she went on. "That much we know. But they didn't leave any fingerprints or other clues. Only, uh, one shaky eyewitness identification."

"What was the motive?"

"Oh, robbery. The whole thing was motivated by greed. My parents had an extensive art collection. I know you saw the painting in the dining room the other day and probably figured out our mother was a brilliant artist. She also had many close friends in the art community who gave her gifts of their work or sold them to her at a steep discount."

A brazen art theft here in quiet Pine Gulch. Of all the things he might have guessed, that was just about last on the list.

"It was a few days before Christmas. Eleven years ago tomorrow, actually. None of the boys lived at home then, only me. Ridge was working up in Montana, Trace was in the military and Taft had an apartment in town. No one was supposed to be here that night. I had a Christmas concert that night at the high school but I…I was ill. Or said I was anyway."

"You weren't?"

She set her fork down next to her mostly uneaten pizza and he felt guilty again for interrupting her meal with this tragic topic. He wanted to tell her not to finish, that he didn't need to know, but he was afraid that sounded even more stupid—and besides that, he sensed some part of her needed to tell him.

"It's so stupid. I was a stupid, selfish, silly sixteen-year-old girl. My boyfriend, Cody Spencer—the asshole—had just broken up with me that morning in homeroom. He wanted to go out with my best friend, if you can believe that cliché. And Sarah Beth had wanted him ever since we started going out and decided dating the captain of the football team and president of the performance choir was more important than friendship.

I was quite certain, as only a sixteen-year-old girl can be, that my heart had broken in a million little pieces."

He tried to picture her at sixteen and couldn't form a good picture. Was it because that pivotal event had changed her so drastically?

"The worst part was, Cody and I were supposed to sing a duet together at the choir concert—'Merry Christmas, Darling.' I couldn't go through with it. I just…couldn't. So I told my parents I thought I must have food poisoning. I don't think they believed me for a minute, but what else could they do when I told them I would throw up if I had to go onstage that night? They agreed to stay home with me. None of us knew it would be a fatal mistake."

"You couldn't have known."

"I know that intellectually, but it's still easy to blame myself."

"Easy, maybe, but not fair to a sixteen-year-old girl with a broken heart."

She gave him a surprised look, as if she hadn't expected him to demonstrate any sort of understanding. Did she think him as much an asshole as Cody Spencer?

"I know. It wasn't my fault. It just…feels that way sometimes. It happened right here, you know. In the kitchen. They disarmed the security system and broke in through the back door over there. My mom and I were in here when we heard them outside. I caught a quick glimpse of their faces through the window before my mother shoved me into the pantry and ordered me to stay put. I thought she was coming in after me so I hid under the bottom shelf to make room for her, but…she went back out again, calling for my father."

She was silent and he didn't know what to say, what to do, to ease the torment in her eyes. Finally, he settled for resting a hand over hers on the table. She gave him another of those surprised looks, then turned her hand over so they were palm against palm and twisted her fingers in his.

"The men ordered her to the ground and…I could hear them arguing. With her, with themselves. One wanted to leave but the other one said it was too late, she had seen them. And then my father came in. He must have had one of his hunting rifles trained on them. I couldn't see from inside the pantry, but the next thing I knew, two shots rang out. The police said my dad and one of the men must have fired at each other at the same moment. The other guy was hit and injured. My dad… died instantly."

"Oh, Caidy."

"After that, it was crazy. My mom was screaming at them. She grabbed a knife out of the kitchen and went after them and the…the bastard shot her too. She…took a while to die. I could hear her breathing while the men hurried through the house taking the art they wanted. They must have made about four or five trips outside before they finally left. And I stayed inside that pantry, doing nothing. I tried to help my mother once but she made me go back inside. I didn't know what else to do."

Outside the kitchen he could hear laughter from the children at something on the show they were watching. Caidy's fingers trembled slightly, her skin cool now, and he tightened his hand around hers.

"I should have helped her. Maybe I could have done something."

"You would have been shot if they'd known you were here."

"Maybe."

"No 'maybe' about it. Do you think they would have

hesitated for a moment?" He couldn't bear thinking about the horrific possibility.

"I don't know. I... When I finally heard them drive away, I waited several more minutes to make sure they weren't coming back, then went out to call nine-one-one. By then, it was too late for my mother. She was barely hanging on when Taft and the rest of the paramedics arrived. Maybe if I had called earlier, she wouldn't have lost so much blood."

Everything made so much sense now. The close bond between the siblings masked a deep pain. He had sensed it and now he knew the root of it.

Did that explain why she was still here at the River Bow all these years later, why she hadn't finished veterinary school? Did guilt keep her here, still figuratively hiding in the pantry?

Was this the reason she didn't sing anymore?

He curled her fingers in his, wishing he had some other way to ease her burden. "It wasn't your fault. What a horrible thing to happen to anyone, let alone a young girl."

"I guess you understand now why I don't like Christmas much. I try, for Destry's sake. She wasn't even born then. It doesn't seem fair to make her miss out on all the holiday fun because of grief for people she doesn't know."

"I can see that."

Much to his disappointment, she slid her hand out from underneath his and rose to take her plate to the sink. Though he sensed she was trying to create distance between them again, he cleared his own dishes and carried them to the sink after her.

She looked surprised. "Oh, thanks. You didn't have to do that. You're a guest."

"A guest who owes you far more the few moments it takes to bus a few dishes," he countered before returning to the table to clean up the mess of plates and napkins and glasses the children had left behind.

She smiled her thanks when he carried the things to the sink and he wanted to think some of the grimness had left her expression. She still hadn't eaten much pizza but he decided it wasn't his place to nag her about that.

He grabbed a dish towel and started to dry the few dishes in the drainer by the sink. Though she looked as if she wanted to argue, she said nothing and for a few moments they worked in companionable silence.

"My mom really loved the holidays," she said when the last few dishes were nearly finished. "Both of my parents did, really. I think that's what makes it harder. Mom would decorate the house even before Thanksgiving and she would spend the whole month baking. I think Dad was more excited than us kids. He used to sing Christmas songs at the top of his lungs. All through December—after we were done with chores and dinner and homework—he would gather us around the big grand piano in the other room to sing with him. Whatever musical talent I had came from him."

"I'd like to hear you sing," he said.

She gave him a sidelong look and shook her head. "I told you, I don't sing anymore."

"You think your parents would approve of that particular stance?"

She sighed and hung the dish towel on the handle of the big six-burner stove. "I know. I tell myself that every year. My dad, in particular, would be very disappointed in me. He would look at me underneath those bushy eyebrows of his and tell me music is the medicine of a broken heart. That was one of his favorite sayings. Or he would quote Nietzsche: 'without music, life is a mistake.' I know that intellectually, but sometimes what we know in our head doesn't always translate very well to our heart."

"Tell me about it," he muttered.

She gave him a curious look, leaning a hip against the work island.

He knew he should keep his mouth shut but somehow the words spilled out, like a song he didn't realize he knew. "My head is telling me it's a completely ridiculous idea to kiss you again."

She gazed at him for a long, silent moment, her eyes huge and her lips slightly parted. He saw her give a long, slow inhale. "And does your heart have other ideas? I hope so."

"The kids—" he said, rather ridiculously.

"—are busy watching a show and paying absolutely no mind to us in here," she finished.

He took a step forward, almost against his will. "This thing between us is crazy."

"Completely insane," she agreed.

"I don't know what's wrong with me."

"Probably the same thing that's wrong with me," she murmured, her voice husky and low. She also took a step forward, until she was only a breath away, until he was intoxicated by the scent of her, fresh and clean and lovely.

He had to kiss her. It seemed as inevitable as the sunrise over the mountains. He covered the space between them and brushed his mouth against hers once, twice, a third time. He might have found the willpower to stop there but she sighed his name and gripped the front of his shirt with both hands, leaning in for more, and he was lost.

She tasted of root beer—vanilla and mint. Delicious. He couldn't seem to get enough. He forgot everything when she was in his arms—his exhaustion, the music she didn't sing, the children in the other room.

All he could think about was Caidy, sweet and warm and lovely.

There was something intensely *right* about being here with her. He couldn't have explained it, other than he felt as if with every passing moment, some dark, empty corner inside him was being filled with soothing light.

She thought their first kiss that night at the clinic had been fantastic. This surpassed that one. The physical reaction was the same, instant heat and hunger, this wild surge of desire for more and more.

But she had barely known him that first time. Now she wasn't only kissing the very sexy veterinarian who had saved Luke's life. She was kissing the man who treated sweet Maya with such kindness, who looked adorably out of his depth making pizza but who trudged gamely on, who listened to her talk about her past without judgment or scorn but with compassion for the frightened young girl she had been.

She was kissing Ben, the man she was falling in love with.

She wrapped her arms around him, wanting to soak up every moment of the kiss. They kissed for several moments more, until his hand had slipped beneath the edge of her shirt to trace delicious patterns on her bare skin at her waist.

They might have continued kissing there in the

quiet kitchen for a long time but the children suddenly laughed hard at something in the other room and Ben stiffened as if someone had dropped snow down his back.

He slid his mouth away from hers. "We've got to stop doing this." His voice sounded ragged and his chest moved against her with each rapid breath.

"We...do?" She couldn't seem to make her brain work.

"Yes. This... I'm not being fair to you, Caidy."

Something in his tone finally penetrated the haze of desire around her and she took a deep breath and stepped away, willing herself to return to sensible thought.

"In what way?" She managed to make her voice sound cool and controlled, at odds with the tangled chaos of her thoughts.

He raked a hand through his hair, finishing the job of messing it that her own hands had started. "As much as I obviously...want you, I can't have a relationship right now. I'm not ready, the kids aren't ready. I've thrown too many changes at them in a very short time. A new town, a new school, a new job. Eventually a new house. I can't add another woman into the mix."

His words doused the last embers of heat between them. She shivered a little and pulled her shirt down while she struggled to chase after the tattered ends of her composure.

What could she say to that? He was right. His children had survived a great deal of tumult in a short time. The last thing she wanted to do was hurt Ava and Jack. They were great kids and she already cared for them. Just that afternoon, she felt as if she'd had a breakthrough with Ava when she had helped her ride around the practice ring on one of their more gentle horses.

Ben was the children's father. If he felt as though a relationship between him and Caidy would be harmful to his children, how could she argue?

He had obligations bigger than his own wants and needs. She had to accept that, no matter how painful.

Much to her horror, she could feel the heavy burn of tears. She never cried! She certainly couldn't remember ever crying over a *man*. Not since that idiot Cody Spencer when she was sixteen.

She took a deep breath and then another, concentrating hard on pushing the tears back. She didn't dare speak until she could trust her voice wouldn't wobble.

"I'm really glad we're on the same page here," she said, pretending a casual, breezy tone. "I'm not looking for a relationship right now. This attraction between us is…inconvenient, yes, but we're both adults. We can certainly ignore it for the short time you'll be living on the River Bow. After that, it shouldn't be a problem. I mean, how often do I need to take one of the dogs to the vet? We'll hardly ever see each other after you move into your new house."

Instead of reassuring him as to her insouciance, her words seemed to trouble him further. His brow furrowed and he gave her a searching look.

"Caidy—" he began, but Des came into the kitchen before he could complete the thought.

"You're still in here making pizza? This kitchen is so hot!"

Isn't that the truth? Caidy thought.

"You didn't even come in and watch the show with us and now it's almost over."

She seized on the diversion. "You really left the movie before the end?"

"Jack wanted more root beer. I told him I'd take care of it."

Ben made a face. "Jack has probably had all the root beer one kid needs for a night. How about we switch his beverage of choice to water? If he complains, you can tell him his mean old dad said no."

Destry grinned. "Right, Dr. Caldwell. Like anybody would believe you're mean. Or old."

"You'd be surprised," he muttered.

"Why don't you watch the end of the show with the kids?" she suggested.

"What about you?"

"I have a few things to take care of in here. After that, I'll be right in."

After a moment's hesitation, he nodded. "I can take Jack's water, if you'd like," he said to Destry, who handed over the cup and led the way to the television room.

When he was gone, taking all his heat and vitality and these seething emotions between them, Caidy slumped into a chair at the kitchen table and just barely refrained from burying her head in her hands.

She was becoming an idiot over Ben. All he needed to do was give her that rare, charming smile and her insides caught fire and she wanted to jump into his arms.

Worse than that, she was developing genuine feelings for him. How could she not? She remembered him at dinner with Maya and her heart seemed to melt.

She had to stop this or she would be in for serious heartbreak. He wasn't interested in a relationship. He had made that plain twice now. He didn't want anything she had to offer and she would be a fool if she allowed herself to forget that, even for a moment.

Okay, she could do this. A few more weeks and he would be gone from her life, for the most part. She would just have to work hard these remaining weeks while he was still on the River Bow to guard her emotions. Ben and his children could easily slip right past her defenses and into her heart. She was just going to have to do everything she could to keep that from happening, no matter how hard it might be.

Chapter Twelve

Three more days.

She could smile and make conversation and pretend to be excited about Christmas for three more days.

Less than three days actually. Two and a half, really. This was Sunday evening, the day before Christmas Eve. She had tonight, Christmas Eve and then Christmas Day to survive, and then she could toss another holiday into her personal history book.

Okay, that didn't count the week leading up to New Year's, but she wasn't going to think about that. Once Christmas itself was over, she usually could relax and enjoy the remaining days of the holidays and the time it gave her with her family.

For now, she had to survive this particular evening. Caidy stepped out of her bedroom wearing her best black slacks and a dressy white silk blouse she had worn only once before, to the annual cattleman's harvest dinner a few years earlier. With it, she wore a triple strand of colorful glass beads she had picked up at a craft fair that summer.

This was about as dressed up as she could manage. Was it too much? Not enough? She hated trying to figure out proper attire for parties, especially this one.

She fervently wished that she could stay home, pop a big batch of buttery popcorn and find something on TV that wasn't a sappy holiday special.

She had an excuse just about every year to avoid going to the big party Carson and Jenna McRaven had been hosting the past few years at Carson's huge house up Cold Creek Canyon, but Destry had begged and pleaded this year with both Ridge and Caidy.

Destry had trotted out a dozen reasons why they should make an exception and attend this year: all her friends were going. It was going to be *a blast*. Attending was the neighborly thing to do. The McRavens would think the Bowmans didn't like them if they continued to decline the invitation every year.

Finally, she pulled the "you just don't want me to have any fun" card and Ridge had reluctantly accepted his fate and agreed to go. Though she knew it was ridiculous, Caidy had felt obligated to accompany them both.

She wasn't looking forward to any aspect of the party except the food. Jenna was a fantastic cook and catered events all over the county. Her friend, though, tended to go a little overboard when it came to Christmas. Her very gorgeous husband did too. Raven's Nest was always decorated to the hilt for the holidays and the McRavens loved hosting holiday gatherings for family and friends.

She could get through it, she told herself. Less than seventy-two hours, right? With that little pep talk firmly in mind, she headed for the kitchen for the two Dutch apple pies she had baked that morning and found both Destry and Ridge there.

"Oh, you look beautiful, Aunt Caidy!" Destry exclaimed.

Ridge gave one of his rare smiles. "It's true, sis. You do. Much too fancy to be saddled with the likes of us."

Her oldest brother looked handsome and commanding, as usual, in a Western-cut shirt and one of his favorite bolo ties while Destry wore her best pair of jeans and the cute wintry sweater they had bought in Jackson the last time they went shopping together.

At the neckline, Caidy could see the flowered straps of her swimming suit peeking through.

"You're all set to swim?"

The McRavens had the only private indoor pool in town and it was a big hit among the area kids. The stuff of legend.

Destry lifted a mesh bag off the table. "I've got everything here. I can't wait. I've heard it's a superawesome pool. That's what Tallie and Claire told me. I just hope Kip Wheeler isn't too much of a tease. He can be *such* a pest."

Kip was Jenna's son from her first marriage, which had ended in the tragic death of her husband several years ago. He and his two older brothers and younger sister had been adopted by Carson McRaven after he married Jenna. They now had a busy toddler of their own, who kept all of them hopping.

"Everybody ready?"

"I am!" Destry jumped up and threw on her coat.

"As I'll ever be," Caidy muttered. Ridge gave her a sympathetic look as he lifted one of the pies and carried it out to the Suburban.

A light snow speckled the windshield, reflecting the

colorful holiday light displays they passed on their way
to the McRavens' house. They approached the house
through a long line of parked cars on either side of the
curving driveway. It looked as if half the town was inside the big house. She recognized Trace's SUV and
Taft's extended-cab pickup. Apparently, even when
they canceled the regular Sunday night Bowman dinner for a special occasion, the family couldn't manage
to stay apart.

"I'll let you two off near the door, then find a place
to park," Ridge said.

She wanted to tell him to forget it, but because she
was wearing her completely impractical high-heeled
black boots, she didn't argue.

"Want me to take a pie inside?" Destry asked.

"You've got your swim stuff. I can manage," she
answered.

As she expected, the entrance to the McRavens'
house was beautifully decorated with grapevine garlands entwined with evergreens and twinkling lights.
A trio of small live trees was also adorned with lights.

The door opened before they could even knock
and Jenna McRaven answered. She smiled, pretty and
blonde and deceptively fragile-looking. "Oh, Caidy. You
made it! I thought the day would never come when we
could convince you to come to our Christmas party."

Carson joined her at the door and gave all of them a
wide, charming smile. He was vastly different from the
cold man she remembered coming to town five years
ago.

"Caidy, great to see you." He kissed Caidy's cheek
before slipping an arm around his wife. The two of
them plainly adored each other. Caidy had noticed before that when they were together, scarcely a moment

passed when one of them didn't touch the other in some way. A hand on the arm, a brush of fingers.

She told herself she had no right to be envious of their happiness together.

"And you brought food!" Carson exclaimed.

"Where would you like the pies?"

"Besides in my stomach?" Carson asked. "They look fantastic. We can probably find room on the dessert table. What am I saying? There's always room for pie."

"I'll help you," Jenna said, taking one of the pies. "Carson, will you show Destry where she can change into her swimming suit?"

"I've already got it on," Des proclaimed, yanking the neck of her sweater aside to show the swimming suit strap.

"Good thinking." Carson smiled at her. "I'll just show you where you can leave your things, then."

They walked away and Jenna led her into the opposite direction, into the beautiful gourmet kitchen of the home, which currently bustled with about a dozen of her friends.

"Hey, Caidy!" Emery Cavazos greeted her with a smile, looking elegant and composed as always while she transferred something chocolate and rich-looking onto a tray.

"Hi, Em."

Nothing to worry about in here, she thought. She loved these women and got together with them often at various social functions. She could just pretend this was one of their regular parties.

"You know, Caidy would be perfect for that little matter we were discussing earlier," Maggie Dalton exclaimed.

"What matter?" she asked warily. With the Cold Creek women, one could never be too careful.

"We've all been admiring the new vet—a gorgeous widower with those two adorable kids," Jenna said. "We were trying to figure out someone we could subtly introduce him to."

"We've already met." And locked lips. More than once. She decided to keep that tidbit of information to herself. If she didn't, the whole town would join her brothers in trying to hook her up with Ben, who had made it quite plain they would never be matched.

Caroline Dalton—married to the oldest Dalton brother, Wade—tilted her head and gave Caidy a long, considering look. "You know, Mag, I think you're absolutely right. She's perfect for him."

"I...am?"

"Yes! You both love animals and you're wonderful with children."

"We need to figure out some way to get them together." Emery, the traitor, joined into the scheming.

Had she become such an object of pity that all the women in town felt they had to step in and take drastic action to practically arrange a marriage for her? It was a depressing thought, especially because Ben had made it clear he wasn't even interested in *kissing* her.

"Thank you, but that's not necessary," she said quickly, hoping to cut off this disastrous conniving at the pass. "As I said, Dr. Caldwell and I have met. He treated a dog of mine who was injured a few weeks ago. And in case you didn't know, he's currently living on the foreman's cottage at the River Bow."

"Oh, I hadn't heard he and the children moved out of the inn," exclaimed Jenny Boyer Dalton, principal of the elementary school. "I'm so happy they're not staying there for Christmas. No offense, Laura."

"None taken," Caidy's sister-in-law said. "I agree."

"That was a brilliant idea," Caroline said. "See, you *are* perfect for him!"

She could see this whole situation quickly spiraling out of control, with everybody in town jumping on board to push her and Ben together. What a nightmare that would be. He would hate it, especially when he had clearly brushed her off two nights ago after that stunning kiss.

In desperation, she hurried to try a little damage control. "I think you all need to give Ben a break and let him settle into Pine Gulch before you start picking out china patterns for him. The poor man hasn't even had the chance to move into his own house yet."

He would be going soon, though. The house he was building would be finished after the holidays and he and the children would be moving off the River Bow. The thought of not seeing those lights gleaming in the windows of the foreman's cottage—of not having the chance to listen to Jack's knock-knock jokes or being able to tease a reluctant smile from Ava—filled her with a poignant sense of loss.

The rest of winter stretched out ahead of her, long and empty. Not just the winter. The months and years to come, each day the same as the one before.

She would miss all of them dearly. How would she live in Pine Gulch knowing he was so close but out of her reach?

Maybe the time had come for her to take a different path. She could probably find a job somewhere outside Pine Gulch. Separating from her family would be painful but she wasn't sure which would hurt more—leaving or staying.

"Only friends, huh? That's too bad." Maggie Dalton gave a rueful sigh. "Don't you think if you tried, you could stir up a little interest in more? I mean, the man is *hot*."

Yes, she was fully aware of that—and was positive none of these women had known the magic of his kiss. The problem wasn't how attractive she found Ben Caldwell. He didn't feel the same way about her and she couldn't figure out a darn thing to do about it.

She wanted to cry, suddenly, right here in front of her dearest friends—each of whom had the great fortune to be married to a wonderful man who loved her deeply. They were all so happily married, they wanted everyone else to know the same joy. Caidy didn't know how to tell them the likelihood of that happening to her was pathetically slim.

Not that she wanted that. She was perfectly happy right now.

"You'd be surprised how often friendship can develop into more," Emery said. "Dr. Caldwell really does seem like a nice guy. We don't get all that many available men in Cold Creek besides the guys who come to snowmobile or fish. Maybe you should think about seeing if he wants to be more than friends."

Those tears burned harder behind her eyelids. Coming to this party was a phenomenally bad idea. If she'd had any idea she would face a gauntlet of matchmakers, she would have hidden in her room and locked the door.

"Don't, okay? Just…don't. Ben and I are friends. That's all. Not everyone is destined to live happily ever after like all of you are. Is it so hard to believe that maybe I like my life the way it is? Maybe Ben does too. Back off, okay?"

Her friends gaped at her and she could tell her vehemence had shocked them. She wasn't usually so firm, she realized. Now they were going to wonder why this was such a hot button for her.

Damn.

And Laura knew she and Ben had kissed. She was going to have to hope her beloved sister-in-law didn't decide to mention that little fact to the rest of the women.

She just couldn't win. Sometimes escaping with the remains of her dignity was the best option.

"I need to take one of my pies out to the dessert table. What about that tray, Emery? Is it ready to go out?"

"Um, sure." Her friend handed the delicious-looking bar cookies to her without another word. Feeling the heat of all their gazes on her back, Caidy escaped from the kitchen.

The party was crowded and noisy. For all its size, having a hundred people, many of them children, crammed into the McRavens' house didn't lend itself to quiet, relaxing conversation. Several neighbors and friends greeted her on her way to the food tables and she tried to smile and talk with them for a few moments but quickly broke away, using the excuse of the treats.

The tables were covered with all manner of culinary delights, as she had expected. Jenna loved to cook and loved coming up with new recipes for her clients and family. Caidy didn't have much appetite but she filled a small plate with a few possibilities—to have something to hold, more than anything.

"Those look good. Any idea what they are?"

At the deep voice at her elbow, she whirled and her heart stuttered. How had she missed Ben's approach?

Probably a combination of the crowd and her own distraction.

"I'm not sure. Jenna is famous for her spinach pinwheels, so that's what I'm hoping for. I should tell her to put signs up so we know what we're eating."

He smiled and she wanted to drink in the sight of him, tall and gorgeous and dearly familiar.

"I hadn't realized you were coming to the McRavens' party," she said rather inanely. As always, she felt as if she were operating on half-brain capacity around him. "It's a bit of a legend around here."

"Mrs. McRaven invited us when they brought their dog Frank in to me last week. Apparently he swallowed a Lego, but the trouble, uh, passed. I thought coming to the party might be a good way to get to know some of the neighbors."

He tilted his head and studied her and she could feel herself flush. She had to hope none of her friends decided to come out of the kitchen just now to see her standing flustered and off balance next to Ben Caldwell.

"What about you?" he said. "I didn't expect to see you here. It's kind of hard to escape the holiday spirit in a crowd like this."

Had he *wondered* if she would come? She wasn't sure she wanted to know.

"Destry begged and begged this year. All her cousins and most of her friends were coming."

Before he could respond, someone jostled her from behind. She wobbled a little in her impractical boots and would have fallen if he hadn't reached out and grabbed her. For a charged moment, they stared at each other and she saw heat and hunger leap into his eyes.

The noise of the crowd seemed to fade away as if someone had switched down the volume, and she was

aware of nothing but Ben. Of his arms, strong and comforting, of his firm mouth that had tasted so delicious
against hers, of his eyes that studied her with desire
and something else, something glittery and bright she
couldn't identify.

"Oh. I'm so sorry. Are you all right, my dear?"

She recognized Marjorie Montgomery's voice
and realized the mayor's wife—and the Dalton boys'
mother—must have been the one who bumped into
her. Still breathless—and grateful she had just set her
plate on the table before she was jostled, so at least she
didn't have spinach pinwheel smeared all over both of
them—she managed to extricate herself from Ben's
arms and turned.

"I'm fine. No problem."

Marjorie smiled innocently at her but she thought
she saw a crafty light in the older woman's eyes. Oh,
great. She and Ben would have no peace now that her
friends had decided they were destined for each other.
She wondered if she ought to warn him but decided that
would just be too awkward.

"It's crazy in here," Ben said. "I saw some open
chairs over by the French doors into the pool if you're
looking for a place to sit down."

She didn't miss the delight in Marjorie's eyes. The
woman probably thought her transparent ploy was paying off. She ought to politely decline and keep as far
away as she could from Ben. The last thing she wanted
to do was give anybody else ideas about linking the
two of them.

But she was weak when it came to him and she
couldn't resist spending whatever time she had with
him, even though he had made it quite clear they

couldn't have a relationship. Maybe, like her, he knew he should stay away but couldn't quite manage it.

She probably shouldn't find that so heartening.

"Sure." She picked up her plate and a glass of water and headed with him toward the chairs he indicated.

"Where are the kids?"

"Where else? In the pool." He gestured through the glass doors and she saw Jack playing in the shallow end with Laura's son, Alex. Ava was huddled with a group of girls, including Destry and Gabi.

"Taft offered to keep an eye on them for me so I could grab something to eat, since he was watching Alex and Maya anyway. I figured they were pretty safe with the fire chief on lifeguard duty."

They lapsed into silence and she nibbled at a little delicacy that tasted of pumpkin and cinnamon.

"So are you ready for Christmas?" she finally asked when the silence grew awkward. She regretted the words the instant they left her mouth. Good grief, could she sound any more mindless?

"No. Not at all," he answered with a slight note of panic in his voice. "I should be home wrapping presents right now. I don't know the first thing about how to do that. My wife usually took care of those details and then Mrs. Michaels has stepped in since Brooke died. Maybe I'll tell the kids Santa decided not to wrap the presents this year and just jumble them under the tree."

"You can't do that! The mystery and anticipation of unwrapping the gifts is part of the magic!"

He raised an eyebrow. "Says the woman who would like to forget all about the holidays."

"Just because I don't particularly enjoy Christmas doesn't mean I don't know what makes the day a perfect one, especially for children," she protested. "Destry's gifts have been wrapped and hidden away since Thanksgiving."

He was quiet for a long moment and then he shook his head. "You're remarkable, aren't you?"

His words baffled her. Was he making fun of her? "Why do you say that?"

"You hate Christmas but wouldn't think for a moment of short-shrifting your niece in any way. I just find that amazing. You really love her, don't you?"

She watched Destry through the glass, now playing ball with the other girls. "I do. She's the daughter I'll probably never have."

"Why not? You're young. What makes you think you won't have a family of your own someday?"

She wanted to answer that she was very much afraid she was falling in love with a veterinarian who had made it plain he was only interested in friendship, but of course she couldn't. "Some of us are just meant to be favorite aunts, I guess."

Before he could respond to what she suddenly realized sounded rather pathetic, she quickly changed the subject. "Do you want some help with the children's presents? I can sneak over after they're in bed tonight and help you wrap them. How long would it take? An hour, maybe. Tops."

He stared at her for a long moment, then shook his head. "I'm sure that's not necessary. I'll probably fumble my way through. Or just leave things unwrapped. It won't be the end of the world."

Another rejection. She almost sighed. She should be used to it by now. This time she had only been offering to help him but apparently even that was more than he wanted from her.

"No problem. I wouldn't want to impose."

"That's my line. I don't want you to feel obligated to come over at midnight on a pity mission to wrap presents for the inept single father."

"I never even thought of it that way!" she exclaimed. "I only wanted to… I don't know. Ease your burden a little."

He opened his mouth and then closed it again, an odd light in his eyes. "In that case, all right," he said after a long moment. "Everything is so crazy this year, with the rented house and Mrs. Michaels gone. I probably should try to keep the rest of our holiday traditions as consistent as possible. Santa Claus has always wrapped their gifts. I'm sure Jack won't care but Ava will probably consider it another failing of mine if I don't do things the way she's used to."

He paused. "I'm afraid my ledger of debt to you is growing longer and longer."

She managed a smile. "Friends don't keep track of things like that, Ben."

Because that's all they apparently would ever be, at least she could be the best damn friend he'd ever had.

"Thank you."

She couldn't sit here and make polite conversation with him, she decided. Not when she wanted so much more.

"Oh, there's Becca and Trace. I promised Becca I would talk to her about the menu for Christmas dinner. I should go do that. Will you excuse me?"

He rose. "Sure."

"I'm serious about helping you with the presents. Why don't you call me after the kids are asleep and I'll run over?"

He looked rueful. "I should refuse. This is something

I should probably be able to handle myself, but the truth is I'm grateful for your help."

She smiled, doing her best to conceal any trace of yearning, and walked away from him.

She was twenty-seven years old and had just discovered she must have a streak of masochism. Why else would she continue to thrust herself into situations that would only bump up her heartache?

Chapter Thirteen

Ben gazed at his phone, at the OK. They're asleep text message he had typed but hadn't sent.

He should delete it right now and tell her he had changed his mind. Caidy Bowman was dangerous to him, especially at ten-thirty at night.

He thought of how beautiful she had looked at the McRavens' party, sweetly lovely, like a spun sugar Christmas angel. The first moment he saw her at the party, standing by the refreshment table, he had been stunned by his desire to whirl her around and into his arms. As ridiculously medieval as it sounded, he had wanted to kiss her soundly and claim her as his for everyone at the party to see.

"I'm crazy, Tri, aren't I?"

The chihuahua cocked his head and appeared to ponder the question.

"Never mind. It was rhetorical. You don't have to answer."

Tri yipped and jumped into his lap with amazing agility for a three-legged dog. Resilient, the little dog, adjusting to whatever challenges life delivered to him. Ben could only wish for a small portion of the dog's courage.

He glanced at his phone again and without taking time to think it through, he hit the send button before he could change his mind.

Her answer came instantly, as if she had been waiting for him: Be right there.

Something in his chest gave a silly little kick and he shook his head, reminding himself of all the very valid reasons he had given her a few nights earlier. He wasn't in a good place for a relationship with her. His kids were struggling enough with this move. He couldn't suddenly throw a woman into the chaos to distract his attention from their needs.

This would be the last time, he told himself. He would accept her help with his presents and then he had to do a better job of maintaining a safe distance from her. He had talked to his contractor at the party and learned the house was on schedule to be finished in about ten days, just after the New Year. Maybe when he moved a few miles away, he could regain a little perspective and be able to spend a few moments of the day without thinking about her, longing for her.

"Yeah, I'm crazy," he said to Tri. He set the dog onto the ground and headed for Mrs. Michaels's room, where all the children's presents were hidden in her locked closet.

Before she left, she had wrapped a few of the presents. He found plenty of wrapping paper, tape and scissors in the closet. *Efficient Anne,* he thought fondly, missing her calming presence in his life. If not for the chaos of living in a hotel and then moving here to the ranch, his housekeeper probably would have finished the job weeks ago.

He carried the wrapping supplies down to the table in the kitchen. After a careful look inside the children's room to make sure they were soundly sleeping, he made a few more quiet trips up and down the stairs to transport the unwrapped gifts to the table.

Just as he finished the last load, he saw a flicker of movement outside and then Caidy approaching from the ranch house, making her way through the lightly falling snow. She had a couple of dogs with her and carried two large reusable shopping bags that piqued his curiosity. As she neared the porch steps, she gestured with one of her hands and gave an order to the dogs. Though he couldn't hear what she said, he guessed she was telling them to go back home. One of the dogs moved with eagerness ahead of the other, which seemed to trudge behind more slowly.

Caidy watched the dog in the moonlight for a moment and when she turned, he thought she looked worried about something but he didn't have time to wonder about it before she climbed the steps and knocked softly on the door.

She was bundled up from head to toe in a heavy wool coat and nubby red scarf and hat. With her cheeks rosy from the cold, she looked delicious.

"Hi," she said, her voice pitched low, probably afraid of waking the children.

"Hello," he murmured and was struck by the quiet intimacy of the night. With the fire crackling in the living room and the snow falling softly, it would be easy to make the mistake of thinking they were alone here, tucked away against the world.

Tri greeted her with a few eager sniffs of her boots and she smiled at the dog. "Hi there. How are you, little friend?"

The dog seemed to grin at her and Ben wished for a little of that easy charm.

"What's all this?" he asked, gesturing to her shopping bags.

"Christmas dinner. My arms are going to fall off if I don't set it down. Can I put it in the kitchen?"

"Of course. What do you mean, Christmas dinner?"

"It's not much. We had an extra ham and I always keep mashed potatoes in the freezer. You just have to add a little milk when you reheat them in the microwave. And then I always make too much pie so I brought one of those too. Without Mrs. Michaels, I wasn't sure if you would have had much time to think about fixing something nice for you and the kids."

Right now he couldn't think much beyond the next meal he had to fix for the kids. Christmas dinner. She went to all that trouble?

Against his will, warmth seeped through him. Her thoughtfulness astounded him and he didn't quite know what to say.

"Thank you," he finally managed to say. "Wow. Just…thank you."

She smiled and the sweetness of it nearly took his breath away. "You're welcome. Shall I put it in the refrigerator?"

He stirred himself to reach for the bags. "That would be great."

Caidy Bowman astonished him. She had endured unimaginable horror and pain. Despite it, she was a nurturer, doing her best to make the world around her a little brighter.

For the next few moments, he pulled out package after package. It was more than just ham and potatoes. She had sent a jar of homemade strawberry jam, some frozen bread dough with instructions for thawing and baking written on them, even a small cheese ball and a box of crackers.

He was sure he would have muddled through some kind of dinner with the children, but the fact that she had thought far enough ahead to help touched something deep inside him.

I just want to help lift your burden a little, she had said earlier in the evening. He couldn't remember anybody ever spontaneously offering such a thing to him. Mrs. Michaels helped him tremendously but he paid her well for it. This was pure generosity on Caidy's part and he was stunned by it.

"Shall we get started with wrapping?"

He wasn't sure he trusted himself right now to spend five minutes with her, but because she had come all this way—and brought Christmas dinner to boot—he didn't know how to kick her out into the snow.

"I've brought everything down, including all the wrapping paper I could find."

"Perfect."

She took in the pile of presents with a slight smile dancing across that expressive mouth. "Looks like the children will have a great Christmas."

He hurried to disabuse her of the notion that he ought to win any Father of the Year awards. "Mrs. Michaels did a lot of the shopping, though I did buy a few things online. So where do we start?"

"I guess we just dive in. You know, I can handle this, if you have something else to do."

Did she want him to leave? For an instant, he was unbelievably tempted to do just that, escape into another room and leave her to it. But not only would that be rude, it would be cowardly too, especially when she had gone to all this trouble to walk down in the snow—and carrying a sumptuous meal too.

"No. Let's do this. With both of us working together, it shouldn't take long. You might have to babysit me a little."

"Surely you've wrapped a present before."

He racked his brain and vaguely remembered wrapping a gift for his grandparents that first Christmas after they had taken him in, a macaroni-covered pencil holder he had worked hard on in school. His grandfather hadn't even opened it, had made some excuse about saving it for later. Christmas night when he had taken out a bag of discarded wrapping paper, he had seen it out in the trash can, still wrapped.

"I probably did when I was a kid. I doubt my skills have improved since then."

"How can a man reach thirtysomething without learning how to wrap a present?"

"I rely on two really cool inventions. You may have heard of them. Store gift-wrapping and the very handy and ubiquitous gift bag."

She laughed, and the sound of it in the quiet kitchen entranced him. "I'll tell you what. I'll take care of all the oddly shaped gifts and you can handle the easy things. The books and the DVDs and other basic shapes. It's a piece of cake. Let me show you."

For the next few moments, he endured the sheer torture of having her stand at his side, her soft curves just a breath away as she leaned over the table beside him.

"The real trick to a beautifully wrapped present is to make sure you measure the paper correctly. Too big and you've got unsightly extra paper to deal with. Too small and the package underneath shows through."

"Makes sense," he mumbled. He was almost painfully aware of her, but beneath his desire was something deeper, a tenderness that terrified him. He meant his words to her earlier in the evening. She was an amazing person and he didn't know how much longer he could continue to ignore this inexorable bond between them.

"Okay, after you've measured your paper, leaving an extra inch or two on all sides, you bring the sides up, one over the other, and tape the seam. Great. Now fold the top and bottom edges of the end on the diagonal like this—" she demonstrated "—and then tape those down. Small pieces of tape are better. Can you see that?"

Right now, he would agree to anything she said. She smelled delicious and he wanted to pull her onto his lap and just nuzzle her neck for a few hours. "Okay. Sure."

"After that, you can use ribbon to wrap around it or just stick on a bow. Doesn't it look great? Do you think you can do it now on your own?"

He looked down blankly at the present. "Not really," he admitted.

She frowned, so close to him he could see the shimmery gold flecks in her eyes. "What part didn't you get? I thought that was a great demonstration."

He sighed. "It probably was. I only heard about half of it. I was too busy remembering how your mouth tastes like strawberries."

She stared at him for a long charged moment and

then she quickly moved to the chair across the table from him.

"Please stop," she said, her voice low and her color high.

"I'd like to. Believe me."

"I'm serious. I can't handle this back-and-forth thing. It's not fair. You flirt with me one minute and then push me away the next. Please. Make up your mind, for heaven's sake. I don't know what you want from me."

"I don't either," he admitted. He was an ass. She was absolutely right. "I think that's the problem. I keep telling myself I can't handle anything but friendship right now. Then you show up and you smell delicious and you're so sweet to bring dinner for us. To top it all off, you're so damned beautiful, all I can think about is kissing you again, holding you in my arms."

She stared at him, her eyes wide. He saw awareness there and something else, something fragile.

He wanted her fiercely. Because she trembled whenever he touched her, he suspected she shared his hunger. He could kiss her—and possibly do more—now, but at what cost?

She was a vulnerable woman. He was no armchair psychologist, but he guessed she was hiding herself away here on this ranch because she saw only weakness and fear in herself. She saw the sixteen-year-old girl who had cowered from her parents' killers. She didn't see herself as the strong, powerful, desirable woman he did.

He could hurt her—and that was the last thing he wanted to do.

"Sorry. Forget I said that. We'd better get these presents wrapped so you can go home and get some sleep."

She stared at him, her eyes wide and impossibly

green. Finally she nodded. "Yes. I would hate to be down here wrapping gifts if one of the children woke up and came down for a drink of water or something."

She turned her attention to the task at hand. He fumbled through wrapping a book for Ava and did an okay job but nothing as polished as Caidy's presents. After a few more awkward moments with only the sound of rustling paper and ripping tape, he decided he needed something as a buffer between them.

He rose from the table and headed for Mrs. Michaels's radio/CD player in the corner. When he turned it on, jazzy Christmas music filled the empty spaces. She didn't like holiday songs, he remembered, but she didn't seem to object so he left the station tuned there.

The pile dwindled between them, and at some point she started talking to him again, asking little questions about the gifts he and Mrs. Michaels had purchased, about the children's interests, about their early Christmases.

When he left to look for one more roll of paper in Mrs. Michaels's room, he returned to find her humming softly under her breath to "Angels We Have Heard on High," her voice soft and melodious.

He stood just on the other side of the doorway, wondering what it might take for her to sing again. She stopped abruptly when she sensed his presence and returned to taping up a box containing yet another outfit for Ava's American Girl doll.

"You found more paper. Oh, good. That should help us finish up."

He sat back down and started wrapping a DVD for Jack.

"Tell me about Christmas when you were a kid," she said after a moment.

That question came out of left field and he fumbled for an answer. "Fine. Nothing memorable."

"Everybody has some fond memory of Christmas. Making Christmas cookies, delivering gifts to neighbors. What were your traditions?"

He tried to think back and couldn't come up with much. "We usually had a nice tree. My grandmother's decorator would spend the whole day on it. It was really beautiful." He didn't add that he and Susie weren't allowed to go near it because of the thousands of dollars in glass ornaments adorning the branches.

"Your grandmother?"

Had he said that? "Yeah. My grandparents raised my sister and me from the time I was about eight until I left for college."

"Why?"

He could feel her gaze on him as he tried to come up with the words to answer her. He wanted to ignore it but couldn't figure out a way to do that politely. And suddenly, for a reason he couldn't have explained, he wanted to tell her, just like in his office earlier in the week when he had told her about Brooke.

"My childhood wasn't very happy, I guess, but I feel stupid complaining about it. I don't know who my father is. My mother was a drug addict who dumped my half sister and me on her parents and disappeared without a word. She died of an overdose about three months later."

Her eyes darkened with sympathy. "Oh, no. I'm so sorry. What a blessing that you had your grandparents to help you through it."

He gave a rough laugh. "My grandparents were extremely wealthy and important people in Chicago social circles but they didn't want to be saddled with the obligation of raising the children of an out-of-control daughter they had cut off years earlier. They probably would have chucked us into the foster care system if they weren't afraid of how it would look to their acquaintances. Sometimes I wish they had done just that. They didn't have the patience for two small children."

"Then it's even more wonderful that you work so hard to give your children such a great Christmas," she said promptly. "You've become the father you never had."

Her faith in him was humbling. At her words, he felt this shifting and settling inside his heart.

This wasn't simply attraction. He was in love with her. The realization settled over him like autumn leaves falling to earth, like that snow drifting against the windows.

How had *that* happened?

Perhaps during that sleigh ride, when he had seen her holding her sweet niece Maya on her lap, or when she had come to the door the other night, flour on her cheek from making three pizzas for a houseful of children. Or maybe that first night at the clinic, when she had knelt beside her injured dog and hummed away the animal's anxiety.

Oblivious to his sudden staggering epiphany, she tied an elaborate bow on the gift she was wrapping and snipped the ends. "There. That should be the last one."

Through his dazed shock, he managed to turn his attention to the pile of presents. Somehow he, Mrs. Michaels and Caidy had managed to pull off another Christmas.

She was right. He was a good father—not because he could provide them a pile of gifts but because he loved them, because he was doing his best to provide a safe, friendly place for them to grow, because he treated them with patience and respect instead of cold tolerance.

"Thank you." The words seemed inadequate for all she had done for him this holiday season.

She smiled and rose from the kitchen table. She stretched her arms over her head to work all the kinks out from being huddled over a table for nearly an hour, and it took all his strength not to leap across the table and devour her.

"Just imagining their faces on Christmas morning is enough thanks for me. You've got a couple of really adorable kids there, Ben."

"I do." His voice sounded strangled and she gave him an odd look but shrugged into her coat. He knew he should help her, but right now he didn't trust himself to be that close to her.

"Good night."

As she started for the door, he came to his senses. "I forgot you walked down here. Let me grab my coat and I'll walk you back to your house."

"That's not necessary."

It was to him. In answer, he pulled his coat down from the hook and drew it on while she watched him with a disgruntled expression.

"I've been walking this lane my whole life. I'm fine. You shouldn't leave the children."

"I'll be gone five minutes, with the house in view the whole time."

She sighed. "You're a stubborn man, Dr. Caldwell."

He could be. He supposed it was stubbornness that had kept him from admitting the truth to himself—that he was falling for her. As they walked out into the light snow, Tri hopping along ahead of them, he was struck again by the peace that seemed to enfold him when he was with her.

She smiled at the little dog's valiant efforts to stay in front as leader of the pack, then lifted her face to let snowflakes kiss her cheeks. Tenderness, sweet and healing, seemed to wash through him. He wanted to protect her, to make her smile—to, as she had said earlier, lift her burdens if she would let him.

His marriage hadn't quite been that way. He had loved Brooke but as he walked beside Caidy, he couldn't help thinking that in many ways it had been an immature sort of love. They had met when he had been in veterinary school and she had been doing undergraduate work in public relations.

For some reason he still didn't quite comprehend, she had immediately decided she wanted him, in that determined way she had, and he hadn't done much to change the course she set out for both of them.

He had come to love her, of course, though his love had been intertwined with gratitude that she would take a lonely, solitary man and give him a family and a place to belong.

He thought he would never fall in love again. When Brooke died, he thought his world was over. It had taken all these months and years for him to feel as though he could even think about moving forward with his life.

Here he was, though, crazy in love with Caidy Bowman and it scared the hell out of him. Could he risk his heart, his soul, all over again?

And why was he even thinking about this? Yes, Caidy responded to his kisses, but she had spent her adult life pushing away any relationship beyond her family. She might not even be interested in anything more with him. Why would she be? He didn't have that much to offer in the relationship department. He was surly and impatient, with a couple of energetic kids to boot.

"I wonder if I can ask you a favor," she said after they were nearly to the barn. "If you have time this week, could you take a look at my Sadie? I'm worried about her. She's not been acting like herself."

He pictured her old border collie, thirteen years old and moving with slow, measured movements. "Sure. I can come over tomorrow morning."

"Oh, I don't think it's urgent. After Christmas would probably be fine."

"All right. First thing Wednesday. Or if the kids and I feel like taking a walk after they open presents, maybe I'll stop up at the house to take a look."

"Thank you. You should probably go back. You left a fire in the fireplace, don't forget."

"Yes." He wanted to kiss her, here in the wintry cold. He wanted to tuck her against him and hold her close and keep her safe from any more sorrow.

He didn't have that right, he reminded himself. Not now. Maybe after the holidays, after he and the children moved into the new house and Mrs. Michaels came back, he could ask her to dinner, see where things might progress.

"Thank you again for your help with the gifts."

"You're welcome. If I don't see you again, merry Christmas."

"Same to you."

She gave that half smile again. Against his better judgment, he stepped forward and brushed a soft kiss on her rosy cheek, then turned around, scooped up his little dog and walked swiftly away through the snow— while he still could.

Chapter Fourteen

"Hang on. Just a few more moments. There's my sweet girl. Hang on."

Icy fear pulsed through Caidy as she drove her truck through the wintry Christmas Eve in a grim repeat of a scene she had already played a few weeks earlier with Luke. She was much more terrified this time than she had been with the younger dog, and the quarter mile to the foreman's cottage seemed to stretch on forever.

Sadie couldn't die. She just couldn't. But from the instant she had walked into the barn just moments earlier and found her beloved dog lying motionless in the straw of one of the stalls, all her vague concerns about the dog's health over the past few days had coalesced into this harsh, grinding terror.

Sadie, her dearest friend, was fading. She knew it in her heart and almost couldn't breathe around the pain.

She couldn't seem to think straight either. Only one thought managed to pierce her panic.

Ben would know what to do.

She had picked up the dog, shoved her into the bed of the nearest vehicle, Ridge's pickup, pulled the spare key out of the tackroom and drove like hell to Ben's place.

Now that she approached the house nestled in the pines, reality returned. It was nearly midnight on Christmas Eve. The children would be sound asleep. She couldn't rush in banging on the door to wake them up, tonight of all nights, when they would never be able to go back to sleep.

Adrenaline still shooting through her, she pulled up to the front door, trying to figure out what to do. The Christmas tree lights still blazed through the window. Maybe Ben was still awake.

Sadie hadn't made a sound this entire short trip, though Caidy could see her ribs still moving with her shallow breathing.

Caidy opened her door and was just trying to figure out which bedroom was his, wondering if she could throw a snowball at it or something in an effort to wake only him, when the porch light flicked on and the front door opened. An instant later, he walked out in stocking feet, squinting into the night.

"Caidy!" he exclaimed when he recognized her. "What is it? What's wrong?"

Relief poured through her, blessed relief. Ben would know what to do.

"It's Sadie," she said on a sob, hurrying to the passenger side of the pickup. "She's... Oh, please, Ben. Help me."

He didn't even stop to throw on shoes—he just raced

down the frozen sidewalk toward her. "Tell me what happened."

"I don't know. I just… After Destry and Ridge went to bed, I was just sitting by the Christmas tree by myself and I…I decided to go out to the barn. It's a…sacred sort of place on Christmas Eve, among the animals. Peaceful. I needed that tonight. But when I got there, I found Sadie lying in the straw. She wouldn't wake up."

She choked back her sob, knowing she needed to retain control if she had any hope of helping her beloved dog.

"Let's get her inside out of the cold and into the light so I can have a look at her."

He scooped the old dog into his arms and carried her back across that snowy walk. Caidy followed. Her heart felt as fragile as her mother's antique Christmas angel. How would she bear it if Sadie died tonight, of all nights?

No. She wasn't going to think about that. Only positive thoughts. Ben would take care of things, she was sure of it.

She thought of that day when she had taken Luke to the clinic, battered and broken. She had thought Ben so cold and uncaring. As she watched him gently lay Sadie on a blanket she had quickly grabbed from the sofa to spread in front of the still-glowing fireplace, she wondered if she had ever so poorly judged a person.

He was kind and compassionate. Wonderful. How could she ever have imagined that first day that he would become so dear to her?

"What's going on, girl?"

At least Sadie opened her eyes at his voice, but she didn't move as the veterinarian's hands moved over her, seeking answers.

"You said she hasn't been acting like herself. What have you seen?" he asked her.

She tried to think back over the past few days. The truth was, she had been so busy coping with the stress of Christmas, she hadn't paid as much attention to her dog as usual.

"She's been lethargic for three or four days. And it seems like on the nights when she wanted to sleep inside, she was always having to go out to pee. She hasn't eaten much, but she has been more thirsty than usual."

He frowned. "Exactly what I suspected."

"What?"

He looked at her with such gentleness, she wanted to weep. "I'll have to do labwork to be sure but I suspect she's having chronic kidney failure. It's not unusual in older dogs."

She drew in a heavy breath. "Can you…can you fix it?"

"The good news is, I can probably help her feel better tonight. She needs fluids and I always keep a few liters in my emergency kit. I can give her an IV right here."

"The bad news?"

"It's called chronic kidney failure for a reason," he said, his eyes compassionate. "There's no miracle cure, I'm afraid. We can perhaps make her more comfortable for a few months, but that's the best we can do. I'm so sorry, Caidy."

She nodded, those tears threatening again. "She's thirteen. I've known it was only a matter of time. But… even a few more months with her would be the greatest gift you could ever give me."

"I don't know for sure it's kidney failure. It could be something entirely different, but from the symptoms you describe and the exam, I'm ninety-nine percent certain. If you want me to, I can wait to treat her until I run bloodwork."

"No. I trust you. Completely." She paused. "I knew you would be able to help her. When I found her in the barn, all I could think about was bringing her to you."

He appeared startled at that, then gave her an unreadable look. "I'll go grab the supplies for an IV, then."

After he left the room, she knelt down beside the sweet-natured border collie, who had provided her with uncomplicated love and incalculable solace during the darkest moments of her life, when she had been a lost and grieving sixteen-year-old girl.

"Ben will help you," she told the dog, stroking her head softly. "You'll feel better soon. We can't have you missing your Christmas stocking. Here's a secret. Don't tell any of the others but I got you a new can of tennis balls. Your favorite."

Sadie's tail flapped halfheartedly on the carpet. It was a small sign of enthusiasm, yes, but more than Caidy had seen from the dog since she walked into the barn.

What would have happened if she hadn't found Sadie in time? The dog would never have made it. She was certain of that. When she and Destry and Ridge went out for chores on Christmas morning, they would have discovered her cold, lifeless body.

Just the thought of it made her stomach clutch. She *had* found her, though. Something had prompted her to brave the weather so she could find the dog in time and bring her here, to Ben, who knew just what to do.

Why *had* she gone out to the barn? Yes, she had found peace and solitude in the barn a few times before on Christmas Eve over the years, but it wasn't as if she made a habit of it.

She had been standing at the window gazing out at the cottage lights flickering in the trees, ready to collapse in her bed after a long day with her family, when some impulse she still didn't understand had compelled her to slip into her coat and head outside.

Coincidence? Maybe. Somehow she didn't think so. More like inspiration. Perhaps her own little miracle.

The thought raised chills on her arms as she gazed down at her beloved dog. What else could she call it? She had gone to the barn just in time to save a life. Even more miraculous, a wonderful veterinarian who knew just what to do lived just a quarter mile away—and he had the ready supplies necessary to help her dog.

Yes. A miracle.

A sweet sense of peace and love trickled over her, healing and cleansing, washing away the fear and sadness that had become so much a part of Christmas for her.

The clock on the mantel chimed softly. Midnight. It was Christmas. What better time for miracles, for second chances, for hope and light and life?

She leaned down to Sadie and began to hum one of her favorite Christmas songs, "It Came Upon a Midnight Clear." After a few bars, the words seemed to crowd through her heart, bursting to break free.

And for the first time in eleven years, she began to sing.

With the IV bag in his hand, Ben stood outside the room, afraid to move, to breathe, as he listened to the soft strains filling the air. He needed to help her dog quickly but surely he could wait a few more seconds.

Caidy was singing to her dog and her voice was the

most beautiful sound he had ever heard, clear and pure and sweet.

"The world in solemn stillness lay, to hear the angels sings."

As she finished the song, he forced himself to move into the room and knelt beside her and the dog. She glanced over, color soaking her cheeks.

"You don't have to stop," he said as he pulled on surgical gloves and went to work finding a spot for the IV. "In fact, I hope you don't. It appeared to comfort her."

She was silent for a moment and then she began to sing "Away in a Manger" in her sweet, lovely soprano. The song seemed to shimmer through the air.

"Your brother is right," he said when she sang the last note of the third verse. "You do have a beautiful voice. I feel blessed I had the chance to hear it."

She smiled a little tremulously. "I can't tell you how strange it feels to sing. Strange and wonderful. All this time, the music has been there, just waiting for me to let it out."

"I didn't know them but I can only imagine your parents would be happy you found your voice again." He knew he was taking a chance reminding her of the sadness that had become so much a part of her holidays.

To his relief, she nodded. "You're right. I know you're right."

Moving forward took tremendous courage. He was consumed with love for her and wanted to tell her so but the moment didn't seem right, when her beloved dog was struggling for life.

"Is there anything I can do right now for Sadie?"

He turned his full attention back to her dog. "I'm giving her a bolus now—a great deal of fluid in a short amount of time—and then we'll slowly drip the other bag over the next hour or so. I've also given her some medication in the IV that will help perk her up. We should see results fairly quickly. I'm afraid I'll have to keep her here for the night. Do you mind?"

"Mind?" She gave a rough laugh. "I don't know what I would have done without you, Ben."

"I guess it was my turn to ease your burden a little for a change."

Though she smiled, the Christmas lights from the tree she had given them reflected in green eyes that swam with tears. One dripped free and slid down her cheek and Ben reached his thumb out and brushed it away from her warm, silky skin. "Please don't cry."

"They're happy tears," she promised him. "Well, maybe a little bittersweet. I know she won't be here forever. But she's here now because of you. That's what matters—she's here. I don't think I could be strong enough to endure losing her on Christmas Eve."

"It's not Christmas Eve anymore. It's past midnight. Merry Christmas."

Her smile took his breath away and she leaned slightly into his hand. "Merry Christmas, Ben."

He caressed her cheek with his thumb, tenderness and love pulsing through him. Unable to resist, he framed her face with his hands and kissed her gently. She sighed softly and her arms slid around him.

The moment was so perfect there in his borrowed living room with the Christmas tree as a backdrop and he didn't want to do anything to break the spell, but he knew she couldn't be comfortable for long on her knees like that. He eased them both back against the armchair and sat there on the floor, pulling her almost onto his lap.

They kissed for a long moment with aching softness

and it was more magical than any Christmas morning
he had dreamed about when he was a lonely boy. Love
poured through him as sweetly as the notes of her song.

He loved this strong, courageous woman and needed
her in his life. Jack and Ava did too. All his carefully
constructed reasons for taking his time, moving slowly,
seemed to fade into insignificance.

Yes, this might present another huge change for all
of them, but he knew his children were resilient. They
both liked Caidy already. Even Ava had said as much
after the pizza night. It wouldn't take long for them to
love her.

Finally she slid away, her eyes glimmering. She
opened her mouth to speak and then must have decided
she didn't want to disturb the peace of the moment. She
turned slightly in his arms to check on Sadie. He held
her as they both listened to the steady pump of the IV
and watched the colored lights of the tree reflected in
the window and plump snowflakes begin to fall.

After a few moments, Tri hopped in, probably
emerging from his favorite sleeping spot at the foot of
Ben's bed to wonder where he was. The little dog wandered over to Sadie, who was lying in front of the fire.
Ben was about to call him off but Sadie's tail began to
wag and she stirred herself to sniff at the other dog.
Tri licked at her muzzle and then settled in next to her.

"Look at her." Caidy's laugh was filled with wonder.

"The medication metastasizes in her system fairly
quickly. I imagine by the time the kids wake up, she'll
have as much energy as they do."

"It's amazing. *You're* amazing."

When she looked at him that way, he felt like the
most brilliant veterinarian in the country. She kissed
him and though he knew some part of it was motivated

by gratitude, he sensed something else in the way her mouth moved across his, the way her arms tightened around his neck.

Finally he knew he couldn't remain quiet any longer. "Do you think it's any kind of conflict of interest for a veterinarian to be in love with his patient's human?"

Caidy stared at him, certain the stress of the past half hour—coupled with her abject relief—must be playing tricks with her hearing. Did he just say…?

Her heart pounded as if that belligerent bull that had started this whole thing had just caught her in his sights and she couldn't seem to catch hold of any coherent thought. "Is that a hypothetical question?" she finally said, her voice low and thready.

Ben—wonderful, strong, brilliant Ben—tightened his arms around her, a soft, tender light in his eyes that made her catch her breath.

"I think you know the answer to that. I've been fighting this like crazy for a hundred different, stupid reasons. But tonight when I listened to you sing, I realized none of them matter. I love you, Caidy. I wasn't looking for it. Especially not now, when my life has so much chaos in it. I told myself I didn't want to take that kind of risk again."

He smiled at her and she felt as bright and sparkly as that angel on the top of the tree. "But here's the thing. Somehow, you calm the chaos. I don't know how you did it, but you burst into my life with your fierce courage and your dogs and your smile and turned everything I thought I wanted spinning into an entirely different direction."

"Ben," she said softly, unbelievably touched that the

man she thought so taciturn and hard that first day could be saying these words to her.

"I think I started to fall in love with you that day you came to the clinic, so determined to get the very best care for your dog. I knew for sure when you came here to help me wrap the children's presents the other night, even though you don't like Christmas."

"I don't know. I think my perspective on that is changing a little."

He laughed and kissed her again. When she slid away a few moments later, Sadie was sitting up, gazing around the room alertly while Tri teased at her ear. Caidy didn't know how her heart could contain more joy.

"To answer your question," she said, "I don't believe there is a conflict of interest at all as long as said veterinarian doesn't mind that the human in question is also very much in love with him."

"Is she?"

"Oh, yes. I love you. More than I can say. And Ava and Jack too. I thought I was content with my life here on the ranch helping Ridge, but over the past few weeks, I've come to realize something good and right has been missing. You. All this time, I think I've just been waiting for you."

He gazed at her for a long moment, his eyes fiery and bright, then with aching softness he picked up her hand and kissed her palm. "I'm here now. And I'm not going anywhere."

She couldn't contain the joy bubbling through her. Sadie would be all right, at least for now. It was Christmas morning, the time for miracles and hope, and she had eleven years of Christmases to make up for. What

better place to do it than in the arms of the man she
loved fiercely?

She wrapped her arms around him and Ben laughed
softly, almost as if he couldn't help himself, then kissed
her again while the Christmas tree lights gleamed and
the two dogs snuggled by the fire and her heart sang.

Epilogue

"**I** just love Christmas weddings," Laura exclaimed as she adjusted one of the pins keeping Caidy's snowy-white veil in place.

"It's not Christmas," Maya said, with irrefutable logic. In the mirror, Caidy had a clear view of the little girl sitting on a bench in the room reserved for brides at the small church in Pine Gulch, carefully holding Trace and Becca's chubby six-month-old son, who was gumming his fingers.

"Santa doesn't come for five more days," Maya pointed out.

"True," her mother answered with a grin. "I should have said I love Christmas*time* weddings. Is that better?"

"Yes." Maya smiled, looking sweet and adorable in her blue-and-silver flower-girl dress.

"The church looks beautiful," Becca said, hurry-

ing in to scoop little Will out of Maya's lap with unerring instincts, just as both of the children started to
get bored with the arrangement. "It looks like a snowy
wonderland with all those silvery snowflakes and the
blue ribbons. Such a better choice than the traditional
red and green. As lovely as it is out there, it doesn't hold
a candle to our blushing bride here. You look fantastic.
Are you happy, Caidy?"

She smiled at her brothers' wives. She did feel a
small pang that her mother wasn't there on her wedding
day, but this was a time for joy, not sadness. She might
not have her mother with her, and that would always
hurt, but she did have these wonderful women who had
become so dear to her.

"*Happy* doesn't come close to covering it. I don't
think I have room inside me to hold all the joy."

"I don't either," Ava said, looking lovely in the
bridesmaid dress she was so very enthralled to be wearing.

"Same here," Destry, in a matching dress, added.

Caidy smiled and squeezed both girls' hands, the
daughter of her heart and the daughter she would be
gaining officially in a matter of moments.

Sometimes she couldn't take in the changes in her
life from last Christmas. Over the years, she had told
herself she was happy living at the ranch, helping her
brother with Destry, raising her dogs and her horses.
Now she could see how much power she had given one
horrible, violent event over her life. She had been hiding out there, slowly suffocating in her fears, afraid to
take any chances.

Ben had changed that. This past year had been filled
with more happiness than she could ever have imagined.
A little sadness too, she had to admit. After her miracu-

lous Christmas recovery, Sadie had made it to spring-time. Her last months she had shown more energy than she had in years, but one April morning Caidy had found her under the flowering branches of the crab-apple tree beside the house. Ben had helped her bury her friend on a hillside overlooking the ranch and the river and had held her while she wept.

The two of them had taken their time this past year, moving slowly to give the children time to adjust to the idea of her being a regular part of their lives.

Jack, with his sunny nature, had no problem accept-ing her. As she might have expected, Ava had been a little more resistant. At first, the girl had fought the idea of anyone wanting to replace her mother in their lives. But now, a year after she and Ben started dating, Caidy believed she and Ava had developed a strong, solid relationship.

A December wedding had been his idea, to give her something joyful to remember—instead of pain and fear—during this time of hope and promise.

Waiting all this time to start their lives together had seemed endless. The day was finally here and she couldn't imagine anything more perfect.

"I think you're ready now," Laura said. "Oh, Caidy. I'm so happy for you."

Taft's wife hugged her, though at four months preg-nant, she was beginning to bump out a little.

"Same here," Becca said, kissing her cheek and squeezing her hands. "You deserve a wonderful guy like Ben. I'm really glad he turned out not to be a rude, arrogant, opinionated jerk."

Caidy cringed, remembering her stupid words about him so long ago. "None of you will let me forget that, will you?"

"Probably not." Laura smiled.

A knock sounded on the door. When Ava opened it, Ridge poked his head in, looking big and tough and gorgeous in his black Western-cut tuxedo. "Are we ready in here? I know a certain veterinarian who's a little impatient out there."

She drew a breath and adjusted her dress. "I think so."

"Come on, girls. Time to get in your places," Becca said.

Laura gave Caidy's veil one more adjustment, then stood back. "Okay. Perfect."

With a deep breath, Caidy slipped her hand in the crook of her brother's arm.

Ridge reached his other hand over and squeezed her fingers. "You're stunning," he said. "Mom and Dad would have been so proud of the beautiful woman you've become. Inside and out."

"Don't make me cry," she said, her throat thick with emotion.

"It's true. They would have liked Ben too. He's a good man. The highest praise I can give him is that I think he's almost good enough for you. I'm so glad you're happy."

She gave her brother a tremulous smile. "I am. It took me a while to get here but I really am."

"Let's do this, then."

The small but earnest church choir she now joined on Sundays broke into singing Pachelbel's "Canon in D Major" and she drew a deep breath, nerves skittering through her. As she and Ridge started down the aisle behind the bridesmaids, she looked down and saw the gruff, sometimes taciturn veterinarian she loved be-

yond measure smiling broadly. The best man—Jack—
was holding his hand.

Her heart aching with love for him and for his children, Caidy walked down the aisle beside her brother to
the beautiful strains of the music toward a future filled
with joy and laughter and song.

* * * * *

She gazed at him, her eyes soft, and he felt something sparkle to life in his chest as if someone had just plugged in a hundred Christmas trees.

He was falling hard for this lovely woman, who treated his daughter with such kindness.

Fear not.

That little phrase written in his father's hand seemed to leap into his mind.

Fear not.

He was pretty sure this wasn't what his father had meant—or the angels on that first Christmas night, for that matter—but he didn't care. It seemed perfect and right to fearlessly take her mug of cocoa and set it on the side table next to his own, to lean across the space between them, to lower his head, to taste that soft, sweet mouth that had tantalized him all day.

A COLD CREEK CHRISTMAS SURPRISE

BY
RAEANNE THAYNE

First published in Great Britain 2013
by Mills & Boon, an imprint of Harlequin (UK) Limited,
Eton House, 18-24 Paradise Road, Richmond, Surrey TW9 1SR

© RaeAnne Thayne 2013

ISBN: 978 0 263 90164 1

23-1213

Harlequin (UK) policy is to use papers that are natural, renewable and recyclable products and made from wood grown in sustainable forests. The logging and manufacturing processes conform to the legal environmental regulations of the country of origin.

Printed and bound in Spain
by Blackprint CPI, Barcelona

RaeAnne Thayne finds inspiration in the beautiful northern Utah mountains, where she lives with her husband and three children. Her books have won numerous honors, including RITA® Award nominations from Romance Writers of America and a Career Achievement Award from *RT Book Reviews*. RaeAnne loves to hear from readers and can be contacted through her website, www.raeannethayne.com.

To my wonderful readers. You constantly awe
and inspire me with your passion, loyalty and heart.

Chapter One

The River Bow had never seemed so empty.

Ridge Bowman stomped snow off on the mat as he walked into the mudroom of the ranch house after chores. The clomping thuds of his boots seemed to echo through the big rambling log home he had lived in most of his life, but that was the only sound.

He was used to noise and laughter—to his sister Caidy clanging dishes or singing along to the radio in the kitchen, to his daughter watching television in the family room or talking on the phone to one of her friends, to barking dogs and conversation.

But Caidy was on her honeymoon with Ben Caldwell and Destry had gone to stay with her cousin and best friend, Gabi.

For the first time in longer than he could remember, he had the house completely to himself.

He didn't much like it.

He slipped out of his boots and walked into the kitchen. A couple of barks reminded him he wasn't completely alone. He was dogsitting for Ben's cute little pooch, a three-legged Chihuahua mix aptly named Tripod. Most of the dogs at the River Bow slept in the barn and lived outside, even Luke now—Caidy's border collie, who had been injured the Christmas before—but Tri was small and a bit too fragile to hang with the big boys.

The dog cantered into the mudroom and planted his haunches by the door.

"You need to go out? You know you're going to disappear in all that snow out there, right? And by the way, next time let me know before I take off my boots, would you?"

He opened the door and watched the dog hop out with his funny gait to the small area off the sidewalk that Ridge had cleared for him.

Tri obviously didn't like the cold, either. He quickly took care of business then hopped back to Ridge, who stood in the doorway. The dog immediately led the way back toward the kitchen. Ridge followed, his stomach rumbling, wondering what he could scrounge from the leftover wedding food for breakfast. Maybe a couple of Jenna McRaven's spinach quiche bites he liked so much, and there were probably a few of those little ham-and-cheese sandwiches. Ham was close enough to bacon, right?

He managed to add a yogurt and a banana, missing the big, hearty, delicious breakfasts his sister used to fix for him. Fluffy pancakes, crisp bacon, hash browns that were perfectly brown on the outside.

Those days were over now that Caidy was married.

From here out, he would just have to either fend for himself—and Destry—or hire a housekeeper to cook his breakfast. Too bad Ben's housekeeper, Mrs. Michaels, wanted to move back to be near her grandchildren in California.

He was happy for his little sister and the future she was building with Pine Gulch's new veterinarian. She had put her life on hold too long to help Ridge out here at the ranch after Melinda left. At the time—saddled with a baby he didn't know what to do with, right in the middle of trying to rebuild the ranch after his parents' deaths—he had been desperately grateful for her help. Now he was ashamed that he had come to rely on her so much over the years and hadn't tried harder to insist she move out on her own years ago.

She had found her way, though. She and Ben were deeply in love, and Caidy would be a wonderful stepmother to his children, Ava and Jack.

All his siblings were happily married now. He was the last Bowman standing, which was just the way he liked it.

He nibbled on one of Jenna's delicious potato puffs then had to stop for a huge yawn. The obligations of running a ranch didn't mix very well with wedding receptions and dances that ran into the early hours of the morning.

"Is it still a disaster out there, Tri?"

The little dog, curled up in a patch of morning sunlight trickling in from the window, lifted his head and flapped his tail on the kitchen tile, then went back to sleep, oblivious.

Ridge knew from his walk down the stairs that morning that the kitchen was just about the only clean part of the house right now. Jenna's catering crew had done a good job in here and had wanted to go to work on the rest of the house, but he hadn't let them. He had also had to shove his sisters-in-law out the door at 2:00 a.m. when they started wandering around with garbage bags. He loved Becca and Laura dearly, but by then he just wanted everybody to go before he fell over, knowing he had to get up in three hours to start his day.

Given the choice between sleep and a pristine house, he had opted for the former, especially since he knew damn well that Caidy, ever efficient, had made arrangements for a cleaning crew to come in today to mop up after the big party.

He grabbed his improvised breakfast and whistled to Tri, then headed through the party carnage into his office, doing his best to ignore the mess as the dog hopped along behind him.

Though it was Saturday, Ridge had plenty of work to catch up on, especially since the past few weeks leading up to his sister's wedding had been so chaotic. He had several emails to deal with, a phone call to a cattle broker he worked with, ranch accounts to reconcile. Finishing off the last bite-sized ham sandwich on his plate sometime later, he glanced up at the clock and was shocked to realize two hours had passed.

He frowned. Where was the cleanup crew? He was positive Caidy had said they would be here at ten, but it was nearly noon.

As if on cue, the doorbell suddenly rang, and Tri jumped up, gave one little well-mannered bark and raced to the front door as fast as his little hoppy, butt-bouncing gait would take him.

The housecleaners really had their work cut out for

them, he thought as he walked back through the house. He only hoped they could finish the job before midnight.

With Tri waiting eagerly to see what exciting surprise waited on the other side of the door, Ridge opened it.

Instead of the team of efficient-looking workers he expected to find, he found one woman. One small, delicate-looking woman with big blue eyes and a sweep of auburn hair that reminded him of the maple trees down by the creek at the first brush of fall.

She wore jeans and a short black peacoat with a scarf tied in one of those intricate knots women seemed to like.

Overall, he had the impression of fragile loveliness, and he wondered if the scope of the cleanup job would be too much for her. He pushed the thought away. He had to trust that Caidy had hired a reputable company and that she knew what she was doing. He sure as hell didn't want to clean the mess up himself, especially after he had rebuffed everybody else's offers to help.

"Mr. Bowman?"

"Yes."

"Hello. My name is Sarah Whitmore. I'm sorry to…"

He didn't wait for her apology, he just opened the door wider for her. "You're here now. That's the important thing. Come in."

She gazed at him for a moment, her mouth slightly open and an odd expression on delicately pretty features. After a slight pause, she walked inside.

"I thought you were supposed to be here two hours ago."

"I…was?"

The cleaning service must have mixed up the time. While he was usually hard-nosed about punctuality,

she appeared so befuddled and a little overwhelmed—
probably at the mess confronting her inside the house—
that he decided not to sweat it.

"As long as you put in an honest day's work and do
what you were hired to do, I don't see why I need to tell
the company about this."

"The...company."

With a slight blush staining her cheeks, she gazed
around at the muddle of crumbs, discarded napkins,
empty champagne bottles. "Wow. What happened here?"

Man, he would have to talk to Caidy about her choice
in cleaning services. The woman's bosses really should
have filled her in about the particulars of the situation.

"Wedding reception. My sister's, actually. It was after
two when the party finally broke up, and since I had
ranch chores to deal with early this morning, you can
probably tell I just left things as they were."

"It's certainly a mess," she agreed.

"Nothing you can't handle, though, right?"

"Nothing I can't..."

"It's not as bad as it looks," he assured her quickly. He
really didn't want to clean all this up by himself. "The
catering crew took care of the kitchen, so there's nothing to do in there. Just this space, a few of the bedrooms
where guests changed clothes and the guest bathrooms
here and on the second floor. You should be done in
three, four hours, don't you think?

She gazed at him, a little furrow between her brow,
her bottom lip tucked between her teeth.

Completely out of nowhere—like a sudden heat wave
in January—he had a wild urge to be the one nibbling
on that delectable lip.

The urge shocked him to his toes. What the hell was

wrong with him? He hadn't responded like this to a woman in a long, long time but something about her soft, lovely features, the soft eyes and that silky spill of auburn hair sent raw heat pooling in his gut.

He set his jaw, shoving away the inappropriate, wholly unexpected reaction.

"Cleaning supplies are in the closet in the mudroom, which is just off the kitchen back there. You should find everything you need. I'll be in my office or out in the barn if you have any questions," he said, already heading in that direction in his eagerness to get away from her.

He thought the dog would follow him, but Tri seemed more interested in the new arrival. Not that Ridge could blame the dog for a minute.

"But, sir," she called after him, a slight note of panic in her voice. "Mr. Bowman. I'm afraid—"

The phone in his office rang at just that moment, much to his relief. He didn't want to stand here arguing with the woman. She was being paid to do a job, and he wasn't the sort of boss who stood around like a hall monitor, making sure his people did what was expected of them. She could ask any of his ranch workers and they would tell her the same thing.

The phone rang again. "I've got to take this," he said, which wasn't really a lie, as it was probably the hay supplier he'd been trying to reach. "Thank you for doing this. You have no idea what a godsend you are. Let me know if you need anything."

He left her with her mouth slightly ajar and that look of dismay still on her features.

Okay, so he had run away like he was twelve years old at a school dance and the girl he liked had just asked him to take a spin around the floor with her. It was strictly self-preservation.

The last time he had been so instantly tangled up by a woman, he had ended up married to her—and look how delightfully *that* had turned out.

All he could think was that it was a good thing she would only be there for a few hours.

Sarah now understood the definition of the word *dumbfounded*.

After Ridge Bowman—at least she assumed it was Ridge Bowman—hurriedly left her alone with a funny-looking little three-legged dog, Sarah stood motionless in the big, soaring great room of the River Bow ranch house trying to catch her breath and figure out what had just happened.

Okay, this did *not* go the way she had anticipated.

She wasn't sure what she expected, but she certainly had never guessed the man would mistake her for someone else entirely.

She stood with her hands in her pockets, gazing down at the little dog, who was watching her curiously, as if trying to figure out what move she would make next.

"I would love to know the answer to that myself," she said aloud, to which the dog cocked his head and studied her closer.

The cold knot that had lodged under her breastbone a week ago as she stood inside that storage unit seemed to tighten.

She *ought* to chase after the man and explain he had made a mistake. She wasn't from a cleaning crew. She had flown out from California expressly to talk to him and his siblings, though she would rather have been any-where else on earth.

She drew in a breath, her nails digging into her palms. *Do it. Move. Tell him.*

The annoying voice of her conscience urged her for-ward in the direction the ruggedly handsome rancher had gone, but she stood frozen, her attention suddenly fixed on a wall of framed family pictures, dominated by a smiling older couple with their arms around each other.

Sarah screwed her eyes closed. When she opened them, she looked away from the pictures at the great room, with its trio of oversize sofas and entwined ant-ler light fixtures.

He really did need help. The house was a disaster. The wedding of Caidy Bowman must have been quite a party, at least judging by the disarray left behind.

Why couldn't she help him?

The thought sidled through her. In that brief interac-tion, she had gained the impression of a hard, uncom-promising man. She couldn't have said how she was so certain. If she helped him tame some of the chaos in his house, he might be more amenable to listening to her with an open mind.

As a first-grade teacher used to twenty-five six- and seven-year-old children, she was certainly used to clean-ing up messes. This wasn't really all that unmanageable.

Besides that, she wasn't in a particular hurry to chase after him. If she had her way, she would put off telling him what she had found in that storage locker as long as humanly possible.

The truth was, the man terrified her. She hated to admit it, but it was true. He was just so *big,* a solid six feet two inches of ranch-hardened muscle, and his features looked etched in granite.

Gorgeous, yes, okay, but completely unapproachable.

He hadn't smiled once during their brief interaction—though she couldn't necessarily blame him for that since he thought she was a tardy cleaning service. She dreaded what he would say when she told him why she had *really* come to the River Bow ranch.

What would it hurt to help the man clean his house for an hour or two? Afterward, they could have a good laugh about the misunderstanding. Who knows? He might even be more favorable to what she had to say.

Okay, good plan.

She tried to tell herself she was only being nice, not being a total wuss. She unbuttoned her coat and hung it on a rack by the door, grateful her extensive wardrobe debate with herself had resulted in simple jeans and a lovely wool sweater. As much as she loved the sweater, wool always made her itch a little so she wore a plain and practical white long-sleeved T-shirt underneath.

She pulled the sweater over her head, rolled up the sleeves of the T-shirt to just below her elbows and headed into the kitchen for the cleaning supplies.

He was right about the kitchen. The big, well-designed space sparkled. She headed into the area she guessed was the mudroom and found an organized space with shelves, cubbies and a convenient bench for taking off boots. A big pair of men's lined boots rested in a pile of melting snow and she picked them up and set them aside before quickly drying the puddle.

She easily found the cleaning supplies stored in one of the cubbies in a convenient plastic tote. She picked the whole thing up and carried it back through the house.

First things first, the clutter of garbage all around, then she could start wiping down surfaces and work on the bathrooms.

As she walked through the big, comfortable great room picking up party detritus, she wondered about the Bowman family.

She knew a little about the family from her initial research, the quick web search she had done after finding that storage unit that had led her to this place and this moment. She had learned a little more after her arrival in Pine Gulch, Idaho last night, thanks to a casual conversation with the young, flirtatious college student working as desk clerk at the Cold Creek Inn where she had stayed the night before.

She knew, for instance, that the charming inn where she stayed was actually owned, coincidentally, by the wife of Taft, one of the Bowman brothers.

From the clerk, she had discovered there were four Bowman siblings. Ridge, the hard, implacable rancher she had just met, was the oldest. Then came twins Taft and Trace, the fire chief and police chief of Pine Gulch, respectively. And finally the daughter, Caidy, the one who had been married the day before—much to the chagrin of the desk clerk, who she quickly deduced had nurtured an ill-fated secret crush on Caidy Bowman, now Caldwell.

The ranch appeared to be a prosperous one. All the buildings were freshly painted, and the big, comfortable log home could easily have doubled as a small hotel itself. It was large enough to host a wedding reception, for heaven's sake.

The Christmas tree alone was spectacular, at least eighteen feet tall and decorated to the hilt with ribbons, garland, glittery ornaments. More evergreen garlands twisted their way up the staircase and adorned the raw wood mantel of the huge river-rock fireplace.

This was more than just a showplace. She could tell. This was a home, well maintained and well loved.

As she headed up the stairs to collect a pile of napkins she could see on a console table in an upper hallway, Sarah had to fight down a little niggle of envy. She couldn't help comparing the splendid River Bow ranch house to the small, cheerless apartments where she had lived with her mother after the divorce.

What child wouldn't have loved growing up here? Sliding down that banister, riding the horses she had seen running through the snow-covered pastures, gazing up at those wild mountains out the wide expanse of windows?

She frowned as she suddenly remembered the rest. A lump rose in her throat.

Oh. Right.

She knew more about Ridge Bowman than how many siblings he had and the outward prosperity of his ranch. She knew he and his brothers and sister had suffered unimaginable tragedy more than a decade earlier, the violent murder of their parents in a home-invasion robbery.

She could only guess how the tragedy must still haunt them all.

That ever-present anxiety gnawed at her stomach again, as it had since she walked into that storage unit, and she pressed a hand there.

She had to tell him. She couldn't keep stalling. She had come all the way from Southern California, for heaven's sake. This was ridiculous.

With fresh determination, she gripped the now-bulging garbage bag and started down the stairs.

She wasn't quite sure what happened next. Perhaps her heel caught on the edge of a stair or the garbage bag interfered with her usual balance. Either way, she somehow missed the second stop down.

She teetered for a moment and cried out, instinctively dropping the bag as she reached for the banister, but her hand closed around air and she lost what remained of her precarious balance.

Down she tumbled, hitting a hip, an elbow, her head—and finally landing at the bottom with a sickening crunch of bone as her arm twisted beneath her.

Chapter Two

At the first hoarse cry and muffled thud from the distant reaches of the house, Ridge shoved back his chair so hard it slid on the wood floor a few inches. He recognized a sound of pain when he heard it.

What the hell?

He jumped up and raced out of his office. The instant he entered the great room, he found a slight form crumpled at the bottom of the stairs, a bag of garbage spilling out next to her and Tripod anxiously whining and licking her face.

"Go on, Tri. Back up, buddy."

The little dog reluctantly hopped away, allowing Ridge to crouch down beside the woman. Her eyes were closed, and her arm was twisted beneath her in a way he knew couldn't be right.

What was her name again? Sarah something. Whitmore. That was it. "Sarah? Ms. Whitmore? Hey. Come on, now. Wake up."

She moaned but didn't open her eyes. As he took a closer look at that arm, he swore under his breath. Maybe it was better if she *didn't* wake up. When she did, that broken arm would hurt like hell.

He had known a couple of broken arms in his day and had enjoyed none of them.

The woman had appeared fragile and delicate when she showed up at his house, too delicate to properly handle the job of cleaning up the wedding mess by herself. Now she looked positively waiflike, with all color washed from her features and long brown lashes fanning over those high cheekbones. Already, he could see a bruise forming on her cheek and a bump sprouting above her temple.

He looked up the stairs, noticing a few pieces of garbage strewn almost at the very top. Must have been one hell of a fall.

All his protective instincts urged him to let her hang out in never-never land, where she was safe from the pain. He didn't want to be the cause of more, but he knew he had to wake her. She really needed to be conscious so he could assess her symptoms.

A guy couldn't grow up on a busy Idaho ranch without understanding a little about first aid. Broken arms, abrasions, contusions, lacerations. He'd had them all— and what he hadn't suffered, the twins or Caidy had experienced. Judging by her lingering unconsciousness, he was guessing she had a concussion, which meant the longer she remained out of it, the more chance of complications.

"Ma'am? Sarah? Can you hear me?"

Her eyes blinked a little but remained closed, as if her subconscious didn't want to face the pain, either. He carefully ran his hands over her, avoiding the obvious arm fracture as he checked for other injuries. At least nothing else seemed obvious. With that basic information, he reached for his cell phone and quickly dialed 911.

He could drive her to the Pine Gulch medical clinic faster than the mostly volunteer fire department could gather at the station and come out to the ranch, but he was leery to move her without knowing if she might be suffering internal injuries.

As he gave the basic information to the dispatcher, her eyes started to flutter. An instant later, those eyes opened slightly, reminding him again of lazy summer afternoons when he was a kid and had time to gaze up at the sky. He saw confusion there and long, deep shadows of pain that filled him with guilt.

She had been cleaning his house. He couldn't help but feel responsible.

"Take it easy. You'll be okay."

She gazed at him for an instant with fright and uncertainty before he saw a tiny spark of recognition there.

"Mr.…Bowman."

"Good. At least you know *my* name. How about your own?"

She blinked as if the effort to remember was too much. "S-Sarah. Sarah M—er, Whitmore."

He frowned at the way she stumbled a little over her last name but forgot it instantly when she shifted a little and tried to move. At the effort, she gave a heartbreaking cry of pain.

"Easy. Easy." He murmured the words as softly as he would to a skittish horse—if he were the sort of rancher to tolerate any skittish horses on the River Bow. "Just stay still."

"It hurts," she moaned.

"I know. I'm sorry. I'm afraid you broke your arm when you fell. I've called an ambulance. They should be here soon. We'll run you into the clinic in Pine Gulch. Dr. Dalton should be able to fix you up."

Her pale features grew even more distressed. "I don't need an ambulance," she said.

"I hate to argue with a lady, but I would have to disagree with you there. You took a nasty fall. Do you remember what happened?"

She looked up the stairs and her eyes widened. For a minute, he thought she would pass out again. "I was going to talk to you and I…I tripped, I guess. I'm not sure. Everything is fuzzy."

"You were coming to talk to me about what?"

A couple of high spots of color appeared on her cheeks. "I…can't remember," she said, and he was almost positive she was lying. On the other hand, he didn't know the woman; she had just suffered a terrible fall and was likely in shock.

She shifted again, moving her head experimentally, but then let it back down.

"My head hurts."

"I'm sure it does. I'm no expert, but I'm guessing you banged it up, too. You've probably got a concussion. Have you had one before?"

"Not…that I remember."

Did that mean she hadn't had one or that she just couldn't remember it? He would have to let Doc Dalton sort that one out from her medical records.

She started to moan but caught it, clamping her lips together before it could escape.

"Just hang on. Don't try to move. I wish I could give you a pillow or some padding or something. I know it's not comfortable there on the floor but you're better off staying put until the EMTs come and can assess the situation to make sure nothing else is broken. Can you tell me what hurts?"

"Everything," she bit out. "It's probably easier to tell you what *doesn't* hurt. I think my left eyelashes might be okay. No, wait. They hurt, too."

He smiled a little, admiring her courage and grit in the face of what must be considerable pain. He was also aware of more than a little relief. Though she grimaced between each word, he had to think that since she was capable of making a joke, she would probably be okay, all things considered.

"Is there somebody you'd like me to call to meet us at the hospital? Husband? Boyfriend? Family?"

She blinked at him, a distant expression on her face, and didn't answer him for a long moment.

"Stay with me," he ordered. Fearing she would lapse into shock, he grabbed a blanket off the sofa and spread it over her. For some reason, the shock first aid acronym of WARRR rang through his head: Warmth, Air, Rest, Reassurance, Raise the legs. But she seemed to collect herself enough to respond.

"No. I don't have…any of those things. There's no one in the area for you to call."

She was all alone? Somehow, he found that even more sad than the idea that she was currently sprawled out in grave pain on the floor at the bottom of his stairs.

His family might drive him crazy sometimes, but at least he knew they always had his back.

"Are you sure? No friends? No family? I should at least call the company you work for and let them know what happened."

If nothing else, they would have to send someone else to finish the job. With that broken arm, Sarah would have to hang up her broom for a while.

"I don't—" she started to say, but before she could finish, the front door opened and a second later an EMT raced through it, followed by a couple more.

Somehow he wasn't surprised that the EMT in the front was his brother Taft, who was not only a paramedic but also the town's fire chief.

He spotted the woman on the floor, and his forehead furrowed with confusion before he turned to Ridge.

"Geez. I just about had a freaking heart attack! We got a call for a female fall victim at the River Bow. I thought it was Destry!"

"No. This is Sarah Whitmore. She was cleaning the house after the wedding and took a tumble. Sarah, this is my brother Taft, who is not only a certified paramedic, I promise, but also the town's fire chief."

"Hi," she mumbled, sounding more disoriented

"Hi, Sarah." Taft knelt down to her and immediately went to work assessing vitals. "Can you tell me what happened?"

"I'm…not sure. I fell."

"Judging by the garbage at the top of the stairs, I think she fell just about the whole way," Ridge offered. "She was unconscious for maybe two or three minutes and has kind of been in and out since. My unofficial diagnosis is the obvious broken arm and possible concussion."

"Thank you, Dr. Bowman," Taft said, his voice dry.

His brother quickly took control of the situation and began giving instructions to the other emergency personnel.

Ridge was always a little taken by surprise whenever he had the chance to watch either of his younger brothers in action. He still tended to think of them as teenage punks getting speeding tickets and toilet papering the mayor's trees. But after years as a wildlands firefighter, Taft had been the well-regarded fire chief in Pine Gulch for several years, and his twin, Trace, was the police chief. By all reports, both were shockingly good at their jobs.

Ridge gained a little more respect for his brother as he watched his patient competence with Sarah: the way he teased and questioned her, the efficient air of command he portrayed to the other EMTs as they worked together to load her onto the stretcher with a minimum of pain.

As they started to roll the stretcher toward the front door, Ridge followed, grabbing his coat and truck keys on the way.

Taft shifted his attention away from his patient long enough to look at Ridge with surprise. "Where are you going?"

He was annoyed his brother would even have to ask. "I can't just send her off in an ambulance by herself. I'll drive in and meet you at the clinic."

"Why?" Taft asked, clearly confused.

"She doesn't have any friends or family in the area. Plus she was injured on the River Bow, which makes her my responsibility."

Taft shook his head but didn't argue. The stretcher

was nearly to the door when Sarah held out a hand. "Wait. Stop."

She craned her neck and seemed to be looking for him, so Ridge moved closer.

"You'll be okay." He did his best to soothe her. "Hang in there. My brother and the other EMTs will take good care of you, I promise, and Doc Dalton at the clinic is excellent. He'll know just what to do for you."

She barely seemed to register his words, her brow furrowed. Taft had given her something for pain before they transferred her, and it looked as if she was trying to work through the effects of it to tell him something.

"Can you… There's a case on the…backseat of my car. Can you bring it inside? I shouldn't have left it out in the cold…for this long. The keys to the car are…in my coat."

"Sure. No problem."

"You have to put it…somewhere safe." She closed her eyes as soon as the words were out.

Ridge raised an eyebrow at Taft, who shrugged. "It seems important to her," his brother said. "Better do it."

"Okay. I'll meet you at the clinic in a few minutes. I'll bring her coat along. Maybe I can find a purse or something in the car with her medical insurance information."

She hadn't been carrying anything like that when she came to the door, he remembered. Perhaps she found it easier to leave personal items in her vehicle.

He found her coat and located a single key in the pocket, hooked to one of the flexible plastic key rings with a rental car company's logo on it. He frowned. A rental car? That didn't make any sense. He headed outside to her vehicle, which was a nondescript silver sedan that did indeed look very much like a rental car.

He found a purse on the passenger seat, a flowered cloth bag. Though he was fiercely curious, he didn't feel right about digging through it. He would let her find her insurance info on her own.

In the backseat, he quickly found the case she was talking about. It was larger than he expected, a flat portfolio size, perhaps twenty-four inches by thirty or so.

Again, he was curious and wanted to snoop but forced himself not to. As she had requested, he set it in a locked cupboard in his office, then locked the office for good measure before heading to the clinic in town to be with a strange woman with columbine-blue eyes and the prettiest hair he'd ever seen.

As far as weird days went, this one probably just hit the top of the list.

Sarah hurt everywhere, but this was a muted sort of pain. She felt as if she were floating through a bowl of pudding. Nice, creamy, delicious chocolate pudding—except every once in a while something sharp and mean poked at her.

"All things considered, you got off easy. The concussion appears to be a mild one, and the break is clean." A man with a stethoscope smiled at her. No white coat, but white teeth. Handsome. He was really handsome. If she didn't hurt so much, she would tell him so.

"Easy?" she muttered, her mind catching on the word that didn't make sense.

The doctor smiled. "It could have been much worse, trust me. I've seen that staircase inside the River Bow. It has to be twenty feet, at least. It's amazing you didn't break more than your arm."

"Amazing," she agreed, though she didn't really know what he was talking about. What was the River Bow?

"And it's a good thing Ridge didn't move you right after you fell. I was able to set the arm without surgery, which I probably wouldn't have been able to do if you had been jostled around everywhere."

"Thank you," she said through dry lips, because it seemed to be the thing to say. She just wanted to sleep for three or four years. Why wouldn't he let her sleep?

"Can I go home?" she asked. Her condo, with its four-poster bed, the light blue duvet, the matching curtains. She wanted to be there.

"Where, exactly, is home?"

She gave the address to her condo unit.

"Is that in Idaho Falls?"

"No!" she exclaimed. "San Diego, of course."

He blinked a little. "Wow. You traveled a long way to take a cleaning job."

She frowned. Cleaning job? What cleaning job?

She wanted to rub away the fierce pain in her head even as she had a sudden image of a garbage bag with cups and napkins spilling out of it.

She had been cleaning something. Why? Is that when she fell? Her memories seemed hazy and abstract. She remembered an airplane. An important suitcase. *Hand-screen it, please.* An inn.

"I'm staying at the Cold Creek Inn," she said suddenly. Oh, she should have told them pain medication made her woozy. She always took only half. How much had they given her?

And how *had* she hurt her arm?

"The Cold Creek Inn." The nice doctor with the white teeth frowned at her.

"Yes. My room has blue curtains. They have flowers on them. They're pretty."

He blinked at her. "Good to know. Okay."

Oh, she was tired. Why wouldn't he let her sleep?

She closed her eyes but suddenly remembered something important. "Where's my car? Have you got my car? I have to take it back to the airport by Monday at noon or they'll charge me a *lot*."

"It must still be at the River Bow. I'm sure your car is fine."

"I have to take it back."

The car was important, but something else mattered more. Something in the car. But what?

Her head ached again, and one of those hard, ugly pains pierced that lovely haze.

"My head hurts," she informed him.

"That's your concussion. Just close your eyes and try to relax. We'll make sure the rental car goes back, I promise."

"Monday. Noon."

She needed something from inside it. She closed her eyes, seeing that special black suitcase again.

Oh.

Ridge Bowman. She had told Ridge Bowman to take it out of the backseat. Too cold. Not safe.

He would take care of it.

She wasn't sure how she knew, but a feeling of peace trickled over her, washing away the panic, and she let it go.

Chapter Three

"The Cold Creek Inn? Really?" Ridge stared at Jake
Dalton, trying to make sense of a situation that seemed
to be rapidly spinning out of his control.

"That's what she said. She was quite firm about it."

Pine Gulch's only physician had no reason to make
up crazy stories but none of this was making any sense
to him. "That's easy enough for me to verify. I can always give Laura a call."

Under normal circumstances, Taft's wife wouldn't
disclose information about her guests, but this certainly
classified as an emergency.

"Her car was a rental. I noticed that."

"Yes, it needs to be returned soon. She was quite em-
phatic on that score," Jake said.

"What the hell? She's staying at the Cold Creek Inn

and driving a rental car, and she shows up for a cleaning job? It doesn't make any sense."

"I'm only telling you what she said. That's not the important part, really. The fact is, if she indeed has no friends or family nearby, as she told you, I can't let our mystery woman go back to a hotel by herself tonight. She's suffered a concussion. She's going to need someone close by to make sure she doesn't suffer any complications. I can't say she really needs an overnight stay in the hospital in Idaho Falls, but I don't feel comfortable sending her back to a hotel to spend the night by herself."

While Ridge might've been baffled about the situation and why a woman paying for a decent hotel room and driving a rental car would take a low-paying cleaning job in the middle of nowhere, he wasn't at all confused about the right thing to do.

"She'll stay at the ranch house," he said firmly. "She can take Caidy's room, no problem. That way she won't have to tackle any stairs. Destry and I can keep an eye on her."

"Are you sure about that?" Jake asked in surprise. "You don't even know the woman."

True enough. All he knew was that she was lovely, that she smelled like vanilla and June-blooming lavender and that she brought out all his protective instincts.

He didn't think Jake Dalton needed those particular observations. "She was hurt in my house while technically working for me. That makes her my responsibility. If she had been hurt at the Cold Creek Ranch, you know any of you Daltons would jump up to take care of her. Wade and Seth would probably come to blows over who would help her, unless their wives stepped in first."

"You've got me there. The fact is, if my wife were

home, Ms. Whitmore could come stay at our place. But Maggie and her mother took an overnight trip to Jackson to do some Christmas shopping. I'm on my own with the kids and have my hands more than full."

The doctor grinned at him. "On second thought, sure you wouldn't like to trade? How about I come out to the quiet River Bow and keep an eye on our concussed woman of mystery and you can head over to my place and entertain three crazy kids hopped up on sugar and Christmas?"

He laughed. Jake and Maggie Dalton had three of the most adorable kids around, but they did have a lot of energy. "Well, that is a kind offer, I'm sure, but I would hate to deprive you of all that father–kid bonding time."

"Well, you've got my cell number. Call me if you have any concerns, particularly if you find any altered mental status or confusion." He paused and gave a little laugh. "I should probably warn you, though, she's a little, er, dopey from the pain meds. This doesn't count."

Jake's cautionary words made him more than a little curious. Sarah had seemed so contained back at his house. Even when her arm had to be screaming pain at her, she had fought tears and tried to be tough through it.

He walked into the treatment room, not quite sure what to expect.

Dopey was an understatement. Sarah Whitmore was higher than a weather balloon in a windstorm.

As soon as he walked into the room, she beamed at him like he had just rescued a basketful of kittens from a rampaging grizzly.

"Hi. Hi there. I know you, right?"

He glanced over at the doc, who just barely managed

to hide a grin. "Er, yes. I'm Ridge Bowman. You fell down my stairs a couple of hours ago."

"Oh. Riiiight." She beamed brightly at him. "Wow, you are one good-looking cowboy. Has anybody ever told you that?"

Jake made a sound halfway between a cough and a laugh. Ridge glared at him before he turned back to Sarah. "Er, not lately. No."

"Well, you are. Take it from me. Of course, what do I know? I don't know many good-looking cowboys. Or that many good-looking noncowboys, for that matter." She frowned, her features solemn. "I really need to get out more."

Jake laughed out loud, and Ridge gave him a quelling look. "Geez, how much did you give her?"

"Sorry," the physician said. "The dose was absolutely appropriate, but I'm thinking she must be one of those people who are hypersensitive to certain narcotics. Sometimes you have to titrate to an individual's particular sensitivities."

"Apparently. Okay, Sarah. Let's get you back to the ranch."

She started to stand up, but Jake laid a restraining hand on her shoulder. "Easy there. We'll bring in a wheelchair to get you out to the car."

"I can walk. I broke my arm, not my legs." She didn't precisely call Jake stupid, but her tone conveyed the same message.

"It's a clinic rule. Sorry, Sarah."

"Well, it's a dumb rule."

He chuckled. "I'll take it up with the clinic director when she gets back from shopping with her mother in

Jackson. Joan, can you bring a wheelchair?" he called out into the hall.

A moment later, one of the clinic nurses pushed in a chair. Jake and Ridge helped her transfer into it, with much grumbling on Sarah's part.

While Jake and the nurse pushed her toward the front of the clinic, Ridge went out to pull his truck up to the doors. Wishing he had brought the ranch SUV, which had a lower suspension and was easier to climb into, he tried to help her up into the cab. In the long run, he settled on lifting her up when she couldn't quite manage to navigate the running boards.

When she was settled, he shut the door to keep in all the heat and turned back to Jake.

"What else do I need to know?"

"You're going to want to make sure she drinks plenty of fluids tonight and keeps on a regular cycle of the pain meds, though you might want to dial that down a little. She'll probably sleep off most of what we gave her here. You'll want to check on her every couple of hours, make sure she's still lucid. Any problems, again, call my cell number. I should be home all night and can run to your place in a minute, though I might be dragging three kids along with me."

Ridge reached out to shake his hand, grateful for the other man. Jake Dalton had been good for Pine Gulch. He had the skills and the bedside manner that could probably have built a lucrative family medicine practice anywhere. Instead, he had chosen to come back to his own small hometown. In the years since, he and his wife, Magdalena Cruz, had really thrown their hearts into helping the community, sponsoring free clinics out of their own pockets and taking anybody who needed health care.

"I'm not worried. We should be fine."

"Are you sure? Maybe Becca or Laura can help," Jake suggested, referring to Ridge's sisters-in-law.

"I'll keep trying the cleaning company in Jackson. They might have an emergency contact number on her employment records."

"Good thinking. Drive safe. I think the storm is going to be here earlier than the weather forecasters said. No question about Pine Gulch having a white Christmas this year, I guess."

"Is there ever?" he said drily as he climbed into the pickup truck.

After making sure his guest was safely buckled in, he waved to Jake and backed out of the parking lot then headed toward the River Bow, a few miles out of town, through a lightly falling snow.

"Your truck smells like Christmas," she said, rather sleepily.

He pointed to the little air freshener shaped like an evergreen tree that hung from the rearview mirror. "You can give my daughter credit for that. She complains that it usually smells like shi—er, manure."

"You have a daughter?"

He nodded. "Yep. Destry's her name. She'll be twelve in a couple of months."

"Like the movie with James Stewart."

"Something like that." His late ex-wife had been fascinated with the old western *Destry Rides Again,* probably because she fancied herself a Marlene Dietrich wannabe. She had loved the name, and at that point, he would have done anything to try saving his marriage.

"Where is she?"

"Er, who?"

"Your daughter. Destry."

Ah. That was easy. Explaining that his ex-wife took off a few months after their daughter was born would have been tougher.

"She stayed at her cousin's house last night, but she's supposed to come home later tonight."

"Oh, that's nice. I have twenty-four kids."

He jerked his gaze from the road just long enough to gape at her. "Twenty-four?"

"Yes. Last year it was only twenty-two. The year before that, I had twenty-five. I had the biggest class in the first grade."

"You're a teacher?"

She nodded, though her head barely moved on the headrest and her eyes began to drift closed. "Yes," she mumbled. "I teach first grade at Sunny View Elementary School. I'm a great teacher."

"I'm sure you are. But I thought you worked for the cleaning service."

She frowned a little, opening her eyes in confusion before they slid shut again. "I'm soooo tired. My head hurts."

Just like that, she was asleep.

"Sarah? Ms. Whitmore?"

She snorted and shifted in her sleep. The mystery deepened. The woman was staying at the inn, drove a rental car and apparently taught first grade.

He knew teachers weren't paid nearly enough. Maybe she had picked up extra work during the school break, but that didn't explain the inn or the rental car.

His cell phone rang just as he pulled into the long,

winding lane that led from the main road to the ranch house. "Ridge Bowman," he answered.

"Oh, Mr. Bowman," the flustered voice on the other end of the line exclaimed. "This is Terri McCall from Happy House Cleaners in Jackson. There's been a terrible mix-up. I'm so sorry! You would not *believe* the day we've had here."

He glanced at the woman sleeping on the bench seat beside him. "Mine hasn't been exactly a walk in the park, either."

"It's been chaos from the moment I walked in this morning. Our power was knocked out in the night and we're only just getting back up. Meantime, all the computers were down. I just saw your name on my caller ID and realized we had your dates wrong, so I've been scrambling to find someone else. I had you down for party cleanup tomorrow. I'm *so* sorry. I'm sending someone right now. She should be there within the hour, I promise, and we'll have you sorted out."

He gazed at the woman sleeping beside him. "Wait a minute. What about Sarah?"

He was met with a little awkward pause. "The woman I'm sending is Kelli Parker. She'll do a fine job. I'm afraid I don't know a Sarah."

"Sarah. Sarah Whitmore. I left you a message about her. We're just coming from the doctor. She broke her arm and had a concussion in the fall."

"Oh, I'm sorry. I haven't had time to listen to my messages, with everything that's been going on. Do you need us to clean her house, too?"

"No. She works for you! She showed up this morning to clean for me. In the process, she tripped and fell down my stairs."

"This is all very strange." The woman sounded baffled and a little concerned. "We don't have anyone named Sarah working for us and, as I said, we had the dates switched."

"You didn't send someone."

"Yes. Just now," she said patiently. "Not earlier this morning. Kelli Parker. She's very efficient. One of our very best, I promise you."

"So if you didn't send someone to clean my house, who the hell is this woman sitting next to me with the broken arm and the concussion?"

"I'm sure I don't know. She's not my employee, I can promise you that. Why would anybody want to pretend to be? Perhaps you had better call the police."

He pulled up in front of the ranch house and sat in the truck for a moment, the phone still pressed to his ear. He didn't want to call the police. In Pine Gulch, the police meant his brother Trace. Bad enough that Taft had to come out on the emergency call and find a strange woman crumpled at the bottom of the stairs. Trace would never let him hear the end of this one.

"Okay. Thank you. I'll watch for your actual employee."

"I'm sorry again for the mix-up. I don't want you to think we usually conduct our business in this scatter-brained way. The holidays have been crazy anyway, with everybody wanting sparkling houses for their parties and overnight guests, and six hours without electricity or computers didn't help matters."

"No problem. Thanks."

He hung up and looked across the cab at Sarah. A strand of auburn hair had drifted across her cheek, accentuating the complexion that was still too pale for his liking.

He would sure like to figure out just what the hell was going on, but he wasn't quite ready to call the police. Trace had an annoying tendency to take over in matters of an investigative nature, and Ridge was feeling oddly territorial about this woman.

He figured he could get her settled and then if she was still out of it, he could go through her purse and try to find out why a woman who claimed she taught first grade at Sunny View Elementary School decided to spend a little time cleaning up the party mess at a ranch house in some small backwater Idaho town.

She didn't appear to wake even after he shut off the engine and walked around to the passenger door. "Here we are. Let's get you inside. Can you walk, or do I have to carry you?"

She opened her eyes for just a moment before closing them again. That was apparently all the answer he was going to get. He sighed and scooped her into his arms, thinking again how slight and delicate she was. She hardly weighed more than Destry.

She was definitely a curvy little handful, though. He tried not to notice, tried to remind himself she was a mysterious stranger who had entered his home under false pretenses, tried not to remember how very long it had been since he'd held a sweet-smelling woman in his arms.

He carried her up the stairs to the mudroom and then through the kitchen to the hallway that led to Caidy's downstairs bedroom.

In contrast to everything else about his hard-riding, horse-training, dog-loving sister, her bedroom was soft and feminine, with a lavender and brown quilt joining a flurry of pillows on the bed and lace curtains spilling from the window.

The room might have been made for Sarah. She had a kind of sweet, ethereal beauty that fit perfectly with all of Caidy's frills.

She moaned a little when he lowered her to the bed and he quickly propped one of Caidy's hundreds of throw pillows underneath her casted arm.

"There. Is that better?"

Her eyes fluttered open, and she looked around, still with that vaguely unfocused look.

"This isn't my hotel room," she said, her voice a husky rasp.

"No. You're temporarily staying at the River Bow ranch."

"I need to talk to the Bowman family," she stated, still dreamily. "It's really important."

This whole thing was so strange. What was she doing here? What did she need to talk to his family about? He frowned as he eased away from her, but she had already closed her eyes again.

She didn't look at all comfortable. After a pause, he reached down and slipped off her shoes, but that was about as far as he dared go.

He grabbed a soft fleece blanket from the foot of the bed and tucked it under her chin, then stood back and studied her.

What an odd day. Why couldn't he shake the strange feeling that something momentous was happening? He didn't like it, especially because he didn't understand it.

After a moment, he gave her one more careful look then turned and walked from the bedroom. The sun went down early on a late-December afternoon. In another hour, it would be dark, which meant he needed to hustle out to take care of chores. He was a rancher, which meant he didn't have all day to stand and look at his mysterious guest, no matter how lovely she might be.

Chapter Four

Sarah awoke to a mouth as dry as the Mojave in August and, conversely, a desperate need to use the bathroom.

She opened her eyes slowly and tried to make sense of where she was, why the room didn't look familiar. A lamp glowed beside the bed, illuminating a comfortably feminine room. A plump armchair stood in one corner and just next to it, she could see an open doorway that looked like it contained the facilities she needed.

When she sat up, a grinding wave of pain washed over her. Her head and her left arm seemed to be the focus of most of the pain but the rest of her body felt as if she had just ridden out the permanent press cycle on a front-loading washing machine.

By the time she hobbled back out of the nicely decorated en suite bathroom, vague, rather unsettling memories were beginning to filter through.

She was at the Bowman family's River Bow ranch—
she could tell by the log walls and the general decor of
the place. She had fallen down the stairs while she was
cleaning the ranch house after Caidy Bowman's wedding.

She remembered Ridge Bowman, suddenly—piercing
green eyes, hard features, broad shoulders. He thought
she was from a cleaning company, and she had been too
much of a coward to tell him otherwise.

She remembered an ambulance ride with a man who
had Ridge Bowman's same handsome features and those
stunning green eyes.

The actual trip from the clinic to the ranch house was
mostly a blur of random impressions, pain and confusion and embarrassment. There had been a kind doctor,
a painful procedure and then the rest was a blur.

Why was she back at the River Bow and not at her
room at the Cold Creek Inn? And how had she ended
up in that bed with her shoes off and a pillow tucked
under her arm?

It must have been Ridge. Who else? Her stomach
trembled when she thought about him taking care of
her. Had he carried her inside? Slipped her onto the bed?
Covered her with that blanket?

She could hardly imagine it.

She had to talk to him, right away, before things became even more complicated. She wouldn't be in this
mess if only she had been able to find the courage to tell
him everything when she showed up on his doorstep,
instead of letting her fear at what he might think of her
overwhelm all her good sense.

How long had she slept? She couldn't see anything
outside the fragile lace curtains. She found the clock

radio beside the bed and was shocked to discover it was after 9:00 p.m. She must have been out of it for hours, though she wasn't exactly sure how long she had been at the clinic in Pine Gulch.

She was just trying to gather the energy and the courage to go in search of her unwilling host when she heard a knock on the door.

"Ms. Whitmore? Are you awake?"

Nerves trembled through her to join the aches and pains. "Yes. Come in."

He pushed open the door and stood there wearing a soft-looking blue shirt and jeans.

You are one great-looking cowboy.

The words seemed to echo through her memory, and she frowned, wondering where they came from. Not that it mattered—they were absolutely true. Ridge Bowman was even more handsome than she remembered, tough and rugged, with shoulders that looked as if they could bear the weight of the world.

"I'm under orders from Doc Dalton to keep an eye on you through the night. I guess I'm supposed to make sure you're not delusional or anything."

She thought of the crazy choices she had made since she showed up at the ranch that morning. Really. Cleaning the man's house as an avoidance method. Could she *be* any more ridiculous?

"I was half hoping this whole thing was some kind of wild nightmare," she said. "Does that count as delusional?"

The corner of his mouth danced up just a bit as if he wanted to smile, but he quickly straightened it again. "I'm supposed to check. Do you know your name?"

"Yes. Sarah Whitmore."

"That's what your driver's license says."

He was holding out her bag, which looked incongruously feminine in his big, masculine hand.

"You looked through my purse?"

"I was trying to find a cell phone that had an emergency contact on it. I couldn't find one."

She didn't go *anywhere* without her cell phone. She frowned, trying to remember. "Did you check the car? It might be there. Otherwise, I probably left it at the hotel."

"I'll look through the car again. Maybe it fell on the floor. I can also have Laura look at the hotel."

"Why don't you just take me back to the hotel and I can look for myself?"

He looked sternly implacable. "You can't stay on your own tonight. Doctor's orders. And as great as the service is now at the Cold Creek Inn since Laura took over, she just can't send a desk clerk to your room every couple of hours to check on you. I'm afraid you're stuck here, at least overnight."

She wanted to argue, but she couldn't come up with the words, between the pain and her angst.

Some of her distress must have shown on her features. He held out a water glass she hadn't noticed before, along with a bottle of medication.

"You're also late for your pain pill. Sorry about that. I was supposed to give it an hour ago, but I had a problem down at the barn and now I'm running late."

She didn't want to take it—she and pain medication didn't always get along—but she could hardly think around the pain in her head and her arm.

"Maybe I had better only take half. I sometimes get a little, er, wacky on pain meds."

"Do you?"

Again, that little corner of his mouth twisted up, and she had to wonder what had happened during the time she couldn't remember.

He broke the pill in half and held it out to her. She swallowed it quickly, more grateful for the water than the narcotic, at least right at that moment.

She drained the glass then handed it back to him. "Thank you."

"Need something to eat? I've got plenty of leftover food from the wedding last night and you haven't had a thing for hours."

"I'm not really hungry," she said honestly.

"I'll bring you a couple of things anyway. That pain medication will sit better in your stomach if you've got something else in there."

He was gone for only a few moments. When he returned, he had a plate loaded with little sandwiches, puff pastries, tiny bite-sized pieces of cake. He was also accompanied by the cute little Chihuahua who hopped in on three legs.

"Your dog is adorable."

"Destry and I are supposed to be dogsitting, but she stayed another night at her cousin's. This is Tripod, who belongs to my new brother-in-law and his kids."

"Hi, Tripod," she said to the dog, who hopped over to greet her with gratifying enthusiasm, though he might have been more interested in the plate of food on her lap.

She took a little sandwich and nibbled on it, discovering some kind of chicken salad that was quite delicious.

"These are really good."

"We had a great caterer," he said.

She suddenly remembered what had started all this. "Oh. I didn't finish cleaning."

He gave her a long look. "Happy House Cleaners and I have worked all that out. Their real employee just left about an hour ago. I'm surprised you didn't hear her vacuuming. I guess you were really out of it."

Apparently she didn't need to tell him as much as she thought, if he knew she hadn't really been hired to help clean his house.

"I've made a terrible mess of everything, haven't I?"

"You're a woman of mystery, that's for sure. Who are you, really, Ms. Whitmore?"

She nibbled at another of the little sandwiches. "You looked through my purse. You tell me."

He gave her a long look, filled with curiosity and something else—something almost like male interest, though she knew she had to be mistaken. From a quick look in the bathroom mirror while she washed her hands, she knew she was a mess. Her hair was flattened on one side where she had been sleeping, she had a couple of really ugly bruises and her eyes looked inordinately huge in her face. Like she was some kind of creepy bug or something.

"Didn't tell me much, if you want the truth," he answered. "You like cinnamon Altoids. You live in Apartment 311 of the Cyprus Grove complex in San Diego. You have a school district ID card, and your birthday is March 14, when you'll be twenty-nine years old. Funny, but I couldn't find a single thing in your purse that might explain why you showed up at my ranch out of the blue and started cleaning up for me."

She could feel her face heat with her ready blush, the redhead's curse. "You assumed that's why I was here. I tried to tell you otherwise but you seemed in a rush to go back to your office. Besides, I could tell you really did need help."

"I absolutely did, which is why I hired someone who wasn't you to take care of it," he pointed out. "Since you weren't here to clean, why *did* you show up on my doorstep?"

She chewed her lip, trying to figure out the best way to explain.

"Oh! I have a case in my rental car," she exclaimed suddenly, horrified at her negligence. "I need to bring it in from the cold. Oh, I can't believe I forgot it!"

"Relax. You didn't forget. It's locked in my office right now. Don't you remember telling me to bring it inside just as Taft and the other paramedics were carrying you out to the ambulance?"

She had a vague memory that seemed to drift in and out of her mind like a playful guppy.

She exhaled with relief. "Oh, good."

"So is the mysterious case the reason you're here?"

She sighed, knowing she couldn't avoid this any longer. "Could you get it?"

He eased away from the door frame, his expression wary. After a moment, he left the room. As she waited for him to return, she closed her eyes, dreading the next few moments.

The past five days had been such a blur. From the moment she found the receipt for a storage unit while clearing out her father's papers, she felt as if she had been on a crazy roller coaster, spinning her in all directions.

After seeing the contents of that storage unit, she had a hundred vague, horrible suspicions but they were all surreal, insubstantial. None of it seemed real—probably because she didn't *want* it to be real.

Her research online had unearthed a chilling story, one she still couldn't quite comprehend, and one she didn't want to believe had anything to do with her or any member of her family.

She had packed up one piece of evidence and brought it here in hopes of finding out the truth. Now that she was here, she realized how foolish her hopes had been. What was she expecting? That she would find out everything had just been a horrible mistake?

She waited, nerves stretched taut. When he returned, the black portfolio looked dark and forbidding in his arms.

"Here you go." He handed it to her, and she moved to the bed.

"Did you look inside, like you looked in my purse?"

He shook his head. "I didn't want to invade your privacy, but circumstances didn't leave me much choice."

She was glad for that, at least. With her only workable hand, she opened the case and slid out the contents, resting it on the blanket.

The loveliness still caught her breath—a beautiful painting of a pale lavender columbine so real she could almost smell it, cupped in both hands of a small blonde girl who looked to be about three years old.

Ridge Bowman's expression seemed to freeze the moment he caught sight of the painting. His jaw looked hard as granite.

"Where did you get that?" he demanded, his voice harsh.

Instinctively, she wanted to shrink from that tone. She hated conflict and had since she was a little girl listening to her parents scream at each other.

She swallowed hard. "My…father recently died, and I found it among his things."

He wasn't angry, she suddenly realized. He was overwhelmed.

"It's even more beautiful than I remember," he said, his tone almost reverent. He traced a finger over the edge of one petal, and she realized with shock that this big, tough rancher looked as if he was about to weep.

Who was this man who looked as if he could wrestle a steer without working up a sweat but who could cry over a painting of a little girl holding a flower?

"It…belonged to your family, then?"

He looked up as if he had forgotten she was there. "This is why you came to the ranch?"

She nodded, a movement that reminded her quite forcibly of her aching head. "When I found it," she said carefully, "I immediately did a web search for the artist. Margaret Bowman."

"My mother."

He looked at the painting again, his expression more soft than she had seen it.

As she watched him, Sarah was suddenly overwhelmed with exhaustion, so very tired of carrying the weight of her past and trying to stay ahead of demons she could never escape.

She shouldn't have come here. It had been foolishly impulsive and right now she couldn't believe she ever thought it might be a good idea to face the Bowman family in person.

If she had been thinking straight, she simply would have tracked down an email address and sent a photograph of the painting with her questions. Better yet, she should have had her attorney contact the Bowman family.

Her only explanation for the choices that had led her here had been her own reaction to the paintings. She had been struck by all of them, particularly this one— by its artistic merit and the undeniable skill required to make simple pigment leap from the canvas like that, but also by the obvious love the artist had for the child in the painting.

"Do you have any idea where your father obtained this painting?" Ridge asked her.

Suspicions? Yes. Proof, on the other hand, was something else entirely. She shook her head, which wasn't a lie.

"It means a great deal to you, doesn't it?" she said carefully.

"If you only knew. I thought we would never see it again. Of everything, this is the one I missed most of all. That's my sister, Caidy, in the painting. The one whose wedding we had here yesterday."

She had suspected as much. Somehow that made everything seem more heartbreaking. "She was a lovely child," she said softly.

"Who grew into an even lovelier woman." He smiled, and she was suddenly aware of a fierce envy at the relationship between Ridge Bowman and his family members. The family was obviously very close, despite the tragedy that must have affected all of them.

She thought of her half brother and their tangled relationship. She had loved him dearly when she was young, despite the decade age difference between them. In the end, he had become a stranger to her.

"How much do you want for it?" Ridge asked abruptly. "Name your price."

"What?" she exclaimed.

"That's why you came, isn't it?" He raised an eyebrow, and she didn't mistake the shadow of derision in his eyes that hadn't been there before.

He thought she was trying to extort money from the family, she realized with horror. She was so startled, she didn't answer for several seconds.

He must have taken her silence for a negotiation tactic. His mouth tightened and he frowned. "I should be coy here, pretend I don't really want it, maybe try to bargain with you a little. I don't care. I want it. Name your price. If it's at all within reason, I'll pay it."

She shook her head. "I—I don't want your money, Mr. Bowman."

"Don't you?"

"When I read the stories online about your parents and their…" Her voice trailed off, and she didn't quite know how to finish that statement.

"Their murders?"

She shivered a little at his bluntness. "Yes," she said. "Their murders. When I read the news reports and realized the artist of that beautiful painting had died, I knew I had to come. The painting is yours. I won't let you pay me anything. I fully intended to give it back to you and your family."

"You what?" He clearly didn't believe her.

"I have no legal or moral claim to it. It rightfully belongs to your family. It's yours."

He stared at her and then back at the painting, brow furrowed. "What's the catch?"

"No catch. It's yours," she repeated.

She didn't add the rest. Not yet. She would have to tell him, but he was so shocked about her volunteering this painting to him, she wasn't quite ready to let him know everything else.

"I can't believe this. You have no idea. It's like having a piece of her back. My mother, I mean."

The love in his voice touched a chord somewhere deep inside. She thought of her own mother, bitter and angry at the world and the cards she had been dealt. Her mother had raised her alone from the time Sarah was very young, working two jobs to support them because she wouldn't take money from her ex-husband. Sarah had loved her but accepted now that her mother had never been a kind woman. Barbara didn't have a lot of room left over around her hatred of Sarah's father to find love for the daughter they had created together.

"Can you tell me," she asked him, "was this piece part of the...stolen collection?"

After a moment, he nodded, his features dark.

What other answer had she expected? Sarah pressed her lips together. She couldn't tell him the rest. The dozens of pieces of art she had found in that climate-controlled storage unit.

She also couldn't tell him what she suspected.

She was suddenly exhausted, so tired her eyes felt gritty and heavy. She wanted nothing but to sleep again, to ease the pain of her injuries and the worse pain in her heart.

"Do you have any idea how your father obtained it?" he asked. "We've only found two or three pieces from the stolen collection in all these years. They seem to appear out of thin air, and we can never trace them back to the original seller. This could be just what we need to solve the case."

She couldn't tell him that. She didn't have the strength or the courage right now when she was hurting so badly. She would have her father's estate attorney deal with all the particulars, as she should have done from the beginning.

He would eventually know everything, but she wouldn't have to face those piercing green eyes during the telling.

"I've told you all I can. I found it among my father's things, as I said, and now I would like you and your family to have it. Take the painting, Mr. Bowman. Ridge. Please. Consider it a Christmas gift if you want, but it's yours."

"I can't believe this. I'm…stunned." He smiled at her, a flash of bright joy that took her breath away. "Thank you. Thank you so much. I can't begin to tell you how happy Caidy, Taft and Trace will be. You've given us a gift beyond price."

"I'm glad." She mustered a smile, even though it made her cheeks ache. "I'm so tired. Can I rest now?"

"Yes. Of course." He picked up the painting from the bed and held it gingerly, as if he couldn't quite believe it was in his hands again. "Caidy left a lot of her clothes here. Would you like me to find a nightgown for you to change into so you can be more comfortable?"

"I can do that. Thank you."

"You have nothing to thank me for. Not after this." He gestured to the painting in his hands. "I'm supposed to check on you a couple more times in the night. I'll apologize in advance for waking you."

"Apology accepted."

He headed for the door. "If you need anything else, call out. I'll probably sleep on the sofa in the family room off the kitchen."

She wanted to tell him that wasn't necessary, that she would be fine, but she was just too exhausted to argue—especially when she somehow knew he wouldn't listen anyway.

Chapter Five

Ridge closed the door behind him with one hand, the other still holding the miraculously returned painting. He stood in the hallway for a long moment and just gazed down at it, wondering what on earth had just happened in there.

He felt odd, off balance, not sure what to think or feel.

Something major had just happened. It wasn't only that she had returned this painting he thought he would never see again. He had felt a link between them, a tensile connection that seemed to seethe and pulse between them.

Or maybe that had been a figment of his imagination. Maybe it was simply late and he was tired after a long, strange day.

He carried the painting to his office and propped it

on a chair across from his desk where he could look at it and remember.

The painting was created with tenderness, out of a mother's love. That came through in every single brush-stroke. Caidy would be so pleased to have it back in the family. She should really be the one to have it. Though he supposed it wasn't technically his to give, as it belonged to all of them as joint heirs to their parents' estate, maybe he could talk to Taft and Trace about the three of them giving it to their sister as a wedding present.

He looked at that sweet little girl in the painting cupping a fragile flower and her whole future in her hands and couldn't help but think of his own sweet little girl. Destry had grown up without a mother's love—though not really, when he thought about it. Caidy had stepped up to play that role after Melinda left, and had done an admirable job.

He frowned, wondering why his thoughts seemed to be so focused on his ex-wife today. He hadn't thought about her this much in months, not since early spring when he had finally paid a private detective to track her down, for Destry's sake.

As he had half suspected all these years, the trail was cold. The private detective had discovered Melinda had died just a year after she left them, killed along with her then-boyfriend in a car accident in Italy, of all places.

He hadn't grieved, only brooded for a few days about his own foolish choices and for a wild young woman who had never wanted to be a mother.

Any grief for his failed marriage had worked its way out of his system a long time ago, as he had rocked his crying child to sleep or put her on the bus by himself on the first day of school.

He suddenly missed his daughter fiercely. The house seemed entirely too quiet without her constant activity—either watching something on TV or chattering with Caidy.

On impulse, he dialed Trace's number. His brother answered the phone on the second ring.

"Missing Destry already?" his brother teased.

"Already?" He stretched back in his chair, suddenly tired from the tumultuous day. "It's been almost twenty-four hours. I missed her as soon as you drove away last night. Aren't you like that with Gabi and Will?"

His wife Becca had given birth over the summer to the most adorable little boy, all big blue eyes and lots of dark hair. Gabrielle wasn't Trace's daughter, she was actually Becca's much-younger sister, but the two of them had legal custody of her and loved her as their own child.

"I guess you're right. I was a mess in the fall when she went away for that school trip to the Teton Science School and that was only four nights."

"Are the girls having a good time?" he asked.

"I don't know. I've been working. I do know everybody's been sneaking around doing Christmassy things all day."

Now that the business of the wedding was over, he supposed he should probably start thinking about Christmas, only three days away.

He wasn't crazy about the holidays. None of the Bowman siblings were, considering their parents had been killed just a few days before Christmas.

Or at least none of them *used* to enjoy the season. It seemed as each of his siblings found love and moved on with life, each had been able to let go of those ghosts and embrace the holidays again. Caidy had even chosen this weekend for her wedding, claiming she wanted to be able to celebrate the season and not continue to mourn.

He gazed across the desk at the sweet little girl in the picture as his brother spoke.

"I hear you had some excitement on the ranch today."

"Did you?"

"I caught the ambulance call on the scanner, and Taft filled me in on the details. What are you doing, trying to kill the hired help?"

He didn't want to go into the whole story, but he suddenly realized he had called his brother's house not just to speak with his daughter but also for Trace's perspective on the situation.

"Sarah isn't the hired help," he explained. "Turns out, we had a little case of mistaken identity. When she showed up this morning, I made a leap and just assumed she was from the cleaning service. Turns out, she wasn't. When she saw what a mess the house was in after the wedding, she pitched in anyway to help me out and that's how she was injured."

"Wait a minute. She wasn't even from the cleaning company?"

Trace sounded both skeptical and suspicious. Justifiably so, he supposed.

"No. They had a mix-up in dates, but it's all been taken care of now. They sent somebody else this afternoon."

"So who is the injured lady and why was she there?"

"That is kind of a long story," he began, not quite sure how to explain what sounded implausible even to him.

"Yeah?"

"It's the craziest damn thing." He shifted in his seat. "She brought us one of the paintings."

A long pause met his words. "Which one?" Trace finally asked.

"One of Mom's. The one she did of Caidy up on the Pine Bend trail, with the columbine."

Trace was again silent. When he spoke, his voice was soft, with the same sort of reverence Ridge felt about it.

"I always loved that one," he said.

"Same here. It's even better than I remembered. She had amazing talent. It's no wonder her paintings sell for so much now."

The few paintings in circulation—those she had sold or given to friends before her death—were beginning to fetch in the high five figures, something that would have astonished their mother.

They had been able to track down a few pieces from the collection and had purchased what they could over the years but the few available were becoming as valued as they were rare.

"So let me get this straight," Trace said, his voice hard. "A woman just shows up out of the blue, almost exactly on the anniversary of the murders, with one of the paintings...and then supposedly injures herself while pretending to be something she isn't?"

He instinctively wanted to defend Sarah against the suspicions, even though he understood it and knew just where it originated. He couldn't blame his brother for questioning the situation.

Becca and Gabi's estranged mother, Monica, was an amoral con artist who had played a part, albeit a small one, in the planned robbery of the Bowmans' extensive art collection twelve years earlier.

Trace had a right to be mistrustful—though in Sarah's case, Ridge was quite certain it was unfounded.

"She broke her arm, Trace. Jake Dalton x-rayed it. If she's running a con, she certainly ramped things up a level or twelve by purposely fracturing her own arm."

He decided not to mention to his brother that too much pain medication made her act like a woozy sorority girl during pledge week. Any savvy con artist likely knew that about herself and would have taken pains to avoid it.

"I'm just saying the whole thing seems a little odd," Trace said. "Where did she say she obtained the painting?"

"Her father recently died and she found it among his things."

"Convenient."

He frowned, becoming annoyed now at his brother's tone. "Say what you want, but she came to the River Bow to return the painting to the family. She says it rightfully belongs to us, and she can't in good conscience keep it. She came all the way from California to give it back to us."

Even as he heard the words, he sensed how incredible they sounded. A little doubt began to creep in. Was she keeping something else from them? No. He didn't believe it. She was lovely and sweet, and he hadn't had nearly enough lovely, sweet things in his life lately.

"Where is she staying?" Trace asked. "At the inn?"

He again shifted in his chair. He wasn't about to lie to his brother, though he seriously disliked feeling like he was being interrogated here.

"She's here. In Caidy's room. Not only did she break her arm falling down the stairs but she also suffered a concussion. Doc Dalton didn't want her to stay by herself at the inn."

Trace didn't say anything, but Ridge could still feel the disapproval radiating from him.

"Be careful," his brother said. "That's all. Just be careful."

"Thanks for the advice, Mom. You mind if I talk to my daughter now?"

"I'll get her."

He drummed his fingers while he waited for Destry to come on the line.

"Hey, Dad! I heard you had some excitement there today. Trace told Aunt Becca you had to call the ambulance. I'm super glad you weren't the one who broke your arm! That would have been hard at Christmas."

One of his life's greatest joys was the knowledge that his daughter was growing to be a compassionate human being, who cared more about others than herself. Three Christmases ago, she had wanted to give all the money her family would have spent on her Christmas gifts to Gabi. He grinned at the sudden memory. At the time, Gabi had been a confused and scared young girl, abandoned by a ruthless mother. She had been trying to find her way in the world and had convinced Destry and all her little friends that she was dying and her family couldn't afford the surgery that would save her life.

Gabi had come such a long way now that she lived in a safe, comfortable home where she never doubted she was safe. She had become a healthy, well-adjusted young woman, and he loved her as if she were indeed his niece.

"So the cleaning lady was pretty hurt, huh?" Destry asked now.

He sighed. Apparently he would have to give the report to everybody in the family. It would have been easier to get them all on a blasted conference call. "She's doing all right. She's staying here for tonight, in Caidy's room. It's a long story."

"Okay," Destry said. Her easy acceptance made him smile.

"You really want to stay another night? I can run in and get you, no problem."

"We're in the middle of making a couple of Christmas projects—don't ask me what because I won't tell you. They won't be done until tomorrow. If you really need me, I guess Gabi can finish up on her own."

"No. It's fine. The house is just quiet with both you and Caidy gone."

"I'll be back tomorrow."

"Well, have a great time. Don't keep your aunt and uncle up all night with your giggling."

"Who us? Gabi and I don't giggle."

Ridge could just picture her batting her eyes innocently. He harrumphed. "Yeah, like I don't snore."

She laughed. "You're a nut. Good thing I love you, isn't it?"

"Good thing. I love you, too, ladybug. I'll see you tomorrow."

He hung up, missing her all over again. Though his marriage had been a mistake from the beginning, he would do it all over again in order to have Destry for a daughter.

Melinda had never been cut out for marriage to a rancher—neither the marriage part nor the living-on-a-ranch part.

His parents had seen it from the beginning and had tried to warn him, but he wouldn't listen, too enamored of this vibrant, beautiful woman who claimed to adore him.

He met her while he had taken a temporary job in Montana consulting with a movie star trying to start a hobby ranch. Melinda had been the personal assistant to the movie star's wife. She had been fascinated by cowboys and the West, and to his shocked delight, this wild, beautiful creature had somehow been fascinated with *him*.

For a month or so they had what he thought of as a fling, fiery and exciting. All that heat had already started to burn itself out when she came to him one night and told him she was pregnant. She had treated it with a casualness that had shocked him—"Oh, by the way, I missed my period. The pregnancy test was positive. Isn't that funny?"—as if the world hadn't just been shaken on its axis at the reality that the two of them had created life together.

He snorted now, remembering how he had automatically assumed they would marry. The way he was raised, that was just what a man did: he stepped up to take care of his responsibilities.

She had laughed at him and treated him like the provincial cowboy he was, but eventually he had persuaded her they could build a life together, for the sake of their child.

His parents hadn't approved of her or their marriage.

He eyed that painting again. The memory still burned. At the time of their deaths, the relationship between them had been strained and distant. Just the night before their murders, he had yelled at his father on the phone when Frank suggested maybe they hadn't known each other long enough for such a big step.

It was a hell of a thing that he let things become so tense between them without trying to heal the rift. He hated knowing his father died with Ridge's ugly words still ringing in his ears.

The worst part was, they were absolutely right about her. She *wasn't* cut out for this life, and both of them knew it. After his parents' deaths, he had no choice but to return to the River Bow to take over the ranch. Neither Taft nor Trace was in a position to do it, even if they'd wanted to.

He wanted to think Melinda had done her best, but a year after they moved to Pine Gulch and the River Bow, she had grown tired of being both a mother and a wife. Or at least being *his* wife. She had left both him and Destry one night with a hastily scribbled note that she was sorry but she couldn't do it anymore. She signed over full custody of Des, sent him divorce papers a few weeks later and disappeared.

For six months or so, she would send him emails from this spot or that one and then the correspondence became increasingly infrequent before it ended abruptly. He had suspected something had happened to her, but none of her friends could even tell him where she was when they heard from her last, and he didn't know how to start looking.

He really should have tried harder to find out, for Destry's sake if not his own, but he really wasn't sure he wanted to know the truth.

His thoughts turned to his unwilling houseguest. She was from California, too. She was also beautiful and soft. He wanted to think that was the extent of the similarities between her and Melinda—but he had learned his lesson well.

His ranch and his family. That's all he had time for, and he intended to keep things that way.

He certainly didn't have room for lovely injured schoolteachers with big blue eyes and secrets they didn't seem inclined to share.

Sarah woke from painkiller-twisted dreams to find a man standing in her doorway, big and hulking in the darkness. For an instant, icy panic swamped her, and her mind froze with nightmare fears of intruders and menacing strangers. A tiny, frightened sound escaped before she could swallow it back.

"Easy. Easy, Sarah. It's only me. Ridge Bowman."

The low, familiar voice acted on her like a comforting cup of chamomile tea. "Oh. Hi."

"Sorry I scared you. I warned you that Doc Dalton wanted me to check on you in the night. That's all I'm doing."

She drew in a calming breath and then another and willed the last shadow of panic to subside. "Of course. I remember."

"Mind if I turn on a lamp?"

"No. Go ahead."

A moment later, he flipped a switch and a small, comforting circle of light from a lamp on one of the bureaus pushed more of her panic away.

"There. Is that better?"

"Much. Sorry, I just woke up disoriented and forgot where I was for a moment."

He moved into the room. "Understandable. You've had quite a day. Anyone would be a little discombobulated, a word my mother used to love."

His mother, who had been murdered. She shivered and drew the quilts up higher as he moved closer to the bed.

"I'm supposed to make sure your brain is still working. Can you tell me what day it is?"

She closed her eyes and tried to think. Her arm and head both still ached, she realized, but without the insistent sharpness of before.

"Um, Saturday, right? Three days before Christmas."

"Technically it's Sunday now, but you're on the right track."

She glanced at the clock by the bed and saw it was after midnight.

"And what's your name again?"

"Sarah Whitmore," she answered promptly.

"What's my name?"

"You just reminded me two minutes ago. Ridge Bowman. Not that I would have forgotten. It's kind of an unusual name."

"That it is."

"Can I ask how you came by it?"

He leaned a hip against the footboard of the bed and she was suddenly keenly aware of him, his solid strength and leashed muscles.

"My parents met in Colorado while both of them were going to school there," he said, a small smile softening the hard lines and angles of his features. "Apparently one day Mom went hiking with her painting gear and ended up taking a bit of a tumble off a steep trail—she didn't fall far and wasn't hurt, but she was stranded on an isolated ledge for a couple of hours."

"Oh, no!"

"My father happened to choose that same day to go for a trail ride—and he happened to have a lariat along. When he came across a pretty damsel in distress in need of help, he did what any smart young cowboy would. He lowered his rope and brought her up to safety. He then did what any young cowboy worth his salt would *also* do and asked her out." He laughed softly at the memory. "The rest was history. Every significant moment in their life since happened in the mountains—he proposed to her on a ridgetop, they were married on another one. She used to say my name reminded her of all the happiest moments of her life and was a symbol of strength and invincibility."

She smiled, charmed by the sweetness of the story, until she remembered what had happened to that young couple.

"Your mother sounds…amazing," she murmured.

"She was," he said simply, then changed the subject with what she was certain was deliberate intent. "How's the arm? Do you need more of the pain meds?"

"Maybe just some ibuprofen. I think I had better take it easy on anything stronger. My head is spinning."

He crossed to the pitcher he had thoughtfully set out for her and poured a glass then brought it over to her, along with a couple of pills. For a gruff rancher, he seemed remarkably comfortable in the role of caregiver. She suspected raising a child probably contributed to that.

She wondered again about the girl's mother. Were they divorced or was he a widower? She wanted to ask but figured she had already filled her nervy quotient for a lifetime when it came to Ridge Bowman.

"I'm sorry I've been such a bother. I'll be out of the way in the morning."

She didn't want to feel this subtle connection to him. She would only find it that much harder to accept when he came to hate her after the truth came out.

"Are you supposed to be catching a flight back to San Diego in the next day or two? The way that snow is coming down, you might have a tough time making it to the airport, not to mention you might be a bit uncomfortable traveling with that broken arm for a day or two."

"My flight isn't until the end of the week. I had planned to stay in Pine Gulch through Christmas."

He looked surprised. "I thought you said you didn't have family around here."

"I don't," she answered. "Here, there or anywhere. Everyone's gone. My mother passed away two years ago and, as I told you, my father died earlier this year."

"You were an only child?"

"No," she said after a moment's hesitation. "I had an older brother but...he died twelve years ago."

She shouldn't have said that. She held her breath, afraid Ridge would probably find it an unusual coincidence that her older brother just happened to have died around the same time as his parents' murders.

She was beginning to suspect it wasn't a coincidence at all.

"So you were going to spend the holidays alone?" he asked.

"I've never minded my own company, Mr. Bowman."

"I enjoy mine, too. But not during the holidays."

He studied her for a long moment, and she had the odd impression he was weighing his words. "You could always spend the holidays here with Destry and me," he finally said slowly.

"What?" She blinked at him, certain she must have misheard.

"The inn is a great place, don't get me wrong. Not like it used to be, when nobody could recommend it. My sister-in-law Laura has worked hard to fix it up and all and make it a warm and welcoming hotel. But it's still a hotel, and you'd still be on your own. We'd love to have you here. As you can see, we've got plenty of room in this old place."

For a long moment, she fought a mix of shock, bemusement and a soft, sweet warmth. Was Ridge Bowman really asking a woman he had just met to spend the holidays at his ranch with him and his daughter?

"I...don't know what to say."

"You don't have to decide right this minute. It's the middle of the night. We both ought to be asleep. Good night."

He headed for the door, but she stopped him before he could reach it.

"Why would you make such an offer? You don't even know me. Why would you want a stranger to intrude in the middle of your family's holiday celebrations?"

He was quiet. "First of all, you wouldn't be intruding. When we were kids, we always had a houseful of people over for the holidays. My parents were known for throwing the River Bow open to anybody in need of a little holiday spirit. I guess in the past few years, we've kind of lost that along the way somehow."

"And?"

He scratched his cheek. "Well, you were hurt falling down my stairs. Seems to me, the least I can do is make you feel welcome here and give you a comfortable place to spend Christmas while you're recovering."

"You don't owe me anything," she exclaimed. "It was my own clumsiness."

"We do," he said. "Even if you hadn't been hurt here, there's the matter of the painting. You gave us

back something we thought was lost forever. I know my
brothers will want to meet you to thank you in person.
You might as well get used to the idea that the Bowman
family now owes you a debt and we always make good."

"I don't—"

"Just think about it. No rush. I'll check on you again
in a few hours when I head out to the barn. Meantime,
try to get some rest. We'll figure everything out in the
morning."

He gave her a lopsided smile, this big, rough cowboy she found so deeply attractive, then headed out of
the room with the little three-legged dog hopping along
behind him.

After he left, Sarah stared at the doorway, overwhelmed by his invitation.

She knew she shouldn't find the idea of staying in
this warm house for the holidays so very tempting. She
didn't belong here at the River Bow. Her whole presence
at the ranch had been a misjudgment on her part and a
case of mistaken identity on his.

No, she couldn't accept. She would have to simply make
her excuses in the morning and return to the Cold Creek
Inn—no matter how depressed that prospect left her.

Chapter Six

As predicted, the snow that had been lightly but steadily falling when he finally tumbled into bed the night before had become a full-on Rocky Mountain blizzard by morning.

After checking on his soundly sleeping guest and leaving a note for her outside her room where she couldn't help but see it, Ridge bundled into all his warmest gear and headed out into a miserable wind that blew ice into every available crevice.

At least a foot of snow had fallen during those few hours of restless sleep, and he couldn't see any sign of it easing up in the foreseeable future. He wouldn't be surprised if they had a good two feet for St. Nick and his reindeer to struggle through. Add in the wind that blew giant drifts to pile up in front of doorways and bury anything uncovered—like certain rental vehicles, for instance—and he didn't see how Sarah would have any other choice but to stay put on the River Bow for now.

He certainly wouldn't be able to take her anywhere for several hours. Most of his day would be spent digging out, clearing paths, repairing any damage from the winds.

Both of his brothers would probably be running all day responding to slide-offs and other weather-related issues in their respective emergency personnel modes, which meant that Destry would likely be stuck at Trace's house, too, at least until evening.

After a few hours of running the plow on the tractor—with many more to go—he decided to take a quick break. He needed more fuel than the quick cup of coffee and yogurt he had grabbed on his way out the door.

The contrast between the howling, bitter wind and the warmth of the mudroom was startling—and so was the tantalizing smell of frying bacon that drifted over him the moment he walked inside.

Hmm. Apparently his hunger was giving him aromatic hallucinations. There was a first.

By the time he shrugged out of his winter gear and walked into the kitchen, he discovered he wasn't imagining things.

Sarah stood at the stove, wearing a deep green robe that must have been one of Caidy's and an apron she must have found hanging in the pantry. Her casted arm looked pale and fragile in contrast.

"What's all this?" he demanded in surprise.

She flipped a strip of sizzling bacon in the pan. "Great timing, that's what it is. I woke up and saw you outside shoveling all that snow. When I came into the kitchen, I couldn't see any sign you'd had breakfast. I thought you might eventually come in to grab a bite so I started cooking. And here you are. I hope you don't mind."

He laughed. "Wrong question to ask a cowboy, if he minds somebody fixing him a meal. The answer to that question will always be no. I had resigned myself to a cold bowl of cereal so this is a great surprise. Just one question. How did you manage all this with a broken wing?"

"I would like to tell you it was easy, but that would be stretching the truth. The trickiest part was opening the bacon package, but somehow I managed."

She gave a rueful smile that completely charmed him—as if the breakfast wasn't enough on its own.

She scooped several perfectly crisp slices of bacon onto a plate and slid it across the island to him, followed by fluffy scrambled eggs and several pieces of toast. She dished out a much-smaller portion for herself.

He poured two glasses of juice from the refrigerator and then sat down across from her at the island, suddenly famished.

"Wow. This is delicious," he said after his first bite of eggs that were perfectly cooked. "Thank you."

She looked pleased. "You're welcome. I like to cook, even one-handed. I don't get the chance to do it for someone else very often."

"I don't mind cooking, either, when I have the time. Our parents made sure we all learned to fend for ourselves if we had to. I just rarely have the time—and I've never much needed to, with Caidy around. All that will change now. I'm looking to hire a housekeeper, but I figured I would wait until Destry and I have a chance to settle into a new routine and see what holes need filling."

"Is your sister moving far with her new husband?"

"Just a few miles away, actually. I imagine Caidy will take pity on us once in a while and throw a meal or two this direction, though she's got two stepchildren to take care of and a busy veterinarian for a husband."

She studied him while she ate a small forkful of scrambled eggs. "You're very close, aren't you?"

He sipped at his juice, remembering how radiant his baby sister had looked when he gave her away. Out of nowhere, he felt a little melancholy. All his siblings were moving on with their lives while he was here shoveling the same damn driveway, repairing the same damn barn roof.

"Hard not to be," he answered. "Caidy has been helping me out with my daughter since Destry was in diapers. We would have been lost without her after my wife took off."

Now why the hell had he told her that? Ridge set down his fork, losing a little of his appetite despite the delicious breakfast. He rarely talked about Melinda anymore. What was the point? Yet here he was blurting out the pleasant news that she had left him alone with a young baby.

"What a loving sister," she murmured.

He found himself unexpectedly amused that she had jumped there instead of the obvious.

"You're not going to ask why my wife left? Seems to me, that would be an irresistible follow-up question for most women I know."

She shrugged as much as she could with one arm in a sling. "I assumed if you wanted me to know, you would have finished the sentence. 'We would have been lost without her after my wife took off to swallow flaming knives with the circus. After my wife took off to become a Radio City Music Hall dancer. After my wife took off to shave her head and join a cult.' That sort of thing."

His burst of laughter seemed to surprise both of them. He tried to picture Melinda shaving her head and couldn't quite pull it off. "Any of those answers would be more interesting than the bare-bones truth. She didn't like ranch life. She hated the wind and the flies and the dirt."

And me, he wanted to add. By the time Melinda walked out, she had hated Ridge for refusing to leave the ranch and had accused him of loving the River Bow more than he loved her. By that point, he had.

"She left her daughter because of that? Her daughter and the, er, man she loved?"

He wanted to think she had loved him once, but he wasn't sure anymore. "We weren't a very good mix from the get-go. And I think some people make choices they later come to regret. All these years, I thought she just abandoned our daughter, but this year I finally had a private investigator search for her and discovered she died about a year after she took off. I like to think she would have reconsidered and tried to reconnect with Des. Guess we'll never know for sure."

"That must be hard on your daughter."

He was touched by her compassion for a girl she didn't even know. Maybe it stemmed from being an educator.

"You know, she's an amazingly well-adjusted young lady. With Caidy's help and the rest of the family's, I think we've managed to do a pretty good job of giving her all the love she needs to thrive, even without a mother."

"She's lucky to have you all," Sarah said softly.

"We're lucky to have each other," he said. "My brothers and their families still come home just about every week for Sunday dinner, though we decided to take a pass this week given the wedding on Friday and Christmas in only a few days. We are getting together for Christmas dinner this week. You'll have a chance to meet them all then."

"About that—" she began.

He knew she was going to argue about staying through Christmas and he suddenly didn't want her to.

"They're going to be so happy to see the painting. I was telling my brother Trace about it last night. We're both really curious about how your father might have come into possession of it."

An odd spark flashed in her eyes, almost like fear, but she quickly looked down at her plate. "I'm...not sure," she said. "To be honest, I didn't know my father well. We were virtual strangers most of my life."

"Oh?"

She sighed. "My parents divorced when I was five and he took custody of my brother, who was several years older than I was. They lived mostly in Las Vegas and rarely came to the coast. I had maybe two mandated weeks with him in the summers and not even that, most of the time. I had little to do with him after I turned eighteen, by my own choice."

"Divorce can be tough on kids." He had a very strong suspicion she didn't talk about this very often, and he was touched that she was willing to discuss it with him. Something about the wind howling under the eaves and the snow falling heavily outside and the homey morning breakfast smells lent a quiet intimacy to the warmth of the kitchen that invited confidences.

"I see that with my students," she answered. "It's only natural for young children to feel like they're responsible somehow. And situations where children are split up between parents can add a special kind of hell to a child's psyche. For a long time, I couldn't understand what I had done wrong that he didn't want me but he wanted Joey. My mother was…bitter about the divorce and the reasons that led up to it. And you know how some people are quietly bitter? That wasn't my mother. By the time they finally divorced, she hated my father, and her anger sat at the dinner table with us every night. She hated that he refused to change, even for her. She always said—"

She broke off the words and suddenly bit her lip. "Sorry. I don't know why I'm rambling on like this. Why should you care about my boring dysfunctional family? Can I get you more bacon?"

She jumped up from the table. In her rush, she moved too quickly and wobbled a little to regain her equilibrium. Out of instinct, he jumped up to catch her before she fell or bumped her arm.

They froze that way, with her arms against his chest and his on her upper arms. She looked up at him, eyes huge. He saw her throat move as she swallowed, and he could swear her gaze flickered to his mouth.

Heat surged through him, wild and urgent. He wanted to kiss her, with an ache that shocked the hell out of him. She felt perfect in his arms, soft and warm, and he knew it was crazy but all he could think about was leaning down, brushing his mouth against hers, tasting those incredibly soft-looking lips….

She barely knew him, he reminded himself. They were alone in his house. Beyond that, she was stranded here, at least for now. He wouldn't take advantage of that and probably completely freak her out by kissing her out of the blue.

He drew on every ounce of self-control hard-won over the past ten years to keep the embrace impersonally helpful instead of yanking her against him as he wanted to do.

"You okay now?"

A very adorable pink blush stained her cheeks. "I... think so. I must have stood up too fast."

"Not to mention, you pushed yourself too hard making breakfast this morning, considering you broke a bone twenty-four hours ago and you've still probably got pain medication on board."

"I'm sure that's true."

What the hell was wrong with him? She was injured and hurting, and all he wanted to do was kiss away that soft, sweet brush of color on her cheekbones.

"You can let go now," she murmured after another moment. "I think I'm okay."

"You sure? This tile floor is pretty hard. Doc Dalton might wonder what's going on out here if you took a header and cracked your head open, too."

"I would tell him it's only me and my usual clumsiness."

She smiled, and he couldn't seem to look away. Almost against his will, he leaned down just a little. He saw her breath catch, saw her eyes widen. Her mouth parted, and he knew he didn't misinterpret the way she leaned toward him, ever so slightly.

A particularly strong gust of wind rattled the windows in the kitchen, and the sound was enough to yank him back to his senses.

With no small amount of regret, he eased his arms

away slowly to make sure she wasn't going to teeter again.

"I hate to leave you, but do you think you'll be okay in here without me for a while? Except for the wind, it looks like the snow is easing up a little. I should really go out and hit the plow again. I might be able to clear the driveway enough for Destry to make it back before dinner."

"I should be fine," she said, quickly veiling her expression, but not before he saw what looked like a little glint of disappointment. "In fact, if your daughter is able to make it out to the ranch, there shouldn't be any reason why I can't go back in the other direction and return to the inn."

He wanted to argue and invite her again to stay at the ranch for the holidays—but given his crazy response to her, maybe that wasn't the best idea.

"We'll see. Take it easy and get some rest. Let's see how you feel this afternoon."

He headed for the mudroom and his winter gear. For once he figured he would welcome the blast of cold air. He needed *something* to cool his fevered thoughts.

As soon as she heard the door close behind Ridge, Sarah covered her overheated cheeks with her palms.

Wow. What just happened?

For a moment there, she had been certain he would kiss her. Had it all been some pain reliever–induced figment of her imagination? No. She couldn't claim to be the most experienced woman on the planet, but he had most definitely leaned closer, until she thought she could feel his heartbeat pulse against her.

What would she have done? She certainly wouldn't

have resisted. She had *wanted* him to kiss her, had ached for it. Her own heartbeat had been racing in her ears and her nerves had shivered in anticipation.

She was fiercely attracted to him, more than she had ever been attracted to anyone in her life. She frowned, astonished at herself and her reaction. This just wasn't like her.

She certainly dated in San Diego and had come close to being engaged to a highly successful attorney, until her mother's debilitating stroke. Michael hadn't been at all supportive during those long months of stress. He resented the hours she felt obligated to stay with her mother at the care center, as Barbara's only living relative. Until then, she had never realized how inherently selfish he was, in that and many other ways. Seeing him filtered through the different light of her own stressful situation made her grateful she hadn't yet agreed to marry him. Breaking up after two years of exclusive dating had been more relief than heartbreak.

Probably because of the comfortable placidity of her near engagement, she found this wild attraction to Ridge Bowman new and disturbing.

This place was to blame, she decided. She hadn't been herself since she showed up at the River Bow. She had this strange sense of belonging here, of homecoming, that made absolutely no sense.

She needed to push that right out of her head. She didn't belong here—and the next time she was tempted to kiss the man, she needed to remember what would happen when Ridge found out the truth. He certainly wouldn't want her in his arms—or anywhere near his ranch or his daughter.

Fighting off a lingering depression, she stood and

began to clear the few breakfast dishes to tidy up. She was loading the last dish in the dishwasher when a familiar ringtone rang through the kitchen. Her phone! He must have found it in the car after all.

The ringing stopped by the time she made it to her purse and pawed through with one hand for her phone—which was much more difficult than she might have expected.

When she recognized her best friend Nicole's name on the recent-call log, she briefly entertained the idea of ignoring it, but perhaps a connection to her regular life might keep her anchored in reality, she thought.

Anyway, Nicki would probably keep calling until she picked up. Her impatient college roommate had always been that way.

She quickly dialed her back. While she waited for Nicki to pick up, she tried to formulate how much she could possibly tell her about the past twenty-four hours.

"There you are! I thought maybe you dropped off the face of the earth," Nicki exclaimed with the gerbil-on-crack energy and enthusiasm that always made Sarah smile.

She always figured the gods of college roommates had been particularly kind the day the two of them had been assigned together freshman year at UCLA. Where Sarah tended to be reserved and cautious, Nicki barged into every situation at full tilt. They had been BFFs since the very first day on campus, when they had stayed up all night exchanging life stories.

"I'm still here."

"Where? I ran by your condo last night, and you weren't home. I stopped again this morning, and you still weren't there. I've got to tell you, my imagination is in overdrive, wondering if you're with some hot guy you didn't tell me about."

She flushed and looked out the window, where she could see the outline of a certain extremely hot rancher shoveling his sidewalk.

Nicki knew more than anyone about her tangled family connections—it was hard to avoid telling her when they had lived together for all four years of school—but Sarah hadn't told her what she found in that storage unit or about her impromptu trip to Eastern Idaho.

"Why the urgency?" she asked, avoiding the question. "What's up?"

"Oh, you know. This and that. Okay, the truth is I have news. *Huge* news. But I don't want to tell you over the phone. Wherever you are, meet me in an hour at the Fishwife for brunch so I can spill."

She sighed, looking out at the vast expanse of mountains and snow out the window, which seemed far away from their favorite beachside restaurant.

"I'm sorry, hon. I can't. I'm afraid you'll have to tell me over the phone. I just had breakfast."

Nicole made a disappointed sound. "Lunch, then. Or coffee. Or pie. I don't care what. I want to see your face when I tell you."

"Does this have anything to do with the certain junior high science teacher you've been dating and perhaps any emotionally and socially significant gifts of jewelry that might have been offered and accepted?"

Nicole snorted. "Forget it. You're not going to break me that easily with your smarty-pants teacher talk. I won't spoil the surprise until I can squeal and hug my maid of honor in person. Just tell me where you are and I'll come to you."

"Doesn't it count if I squeal over the phone and give you a virtual hug?"

"No!" Nicki exclaimed. "Where the heck are you?"

She sighed. Like it or not, she was going to have to tell her friend and deal with the fallout. "I'm sorry, Nic. You know I would be there in a minute to celebrate with you if I could, but I can't. I should have told you, but to be fair, it was a last-minute decision, and anyway, I thought you were going to be spending the holidays in Big Bear with Jason's family."

"Told me what?"

"I'm in Idaho."

A long, echoing silence met her words.

"Excuse me. We must have a bad connection. Did you just say…Idaho."

"Erm, yes."

"As in potatoes."

She had to smile, as she hadn't seen a single tuber since she arrived two days earlier. "Yes. Actually, I'm almost to the Wyoming border. A little town called Pine Gulch."

"And the rest of the story is…"

"Long and complicated. Too long and complicated for me to adequately explain over the phone. I'm so sorry I'm not there to celebrate with the two of you, Nic. I really am."

"You're going to leave me hanging like that? So unfair."

"This, from the woman who won't even tell me she's engaged unless we're face-to-face?"

"How do you know whether I'm engaged or not? That's purely speculative."

She laughed, deeply grateful for one of the people she

loved most in the world. "You're right. I know nothing. I'm probably way off base anyway."

"And I know less than nothing about what you're doing there." Nicole paused. "Wait. Does this have anything to do with your father?"

She shivered a little at her friend's unerring guess. Nicole didn't know the full story of Vasily Malikov's criminal background—not that Sarah did, either—but she had shared enough details over the years with her friend that she could probably guess. Nicole certainly knew Sarah was left with the difficult task of trying to settle his complicated affairs.

She didn't want to talk about her family, so she chose the best method of distraction she could think of on short notice—which happened to be at the forefront of her brain because it was beginning to throb incessantly.

"Oh, I almost forgot to tell you," she said. "When I get back to San Diego, I'm going to have to take a rain check on our Saturday-morning tennis matches for a while. I, um, sort of broke my arm yesterday."

"What?" Nicole exclaimed. "What *else* haven't you told me? Have you got a new husband you haven't bothered to mention? And how does somebody *sort of* break an arm?"

"Okay. I broke my arm. No *sort of* about it. It is a clean break though, apparently, and I should be okay in about four weeks. No surgery necessary. And no new husband, believe me."

To her relief, Nicole let herself be distracted instead of pushing for further explanations about her father and her presence in Pine Gulch, answers Sarah wasn't yet ready to provide.

"Oh, you poor thing! Who's taking care of you? Do

you know somebody there in this Pine Gulch? Let me come get you and take you home where you belong. I'll skip Big Bear. Jason's family will understand."

Her friend's concern somehow made her feel much better about things.

"You know, I think I'll be okay. People here have been very kind. I've even had an invitation to spend Christmas with some people I've met here, and I'm seriously considering taking it."

It was a lie, but she could sort it out with Nicole over waffles at the Fishwife when she returned.

"I wish you would tell me what's going on," her friend said, obvious concern in her voice.

"I will. And please tell a certain seventh-grade science teacher, who might or might not be engaged, congratulations for me. He's the luckiest man I know."

"You promise you'll spill everything?"

"Pinkie promise."

"And you're safe? People are taking care of you?"

"I'm fine, honey. You go to Big Bear and have a wonderful time. Do me a favor, though. Be careful and don't break any bones. I can promise, it's not a great way to spend the holidays."

Nicole reluctantly hung up a short time later. After she disconnected, Sarah sat for a moment in the big, comfortable kitchen, listening to the house settle around her.

Without Ridge's conversation or Nicole's cheerful chatter on the phone, her own company somehow seemed unsettling. At loose ends, she wandered into the great room, dominated by that massive Christmas tree and the festive greenery all around.

Ridge hadn't turned on any of the Christmas lights

before he headed outside to shovel. Though it was late morning already, the day outside was still heavy and dark from the storm and the endless wind. On impulse, she searched until she found a switch. The Christmas tree lights came on as well as the little fairy lights nestled in the greenery above the fireplace and trailing up the staircase.

Immediately, her mood lightened.

She had the oddest feeling in this house. She didn't understand it and assumed it had to be the lingering effects from the pain medication. Nothing else explained why she felt this overwhelming sense of warmth and welcome here, why the very walls of the log ranch house seemed to be urging her to settle in and be comfortable.

She loved her own condo just a few blocks from the ocean and had worked two jobs for a long time to save for the down payment, but she wasn't sure she ever felt the same sense of cozy contentment there.

A picture above the mantel drew her gaze, and she saw it was a mountain scene, with horses in the foreground who looked as if they could run off the painting, and a compelling old cabin with weathered log walls and fluttery lace curtains.

Even before she saw the flowing signature of Margaret Bowman, she knew by the style and skillful use of color and perspective that it must have been painted by Ridge's mother.

That alone was enough to remind her she *didn't* belong here. Like the painting, the feeling was only an artful illusion, and she would do well to remember that.

Chapter Seven

He stayed out in the cold for several hours, plowing neighbors' driveways and digging out mailboxes buried by blowing snowdrifts and the county road crews.

The heater in the tractor cab had stopped working about an hour earlier and he was chilled to the bone. Though the snow had stopped for now, the clouds were heavy and dark, and he expected several more inches would fall overnight.

As Ridge finally drove the tractor up the long, curving lane that led from Cold Creek Road to the ranch house, nestled in the trees, he was greeted by a scene that belonged on a greeting card.

There, shining through the gloom, was the house where he had lived most of his life, the front window gleaming with color and light from the huge Christmas tree Caidy and Destry had spent the entire Thanksgiving weekend decorating.

He stopped the tractor and just savored the view. He loved this place, every last inch of it. The house, the barn, the outbuildings, the acreage. He knew it as well as he knew his own face in the mirror.

His houseguest must have turned on the tree lights. He wondered how she was doing and hoped she had found the chance to rest. Guilt pinched at him, knowing he had left her far too long. He should have checked on her an hour ago.

He meant to earlier, but time had this bad habit of slipping away from him. He could also be honest enough with himself to admit he was also a little leery about facing her again after that moment when he had nearly kissed her in the kitchen.

That hadn't stopped him from thinking about her all afternoon. She was hiding something from him. He was certain of it, though he couldn't have said why.

Hell, he'd only met the woman a little more than twenty-four hours earlier. He didn't really know anything about her, other than that she was lovely as a spring meadow, that she didn't have anywhere else to go for the holidays and that she made him begin to crave all these crazy things he never thought he needed.

Despite their short acquaintance, he still sensed secrets seething beneath her outward calm like rainbow trout darting around under the ice of Cold Creek. He wanted to dip his hand in and catch a few of them.

After enjoying the view for a few more moments, he drove up to the house and parked close. Broken heater or not, he was going to have to go out to plow again before the storm blew itself out and passed away from Pine Gulch. It was an inevitable part of wintertime here on the western slope of the Tetons.

When he walked into the mudroom, he was again met by something tantalizing, rich and hearty. His stomach growled in a rather embarrassing way. He took off his winter clothes and walked in to find an empty kitchen. One of Caidy's slow cookers steamed on the countertop.

Though his sister had often instructed him on the cardinal rule of slow cookers—don't lift the lid!—he was too curious, and, hey, male. He couldn't resist doing just that. To his amazed delight, he discovered one of his very favorite winter meals: a beef stew brimming with onions, potatoes and carrots.

His houseguest must have thrown it together. How had she managed to peel and slice the vegetables with a broken arm?

A warmth that had nothing to do with the furnace seeped through him. After another quick, appreciative sniff, he closed the lid and went in search of her.

He found her snuggled up under a blanket on one of the sofas in the great room, positioned so she could see both the blazing Christmas tree and the fire that sizzled and hummed in the river-rock fireplace.

He opened his mouth to greet her, then realized her eyes were closed, her breathing even. A strand of auburn hair drifted across her cheek and he had to clench a fist to keep from pushing it back.

She looked so peaceful there, lovely and sweet and more relaxed than he had seen her since she arrived at the ranch.

Despite his better instincts, Ridge indulged his cold, achy bones and sank down onto the other sofa. He had a million things to do. Running a cattle ranch left him very little leisure time. He could always find some task to fill his downtime—ranch accounts, ordering supplies, tinkering with the stupid heater on the John Deere.

He hadn't slept much the night before. Just for a moment, he decided to sit by his own fire on a cold, snowy afternoon and relax while the Christmas lights flickered on the tree.

The past week revving up to the wedding had been so crazy, he hadn't had a single moment of downtime. As he sat there with the fire warming his feet, tension he hadn't even been aware of began to trickle away. He exhaled heavily and closed his eyes—just for a moment, he told himself.

Sometime later, the sound of the front door slamming pierced through a hazy, delicious dream that involved a lovely woman with auburn hair and blue-gray eyes and a soft, eager mouth...

"Dad! I'm home!"

He jerked back to full awareness just as his daughter bolted in at full tilt, like a gawky energetic colt.

He blinked a few times. Surely he hadn't been asleep. He *never* took naps. But the fire had burned down and his eyes felt heavy and swollen, so he must have been out for a while.

For a moment, Destry looked mildly surprised to find him sitting on the living room sofa, apparently doing nothing. "Hi, Dad!" she exclaimed.

"Hey there," he said softly. He quickly rose and headed back to the foyer so their guest could keep sleeping.

Destry followed him, dropping her backpack on a chair as she went. "You wouldn't believe the crazy roads. Uncle Trace had to drive like two miles an hour all the way here."

"Is that so?" he murmured softly as Trace walked in carrying an unfamiliar suitcase, Gabi right behind him hauling a mysterious plastic bin whose contents he couldn't discern.

"I didn't think I would see you guys today. I figured you wouldn't be able to make it through the snow."

"You got a lot more out here than we did in town, and we didn't have the wind," his brother said. "Anyway, what's a blizzard when you've got four-wheel drive and a couple of determined girls on your hands?"

Gabi and Destry both giggled, something they tended to do a great deal of whenever they were together. He never minded it. What else were girls their age supposed to do?

"Sorry to make you drive me home in the snow, Uncle Trace," Destry said. "I just have *so* much to do before Christmas, you know? We've only got *two days*. Can you believe it? Now that we finished the, er, things we were making at your place, I wanted to come home to finish the rest. I didn't want you out here by yourself, now that Aunt Caidy's on her honeymoon."

"I'm not by myself," he started to explain, but at that moment, Destry's attention was caught by something in the living room. Sarah, he realized. She had sat up and was looking around the room sleepily, her hair messed up from sleeping on her side.

She looked completely delectable, especially when she flushed a little to find them all looking at her.

"Oh. Hi."

Her voice sounded husky with sleep, and Ridge had to swallow hard at the instant heat that surged through him.

He did his best to ignore the arched eyebrow Trace

sent his way. Sometimes younger brothers were a pain in the ass.

"Sorry we woke you," he said. "Look who showed up. This is my brother Trace, my daughter, Destry, and Trace's sister-in-law, Gabi. Everybody, this is Sarah Whitmore."

Sarah tucked her feet under the blanket. "Hi," she said with a nervous sort of smile. His family could be overwhelming. At least she was meeting them a few at a time.

"Hi, Sarah," Gabi said cheerfully. "Did you really break your arm falling down the stairs?"

Sarah lifted her cast, her expression embarrassed. "Can you believe anybody would be so clumsy?"

"Does it hurt a lot?" Gabi asked. "I sprained my wrist one time playing dodgeball at school, and it hurt like *crazy*. I couldn't use it for like two weeks. I had a cast and everything. It did help me get out of like four tests, since I couldn't write the answers, so that was kind of awesome."

"So that's why you didn't complain more about your injury," Trace said, rolling his eyes at his young sister-in-law. Gabi was quite a character, someone who had grown up learning how to manipulate circumstances to her advantage. "All this time, I thought you were just being brave."

"I was! It still hurt like crazy."

Trace laughed and nudged her with his shoulder. He loved the girl like a daughter, something that warmed Ridge to see.

He didn't look quite as favorably on his brother when Trace turned his attention to Sarah.

"Ridge was telling me last night about the painting

you brought with you to Pine Gulch. He said you wanted to give it back to the family."

"Er, yes. That's the plan." She looked down at her hands, clearly uncomfortable at the direction the conversation had taken.

"That seems like quite a remarkably generous gesture. It's not a masterpiece by any means, but it's still a valuable painting, especially given the history. Were you aware our mother's work is beginning to fetch in the five figures?"

"I can certainly see why," she murmured, gesturing to one of Ridge's favorites on the mantel, one of her earlier works they had been able to purchase a few years ago. "She was very gifted."

"But you still want to give it to us. Complete strangers."

She sent a fleeting glance in Ridge's direction, and her cheeks colored, which he interpreted to mean she didn't consider him a *complete* stranger. Good thing, especially since he'd nearly kissed her a few hours earlier.

"Keeping it wouldn't have been right. The painting never belonged to me," she said quietly. "I'm not sure how my father obtained it, but it appears your family has rightful claim to it. Especially given that history you referred to."

"That's quite an unusual position to take. I'm not sure many people would agree. Possession being nine-tenths of the law in many people's minds."

"I'm sure you would agree, Chief Bowman, that legalities and moralities are sometimes two very different things."

She said the words in that same even tone, and Trace

studied her carefully as if he were weighing every syllable, every expression.

Ridge could tell Sarah was growing increasingly uncomfortable, and he found himself wanting to tell his brother to back the hell off.

"And you really have no idea how or where your father obtained it?" Trace pushed.

"I was estranged from my father for many years before his death."

"And yet he left you what could be a valuable painting."

"Yes," she said, her voice tight, and Ridge had had enough.

"It's in my office. Come on back and take a look."

He said the words in a firm command his brother couldn't mistake.

After a moment, Trace followed him down the hall with clear reluctance. Ridge could tell his brother wanted to push harder for information on the painting's journey into her father's possession, but he wasn't about to let him badger Sarah.

His protective impulse toward her both surprised and alarmed him, but he told himself he would do the same for anybody.

The painting still held a place of honor on the credenza. He saw exactly the moment Trace caught sight of it. His brother's rugged features softened with raw emotion, and he moved to stand directly in front of it. He touched a finger to the edge of the frame as if he couldn't quite believe they had this piece of her back, after all these years.

"I remember the day Mom started this one," he said, his voice low. "We all went for a picnic up by Winder

Lake one evening. Do you remember? Taft and I were probably still single digits. You were maybe twelve. You and Dad and Taft went off fishing, but I had a stomachache and I think I was pissed at Taft for something, as usual, so I stuck with Mom and Caidy."

He paused, his fingers tracing one of the brush marks. "I watched her do a bunch of sketches of Caidy that looked just like this, only more raw. She also did a few of me, as I recall. It was always kind of a miracle to me how she could make somebody come alive on paper with only a pencil."

"She definitely had a gift. Too bad she didn't pass it down to any of us."

"I'm hoping my son will inherit it. He might only be six months old but I'm telling you, he has a great eye for color."

Ridge smiled at the obvious love in Trace's voice whenever he spoke about Will or about Gabi. It was a little odd seeing both of his brothers in these family roles, but he was exceptionally proud of the fathers they had become, probably because they had a damn good example in Frank Bowman.

It was kind of funny that both of the wild twins had settled down to become family men. Trace and his wife, Becca, had taken on responsibility for Gabi before they were married, while Taft had just a year ago formally adopted his wife Laura's two children from her first marriage, the mischievous and energetic Alex and darling little Maya.

"Caidy is going to cry buckets when she sees this. You know that, right?"

"Oh, yeah. At least two or three. I thought maybe

the three of us could give it to her for a belated wedding gift."

"That's a great idea," Trace said. "I'm sure Taft will agree."

"It's good to have it back, isn't it? Admit it."

His brother frowned. "I never said it wasn't. I'm as happy to see it again as you are. But if we knew more about how this woman's father came into possession of a hot painting, we might be a step closer to cracking the case and bringing their killers to justice. Even a tiny clue—a name, a receipt, a wire transfer—could lead us in a new direction."

Trace had never given up his quest to find the murderers. Ridge knew how important that was to his brother, partly because of the role Becca's mother played in the crime. From what little they could piece together, Trace's witch of a mother-in-law had been involved in reconnaissance for the planned art thefts that had unexpectedly turned into a double murder when the Bowmans had surprised the thieves by being home.

Unfortunately, the investigation into the crime stalled after Monica claimed she didn't know who else had been involved. Ridge knew it chafed Trace that he hadn't been able to interrogate the woman further about the crimes. Instead, he had been forced to make the difficult choice of letting Monica go free in exchange for her agreement to sign over permanent custody of Gabi to Becca.

Under the circumstances, he had to respect the decision Trace had made, choosing an innocent young girl's future happiness over his own burning desire for vengeance. He understood and probably would have made the same choice.

While he sympathized with Trace's frustration after

twelve years of dead ends, he wasn't about to let him harass Sarah in his search for those answers.

"She said she doesn't know, and I want you to leave it at that," he said firmly.

"She might know more than she's telling you. Even more than she *thinks* she knows. Sometimes it just takes the right question to bring out unexpected answers."

"Back off," he warned, his voice hard. While his younger brother might be chief of police in Pine Gulch, Ridge still considered himself in charge when it came to matters here at the ranch. And since Sarah was his guest, she was also his responsibility. "I don't want you hounding her about this, you hear me? She's a nice woman, who has done an amazingly generous thing to return the painting to us."

"Maybe it's the cop in me but I don't trust that kind of unprovoked altruism."

He snorted. "She teaches first grade, Trace. She's not some kind of a criminal mastermind. Seriously, let it go."

Trace looked as if he wanted to argue, but he finally shrugged. "You want to take things at face value, fine. I'll let it go. For now."

Ridge supposed he would have to be content with that. "So tell me what Destry and Gabi have been up to."

"Beats the hell out of me. Everybody at my house seems to be keeping secrets right now, even Gabi's ugly dog."

That made two of them, Ridge thought. Apparently there were secrets to spare right now, and he had a feeling not all of them had to do with Christmas surprises.

Sarah fought down her dismay and fear while Ridge and his brother walked out of the room.

She had no idea how to deal with a hard-looking police chief who looked at her with suspicion and mistrust.

Could she be charged with possession of stolen property? She would have to talk to the estate attorney about that.

Abruptly, anger sizzled through the panic. She was furious suddenly at her father for leaving her to clean up this mess.

She ought to just tell Ridge everything. About her father, about Joe. She didn't want to believe it, but she was becoming increasingly convinced her brother had something to do with the Bowman murders.

It couldn't be a coincidence that he died only a few hundred miles from here, just a few days after the murders. That storage unit full of paintings was further proof. Her father must have been involved somehow. The Malikov crime family had probably orchestrated the whole thing—which still made her wonder why her father had never tried to liquidate the art.

How could she tell Ridge about her family background? He would despise her if he knew even a fraction of what she came from. He would no doubt see the daughter of a Russian organized crime figure as something foreign and undesirable.

She would tell him before she left, she promised herself, when she wouldn't have to face the condemnation in his green eyes.

The deception by omission didn't sit comfortably with her, but she pushed it away. Instead, she turned to the two young girls who were watching her with wary curiosity.

"I have to tell you, that Christmas tree is just about

the prettiest one I've ever seen, Destry. Did you help decorate it?"

"Yeah. It took me and my aunt Caidy like two whole days by the time we finished hanging all the decorations. That doesn't count all the time making some and buying others."

"It's really lovely. The whole house is the perfect Christmas home."

"It is pretty cool during the holidays," Destry agreed. "We go cut our own tree up in the mountains right before Thanksgiving. And sometimes my dad hitches up the wagon to the horses, and we go for sleigh rides up and down the road singing Christmas carols."

"That sounds really wonderful."

"I'm sorry you were hurt at our house. How did you fall down the stairs?"

"I wasn't paying attention to where I was walking, I guess. As a result, I missed a step and lost my balance."

"I do that all the time," Gabi assured her. "Trace says I'm always in too big of a hurry and I need to slow down."

"That's probably very good advice. I'll try to work on that. But, really, I'm fine. I've been trying to convince your father, Destry, that I'll be okay back at the inn where I've been staying. So far I haven't had much luck."

"He can be pretty stubborn," the girl said, fully in sympathy. "I've been wanting to start wearing makeup and pierce my ears for like *ages,* and he won't listen. I think he wishes we were pioneers or Amish or something. Becca lets Gabi wear lip gloss and eye shadow. I don't know why I can't."

She didn't feel qualified to comment and decided

to head off the insurrection before it could gather any steam.

"So what's in the box?"

Destry let herself be distracted easily. "A present for my dad," she said, her features bright. "You should see it. It's going to be *awesome*."

"No doubt," she said.

"Show her," Gabi urged.

Destry appeared to hesitate.

"You don't have to show me if you don't want to," Sarah assured her.

"You can't say anything. I want him to be totally surprised."

"My lips are sealed, I swear."

Destry set the box on the sofa beside Sarah and pulled open the lid. Almost reverently, she pulled out a nearly finished throw blanket in shades of brown and green.

"Wow," she exclaimed, impressed. "You made that? Seriously?"

"My aunt Becca taught me to knit. I'm still not very good but I've been working on it for like *weeks*. Last week I realized there was no *way* I would be done in time for Christmas unless I hauled some serious butt, so that's what we've been doing. My fingers literally feel like they're going to fall off."

"He'll love it," Sarah assured her. "Especially because you went to all the trouble to make it."

"I hope so. I dropped a lot of stitches. Aunt Becca was going to show me how to finish it but the baby was being kind of cranky this weekend and she didn't have a chance."

Sarah hesitated, torn between her natural teacher instincts and desire to help and her fear that the more enmeshed she became in the Bowmans' lives, the more difficult it would be to say goodbye to them all.

If she were smart, she would ask Trace Bowman to take her back to the Cold Creek Inn, but she really didn't want to spend more time with the police chief than she absolutely had to. She could spend one more night here, she decided, then drive back herself the next morning.

"I can knit. I'm not super great, either—and now I've only got one hand—but maybe between the two of us, we can figure things out."

"Really? That would be great! Thank you!"

"No problem," she said.

Male voices suddenly heralded the return of Ridge and his brother, and the girls rushed to close the plastic bin before either could sneak a peek.

When the men returned, Sarah tensed, waiting for the police chief to recommence his interrogation. If he did, she would have to tell them all the truth far earlier than she wanted. Unlike the rest of her family, she had never been good at lies or subterfuge.

To her vast relief, Chief Bowman didn't comment again on the painting.

"The snow is starting up again so we should probably start heading back, Gabs. We don't want to be stuck out here on the ranch. I don't know about you, but I wouldn't like to feel Becca's wrath if I have to leave her alone much longer with a cranky baby."

The girl rose. "Okay. See you, Uncle Ridge. Bye, Des. Ms. Whitmore, it was nice to meet you. I'm really sorry about your arm."

"Thank you."

When the two of them left, Sarah suddenly remembered the slow cooker meal she had thrown together before she came back into the great room and fell asleep by the fireplace.

"Are you hungry?" she asked. "I made stew earlier."

"It smells delicious. You mind if I wait awhile? I should probably go try to take a look at the heater on the tractor while I've still got a little daylight. Will you two be okay in here if I head out?"

Destry gave Sarah a sidelong, secretive look. "Go ahead. We'll be just fine," she said, with just a tad too much enthusiasm in her voice.

Ridge looked a little confused but apparently decided to let it go. "Call me if you have any problems. I don't know how late I'll be so go ahead and eat without me."

"Sure," Destry said.

He headed for the kitchen. As soon as they heard the door close, she and Destry went to work.

Chapter Eight

Apparently she had led a safe, sheltered life in San Diego. She had absolutely no idea until now that snow could fall with such relentless abandon.

A few hours later, Sarah sat at the kitchen table at the River Bow, Tripod at her feet, watching Destry roll out bread sticks from dough she had mixed up herself—apparently one of the specialties she had learned from her aunt.

"I can never make them look even," Destry complained. "My aunt Caidy's really good at it but mine are always bulgy on one side, no matter how careful I am. Not that it really matters. My dad eats them anyway, bulgy or not."

Sarah smiled, though she couldn't help searching out the window for further sign of him. He had been gone a long time. Destry seemed unconcerned, but Sarah couldn't help watching for him—despite the fact that she couldn't see more than a few feet past the window.

She had certainly seen news coverage of bad storms that socked in entire states, had read about them in books. But growing up in the mild, constant climate in San Diego hadn't prepared her at all for the raw ferocity of a heavy low-pressure system. What had always seemed a rather abstract concept to her was quickly becoming cold, blowing reality that went on and on.

She wouldn't be going back to town that evening, and possibly not the next.

She knew that should probably upset her but despite her worry for Ridge she had enjoyed the afternoon in the cozy, warm ranch house immensely.

With a fire merrily burning in the great-room hearth, she and Destry had worked together to finish the knitted throw. Sarah was far from an expert, but she had enjoyed teaching the girl. The result was a beautiful blanket that she knew Ridge would cherish, especially knowing his daughter had worked so hard on it.

"We just need to let these rise for a half hour and then we can throw them in the oven," Destry said.

"They look absolutely beautiful. I can't wait to try them."

The girl grinned at her and set the jelly roll pan of bread sticks on the countertop.

"Hey, you want some hot cocoa? My aunt Caidy has like twenty different mixes, and I think she left most of them. Mint chocolate, orange chocolate, caramel chocolate. Whatever you want. She orders them from some fancy gourmet coffee place in Jackson Hole."

"Which one is best?"

"They're all good but I think raspberry is my favorite."

"Sure. Raspberry sounds great. Can I help?"

Destry made a face. "No. If I were making it the hard way, with fresh cream and shaved chocolate and stuff, I might need help, but this is super easy. All you have to do is heat up the water in the microwave, add the mix and you're set."

The hard way sounded absolutely divine, and she vowed to get the recipe from Destry before she returned to San Diego, but right now raspberry cocoa from a mix would be great. She rose to grab four ibuprofen for her aching arm from the bottle by the sink, poured a glass of water and swallowed just as a particularly hard gust of wind hurled flakes against the window and rattled the glass.

She shivered. "Will your dad be okay out there?"

Destry followed her gaze out the window at the swirling, unceasing snow. "He's a rancher. He's used to bad weather. It's part of the life," she said simply.

Sarah considered that quite an insight from a girl who was not yet twelve. "Will he be able to come in for dinner?"

Destry nodded. "Oh, I'm sure he'll come in soon to eat. He usually does. Sometimes he goes back out after dinner, but with this much snow, he might call it a night and start again first thing in the morning."

Their lifestyle was as foreign to Sarah as a Kabuki dancer's but she found a rhythm and peace in it that called to her.

"Do you like growing up on a ranch?" she asked Destry.

Destry furrowed her brow as if she'd never considered the question before. "Sure I do. I mean, what's not to like? I've been riding horses since I was three. I have my own and everything. I love going on roundup in the fall and spring and there are always new puppies and kittens to play with in the barn. It's hard to be bored when we always have things to do."

This very competent, very mature-for-her-age girl set a mug of cocoa in front of Sarah. "I mean, yeah, it might be cool to have a mall closer than Idaho Falls and something bigger than the one there. I'd also like to maybe be able to go to the beach sometime, you know? But I wouldn't trade it here for anything."

Sarah sipped at the delicious cocoa, trying to will away her sharp envy of the girl. She knew adults who weren't as comfortable with their world as this winsome young woman.

"Besides," Destry went on, "I have the *best* family. My dad is like the coolest dad *anywhere*. He's awesome, don't you think?"

Suddenly, she couldn't think about anything else but that moment when he had almost kissed her, right here at the kitchen table. "Yes. Awesome," she murmured, blaming the sudden heat of her cheeks on the steam from the cocoa.

Destry stirred her own mug of cocoa before sliding it onto the table and sitting down across from Sarah. "When I was a little kid, I used to be kind of sad about not having a mom like my friends did. I mean, I had Aunt Caidy and she was great and loved me and took care of me and stuff, but, you know, sometimes you still kind of feel like something's missing, right?"

Sympathy washed over her for this charming girl with the green eyes, freckles and huge capacity for love. "Yes. I completely understand," she said. "My parents divorced when I was small. I never really knew my father other than the occasional weekend."

"I didn't even have that. My mom just took off and then she died. We didn't know that until a while ago. I thought she just didn't want me and left."

"Oh, honey. I'm sure that's not true."

"My aunt Caidy thinks she would have come back eventually if she hadn't died. Who knows?" She sipped at her hot cocoa. "I don't think she was a very nice person. I can tell my aunt Caidy didn't like her. My dad doesn't talk about her at all."

Had Ridge's heart been broken by his ex-wife? she wondered. It wasn't a question she could ask the man's daughter.

"I hope I'm not like her," Destry said, for the first time showing a glimmer of insecurity that broke Sarah's heart.

"There's something else we have in common," she said quietly. "My father wasn't very nice, either. It's taken me a long time to see this, but I'm slowly coming to realize I can't let his decisions and weaknesses define me."

The truth resonated through her. Whatever her father or Joe might have done, none of it was her fault. She knew it, but she was no more eager to share her background or her suspicions with Ridge than she had been.

Destry sipped at her cocoa, swishing a mouthful around in her mouth as if she were testing fine wine.

"Do you want to know something funny? I used to feel really awful sometimes about her leaving, like, I don't know, I wasn't good enough for her to love me enough to stay or something."

Again, her heart was pierced by both the admission

and Destry's willingness to share it. "Oh, honey. You know that's not true, right?"

"Yeah. I do. Her leaving was about her, not me. And I know I could have had things a whole lot worse. Gabi lived with her mom for ten years, and it was a *nightmare*. She's a lot better off since her mom left her with Becca and Uncle Trace. And if she hadn't, Gabi wouldn't be my best friend and part of our family now."

"That's a good way to look at it."

"And I'm lucky, really. I might not have had a mom, but I've always had my dad and Aunt Caidy, which is more than a lot of kids."

She smiled, already crazy about Ridge's daughter. "You're an amazing young woman, Destry. Your family members are the ones who are lucky to have *you*."

Destry grinned. "I guess we're one big, lucky, happy family then, aren't we?"

They were, while Sarah would be returning to her mostly solitary life. She tried not to let that depress her.

"Thanks again for your help today," Destry said. "I never would have been able to finish by Christmas. I can see why you're a teacher. You're really good at it."

"That's the best compliment I've had in a long time. Thank you."

Destry glanced at the clock. "I think the bread sticks have risen enough. Should I put them in or wait for Dad?"

"You would know that better than I do."

"I think I'll throw them in," she decided. "He'll probably come in the minute I pull them out of the oven. Somehow he always seems to know when dinner's ready."

Sure enough, the timer on the oven had only two minutes to go when the back door opened.

Destry giggled. "See? Told you."

A few moments later, Ridge entered the kitchen in stocking feet, bringing the scent of cold with him. His cheeks were rosy and wind-chapped, and she wanted to wrap him in that knitted blanket his daughter made for him and tuck him in by the fire.

"Man, are those bread sticks I smell?"

Destry nodded. "Yep. They're just about done. You've got perfect timing, as usual."

"You truly are the best daughter in the world."

He leaned in and kissed her cheek, and she shrieked. "Ack! You're like a block of ice! Even your eyelashes are frozen!"

"It's shaping up to be a bitter storm out there." He crossed to the sink and turned on the warm water to wash his hands.

"Were you able to get the heater working on the tractor?" Sarah asked him.

"It's not a hundred percent, but at least it's not blowing cold air. How's the arm?"

"It's actually feeling better."

"And the head?"

"Same story. I really think I would be fine on my own."

"Sorry, but I'm afraid we're not going anywhere this evening unless I hitch up a sleigh or drive you in on a snowmobile, neither of which would be very pleasant with that wind and blowing snow."

"Sleepover!" Destry exclaimed. "After dinner, we can roast marshmallows on the fire and have popcorn and watch a Christmas movie in our pajamas."

That idea actually sounded quite appealing while the storm howled and moaned around them. She had to admit, Destry's presence at the ranch left her feeling much less trapped.

"You Bowmans are nothing if not persistent," she said with a laugh.

Ridge smiled at her, and she was happy to see his cold-flushed cheeks already beginning to fade back to their normal tanned shade.

He really was extraordinarily good-looking, with those long eyelashes and the grooves beside his cheeks that she would never dare call dimples.

She found herself fascinated with that firm jawline, the mobile mouth. When she lifted her gaze to his, she found him watching her with an expression she could only call *hungry*. She shivered and looked away.

"Dinner is just about ready, but you still have time to take a shower and warm up the rest of the way." His daughter sounded like a little bustling mother hen, which made Sarah smile.

"I just might do that. Thanks, darlin'." He kissed Destry on the top of her head, gave Sarah a smile and headed out of the kitchen, leaving her head filled with all kinds of inappropriate images. Steamy water. Bare skin. Hard muscles. She took a hurried sip of her hot chocolate, which did absolutely nothing to cool her suddenly over-active imagination.

He couldn't remember an evening he had enjoyed more.

First they had the delicious slow-cooker stew along with hot, crusty bread sticks dripping with parmesan cheese. Dessert was ice cream and a few of the leftover goodies from the wedding.

While the storm howled like a kid having a tantrum, hurling snow at the windows and generally being a whiny, annoying pain in the ass, he and Destry and Sarah—and Ben Caldwell's funny little dog—sat in the cozy family room of River Bow with a fire flickering merrily away in the woodstove, watching Des's favorite Christmas movie, *Elf*.

He had always been partial to *Miracle on 34th Street* or *It's a Wonderful Life* himself—or Ralphie's BB gun travails in *A Christmas Story*, when he was in the mood for a good laugh. But Destry insisted that only *Elf* would do, even though she had watched the movie already at least three times that holiday season.

He didn't care. Right now, he was just happy to be out of the cold with a bowl of popcorn and a couple of pretty females to enjoy the movie with. He settled in to watch the silly but sweet fish-out-of-water movie about an overgrown elf trying to bring a little Christmas spirit to his grinch of a father amid the hustle-bustle of New York City. As always, he had to smile at the way Destry repeated all her favorite lines and laughed in all the same places.

He did his best, but he also couldn't seem to stop sneaking little looks at Sarah all evening. She sat beside his daughter on the sofa, her casted arm propped up on a pillow. When she smiled at the movie, he felt as if a warm sunbeam had just shot right through the window to rest on his shoulders.

He was aware of a sneaky, unexpected feeling of contentment. Winter nights were made for moments like this—the cozy, warm peace of being safe and dry and comfortable while the elements howled and raged outside.

He was one hell of a lucky man.

Their guest fell asleep about two-thirds through the movie, her head back against the sofa cushions and her mouth open just a bit. Poor thing. He wondered if she had had a chance to nap while he had been outside shoveling snow and preparing for the next onslaught. He doubted it. Judging by their animated conversation at dinnertime, Des probably yakked her ears off all day.

The two of them seemed to get along well. Maybe it was the educator in Sarah, but she treated Destry with respect, and his daughter seemed to thrive at the genuine interest she showed.

He would have to remember to thank her for temporarily helping to fill the gap left when Caidy got married. He had a feeling his daughter would miss her aunt—really, her surrogate mother—more than she wanted to admit.

It wasn't as if Caidy was going far, he reminded himself. She and Ben had a house just a few miles away with Ben's two children from his previous marriage and he expected Des would spend as much time there as she did here.

His sister loved his daughter deeply and would always be part of their lives, but Ridge knew this new phase of life for Caidy would be difficult for his daughter.

At least with the distraction of Sarah's company, Destry might be able to make it through the holidays with minimal emotional trauma—until their guest also left the River Bow and took her sweet smile back home to San Diego, anyway.

He didn't want to think about that tonight, especially

when the idea of her leaving left him with a hollow ache in his gut he had no business entertaining.

The closing credits to the movie started to play, and Destry sat up and stretched her arms above her head.

"I just love that one, don't you?" Destry asked the room in general.

Ridge pressed a finger to his lips and pointed to their guest, curled up beside her with her eyes closed.

"Oops," Des whispered with a wince. "Sorry. I didn't know she was asleep."

"She's had a couple of long days," he murmured. "This all has to be pretty unsettling for her, finding herself injured among strangers."

Destry looked thoughtful as she picked up the empty popcorn bowls and drink glasses and carried them into the kitchen. He followed after her.

"I really like her, Dad. She's super nice. We had a lot of fun today while you were out shoveling."

"Thanks again for fixing dinner. It was nice not to have to think of something to make."

"Sarah did the stew. I only made the bread sticks to go with it."

"Either way. Thanks." He glanced at the clock in the kitchen. "Wow, I didn't realize it was so late. You need to head to bed, too."

She made a face. "It's only ten-thirty, and I don't have school tomorrow."

"No, but I'll probably need your help clearing the sidewalk here and maybe at the Turners and Hansens," he said, naming the older neighbors on either side of the ranch who had trouble taking care of their own walks. Destry was a whiz with a snow shovel and she usually enjoyed it.

"Okay," she said promptly. "Hey, since it's Christmas Eve tomorrow, could we go for a sleigh ride later in the day, if the snow clears?"

"We already took all your girlfriends last weekend. You really want another one?"

"Just us and Sarah. She would like it, don't you think?"

He pictured her out in the sleigh with her nose pink from the cold and her eyes sparkling. "We might be able to arrange that. I'll see what condition the sleigh is in."

Usually when he took Destry and her friends, he used a wheeled hay wagon on plowed roads. It held more bodies and was easier on the horses. He hadn't used the smaller sleigh with runners in a few years. She would probably love it.

"Yay. Thanks!" She padded over to him in her silly little fluffy Rudolph slippers and hugged him.

At almost twelve, she was growing up so much, becoming a young lady right in front of his eyes. Before he knew it, she would be in high school, and all the boys would start flocking around her like cattle around the hay truck.

"Should I wake Sarah?" she asked.

"She looks pretty comfortable there by the fire. Let her sleep. I'm going to throw on my gear to take one last look around the ranch for the night to make sure everything is tight and secure in this wind. I'll wake her when I come back inside."

"Okay. Good night, Dad."

She started for the stairs with Tripod in her arms. Seeing her right about where Sarah had landed reminded him of something.

"Hey, I keep meaning to ask you. How would you

feel if Sarah spent the holidays with us? She doesn't have anybody else, and I feel bad thinking about her spending Christmas alone in the hotel, especially with a broken arm."

Destry smiled. "I think it would be great. I like her a lot. She's really nice."

He liked her, too. Perhaps a little too much.

"I'm trying to convince her, but she seems to think she'll impose. Maybe you can help me try to persuade her we have tons of space and would love the company. For most of the holidays, it would just be the three of us—at least until dinner at Taft's place on Christmas Day, and I know Laura won't mind setting out another plate."

"I'll try to convince her. It would be really fun to have her stay and I know *I* wouldn't want to be alone at Christmas."

"Whoever would you talk to, if you were by yourself?" he teased.

"Ha-ha." She made a face. "Good night, Dad. Love you."

"Love you right back."

He watched her pad all the way up the stairs in her silly festive slippers before he headed back to the mudroom for his winter gear again.

What he thought would be a quick fifteen-minute trip outside to make sure all hatches were battened down turned into an hour when he had to scramble to nail a couple of boards over a barn window that had shattered from a falling tree branch.

The welcome warmth of the house and the lingering scent of the apple-wood fire and their movie popcorn greeted him when he walked back inside, his bones aching from the cold and the twenty-hour day.

He loved the River Bow and had never wanted to be anything but a rancher like his father, but these sorts of days were long and hard—and, unfortunately, far from unusual.

He couldn't complain. He was doing exactly what he wanted with his life, something few people could claim. He was damn proud of what he had accomplished with the River Bow in the past twelve years. The ranch had always been prosperous—a rare feat in the transitory agricultural economy—but his father had been traditional, even a little staid, in his practices.

Through a few innovative changes, Ridge had managed to double the size of the herd while tripling the profit.

For all intents and purposes, the ranch was his. His brothers and Caidy loved the River Bow, but none of them was much interested in running it. Before she met Ben the year before and started taking online classes to become a veterinary tech, Caidy had trained horses and dogs and helped out where she was needed, but it had never been her passion.

He bore all responsibility for success or failure—and that was exactly how he liked it, even if it meant long, tough days like this one.

Yawning, he walked into the family room and found Sarah still sleeping there, though at some point in the past hour she had stretched out on the sofa and pulled a blanket over herself.

He gazed at her, lovely and serene in the flickering firelight through the woodstove glass and the multicolored glow from the little Christmas tree Caidy put up in this room.

For one crazy moment, he was overwhelmed with an odd feeling of *rightness* as he looked at her, as if she belonged exactly here.

Whoa. Slow down, he thought, more than a little disturbed at the direction of his thoughts. There was nothing *right* about Sarah Whitmore being on the River Bow. She didn't belong here, any more than Melinda had. She was a guest for only a few days, that was all, and he needed to remember that.

Her presence here was transient, just someone who would be drifting out of their lives as soon as she was up to it.

Yeah, he was fiercely attracted to her. Every time he looked at her, he had a funny little ache in his gut, the same feeling he had whenever he looked at a piece of his mom's art that particularly moved him.

He hadn't been looking for it and he didn't fully understand how he could be so quickly and completely drawn to a woman he still didn't know well. But there it was. He had it bad for her, and each moment they spent together only ratcheted up his aching hunger.

She wasn't for him, he reminded himself again. He needed to keep that clear in his head, no matter what kind of nonsense his gut—and other parts—tried to persuade him about.

With that in mind, he moved closer to the sofa. He hated to disturb her, but she would be far more comfortable in a bed where she could position that arm correctly.

"Sarah. Wake up."

Her eyelids flickered at his soft words, but she gave a delicate little sniff and closed them again. He was seriously tempted to lift her up and carry her to the bedroom like he used to do with Destry when she was small, but he had a feeling that wouldn't earn him any points with his houseguest.

"Sarah," he tried again. "It's late. Come on, wake up. Just for a minute. I'm sure it's cozy in here, but that fire's going to burn out soon and you'll be freezing. I promise you'll be better off in a bed."

"Tired," she muttered, her eyes still stubbornly closed.

He smiled at how very much she sound like Destry just now. Not knowing what else to do, he crouched down on a level with her. "Come on. Wake up. Let's get you to bed."

Unable to resist the beckoning appeal of that silky skin, he touched her cheek lightly with the back of his fingers. Her lashes fluttered once then twice and finally those blue-gray eyes opened.

She gazed at him, sleepy and disoriented. He knew the instant she recognized him. Her lips parted slightly, as if on a breath, and her eyes softened.

"Ridge. Hi." She spoke the words with a sweetness and welcome that stunned him, and for an instant, his emotions soared with such happiness he just wanted to crouch here beside the sofa and soak it in.

The impulse left him startled, even a little bit shaky.

"What time is it?" she asked, her voice a sexy rasp that shivered down his spine as if she'd trailed her fingertips there.

"Heading toward midnight," he answered, his own voice gruff. "Des went to bed more than an hour ago."

She sat up and rubbed at her neck. "Oh! I guess that means I missed the end of the movie."

"Yeah. I wouldn't worry about that at all. Destry will probably watch it all over again with you tomorrow if you want to catch the part you missed. She won't mind a bit, trust me."

She laughed a little and stretched out the arm not in a cast over her head. He had a tough time reminding himself to breathe.

"Come on. I'll take you to bed. Er, *help* you to bed."

He stumbled over the slip, hoping she didn't notice. Her sudden soft, very attractive blush indicated otherwise.

"You don't have to," she assured him. "I'm quite certain I can find my way the twenty feet to your sister's bedroom."

He managed a smile, when what he really wanted to do was press her back against those sofa cushions.

"Humor me. I just want to make sure you're not too wobbly, with that concussion."

She sighed and stood up. "Okay, fine. You can babysit me all the way to the bedroom, if that will make you feel better."

Yeah, he knew exactly what would make him feel better—and a bedroom was definitely involved.

He ground his back teeth, trying his best to force those all-too-appealing images out of his head, and followed her down the hall.

"You look cold," she said. "Have you been outside again in that weather?"

Okay. Good. Something safe to discuss. The intense blizzard was a great topic of conversation guaranteed to cool down his feverish thoughts. "Yeah. I went out to give things one last check before heading to bed myself. It was a good thing I did. A tree limb had knocked out a window in the barn. It took me a few minutes to patch over it."

"It's still snowing?" she asked, incredulity in her tone.

"I'm afraid so," he answered. "We're probably up to two feet by now. I sure do hope people had their Christmas shopping done already because I think most of Pine Gulch will be socked in for the next few days."

He opened her door. "Do you need anything? A glass of water? Midnight snack? More painkillers?"

"I should be fine, especially since your brother brought my clothes."

"Good. That's good." Her skin had to be the softest he'd ever seen on a woman, all creamy hollows and curves that begged for a man's mouth to explore....

"Um, good night, I guess," she said, her voice throaty again.

"Good night."

He gazed down at her, all sleepy, warm woman, and that sultry connection tugged between them.

He angled his head down without really even being aware of it just as she tilted her face up in an invitation he couldn't refuse.

Just one kiss, he told himself, only an experiment to discover if she could possibly taste as delicious as she looked.

His mouth brushed hers once, twice, tasting chocolate and buttery popcorn and Sarah. She didn't move for a long moment, and he was suddenly afraid he'd forgotten how to do this, but then she gave a tiny, sexy little sound and kissed him back.

She couldn't quite wrap her head around the idea that she was really here, kissing Ridge Bowman.

His skin was cool against hers—no wonder, since he had spent most of the day out in the harsh elements, poor man. She wanted to share her warmth with him, to tuck him against her until he absorbed some of her heat.

Any trace of sleepiness had long since disappeared, lost in the sheer wonder of the moment.

She was quite certain she had never been kissed like this, as if he couldn't get enough, as if he had spent a lifetime preparing for the moment their mouths would finally meet.

She wanted to savor every instant, every taste.

"I've been thinking about kissing you all day," he said, the gruff words vibrating through to her core.

"Have you?" she managed. It was a very good thing his arms around her were tough as steel or she probably would have dissolved to the floor in a quivering pile of hormones.

Even as passion flared between them, hot and bright, the tiny corner of her mind that could still string together a coherent thought was touched by the care he took not to jostle her broken arm.

"You're just about the sweetest thing I've ever seen. I can't get you out of my head. Crazy, isn't it?"

"Oh, yes." She didn't know if her breathy response was an agreement or simply a plea that he kiss her again just like that, right there at the corner of her mouth, that he wrap all those hard muscles around her and never let go....

He must have instinctively understood. They kissed for a long time, there in his cozy family room with the little Christmas tree glowing merrily in the corner. This felt so good, so right, she didn't ever want to stop.

Eventually, though, reality began to seep through the

wonder of Ridge's arms. This wasn't real. It was as fragile and insubstantial as silvery tinsel. Yes, he might be
attracted to her right now, but that couldn't possibly last
when he found out about her family.

Letting this continue was vastly unfair to him until
she could find the courage to admit the truth. They stood
on either side of a vast, unbreachable gulf…and she was
too much of a coward to even point it out to him.

Despising herself, she gathered the last ounce of
strength she had and eased away from him. "I… It's
late. We should probably both get some sleep."

For just a moment he froze, his expression still fierce
and hungry, then he drew in a breath, his features closing as if he had slammed a door.

"Yeah. It's been a long day."

His voice was stiffly polite, and she gave an inward
cringe, aware he thought she was rejecting him and
hadn't wanted him to kiss her.

How could she tell him otherwise without telling him
everything else?

She couldn't tell him she had never wanted anything
in her life so much as she had wanted to stand here in
the warm, cozy hallway and continue kissing this hard
rancher whose slow smile turned her insides to soft,
gooey taffy and who treated his daughter with such
kindness.

If she said any of that, he would ask why she had
stopped things—and she would have to tell him.

"Get some rest," he said. "I'll try not to wake you
when I head out early in the morning. I'll leave a note reminding Destry to keep things down in the kitchen, too."

"Thank you," she answered, not knowing what else
to say.

He seemed like a remote, distant stranger now, instead of the intense, passionate man who had kissed her as if he couldn't get enough.

She slipped into his sister's bedroom and closed the door carefully behind her. She waited, heart pounding, for him to walk away. It was another full moment before she heard his footsteps finally recede down the hall.

So he kissed her, Ridge thought as he banked the fire in the woodstove, then did the same in the great room before double-checking the locks and security system.

She was a lovely, unattached woman. He was a healthy male who hadn't been with a woman in entirely too long. Sharing a passionate kiss with her wasn't the end of the world, for crying out loud.

He was taking this rejection harder than he should. He had every reason to be decent about it. Sarah was a guest in his house. Beyond that, she was giving his family a gift of inexpressible worth. He could be polite, friendly, even warm to her, despite his disappointment and, okay, pissed-off attitude.

She hadn't asked him to kiss her. He had taken the initiative all on his own. While she had certainly kissed him back with undeniable enthusiasm—he hadn't been without a woman that long that he didn't recognize a genuine response when it licked his tongue—he still had no business being upset when she erected barriers between them again.

While his bruised ego would like to help her pack up her suitcase and drive her back to the Cold Creek Inn for Christmas, he knew he couldn't do that. He was a big boy. He could handle a little rejection.

He would rather have a little awkwardness between

them than the buckets of guilt he would have to carry around, thinking about her spending the holidays by herself in a hotel room simply because he had his boxers in a twist.

The last thing he did to shut the house down for the night was flip the switch to turn off all the Christmas lights.

He tried not to notice how the house seemed instantly colder—or how that chill suddenly matched his mood.

Chapter Nine

"I've never seen so much snow," Sarah exclaimed on Christmas Eve morning. It created a vast white sea—wave after wave, engulfing fence lines, shrubs, anything in its path. Across the way, snow had piled clear to the eaves of an outbuilding.

"The snowdrifts make it look a lot worse than it is," Destry said, with far more experience than an eleven-year-old girl ought to have.

"Do you think your father is okay out there?"

Destry looked surprised at the question, as if it had never occurred to her before. "Sure. Why wouldn't he be?"

Sarah could think of a dozen reasons. Frostbite. A fall from the tractor. A sudden howling avalanche. She shivered, not wanting to think about any of them.

"You must not have blizzards in San Diego," Destry guessed.

Sarah gave a rough laugh. "No. It's never snowed there in my memory, and I've been there since I was just a little girl. I think I read once it's snowed like five times in a hundred-fifty years. If we get more than a half inch of rain in twenty-four hours, people go into full-fledged panic mode."

"I love big storms like this, especially at Christmas," Destry said, expertly flipping a pancake just right.

The girl was amazing. Sarah knew fellow teachers who weren't as self-sufficient in the kitchen as this eleven-year-old girl.

"Why is that?" she asked.

"Seems like my dad takes a little more time to have fun, you know? We go sledding and ride the snowmobiles and have snowball fights. I like it when he can relax a little more."

Her expression grew a little sad. "Of course, this year won't be quite the same without Aunt Caidy. She and Ben won't be back until after New Year's Day."

"You'll still have a great Christmas. I'm sure of it." Sarah tried for a cheerful tone.

"Yeah. You're probably right. It's going to be different, that's all. We always spend Christmas Eve with just us and then we'll get together with the cousins for lunch tomorrow on Christmas. You'll like everybody, I promise. You already met Gabi and Trace, yesterday."

She nodded. "And Taft. He was one of the paramedics who took me to the hospital after my fall."

"Oh, yeah. Well, Becca and Laura are super nice and they have the *cutest* kids ever. Alex and Maya are Taft and Laura's two. Alex can be a little stinker but even when he drives everybody crazy, we can't help smiling at him. That's just the way he is. And Maya is so sweet.

She has Down syndrome, but that doesn't stop her chasing after Alex for a second."

"They sound adorable."

"They are. And then Trace and Becca had a baby earlier this year. William Frank, after my grandpa. Little Will. He has these big fat cheeks you just want to smooch all over. We all fight to hold him."

It sounded wonderful and warm and perfect. She fought down an aching wave of envy for this girl who knew exactly where she fit into the world, who was surrounded by people who cared about her.

Sarah didn't quite know how to break the news to Destry that she wouldn't be meeting any little fat-cheeked babies or cute little pesky cousins.

She had made up her mind sometime during the night that she would ask Ridge to dig out her rental car so she could return to the inn. The snow had stopped during the night and now the sun was shining. Though the snow seemed impenetrable, she imagined the plows would have a path cleared to town. If she drove slowly, she should be able to make it.

She would just have to be insistent, and if that failed, maybe she could find a taxi or something. At this point, she was even willing to walk.

She had practiced a dozen different arguments through the long, sleepless night.

While she didn't *really* want to leave this warm, comfortable house, she knew it would be for the best.

Yes, she felt an odd sense of belonging here at the River Bow, but she knew it was only an illusion. She could make believe otherwise but that didn't change the cold, hard reality. She was an interloper at the Bowmans' family Christmas and if they knew the truth about her background, none of them would want her anywhere near their adorable children, their holiday traditions.

That was enough of a reason for her to want to leave. Throw in the inevitable awkwardness between her and Ridge she didn't see how to avoid and she had even more incentive to return to Pine Gulch.

"Here you go. Buttermilk pancakes with homemade chokecherry syrup." Destry slid the pancakes onto a serving platter and pulled a little glass pitcher full of ruby-red syrup out of the microwave.

"We pick the chokecherries every year along the river and Caidy and I make jam and syrup. I guess we'll probably do that at her new house now with Ava and Jack. Those are Ben's kids from his first marriage. They're awesome, too, but I didn't tell you about them since I knew they wouldn't be there. They went with Caidy and Ben on their honeymoon."

"They took his children on their honeymoon?"

"And Mrs. Michaels, their housekeeper. They went to Hawaii. Ben and Caidy didn't want to spend Christmas without the kids, so they all went together, then Mrs. Michaels is bringing Ava and Jack back here while Caidy and Ben go to another island. Kauai, I think. I don't know, I've never been to Hawaii. Have you?"

"I went in college with some girlfriends," she said. She and Nicki and a couple of other friends had spent four days crowded into a tiny hotel room on Waikiki. It had been crazy and chaotic—not to mention expensive!—but she had great memories of the trip.

"It's all beautiful," she said. "I'm sure they'll have a great time."

"I guess. Ava was excited to go shopping. But that's Ava."

The Bowmans had this big, wonderful family, filled with interesting personalities. Under other circumstances, she very much would have enjoyed the chance to spend time with them all.

Some things weren't meant to be.

She and Destry were finishing up their pancakes when they heard footsteps coming up the back stairs and the outside door to the mudroom opening.

"That's Dad. I'd better cook a couple more pancakes. He likes his hot."

Destry jumped up while Sarah fought the urge to press a hand to her trembling insides.

A moment later, he came in wearing a green long-sleeve T-shirt and a pair of faded jeans that hung low on lean hips. He must have hurried out without shaving since a day's dark growth shadowed his lower face and made him look appealingly shaggy and disreputable.

"Hey, Dad! I didn't think you'd be in until lunchtime. Are you done?"

He smiled at his daughter—and while the smile might have encompassed her, it wasn't quite as warm as it might have been the day before.

"No. I finished our place and figured that was a good point for a break. I came in for more coffee and to see if you're ready to suit up and help me dig out the neighbors."

"Sure!" she said, with an eagerness that Sarah found amazing in a young girl. "Do you want a pancake or two and some sausage first?"

"Do you even need to ask?" he countered.

Destry laughed and poured more pancake batter onto the still-sizzling griddle. Sarah could only imagine how much fuel it took to power all day long through a physical job like ranching.

"I almost forgot! Merry Christmas Eve," he said to his daughter.

She grinned as she flipped his pancakes. "That's just what I was going to say. I think I like Christmas Eve better than Christmas. I'm always so excited, all day long. Today we're going on a sleigh ride, right?"

"You're relentless, my dear. I haven't had time to look at the sleigh but I'm still going to see what I can do, I promise. *After* we clear snow."

"I know. Work hard, then you can play hard. You tell me that like every single day."

"So I should get to say it twice on Christmas Eve."

She snorted and scooped the pancakes onto a plate for him. "There you go."

He smiled at her with warmth and affection as she turned off the griddle.

"I need to go put on my long underwear," Destry said.

"You can finish your breakfast first. I'm not going to take off without you."

"I'm *stuffed,*" she said. "I had, like, four pancakes and three pieces of sausage. I'm going to be lucky to *fit* in my long johns. Anyway, I want to get the work done so we can hurry to the fun part."

She took a long drink of her milk, wiped her mouth with her napkin then barreled out of the kitchen.

The moment she left, taking all her energy and sweetness with her, an awkward silence descended on Sarah and Ridge.

This was the first she had seen him since that stunning kiss, and she didn't know what to say, where to look.

"Um, have you had a chance to dig out my rental car yet?"

He paused, mug of coffee halfway to his mouth. "Yeah. It's clear. You going somewhere?"

She realized she was fidgeting with her napkin and forced her hands to stop. "The sky is blue, with no more snow in sight for now. I imagine the roads should be clear by this afternoon. I can't see any reason not to return to the inn for the rest of my stay, can you?"

He set the mug down carefully, giving her a searching look. She could feel heat soaking her cheeks and really hoped she wasn't blushing.

"I thought we had you convinced to stay."

"It was a lovely offer and, believe me, I appreciate it. It's just…it's Christmas Eve. A time for families. I'm intruding, Ridge. You have been more than welcoming, but I can't help feeling like I don't belong in the middle of your Christmas celebrations. I had fully intended to spend the holidays on my own. I don't mind. I would be more comfortable back at the inn."

As far as lies went, that was a pretty big one. The idea of spending Christmas by herself, staring at the walls of a hotel room—no matter how warmly decorated—left her feeling bleak and achy from more than her lingering headache and broken arm.

The contrast between that image and the loud, chaotic, *wonderful* Christmas she imagined with the Bowman family was starkly vivid.

But what other choice did she have?

"Is this about what happened last night?" he asked after a long moment.

She flushed. "Are you accusing me of running away?"

"What else would you call it?" he countered.

She rested her hand on her lap, unable to meet his gaze. "Put yourself in my place, would you? Suddenly thrust into the lives of strangers by accident and your own stupidity. You and Destry already had Christmas plans before I showed up, and I've complicated everything. I think the best thing all around would be for me to return to town and leave you to your plans."

A muscle flexed in his jaw, and his chair squeaked a little as he shifted. "And the fact that we shared a pretty hot kiss just a few hours ago has absolutely nothing to do with your sudden eagerness to rush back to the inn?"

The memory of that *pretty hot kiss* flamed through her memory, fierce and bright as a flash fire. She had been up half the night reliving that kiss, his mouth hard and demanding, his fingers tracing patterns on her skin, those strong arms making her feel safe and cherished.

She didn't realize she was gazing at his mouth until his lips parted and he drew in a sharp breath. She jerked her gaze back to her hands.

"Okay, yes," she admitted. "I felt uncomfortable enough before, knowing I had intruded. Now things are even more…awkward."

He sighed heavily. "I'm sorry for that. I take full responsibility, Sarah. I shouldn't have kissed you. You're a guest in my home—and were injured here, to boot. I overstepped and I'm sorry. You shouldn't feel any awkwardness in the least—it's all on me."

"I didn't exactly push you away," she murmured.

Something bright as sunlight sparkling on snow flashed in his eyes. "No. You didn't."

That blasted color flared again, and she knew she must be as bright as one of the shiny glass ornaments on the tree. "I'm sure you agree it would be better for both of us if I returned to the inn."

"Maybe for you and me. But what about Destry?"

She frowned. "What *about* Destry?"

"This is her first Christmas without her aunt here. Her feelings are already tender. She likes you and considers you a friend. The two of you seemed to really hit it off, or am I imagining things?"

"No. She's…she's a wonderful young woman. You've done a great job as her father."

"I can't take much credit. Part of it was just the way she came and my family helped with the rest, but thank you. Our first Christmas without Caidy here is going to hit her hard. If you take off, too, who knows? She might feel abandoned all over again, poor thing. I'm sure you don't want that."

She narrowed her gaze. "You do *not* fight fair, Ridge Bowman."

He grinned suddenly and unexpectedly, looking years younger. "Whoever told you I did? Not my brothers, I'm sure."

She sighed, accepting defeat. While she was sure he was exaggerating his daughter's likely reaction to her leaving, she accepted that the girl missed her aunt in a hundred different little ways. The holidays might, indeed, be a bit of a struggle for her. If Sarah could help distract her for the next few days, how could she walk away?

"Fine. I'll stay a few more days, for Destry's sake. That's the only reason."

"Understood."

And no more kissing, she wanted to say, but she didn't have the courage.

Before she could change her mind or ask herself how she would endure even a few more hours with the two of them when they were already sneaking into her heart, Destry returned to the kitchen, bundled in snow pants, parka, hat, scarf and thick gloves.

"Okay. I'm ready," she declared. "Let's do this quick, before I have to go to the bathroom or something."

"Whew. Good thing I just finished my breakfast since apparently we're on the clock." Ridge set aside his napkin and slid his chair back.

"Will you be okay in here by yourself?" he asked Sarah. "We shouldn't be longer than an hour or so, since I did most of the hard stuff yesterday."

"Sure. I've got Tri to keep me company."

The dog yipped at his name, and Destry and Ridge both smiled.

"Don't worry about breakfast cleanup. Tri and I will take care of it, won't we, boy?"

The dog gave her a *speak-for-yourself* kind of look, as if to indicate he wasn't budging from the warm patch of sunlight on the floor.

"Just leave it," Ridge said. "We'll clean it up when we get back."

She didn't answer, just pointedly picked up her plate and started to scrape it into the kitchen garbage can.

"I mean it, Sarah. Go put your feet up or something."

"You'd better hurry. Those driveways aren't going to shovel themselves."

He gave her a long look, shook his head and then threw on his coat. She heard their murmured voices in the mudroom for a minute then watched out the window as he helped Destry hop up into the cab of the big tractor before following her and closing the door.

* * *

It charmed her more than it should, father and daughter heading out into the cold to help their neighbors together. She loved seeing it.

She thought of the little she knew of her own father from those carefully orchestrated visits. She couldn't imagine two men more different than Ridge and Vasily.

First of all, her father wouldn't have lifted a finger to help a neighbor. Not unless he were trying to steal the tractor right out from under them. Second, even if, by some wild stretch of imagination, he did have a tiny helpful bone in his body, he wouldn't have bothered to include his daughter in his efforts.

He had always treated her and Josef differently. As a young girl, she had grieved that she couldn't be what her father wanted. As the years passed and she realized Vasily was training Joey to follow in his footsteps, she could only be grateful her father had always seen her as lacking.

She pushed away the grim memories as she wiped down the countertops with a rag and dish soap that smelled like warm, juicy pomegranates.

It was Christmas Eve. She still could grab her keys and return to the inn. It was the safest choice, to escape while she still had half a chance to keep her heart intact.

Now that she was alone here in this quiet kitchen with only the sound of the refrigerator humming and the logs creaking and settling around her, she could admit the truth.

She wanted to be here.

She had spent so may cheerless Christmases when her mother was alive, feeling obligated to be with Barbara instead of accepting one of the many invitations that had been extended to her by friends.

This would be her first real family Christmas. She didn't care if she was merely borrowing someone else's holiday traditions. Now that she had made the decision to stay—or rather, now that Ridge had applied a little emotional blackmail to convince her of it—she intended to put aside her misgivings and throw herself into enjoying herself.

She would worry about the cost later.

"Oooh. Something smells good," Destry exclaimed, drawing out the last word to two syllables, as soon as they walked inside the warm house.

He had to agree with her. Cinnamon and vanilla, two of his favorite scents, drifted through the house with sweet, enticing promise.

"Sarah must be baking," he said, unbuttoning his coat.

"Cookies. I bet it's cookies," Des said eagerly.

"You could be right," he said. He took off his hat and shrugged out of his big ranch coat. How had Sarah managed to bake cookies when she only had one working arm? Everything must have been doubly hard, from measuring ingredients to rolling out dough.

Some kind of jazzy Christmas music played from the stereo in the kitchen. Even a grouchy old Scrooge like him could appreciate the perfection of the moment—fresh powder outside and a warm, cozy house that smelled like heaven.

As he slid off his boots, he tried not to think about how eager he was to see her again. She hadn't left his thoughts for more than a minute or two all day.

That heated, intense, surprising kiss the night before had left him restless and achy for things he knew he couldn't have.

She was a transitory part of their lives, he reminded himself. He had managed to convince her to stay another night or two but he had a feeling that wouldn't last long. No matter how he protested that she was very welcome to stay at the house, she seemed stuck on the idea that she was intruding on their family Christmas.

In a few days she would return to San Diego to her life and her students, leaving him to the hard reality of a lonely Idaho winter.

He told himself the sudden ache in his gut was only a pang of hunger that would be quickly dealt with by a cookie or two.

Destry beat him out of her winter gear and hurried into the kitchen. When he followed, he found the two of them with their heads together at the kitchen island, his daughter and the woman who was becoming entirely too important to him.

She flashed a tentative smile at him, looking sweetly uncertain. The ache in his gut intensified.

Okay, maybe he would need three cookies to ease it.

"Hi. How did the plowing go?"

Destry answered for both of them. "We kicked some blizzard butt, didn't we, Dad?"

He forced a chuckle. "Winter cleanup feels like a never-ending job sometimes around here, but I think the work is done for now. What are we baking?"

"Snickerdoodles. I make them with my students every year and I had a sudden craving. I hope you don't mind."

He had plenty of cravings of his own, suddenly. To

whirl her into his arms. To kiss the smudge of flour off her cheek. To press his lips to that soft, warm mouth....

"No," he murmured, his voice a little ragged. "I don't mind at all."

"Can I have one?" Destry asked.

"Of course," Sarah answered with a smile. She handed one to his daughter and then picked one up for him, too.

"Oh, wow. That's really good," Destry exclaimed.

"Will you help me finish baking them?" she asked his daughter. "I'm afraid I mixed up far more dough than the three of us can eat. We might need to freeze some."

"We can take some cookies tomorrow when we head to Taft's place for Christmas dinner," he suggested.

"Okay. There should be plenty. I'm used to cooking for twenty-four children and their families, I'm afraid."

"Hey," Destry exclaimed. "Maybe we could go take some to the Halls' house. I bet they're feeling kind of sad this year without Jason, don't you think, Dad?"

He smiled, touched at Destry's kindness. Caidy had done a good job of helping her think about others.

"Our neighbors' only son is finishing his residency in Utah," he explained. "His wife is having a baby in a few weeks and they can't travel, and the Halls have health issues and can't travel easily, so they're waiting until after the baby to go visit. They've been a little blue about spending the holidays alone."

"We should definitely take them a plate of cookies then," she exclaimed. "It will cheer them up."

"Could we take some to that nice new family that moved into the Marcus house?"

"You know, we were so busy with the wedding this year we skipped our little gifts to the neighbors. These cookies would be great. How about we combine activities? We can take a sleigh ride and distribute cookies on our way."

Sarah and Destry both looked at him with shining eyes that made him feel about twenty feet tall.

"Oh, that would be perfect," Sarah exclaimed. "I love it."

"Dad, you think of the *best* ideas."

He grinned down at his daughter. "I do what I can."

"Can we go after dark so we can see the lights?"

"How about we leave just before twilight? A couple hours from now. Then we can come back and grill our steaks."

"Steaks?" Sarah asked.

"Another Bowman family tradition," he answered. "My dad always fired up the grill on Christmas Eve. Mom would cook a big turkey for Christmas dinner but we always had a steak dinner on Christmas Eve. I guess it was his way of celebrating another year of keeping his cattle operation in the black."

"My mouth is watering already," she said.

When she smiled at him like that, soft and approachable, his mouth watered, too—and not for a juicy cut of beef.

Chapter Ten

"Are you warm enough?"

Sarah wrenched her gaze from the pristine winter scene ahead of them long enough to glance across the seat of the sleigh at Ridge, holding the reins.

He gazed steadily at her and she blushed, for reasons she couldn't have explained. "Oh, yes. We have about five blankets on, don't we, Destry?"

His daughter sat between them on the wide padded seat. "Maybe not quite but I'm not cold at all."

Though there was plenty of room, Sarah wished she was sitting behind them in the second row of seats. She had suggested it, but Destry liked to take a turn with the reins and neither of the Bowmans wanted her to sit by herself in the backseat.

As it made more sense to share the blankets and crowd together for warmth, they all sat together. Ridge wore his big lined ranch coat and a Stetson. He looked like something out of a sexy aftershave commercial, and every time she looked at him, she could feel her skin prickle with awareness.

"What about you?" she asked. "You're not using the blankets. Are you warm enough over there?"

"I'm great," he answered with a slow grin that made her insides jump and whirl like her first-graders after a sugar rush. "If you want the truth, I can't imagine anywhere I would rather be right now."

She had to agree. The night was clear and cold, with a vast expanse of starry sky overhead and a sliver of moon. The previous day's storm would have seemed like a distant memory if not for the deep snow piled up on either side of the road.

The sleigh bells on the big, sturdy horse's harness jingled in the night, the only sound besides the hooves thudding on snow and the steady whir of the sleigh runners.

They—and the prosaically named horse, Bob— seemed to be the only ones out on the cold night. Everyone else was probably hunkered in by the hearth having Christmas Eve dinner, singing carols, opening presents.

Like Ridge, she wouldn't have traded places with them for anything.

"This is magical," she said. "I keep thinking how my students would love to be in my place right now."

"Probably not *right now*," Destry pointed out. "Right now they're probably so eager for Santa to come, they don't want to be anywhere but their own houses. I know I always was that way when I was a little kid."

"You're still a little kid to some of us," Ridge said, earning a hard shoulder nudge from his daughter.

"Watch it or your driver will end up on the ground," he said with a laugh.

"Hey, don't call me a little kid. I'm almost twelve!"

"I know. Ancient. You'll be needing denture cream before you know it."

Sarah smiled at their interaction, charmed all over again by how close the two were. She almost didn't realize Ridge had directed the conversation to her.

"You mention your students all the time," he pointed out. "You must enjoy your work."

"I love being a teacher," she admitted. "The thing is, even when I'm not in the classroom, one part of my brain is always wondering how I can incorporate this experience or that piece of knowledge into my lesson plan. I wish you were closer. I would love to have you and Bob—and you, Destry, of course—come to class so we could have a lesson about horses. Or better still, a field trip to a working cattle ranch would be fantastic, wouldn't it? They would learn how you feed them, how much water they need, how ranching has changed over the time your family has owned the River Bow."

"That would be good. You know any cattle ranchers in San Diego?" he asked.

"No. I'm not sure there are any."

"There are. I can check with a couple of associations I belong to and see if I can find anybody in that area who might want to host a field trip."

"That would be wonderful. Thank you!"

A car approached from the other direction, and he turned his attention back to his driving, presenting her with that strong, handsome profile.

"You could bring them here," Destry said, her voice excited. "Wouldn't that be fun, Dad?"

"Sure," he drawled. "Might be a bit of a bus ride, though."

His words were a firm reminder of how much distance lay between their worlds, literally and figuratively. Some of her ebullient joy in the evening trickled out.

She forced herself to focus instead on how beautiful the Christmas lights looked, glowing through thick blankets of snow.

"I love how so many of your neighbors decorate their houses for the holidays."

"We're a pretty festive community, that's true," he answered. "Des, how many more cookie plates are back there?"

She looked behind him on the second row of seats. "One more. I was thinking we could give it to Mrs. Thatcher."

The girl turned to Sarah. "She's always *so* nice to me. Last time I shoveled her walk, she tried to give me five dollars, even though I told her I wanted to do it for free. I wouldn't take her money, but guess what? She mailed me an online gift card for fifteen dollars. Isn't that funny?"

"Wonderful," she answered with a smile, touched at the warmth and friendliness here in Pine Gulch. She knew a few of her neighbors in the condo unit where she lived in San Diego but this sort of community spirit seemed completely alien to her.

Ridge drove a little farther before reining Bob to a stop. Destry grabbed the last plate of snickerdoodles and hopped down effortlessly. "Be right back," she said.

Without the buffer provided by his daughter, Sarah and Ridge lapsed into silence broken by the jingling of the reins and the wind moaning in the trees.

They both watched Destry ring the doorbell, and a

moment later an elegant-looking older woman with carefully groomed hair opened the door.

"She'll probably want us to come inside, too, I'm afraid," Ridge said. "Don't worry. I'll make some kind of excuse."

"I can't imagine being friends with all my neighbors," she said. "You must love living here."

Though he still sat a Destry-sized space away from her, she could feel the air between them move when he shrugged. "Most of the time, I guess. It's all I've really known."

"Really? You haven't gone anywhere else?"

"Oh, on and off for school, though I finished a lot of my classwork through distance education. I met Destry's mother when I was working at a ranch outside Livingston, Montana, and stayed there a year."

He tilted his head back and gazed up at the stars. She wondered what he was thinking about. Old loves? People he had known and lost? Other starry nights?

"I wouldn't have stayed that long," he said after a moment, "but things were tense with my parents after I got married. They never liked Melinda much. She was too much of a city girl, and they figured she wouldn't be happy on the ranch. Turns out they were exactly right."

"Oh," she said softly. "I'm sorry."

"Just a week before they died, we fought pretty bitterly on the phone and I…said things that haunt me to this day. They wanted us to spend the holidays here that year so they could have the chance to get to know Melinda better. I refused, said it was too late to make nice. If they couldn't embrace my marriage, they could all spend Christmas in hell, as far as I was concerned. Yeah, I was pretty much an ass."

He was silent, gazing up at those stars, and she fought the urge to tuck the blanket around him in an effort to warm those suddenly wintry features.

"I can't stand knowing they died with ugliness between us, thinking I hated them," he said, his voice low.

A hard, sharp ache pinched her chest—for his pain and also for her connection to it. She reached across the space between them to place a hand on his arm. She could feel those leashed muscles even through the heavy lining of his coat.

"I didn't know your parents, but I've met several of your family members. From everything I've learned about Margaret and Frank since I arrived in Pine Gulch, I have to believe they knew you loved them. They strike me as the sort of people who would have been quick to forgive. I'm sure things would have eased between you eventually."

He drew in a long breath and then exhaled it slowly. After a pause, he covered her gloved fingers with his. She couldn't even feel his skin against hers, but the connection seemed profoundly intimate anyway.

"You're right. I know you are. They probably would have tried harder to accept the situation once they found out a baby was on the way."

"They didn't know about Destry?"

"No. I should have told them, but I was too angry at their reaction to Melinda. I didn't want to hear them say that was another strike against my marriage, that we had married for the wrong reasons. I had been thinking I would come for the holidays and tell them, but, well, I was too angry after we fought, especially at my father. Destry was born six months after their deaths. I wish they could have had the chance to know her."

"I'm so sorry."

He gazed down at her, silhouetted against the vast starry sky, and something sweetly tender, bright and glossy as Christmas lilies, bloomed inside her.

She was falling in love with him.

The realization didn't tumble over her like an avalanche, hard and wild and terrifying. Instead, it whispered down like a single, soft, plump snowflake, gentle and pure, followed by another and then another.

She swallowed. Oh. This was certainly unexpected.

She couldn't think or breathe or move. Love. How on earth had *that* happened? She couldn't be in love with him. She had only just met the man.

Common sense told her she was crazy, but she couldn't argue with the fragile tenderness fluttering through her.

Her heart would be broken into tiny jagged pieces when she left Pine Gulch.

She thought she enjoyed her life in San Diego. Her students, dinners out with friends, kayaking in Mission Bay. But right now, on this cold Christmas Eve, the idea of returning to her life seemed bleak and disheartening.

"What's wrong?" he asked softly.

Everything. She swallowed hard again. "Why do you ask?"

"You looked, I don't know, almost *bereft* for a moment. Is it your arm? It's probably aching in this cold, isn't it?"

"A little," she said, seizing on the ready excuse.

"You pushed yourself too hard today. Somebody who's only a few days out from a broken arm shouldn't be making cookies and gift wrapping."

Gift wrapping was probably a stretch to describe the

clumsy job she did packaging the few little things she had managed to find in her luggage to give the two of them.

"It was a wonderful day, Ridge. Thank you for allowing me to be part of it."

"We're the ones who should be thanking you. Those are mighty fine snickerdoodles. I'm really glad I have a couple more to go home to. As soon as Des comes out from chatting with Mrs. Thatcher, we'll head back to the ranch. The spuds you and Destry threw in the oven ought to be just about ready, and it won't take me long to grill up some steaks. Then you can get some rest."

She didn't *want* to rest. In a few days' time she would be back amid the seashore and sunshine of Southern California, and this would all seem like a distant dream. She wanted to savor every moment now, while she could.

As if on cue, Destry opened the door and came out carrying an overflowing basket.

Beside her, Ridge chuckled. "That's Ruthanne for you. She's probably afraid Des and I are going to wither away and starve without Caidy. She doesn't know we have all the leftover wedding food, not to mention about three months' worth of meals my sister stored up in the freezer for us."

Destry's flashlight beam lit up the night as she climbed back into the sleigh. "She's the *nicest* lady. I gave her one plate of cookies and ended up with this huge basket. A loaf of bread, homemade blackberry jam, some of that fancy cheese you like from the dairy in town, Dad. She said she had been planning to run it to the ranch tonight to thank us for shoveling her out."

"Well, then, I'm glad we saved her a trip. She would have slid all over the place with that old sedan of hers."

After much tucking and shifting, Destry was once more snuggled beneath the blankets with Sarah. When she was settled, Ridge glanced down at both of them.

"Well, ladies, should we head back for some Christmas dinner before all the goodies Mrs. Thatcher gave us freeze out here in the cold?"

"I *am* kind of starving," Destry said. "But take the long way back, okay? I want to go past my friend Kurt's house. He texted a picture of this awesome snowman family he and his brothers made."

"Snowmen, coming up." Ridge clicked his tongue to the horse. "Gee, Bob."

With Ridge guiding at the reins, the horse turned a corner at the next street, bells jingling. Sarah snuggled under the blanket and vowed to enjoy every moment of this one magical night she would have with them.

This was turning into his best Christmas ever.

It was loads better than the year he turned seventeen, when his dad had given him the keys to an old Chevrolet Silverado pickup truck. Better, even, than the first Christmas after Destry was born, when he still thought he might have half a chance at salvaging his marriage.

Christmas had always been his parents' favorite season, particularly his mother's. She would decorate the ranch house to the hilt, with trees in every room, fresh-cut garlands dripping from the mantel and the staircases, candles in every window.

Christmas music would play through the house from a few weeks before Thanksgiving through New Year's Day, until none of them could bear to jingle one more damn bell.

After his parents were murdered, the holidays took on a bittersweet tone for each of them.

He thought Caidy might have been most affected—with reason. She had been a sixteen-year-old girl, the only one of them not out on her own. The night of the murders, she had been home with Margaret and Frank and had ended up huddling on the floor of the kitchen pantry where their mother had shoved her at the first sign of intruders, where she had been forced to listen to her mother's dying moments.

For a long time, all of them had pretended to be overflowing with Christmas spirit for Destry's sake.

This year, for the first time since that awful Christmas season, he could actually claim his excitement was genuine.

The evening had been filled with laughter and fun. After the sleigh ride, he and Destry had quickly taken care of Bob and the sleigh and then returned to the house to finish dinner preparations.

The steaks had taken almost no time to grill while the girls performed an impromptu Christmas carol concert at the piano, with Sarah pecking out notes with one hand and Destry singing along.

Now they sat in the dining room with the candles lit and more soft, jazzy Christmas music playing out of the speakers.

"That was a delicious steak," Sarah said to him now, that soft smile lighting up her delicate features. "I enjoyed every bite, though it was a little humiliating that Destry had to cut it up for me."

"Anytime," his daughter said with a grin.

The two of them had developed a fast friendship. All evening, they seemed to have laughed together just as much as Destry did with Gabi. It warmed him to see it, even as he admitted to a few reservations.

His natural paternal instinct was to protect his daughter from hurt, even as he accepted that she needed to navigate a few little bumps in the road along the way in order to become a strong, capable woman and know how to handle the inevitable stresses in life.

But he had already failed to pick a loving woman to be her mother. Because of his poor choice, she would always have that void where her mother should have been.

Like it or not, she had suffered another emotional bump with Caidy's marriage.

How would she deal with one more loss of a friendship, even a fresh one, when Sarah returned to San Diego?

How would he?

He listened to their chatter while he tried to process how she could have become so important to both of them in such a short time.

He thought of those tender moments on the sleigh, the connection that had shivered and seethed between them. He was beginning to care about her deeply—and the idea of it scared the hell out of him.

He hadn't been looking for this. If somebody had asked him, he would have said he was perfectly content with the way his life had been going, that he didn't need anybody.

His marriage to Melinda had been such a hot mess he had just about decided he wasn't good at that sort of thing. Better to just stay single, raise his daughter, build the ranch. Maybe someday, long into the future when Destry was in high school or something, he could start thinking about a relationship. Something safe and solid and comfortable.

Suddenly Sarah tumbled into his life with her warm eyes and sweet smile.

He had it bad. He couldn't be in the same room with her without wanting to kiss her, taste her, touch her.

He pushed away his plate. Spending this magical Christmas Eve with her had only reinforced how empty his world was the rest of the time.

"What now?" Destry asked. "We could watch *Elf* again. Sarah never saw the end."

He enjoyed the movie, but he didn't necessarily want to watch it for the second time in as many days. "How about my favorite? *It's a Wonderful Life.*"

"I guess," Destry said. "I do like that one, too. I'll pop the popcorn."

"After you just had a steak dinner? How about we pass on the popcorn?"

"I'll pop some just in case we want some later," Destry said.

A short time later, they settled into the family room in roughly the same spots they had been for the previous movie, with him in his favorite recliner and the two of them snuggled in blankets on the sofa.

He would have liked to ask Destry to switch places with him but he didn't think either of them would appreciate the suggestion.

The movie was a long one—and, once again, Sarah fell asleep during the last half.

It was quite endearing to watch her try valiantly to stay awake, but finally her eyelids seemed to get heavier and heavier with each blink until she slumped to the side with her mouth open a little.

Destry noticed the same thing after a few minutes and grinned at him. "I guess she has a hard time staying awake in movies," she whispered.

"Looks like," he answered. Maybe she had also struggled to sleep after that stunning kiss they shared. It was probably small of him, but he hoped so.

This time, she woke up just as the little bell on the Christmas tree rang, heralding the angel Clarence earning his wings.

He was watching her more than the movie and enjoyed the sleepy way her eyes blinked open. "Oh," she exclaimed on a yawn, her voice thready with sleep. "I love that part."

The credits started to roll, and she rubbed at her eyes. "I must have dozed off."

"You did!" Destry said. "You tried really hard not to, but I guess you were just too tired."

"How much did I miss?"

"I don't remember. Dad? When did she fall asleep?"

He knew exactly when, right down to the moment in the scene. Would admitting that to her make her wonder just how closely he had been watching?

"Right about the time George Bailey sees how the old crumbling house would have been falling apart without him."

"And finds his beloved wife a lonely spinster," she murmured. As she said the words, color flared in her cheeks, and he wondered at it.

"Yep," Destry said. "That movie just makes me happy. Now I don't know which one is my favorite Christmas movie, *Elf* or *It's a Wonderful Life*. They're both so good."

"No reason you have to decide tonight. In fact, we're

heading for eleven. You should probably go to bed. Remember, Santa Claus can't come unless you're asleep."

She rolled her eyes. "Dad. I'm eleven and a half, remember?"

"So? You think he has different rules for smarty-pants girls who think they're almost teenagers?"

"You're such a dork," she said with a wry grin. Still, she hopped off the sofa. "But I am tired. I guess I should think about bed. Are we going to read the Christmas story first?"

"Why don't you get in your pajamas first, then we'll read in the great room by the fireplace and the big Christmas tree."

"Deal."

She hurried from the room with the same energy she brought to everything.

"We always read the story in Luke," he explained to Sarah when the two of them were alone. "It was kind of a tradition with my parents. You don't have to stay if you don't want to."

"You and Destry are trying to build your own traditions. I can go to bed if you would rather just read the story with your daughter."

"Not at all. You're more than welcome. Come in, and you can help me add a couple more logs to the fire."

Though he knew touching her probably wasn't a good idea, proper host etiquette and simple human courtesy demanded he reach out a hand to help her to her feet.

When she rose, she was only a few inches from him. He could feel the air currents swirl around them with each inhale and exhale.

She gazed up at him, and he thought he saw *something* there, something bright and tender.

"Sarah—" he began, but whatever he meant to say next caught somewhere in his throat, all tangled up in his overwhelming desire to kiss her.

She leaned toward him, her breasts brushing against his chest, lips slightly apart and the flutter of her heartbeat at the base of her neck.

She wouldn't push him away. Not this time.

Call it male arrogance, call it instinct. He didn't know how he knew, but he did.

He leaned down, just enough, but a half second before his mouth would have found hers, they heard footsteps hurrying down the hall.

He eased back again just as Destry raced into the room at full speed.

"All done," she said proudly. "That was the fastest change on record, right?"

"Painfully fast," he muttered. "I didn't even have time to build up the fire."

Sarah made a small sound in her throat that might have been amusement or dismay, he couldn't tell.

"I also need to grab my dad's Bible out of the china cabinet in the dining room."

"I'll find the Bible. I know where it is. I found it when I was helping Caidy look for a few things for the wedding. You two take care of the fire," Destry ordered.

"Yes, ma'am."

As far as he was concerned, they had been doing just that, and he would have liked a chance to get back to it. This was obviously not the moment, with his daughter running around. After a pause, he headed into the great room, where tree lights already glowed, sending a kaleidoscope of color throughout the room. She followed, settling onto the sofa there while he added a few new logs to the fire he had started earlier in the evening.

"Am I supposed to be helping with the fire, according to Destry's script?" she asked.

He laughed. "She tends to want things a certain way. I have no idea where she gets that."

"I can't imagine," she murmured.

He again wanted to sink down beside her on the sofa and leave Destry to sit by herself on the other sofa but he decided that would be entirely too selfish of him.

A moment later, his daughter walked in with her arms wrapped around the black leather Bible Ridge had watched his father read just about every morning of his life after chores.

"Here you go, Dad." She handed him the black King James Version that had Franklin Paul Bowman etched in gilt letters across the front.

He gazed down at it as a hundred memories flooded back to him. Going to Sunday school when he was a kid, his thick wavy hair tamed with copious amounts of gel, pinching the twins to be quiet as they tried to wrestle on the pew. Listening to his father talk about his reverence for the land and his relationship with God while they were out on the tractor.

At the forefront were those last bitter things he had hurled at his father just days before he died—that he was tired of Frank trying to run his life, damn sick and tired of being treated as if he didn't have the brains or the balls to figure things out on his own, that he couldn't respect a man who didn't see his own son was a grown man trying to live his own life.

He pushed that memory away, focusing instead on all those years of his childhood when his family would gather right here and read about babies and miracles and gifts from above.

He opened to the well-worn page in Luke, carefully highlighted in red pencil by his father's hand. He'd read from this Bible every Christmas since coming back to River Bow, but he'd never noticed the small note in the margin at one verse, in his father's handwriting, underlined three times.

"Fear not!" the note read. For some reason, the words seemed to jump off the page at him, as if his father were trying to tell him something.

He gazed at it for a long time, until Destry finally spoke.

"Dad? Aren't you going to read?"

"Um. Yeah. Sorry." He cleared his throat and began reading. "'And it came to pass…'"

When he looked up after reading the last highlighted verse, Destry's eyes were bright with happiness.

"I never get tired of hearing that," she declared.

Sarah's eyes were bright, too, but if he wasn't mistaken, they were shiny with emotion.

"That was lovely," she said, her voice soft. "I don't think I've ever heard the story read so beautifully."

That subtle connection seemed to shimmer around them like a shiny garland.

"I had a good example. My dad read the story as if he had been one of those shepherds suddenly shaken out of their normal world by a host of angels."

She smiled, and he was suddenly deeply grateful for her. If she hadn't been here, would he have found any sliver of Christmas spirit this year? Or would he have simply continued trudging through the motions to make sure his daughter enjoyed the holiday?

Destry gave one of her ear-popping yawns, big enough to show off her back molars.

"You need to be in bed, missy. And no sneaking down to see what Santa brought you before I have a chance to be there with you."

"I won't," she promised. She padded to him in her silly slippers and threw her arms around his neck. "I love you, Daddy. Merry Christmas."

He hugged her, a ridiculous lump in his throat. "Love you right back, ladybug."

She made a face at the name he had called her since she was a toddler. To his surprise, she went to Sarah next.

"Merry Christmas. I'm so glad you were here this year. You made everything more fun."

He saw Sarah's eyes widen with astonishment when Destry threw her arms around her neck. After a shocked moment, she hugged her back.

"I had a wonderful day," she said. "Good night. I'll see you in the morning. Merry Christmas."

When Destry headed up the log staircase to her room, he suddenly realized he was alone with his houseguest again.

"You're probably exhausted, too," he said.

"Not really. That nap sort of took the edge off. Right now I'm not tired at all."

"I've got to wait about an hour until I'm certain she's asleep before I play Santa Claus. Do you want to help?"

"Oh!" she exclaimed, looking intrigued. "That sounds fun."

"I have to admit to being selfish about this part of Christmas. The way things have always worked out in the past—and even this year, with all the craziness of her wedding, if you can believe that—Caidy has always done a lot of the holiday shopping for me. She even wraps most of the presents. She's good at it so I let her, but I always tell her I like to play St. Nick. I always like filling the stockings and setting everything out around the tree. Thank you for keeping me company."

"You're welcome."

"Can I get you something to drink?"

"I've been thinking all day about that delicious raspberry cocoa Destry made yesterday."

"You got it."

Cocoa actually sounded great to him, too. Perfect for a cold Christmas Eve. He quickly heated water and mixed in the gourmet cocoa packets Caidy had left behind—raspberry chocolate for Sarah, mint chocolate for himself. When the mix dissolved, he carried the mugs back to the great room, where he found her gazing at the Christmas-tree lights reflected in the front window.

This time he did sit beside her on the sofa, and she moved her feet a little to make room for him.

They sat in surprisingly companionable silence, especially given the currents that seemed to zing between them.

"These past few days you've had a taste of the Bowman Christmas traditions. What about the Whitmore Christmas traditions?"

She tensed at the question with the mug halfway to her mouth. "What about them?" she asked, her tone far more defensive than he might have expected.

"I'm curious. That's all. I've noticed you have a habit of not talking much about yourself. It's tough to get to know you when you don't share much."

"I told you my parents divorced when I was young,

and that I…didn't have much of a relationship with my father."

"Yes. I'm sorry for that."

"I could tell by the way you cherished your father's Bible this evening how much you miss him. Mine died only a few months ago, and I don't miss him at all. Does that make me a terrible person?"

"It makes you normal, Sarah. You didn't know the man. You can't grieve for someone simply because you happen to share his DNA."

She was quiet, her fingers picking at the edge of the soft fleece blanket she had tucked around her feet. "If I grieve for any loss," she finally said, her voice low, "it's the fantasy I had of a good, loving father who wanted the best for me. The kind of father you are to Destry."

Emotion rose in his throat again, both at the sweetly touching compliment she had just paid him and for everything she had missed in her childhood.

"What about your mother?" he pressed. "Did you have any traditions with her?"

"We went to church every Christmas Eve. I don't remember much besides that. I can tell you that I was never so stirred in a church service as I was tonight by the way you read the simple story."

She gazed at him, her eyes soft, and he felt something sparkle to life in his chest like someone had just plugged in a hundred Christmas trees.

He was falling hard for this lovely woman who treated his daughter with such kindness.

Fear not.

That little phrase written in his father's hand seemed to leap into his mind.

Fear not.

He was pretty sure this wasn't what his father meant—or the angels on that first Christmas night, for that matter—but he didn't care. It seemed perfect and right to fearlessly take her mug of cocoa and set it on the side table next to his own, to lean across the space between them, to lower his head, to taste that soft, sweet mouth that had tantalized him all day.

Chapter Eleven

She knew they shouldn't be doing this, but kissing Ridge Bowman was an irresistible joy and she couldn't seem to summon the strength to stop.

"All day long, I've been thinking about kissing you again."

She shivered at his low words against her mouth. Tenderness for this man—solid, steady, ranch-tough but achingly sweet—fluttered inside her like a tiny, fragile bird.

Her entire life, she had dreamed of a man like him. Someone she knew would cherish her—a man who would see and appreciate her strengths, who would love her despite her weaknesses.

How could she ever have imagined she would find him here—or that she would have to walk away before she really had the chance to savor this unexpected wonder?

She returned the kiss, pouring all the emotions she couldn't tell him into it. He smelled delicious—soap and some kind of outdoorsy aftershave—and tasted even better, of chocolate and mint.

Her casted arm seemed to get in the way, even though he took great care not to jostle it, and she fleetingly wished that she didn't have the bother of it.

As soon as she had the thought, she pushed it away. She never would have believed she could be grateful for breaking her arm. If she hadn't, though, she would have dropped off the painting and returned to San Diego to arrange delivery of the rest of the collection.

She never would have known Ridge or Destry other than as strangers she had once met. She never would have discovered how very appealing she found a man who cared deeply for his daughter and was trying to do right by her under hard circumstances.

She never would have guessed that first day she showed up at the doorstep that she would enjoy the most joy-filled Christmas of her life in company with a tough rancher and his irrepressible daughter.

Yes, leaving them was going to hurt—so badly she didn't know how she would bear it and was already bracing herself for the inevitable pain. But she wouldn't have missed this chance for anything, this rare and infinitely precious moment tangled around him while the tree lights gleamed and the fire crackled beside them.

They kissed for a long time—deep, lingering, intoxicating kisses that left her achy and restless for more.

Finally he drew away and rested his forehead against hers. "I can't believe I've only known you a few days.

You're perfect. The most wonderful woman I've ever met. I feel like I've been waiting for you my entire life. You fit perfectly into our lives, as if you've been at the River Bow forever."

The husky words pierced the soft, delicious haze surrounding her. She had a wild rush of joy that he was beginning to care for her, too, and then the reality crashed down as if the whole Christmas tree had toppled onto the two of them, shattering ornaments and lightbulbs and angels.

Oh. Oh, no. How could she have been so selfish? This wasn't all about her. She had been so wrapped up in thinking about how she would hurt when she left she hadn't given any thought to his feelings. What if he were coming to care for her, too? He would be even more angry when he found out the truth.

Heart aching with the words she couldn't say, she eased away, desperate for space between them.

The tenderness in his gaze raked her conscience with sharp talons. She was here—in his house, in his arms—under false pretenses. When he found out the truth, those kisses she considered sweetly magical would seem tawdry and wrong.

She was making everything worse by pushing her way into their lives, fooling them into beginning to care about her. If she had thought of the consequences, she never would have come here.

"Don't you think we should put the presents out now?" she said, hoping he didn't hear the note of desperation in her voice. "I imagine Destry's asleep by now."

He gazed at her for a long moment, a tiny frown between his brows. "Yeah. You're right," he finally said.

"I've got them all stored in a corner of the attic. Give me a minute to carry them down."

"Do you need my help?" she asked, grateful that her voice wasn't trembling as much as she feared.

"No. I've got it."

She nodded and curled her legs up beside her on the sofa. While she waited for him to return, she gazed into the fire and seriously considered leaving. Just packing her things right now at nearly midnight on Christmas Eve and driving away.

She couldn't do that to Destry. After the wonderful day they'd had today, the girl would be hurt at such an abrupt departure.

But how could she stay, when each moment with Ridge sent her tumbling further and further in love with him?

What a mess.

She pressed a hand to her stomach, wishing on all the Christmas stars in the sky that things could be different.

A moment later, Ridge came down the stairs carrying a huge plastic bin piled high with wrapped presents.

"Here we go," he said, setting the bin down by the tree. "I'll fill the stockings while you set the other presents under the tree."

All over the world, parents who celebrated Christmas were doing this same thing, she thought with a little amazement. Perhaps with only a gift or two, perhaps with grand expensive gestures.

Her part didn't take long, then she turned back to watch Ridge, more charmed than she wanted to admit as she watched him fill a stocking with oranges, candy, small wrapped packages.

"Did you wrap the presents yourself?" she asked him

as she looked at the artful pile of gifts under the massive tree.

"Some of them. I would guess Caidy bought and wrapped about half of them. I did the rest. I'm not sure how she found time to think about Destry's Christmas gifts leading up to the craziness of the wedding, but somehow she managed. She actually starts pretty early in the year and is usually done by Thanksgiving, so that probably helped."

"She sounds like an amazing person."

"She is. I think you'll like her, and I know she'll love you."

That guilt settled low in her stomach. She wouldn't have the chance to meet Caidy Bowman Caldwell. By the time his sister and her veterinarian husband returned from her honeymoon, Sarah would only be a memory to Ridge and his daughter—and not a very pleasant one.

"There. That should do it." He carried the stocking over to the mantel, where a heavy brass stocking holder was already in place, then he returned to the table where he had the little bits and pieces of leftover candy and began to fill two more.

Two. One for himself, she assumed, and one for her.

"You have a stocking for me?"

He looked up, surprised. "Of course."

He held it up and she saw it was a lovely hand-sewn stocking made from a shimmery burgundy material.

"Where did it come from?"

"The attic. I found it in a box of one of the old Christmas things while I was up there. That's what took me so long." He paused and studied her with an expression she couldn't decipher.

"It was my mom's. I figured she would be delighted to share with you."

His mother's. The woman who had created that work of stunning beauty over the mantel and the tender portrait of her daughter that vibrated with Margaret's love for Caidy. The parent who hadn't lived long enough to see her first grandchild—or all the children who had come after, adopted into the family or biological.

As she looked at those big, callused hands holding the delicate thing, thick emotions welled up in her throat and spilled over.

He immediately looked horrified. "Hey. Don't cry. I didn't mean to upset you. I just didn't want you to feel left out and have nothing on Christmas morning."

She let out a hitching little sob. "You've been so wonderful to me. I've never known such a happy Christmas. I mean that. Thank you for sharing your holiday with me, Ridge. I can't begin to tell you how much I have enjoyed every moment."

He gave a rough laugh. "That's funny. You look like your heart is broken or something."

It was cracking apart. Surely he could see the pieces lying there on the floor. "I just…don't deserve your kindness and generosity. I'm a stranger."

"Not anymore, Sarah. Can't you see that? You will always be welcome at the River Bow."

Oh, how she wished that were true. She should tell him everything, right now. The weight on her conscience was becoming more than she could bear.

How could she ruin his Christmas by bringing such dark ugliness into it? Just a few more days, she told herself. Then she would be honest with him for the first time.

She continued the lie by forcing a smile. "Thank you

for that, and for the stocking. It was remarkably kind of you. That's the reason for the tears—your kindness, and the fact that my arm is letting me know it's been a long day. I should probably turn in."

He gave her a searching look, but she forced her features into what she hoped appeared as calm composure.

At all costs, she had to keep the love and tenderness out of her expression. If he knew how much she was coming to care for him and his daughter, everything would be much worse.

"Good night. Merry Christmas."

"Merry Christmas." She smiled, drew in all her strength and kissed the corner of his mouth with feigned casualness, then slipped away before he could pull her into a deeper embrace.

Something was definitely eating her.

Ridge watched Sarah walk to her bedroom, each step measured and her head sagging as if her neck couldn't support the weight of whatever was bothering her.

He had no idea how to bridge the distance she seemed so determined to keep between them.

Maybe he needed to stop trying.

His feelings for her were growing, but that didn't automatically mean she felt the same thing. He closed his eyes. No. He had seen *something* in her gaze, something soft and tender and real, like the star on the very top of the Christmas tree, but then she pulled away before he could reach for it.

With a sigh, he hung the other two stockings then went about his routine of shutting down the house— banking the fire, turning off lights, making sure all the doors were locked.

He left both Christmas trees on, another Bowman family tradition.

"Santa's got to find his way here somehow, doesn't he?" Frank would always say with a wink, even when Ridge and the boys were into their late teens.

Perhaps that was the core of Sarah's misgivings. From the few things she had told him, his heart ached for what sounded like a painful childhood.

Of the two of them, he was far luckier. Yes, his parents had been taken from them all in a terribly tragic way. But at least he had known twenty-four happy Christmases with them—okay, twenty-three and then the one where he'd just been an ass.

Judging by what little she had said, and her astonished joy in everything they did that day, her childhood holidays must have been dry, cheerless affairs.

This year would be different for her, he vowed. Tomorrow he would do everything he could to give her the bright day full of hope and promise that she deserved.

He gave the tree one last look, ran a hand down his father's Bible still sitting on the side table, then headed for the solitary bed he had slept in for the past twelve years, wishing fiercely that things could be different.

Watching Destry Bowman on Christmas morning was a sheer delight, Sarah thought.

The girl was grateful for every gift she opened, from a collection of lip glosses her father confessed to picking out himself to a new eReader she had been wanting "for *ages*," she declared dramatically.

If Destry could be this excited about Christmas at nearly twelve, Sarah could only imagine the girl's reaction a few years earlier.

She loved this glimpse into their lives, seeing the bond between father and daughter. Ridge was a great father—firm but loving.

He should have had more children, she thought, and fought down a pang of sympathy that his life had taken a very different road than he probably expected.

"Looks like there are only a few left," Destry said. From under the tree, she pulled out the big, beautifully wrapped box Sarah knew contained the gift the girl had made for her father.

"Hey, this one's for you," she said in mock surprise. "I wonder what it could be?"

Ridge chuckled. "I have a feeling you know the answer to that."

"Maybe. Well, open it already!"

Ridge looked down at the box. "The wrapping paper is so pretty. Whatever it is, somebody put a lot of time into wrapping it."

"It's from me, okay? Open it, would you?"

He laughed again, clearly enjoying teasing his impatient daughter. "Haven't you ever heard of anticipation? Savoring the journey instead of always rushing headlong to the destination? Maybe you should work on it sometime."

"I will," she promised. "Just not right now. I've been *dying* for you to open my present. You're going to *love* it."

Sarah found it touching, and another mark of excellent parenting on Ridge's—and his sister Caidy's—part that, as excited as Destry had been about opening her own gifts, she seemed even more thrilled to be giving her handmade, from-the-heart gift to her father.

"All right, all right," Ridge finally said. He took the

box on his lap and started carefully removing the wrappings. By the time he pulled off the last bit of wrapping, even *Sarah* was on the edge of her seat with anticipation.

She suddenly had no doubt that he would make love with the same deliberate, focused attention.

She blushed at the inappropriate thought, right here in the middle of a family Christmas. What was the matter with her? Her mind was entirely too unruly when it came to him. She pushed away the thought as he opened the lid to the box and pulled out the richly colored throw.

"Oh. This is beautiful, Des. Did somebody make it for you?"

"No! I made it, all by myself! Well, okay, Becca showed me the stitches and helped me work on it while I was there, and then Sarah helped me finish it. But I did most of it all on my own."

His tough features softened as he looked at his daughter. "Wow! This is amazing. It must have taken you hours!"

"A few," she admitted, quite humbly, since Sarah knew she had spent much more than a few on the project.

He pulled it out and laid it across his lap. "I can't believe you did this."

"I thought my fingers were going to fall off," she confessed, though her cheeks were pink, her eyes shining. She looked as if her father's reaction was everything she had imagined and more.

"Do you know what this is? The perfect thing for lying on the couch and sleeping while I'm pretending to watch a ball game."

"I know! That's just what I thought you could use it for."

He laughed and held out his arms. "Thank you. I *love*

it. It's beautiful, and it means so much more because you took the time to make it. Come here, ladybug."

She hugged him and the love between father and daughter touched a small, lonely part of her heart.

"Thanks for my great Christmas, too," Destry said. "It's all been perfect."

"What about those last few gifts?" Ridge asked.

"Oh, yeah," Destry said. She winked at her father in a not-so-subtle way and then pulled them from beneath the lowest limbs of the tree and carried them both over to Sarah.

She looked down at her name clearly marked on the outside, then back at the two of them.

"Oh. You didn't have to get me gifts," she exclaimed.

"Like you didn't need to give us gifts?" Ridge drawled.

"Mine weren't much," she said, though she could feel her face heat again. "I haven't exactly had a chance to go shopping since I've been here."

The first night she arrived in Pine Gulch, before she had come out to the ranch, she had wandered around the small downtown, peeking her head into a few gift shops. She had been very grateful for her few impulse purchases the night before when she was trying to think of what to give them.

For Ridge, she had given him the book on Pine Gulch history she had purchased on a whim. For Destry, she had a pair of finely wrought silver-and-turquoise hoop earrings and a bottle of scented lotion she had originally purchased for Nicki. She would find something else for her friend.

She opened Destry's gift first, and when she saw it,

her heart swelled. "Oh, honey. It's beautiful. When did you have time to make this?"

"I worked on it the last two nights in my room after I went to bed. You might not have all that many chances to wear scarves in San Diego but maybe once in a while."

She pulled out the colorful scarf, knitted out of soft yarns of variegated green and peach, touched beyond measure to think of the girl working late in her room to make a gift for an unexpected houseguest she just met.

"I'll make the chance," she promised. "And every time I wear it, I'll remember this wonderful Christmas with both of you."

She fastened it around her neck, looping it in half and pulling the ends through.

"Now the other one," Destry said, her eyes bright. "It's from both of us."

This one was rectangular and narrow, roughly eighteen by twenty-four inches. She pulled away a bit of wrapping paper and saw an edge of a black picture frame. Heart pounding, she pulled away the rest of the paper.

"Oh."

She couldn't breathe for a long moment and could feel tears burn her eyes. It was a lovely framed print of the River Bow, obviously painted from the perspective of the foothills above the ranch.

She could see the distinctive log house and the beautiful red barn, as well as the other landmark building she recognized, all painted in a summer scene with wildflowers in the foreground. The silvery bright Cold Creek wound around the edge of the scene, forming the distinctive bow the ranch was named for.

"Your mother painted this one, as well," she said softly. "I recognize her style."

Ridge nodded, shifting a little uncomfortably. "It's one of the few she had made into prints, so we have others of this same scene. I just thought you might like to have something to remember us."

Yes, it might be a print, but she didn't doubt it was also valuable, considering the increasing recognition of Margaret Bowman's rare talent in art circles.

She wanted to tell him she couldn't accept it, that it wouldn't be right. He would probably agree with her once she returned all those other paintings to the family. The words caught in her throat. She couldn't say that now. Refusing the gift would be churlish of her, especially when she very much wanted to keep it.

When she returned to San Diego, she would probably wonder if all of this had been a dream. The art print would be a tangible reminder to her of these amazing few days, to go with all the memories she knew would haunt her.

"Thank you," she murmured solemnly. "I will cherish it always."

Something in her tone seemed to disturb him. He gave her a careful look and tension shivered between them.

"I guess that's it, then," Destry said, beginning to gather up wrapping paper.

"For now. We've got more fun planned at Taft's this afternoon. That breakfast casserole Caidy froze for us should be just about ready to come out of the oven by now. I'll throw some waffles on the iron and then we need to head out for chores."

"Can I help?" Sarah asked on impulse. "With the chores, I mean. I'd like to see what you do."

He looked surprised but not displeased. "Sure thing. I'm sure Caidy's got plenty of winter gear around the house that should fit you fine."

After the delicious breakfast that was more like a quiche, savory and satisfying, along with waffles Ridge made himself, Destry helped her bundle into a pair of snow pants and a parka, along with a pair of heavy boots and gloves.

She added the scarf the girl had given her and then headed out to watch the two of them deliver hay, clean out stalls, deliver feed to the River Bow horses in the barn, drive several heavy bales of hay out to various pastures for the cattle and clean out a couple of stalls.

For two hours, the work was cold and relentless, but Ridge and Destry hardly appeared to notice. They laughed together, sang a couple of silly Christmas carols and otherwise seemed to have a good time, while Sarah mostly tried not to stumble into their way.

When they finally walked back to the house, her cheeks felt chapped, her arm ached from the cold and raw emotion felt huge and unwieldy in her chest.

Seeing Ridge completely in his element left her more in love with him than ever. Both of them, really. She adored Destry. Both of them were as firmly planted in her heart as his heart was planted on this ranch.

What was she going to do? she thought grimly, as they walked into the warm, welcoming embrace of the house. She was in love with a man who would despise everything about her when he learned the secrets she had kept from him.

She had to tell him, soon. As much as it hurt, she had to tell him—and then she would have to figure out how to live with the consequences.

Chapter Twelve

When was she going to tell him?

She mulled over it all day and started to a dozen times, but the moment never seemed right. She didn't want to ruin Christmas morning. Then they were all having too much fun playing some of the games Destry got for Christmas. Then he took a nap on the sofa near the great room fireplace—under the multihued throw knitted by his daughter—and she didn't have the heart to tell him when he first woke. Then they were all busy getting ready for the family meal at his brother's house.

Now, here they were on the way to Taft and Laura's, and she hadn't been able to find the right moment. How could she ruin his family dinner? And if she did, she wouldn't have any way to leave and would be stuck in a miserable situation until he could take her back to the River Bow for her rental car.

Always look for an escape route. One of those subconscious lessons she'd learned from her father.

"Are you sure you're okay?" he said. "You seem tense."

She gave him a sidelong look. "I'm a stranger going to someone else's big family party. Wouldn't you feel a little stretched out of your social comfort zone?"

"Trust me, you won't feel like a stranger for long. Alex will probably try to pull a prank on us the minute we walk through the door. Maya will throw her arms around you and give you one of her awesome hugs to say hello then Laura and Becca will probably kidnap you and haul you into the kitchen to dig out all the dirty details of your life—and probably share way too many embarrassing details of *mine.*"

It all sounded chaotic and terrifying and *wonderful.*

"You love your family, don't you?"

"Every last crazy one of them," he said promptly.

Her chest ached. She wanted this. The noisy chaos, the inquisitive relatives, the sense of belonging to something bigger than she was.

And the man who went along with it. She wanted him most of all.

Not trusting herself to speak, she gazed out at the steep, snow-covered mountains that loomed out the windshield. After a moment, he reached out and gripped her fingers in his.

"It won't be that bad. Don't worry. Everybody will love you, I promise. And if it's all too much for you, let me know and I can take you back to the River Bow."

She forced a smile, touched beyond words at his concern for her.

He squeezed her fingers. "At some point, you're going to tell me what's bothering you, right?"

Was she that obvious? She flushed. Probably. He seemed to know what she was thinking before she even realized it. "Yes," she finally murmured. "But not right now, okay?"

His expression was intense and curious, but he said nothing as they drove across a bridge and headed on a lane through towering, snow-covered evergreen trees.

Finally they pulled up in front of a beautiful two-story home constructed of honey-colored pine logs and river rock with a wraparound porch. White icicle lights dripped from the porch roof and the gables of the house. It reminded her a great deal of the River Bow ranch house, though on a smaller scale.

The scene inside played out just as Ridge predicted. It was as if he'd read the script ahead of time, she thought.

A young dark-haired boy rushed over to greet them the moment they walked through the door.

"Hey, Uncle Ridge. Shake my hand."

"Why?"

"No reason. I just want you to."

Ridge snorted, obviously up to the game, but he played along anyway and held his hand out, then pretended to jump away in shock from a little tingly joy buzzer in the boy's hand, to peals of laughter from Alex.

"Oh, you got me."

"Guess what I got from Santa Claus? A whole box of joke and magic stuff. It's so awesome!"

"Wow. I bet your mom was just thrilled at Santa Claus for that one."

"Yep. Dad thought it was *hilarious*."

"He would," Ridge answered wryly.

"Hey, Destry. Shake my hand," the boy said.

"Forget it, Alex!" she said. "You think I didn't just see you punk my dad?"

"Aw, man." With a disappointed look, Alex rushed off, probably to gear up for another trick.

Before Sarah could catch her breath, an adorable girl with Down syndrome and the sweetest smile she'd ever seen came over and hugged both Ridge and Destry, who clearly adored her.

"Maya, this is our friend Sarah. She teaches first grade, just like you're in. Sarah, this is our Maya."

"Hi," Maya said cheerfully. "I love my teacher. Her name is Miz L."

Just as Ridge predicted, she threw her arms around Sarah's waist without waiting for a response, and Sarah smiled and hugged her back, completely charmed.

The sisters-in-law didn't precisely kidnap her, but they did push her into the kitchen with firm determination, where they set her to work stirring gravy with her good hand, all while subtly and gently interrogating her.

She loved every moment of it.

She had met each of Ridge's brothers separately, but seeing them together, she would have had a tough time figuring out which twin was which if not for the adorably fat baby boy Trace held.

All of them treated her with warm acceptance. By the time they left three hours later—full of delicious food, fun conversation and more holiday spirit than she ever imagined— she felt fully enmeshed into the Bowman family.

How would she ever say goodbye to them all?

* * *

"What a great day," Destry declared when they were in the pickup truck again, prepared to head back to the River Bow. "Best. Christmas. Ever."

He grinned at his daughter. "It was pretty awesome, though I believe I remember you saying the same thing last year."

"That's because every year just gets better and better. Next year will be the best yet because Ben and Caidy will be there with Jack and Ava. I missed them all. Who knows? Maybe Caidy will even have a baby by then."

It was certainly possible, though the idea of his baby sister—the one he had practically raised since she was a teenager—becoming a mother was not a subject he wanted to think too long about.

He had his suspicions in that direction about Taft and Laura, though they hadn't said anything. Laura had a certain unmistakable glow about her, and Taft couldn't seem to keep his eyes off her—not that he ever could. His brother had loved his wife for most of their lives. Ridge loved seeing them all so happy.

In contrast to the Bowman clan, with each mile, the lovely woman beside him seemed to grow more and more quiet.

"Sorry about my crazy family," he said as they neared the River Bow. "I'm afraid they can be a little over-whelming."

She shook her head. "They were wonderful. So kind and welcoming, even though I'm a stranger. Everything was perfect. Destry is right. It was the best Christmas ever."

So why did she seem so sad? he wondered. He wanted

to ask, but the moment didn't seem right with Destry listening in from the backseat.

While she seemed to enjoy herself, he didn't miss the way she maintained a careful distance from the family. She smiled and laughed and chatted, all while keeping something of herself in reserve, as if she didn't want to let them all into her life too far.

That hadn't stopped everyone from falling for her, just like he had. Both Laura and Becca had ganged up to corner him in the kitchen and not-so-subtly dig for information about her and, he thought, to try to sniff out any romantic entanglements between the two of them.

He wanted to think he'd been sly and evasive, but judging by a certain crafty gleam in the expression worn by both of his sisters-in-law, he had a feeling he hadn't been very successful.

He glanced at Sarah again. Her broken arm was clutched to her stomach, and she seemed to be clenching and unclenching the other hand on her thigh.

He thought about what Destry had said…that the next Christmas would be even better for them. How could it possibly beat this one if Sarah wasn't there?

His heart seemed to race as the truth seeped through. He wanted her in his life permanently.

Yeah, it was early, but he had always been a man who knew what he wanted. Things hadn't worked out so well when it came to Melinda, but he knew in his heart that Sarah was different. She was sweet and kind. She loved his daughter and had seemed to enjoy his family.

He didn't know how they could make it work long-distance. With phone, email, Skype, maybe they could figure it out for the short term. He could arrange short visits to the coast, and maybe she could come back here during school vacations.

His mind raced with possibilities. What were the chances she might be willing to relocate? He couldn't leave the ranch, but maybe he could persuade her Pine Gulch had a wonderful elementary school that might be in need of a dedicated first-grade teacher. He would have to talk to the principal of the elementary school, Jenny Dalton, to see if she expected any positions to open up for the next school year....

Whoa. Slow it down, now. As they pulled up to the ranch house, he forced himself to rein in his thoughts as he would old Bob. These powerful feelings seething through him were too new, too raw. He needed time to become accustomed to them—not to mention that she seemed to be fighting this with everything she had.

They could talk later, when Destry was in bed, he vowed as they walked inside the house. They could sit by the fire again in the great room, and he would push until she told him what was bothering her.

Tri hopped to greet them first thing, wagging his tail with excitement.

"Destry, why don't you let Tri out? Then you can help me do evening chores, if you want."

"Sure," she said with that bright eagerness that always warmed his heart. He hoped she never lost that attitude, like helping her old dad feed the stock was a rare and precious treat.

"You're welcome to come down to the barn if you want," he offered to Sarah.

She still seemed subdued and didn't meet his gaze. "I think I'll pass, if you don't mind. My arm is kind of achy."

"No problem. We'll be back up to the house in an hour."

"Okay."

She gave him a smile he thought looked forced.

Yeah, they needed to have a talk. He would listen to her, would try to help with whatever bothered her and then he would tell her he was falling in love with her.

The back door opened just as she was rolling her suitcase one-handed out of her bedroom.

Her heart sank and her insides roiled. She was very afraid she would be sick—and not from the delicious meal she hadn't been able to eat much of at the Bowman family party.

If only she had been ten minutes faster, she would have been gone before they returned from the barn.

Skulking off in the darkness on Christmas night was a stupid and cowardly thing to do, but then she had spent a week being stupid and cowardly, running from this moment. Why ruin a perfect record?

Destry came in first, chattering away to her father about a horseback ride she wanted to take the next day.

She froze when she saw Sarah standing with her suitcase in her hand, stopping so abruptly her father nearly ran into her.

"Hey," Ridge said to his daughter, holding a hand to steady both of them. His gaze lifted, and he saw her and then the suitcase she pulled. For one brief instant, she saw a host of emotions she couldn't read in his gaze, ending in a fierce blaze of anger that he quickly contained.

"Going somewhere?"

She wanted to burst into tears, cover her face and

run out the door, but she had been cowardly enough for a dozen lifetimes.

She squared her shoulders. "Yes. I'm driving into Jackson for the night. I...found a hotel and arranged a flight back to California tomorrow."

Destry made a little sound of distress. "But why?" she wailed. "We were having such a great Christmas."

Her chest ached as if the girl had punched her. Oh, she hated this. "I know, honey. You've been wonderful. I've enjoyed our time together so much. I just... I have to go."

She didn't know what else to say, even as she heard how lame the words sounded.

"Why?" Ridge demanded.

For a fairly innocuous word, it sliced and clawed at her, leaving her emotions in shreds.

"I just do. I don't belong here. You've been kind enough to open your home to me, but...I don't want to overstay my welcome."

"So you're running off at 9:00 p.m. on Christmas night. That really seemed the best time to leave?"

"If you'll remember, I tried to leave a dozen times these past few days. There was always another reason why I should stay."

"And now you've run out of reasons. Is that what you're saying?"

He looked furious again, and something else, something deeper.

He looked hurt.

She thought of the kisses between them, all the unspoken feelings in her heart. More than she had wanted anything in her life—more than every dreamed-of Christmas gift thrown together—she wanted to stay here at the River Bow with him, to give these growing feelings a chance to blossom.

She knew she couldn't. He wouldn't want her here after he knew the truth—and if she was running out of anything, it was the dozens of excuses she had cowardly used to avoid exactly this moment.

"I don't belong here," she tried again, but he cut her off.

"You do and we both know it. You fit into this house—into our *lives*—perfectly."

She sucked in a breath as fresh pain jabbed her. So he sensed it, too, how *right* they could have been together, if things had been different.

Tears burned and she blinked quickly to force them back.

"I don't. I can't. If you knew the truth about me, you would agree."

"Tell me. You've been hiding something since the moment you showed up. What the hell is going on? Don't you even have the guts to tell me as you're walking out the door?"

She pressed a hand to her stomach. She had to tell him. Now. She gazed at Destry, watching the interaction with confused misery on her sweet features, and Sarah's heart broke all over again.

Ridge intercepted her look and shifted his attention to his daughter.

"Destry, will you go to your room, please?"

"But, Dad!"

"Please, Des."

Though she gave her father a mutinous look, she moved through the kitchen with the three-legged little dog hopping along behind her. Just before she left the room, she turned one more time to glare at Sarah.

"I thought we were friends. Friends don't just turn their backs on each other," she said, with all the dramatic flair of a preteen.

"I'm so sorry, Destry. I really am."

The snake-eyed look she received in return told her plainly the girl didn't believe her. She could hear Destry racing up the stairs and slamming her door hard behind her. Each sound only added to her guilt and pain.

"You want to tell me now what the hell is going on?" Ridge said. "You've been trying to run away since the moment you stepped onto the River Bow. Is it because I told you last night I was starting to have feelings for you? Because I'm falling in love with you?"

Joy burned through her, fierce and bright as a Christmas star. For a long moment, she wanted to just bask in it, then reality abruptly doused her elation. Those tears burned harder, and this time she couldn't seem to force them all back.

"You're not in love with me." Her voice sounded ragged, small. "You can't be."

He narrowed his gaze. "Hate to break it to you, sweetheart, but you don't get to decide whether I love you or not."

A tiny sound escaped—a gasp or a sob, she wasn't sure—and then another one. She had to leave soon, while she could still keep her tears contained.

"I didn't want this," she said. "I never should have come here. I'm so sorry."

"You're sorry I love you?" he asked harshly. "Or you're sorry you love me back? Whatever you think of me, I'm not stupid, Sarah. I know you have feelings for me, too."

It would be far easier to tell him he was mistaken,

that she didn't care for him at all. That she was leaving to avoid any further awkwardness between them.

She had lied all this time, but she knew she wouldn't be able to make that blatant a falsehood believable to either one of them.

"Admit it," he pressed. "You care about me, too."

She couldn't answer, could only gaze at him with her heart aching and misery pulsing through her with a heartbeat of its own.

Some of her mute distress must have showed on her features. His anger seemed to ease, and he took a step toward her, his eyes dark with concern.

"Sarah, what's going on? Just tell me. It can't be that bad. I love you. Whatever it is, we'll work it out, I swear."

"Not this," she whispered.

"Tell me."

This was the hardest thing she had ever done. She pressed her broken arm to her stomach, the cold, hard weight of the cast digging into her flesh through her clothes.

She couldn't delay anymore. She owed him an explanation, one she should have given the moment she rang the front doorbell of the River Bow.

She drew in a ragged breath through a throat that sudden burned with emotions and straightened her shoulders.

"Okay, I'll tell you," she said. "I think my brother killed your parents."

Chapter Thirteen

Ridge heard her, but somehow the words didn't seem real.

I think my brother killed your parents.

He couldn't think what to say for several long seconds, and she continued to gaze at him with sheer misery in her eyes.

"What are you talking about?"

His mouth felt numb suddenly and he could barely get the words out.

She pressed her lips together. "Sarah Whitmore hasn't always been my name. It was my mother's maiden name. Until the courts finally allowed us to legally change it when I was twelve, my name was Sarah Malikov. That's the rough translation, anyway. It's spelled completely differently, but Sarah is the English pronunciation."

"You're...Russian?"

"No. I'm American. I was born here and have lived

here all my life. My mother was, as well. My father, on the other hand, was from Moscow."

She drew in a shaky breath and seemed to press her cast farther into her stomach. "He was a *Pakhan* in a Russian *Bratva*. Basically the equivalent of a mob boss."

A mob boss. Her father? She taught first grade! How could this even be possible?

I think my brother killed your parents.

"And your...brother?" he managed.

"Followed right along in his footsteps. I told you we were all separated after the divorce. My father raised Josef—Joe—to be exactly like him."

"You said he was killed twelve years ago," he said. The forgotten half memory surged to the surface.

"He was. Twelve years ago this month, on Christmas Day."

That was only a few days after his parents died, he realized. Was there really a connection?

"He was killed in a hotel room in Boise during an argument with an associate after a criminal operation went wrong. I believe that job was the theft of your parents' art collection."

He tried to put the pieces together, but they were slippery as muddy calves and just as uncooperative.

"Why would you possibly think so? Because you found a painting in your father's things?"

She met his gaze, her blue eyes murky and dark. "Because I found *dozens* of paintings. A storage unit full of them. Your mother's work, as well as other Western artists."

She spoke in a low, emotionless voice, and he heard her words as if from a great distance, as if she were a stranger.

Apparently she was.

Dozens of paintings. It must be his parents' entire collection, or most of it, anyway. She couldn't possibly be making something like that up—but could the paintings actually have been squirreled away in a storage unit somewhere, all this time? It made sense and certainly explained why nothing much had ever turned up on the black market.

Ridge couldn't seem to think straight. His thoughts and emotions seemed to be racketing around like cats after a recalcitrant ball of string—shock, disbelief, anger. Surely it couldn't be true. Surely it was unimaginable that he and his brothers had been looking all these years for the murderers and suddenly a relative of a viable suspect just happened to show up on his doorstep.

Not just *happened to show up*. This had been planned from the beginning. She had come here on purpose. Suddenly Ridge could focus on only one thing that seemed to push away everything else—his deep, aching sense of betrayal.

"You've known. This whole time you were in my house, sleeping in my sister's room, laughing with my daughter—kissing me, damn it, letting me come to care about you—you kept this a secret."

Her mouth seemed to wobble, but she firmed it into a tight line. "Yes."

"Why?"

"I should have told you that first day. I meant to, but then I fell down your stairs and everything became so tangled."

"You still could have told me at any point in the past several days. Instead, you kept your mouth shut. This is one hell of a secret, Sarah. I can't believe this. Why didn't you say anything?"

She had known the answers to all the questions he and his siblings had been asking for a dozen years. He still couldn't seem to wrap his head around it. What if she was wrong? But why else would her father have all the paintings?

What a freaking mess.

"Why did you come here?" he demanded. "Why not just turn the paintings over to the authorities in the first place and let them handle it?"

Sarah didn't know how to answer. She couldn't tell him something had been driving her to come here, to meet the family of the woman who had painted such beautiful work. The moment she had seen those paintings, they had haunted her and then when she found out the deadly provenance, she could only think about giving them all back.

It made no sense, even to her, but it had seemed like the only thing she could do.

"I don't know," she answered, truthfully enough. "I've also asked myself how the artwork came to be in my father's possession in the first place and why he never sold it off, all these years later. Perhaps he sold a piece here or there. I won't know until your family insurance investigators go through the pieces and see if anything is missing. But whatever else anyone can say about Vasily Malikov, he was generally an astute, if absolutely amoral, businessman. He was always looking at the bottom line—so why would he hang on to everything and not sell it along the way?"

"You knew him. I didn't. You tell me."

She hadn't known him. Her father and his lifestyle had been completely foreign to her. She had *hated* visits with him. She used to suffer stomach cramps for weeks before every visit, but her mother would never have defied a court order.

"My father loved two things—my brother and vengeance."

"Vengeance."

He said the word with a grim emphasis that made her shiver.

"Yes. He lived and died by it. If someone crossed him, they paid the price. I'm positive the man who killed Joe wouldn't have made it far before my father found him and took back the stolen artwork he believed was his by rights, in his twisted way. As to why he kept it all these years, I can't say. Perhaps it was some kind of shrine to my brother or a reminder to my father of all that he had lost. Or maybe he was simply waiting until prices went up. I doubt we'll ever know."

"None of that explains why you didn't tell me the moment I answered the door that first day. You lied to me from the beginning."

"Yes," she said.

"Like father, like daughter."

Her face felt cold as blood rushed away at his deliberate cruelty. She had earned his disdain, every drop of it. That didn't make it hurt less.

"I have been trying to escape that legacy my entire life, but perhaps you're right. You understand now why I tried to warn you not to open your home to me. I knew you wouldn't want me here if you had known my family was more than likely involved somehow in your parents' murders."

"You're right about that," he snapped.

She forced herself to breathe around the pain. Her eyes watered, and the family room Christmas-tree lights through the kitchen doorway seemed to glimmer and merge.

Her beautiful Christmas—the best one ever, just as Destry said—lay in ruins like so much torn and tattered wrapping paper.

The season of hope and forgiveness was lovely in the abstract. In reality, it could be just as flimsy and insubstantial as that paper.

"You see now why I was leaving. I knew you would h-hate me when you found out." Despite all her best efforts, her voice wobbled and she had to fight down a sob again. "I'm sorry I didn't tell you. After I broke my arm, everything was so tangled, and by the time I could sort it all out, I already cared about you and Destry so much. I'm sorry to hurt you. So sorry, Ridge. I…thank you for everything. Please tell Destry—all your family—that I'm sorry. My attorney will be in touch."

"Why?"

She gripped her suitcase so hard her fingers felt as if they were fused into the handle. "So I can return the rest of the paintings to you, of course. Why else?"

She didn't think she had room for any more pain, but the shock in his eyes proved her wrong. "Really, Ridge? You honestly think so poorly of me that you think I would keep stolen property?"

He didn't answer, and another arrow found its way home.

"I suppose I can't blame you," she managed through the last of her strength. "As you said, I'm my father's daughter. I hope you can someday see I'm my own person before I am Vasily Malikov's child."

She turned and headed for the door and her rental car. She almost made it outside before he yanked her suitcase away. For one wild, breathless moment she thought he was going to carry it back inside for her.

I love you. Whatever it is, we'll work it out, I swear.

No. Instead, he stiffly walked to her rental car, opened the trunk and shoved the suitcase in.

He held the driver's door open for her. Furious as he was at her, the hard, implacable, *completely wonderful* man held the door open and even helped her inside the car. Then he backed away and stood outside on an ice-cold Christmas night without his coat, arms at his side as he watched her back the rental car out, turn it around and head down the road.

Only after she was certain he couldn't see her did the tears finally burst through.

"You want to tell us what's going on?"

Ridge looked up from his work to find his annoying-as-hell brothers watching him with matching frowns.

"I'm cleaning out the stalls," he growled. "Why don't you grab a couple of shovels and help instead of standing there with your thumbs up your asses?"

Taft raised an eyebrow at Trace before turning back to him.

"You seem to be doing a fine job. Judging by that little remark, I'd say shoveling, er, Shinola is just what you need to be doing right now."

After a sleepless night, he had been up as early as he could, looking for any kind of physical labor to hold back the pain.

"You two don't have anything better to do than come down here and make stupid comments?"

"Not really," Trace said.

"Speak for yourself," Taft muttered. "The kids stayed at their grandma Pendleton's last night. I could be sleeping in with my lovely wife right now. Or not sleeping in."

"So why are you here?" he demanded.

Again, they exchanged looks that made him want to punch one or both of them. In his current mood, he was pretty sure he could take them both without working up much of a sweat.

"Apparently Gabi received a rather frantic call from Destry this morning that Sarah left and now you've gone mental."

He kept shoveling, barely looking up at them. Maybe if he worked hard enough, this ache in his chest would ease. "Did she?"

"Is it true you took down all the Christmas decorations in the middle of the night?" Trace asked.

He let out a huffing sort of sigh. Okay, that *had* been a little mental, a crazy impulse he couldn't really explain. One minute, he'd been sitting by the fire and looking at the Christmas tree, the next, he'd been pulling off ornaments.

"Not everything. Just the big tree in the great room and the garlands. There's still plenty of Christmas crap all over the house. It had to come down sometime, didn't it?"

He shoveled harder, avoiding their gazes and the concern he didn't want to see.

"Why did Sarah leave?" Trace asked, in the same kind of overly solicitous voice a police chief would probably have to use when dealing with people who needed a seventy-two hour hold or something. "Did you two have a fight?"

His whole body ached as if both brothers had taken turns pummeling him. He didn't know how the hell he would ever get past it. "You could say that," he muttered.

"It must have been a pretty good one if you were taking down your Christmas tree at two in the morning on December 26," Trace observed.

He wasn't obliged to explain any of his actions to his younger brothers, so he opted not to answer.

"What did you do to her?" Taft pressed.

He stopped shoveling and gave a steely glare that encompassed both of them. "What makes you think I did anything?"

"Just a wild guess," Taft said. "I thought she seemed really sweet. Laura loved her and kept saying how perfect she was for you."

"I had the same conversation with Becca," Trace offered.

He gritted his teeth as if it took all his force of will and reminded himself it would be juvenile to "accidentally" let a little shit fly on both of his brothers.

"You both misunderstood," he said calmly. "She was a guest in my home. That's all."

A guest there under false pretenses, he wanted to add.

"That doesn't quite explain why you took down your Christmas tree in the middle of the night and have been shoveling out the stalls since before sunrise," Taft drawled.

He wanted to tell them it was none of their damn business, but that would have been a lie. They needed to know about Sarah's deception and her family history.

He had to tell them, but didn't know how. He was ridiculously aware that after everything, part of the reason for his hesitation was a reluctance for them to think poorly of her.

He was suddenly exhausted, so tired he couldn't think straight. He leaned against the half wall of the stall, the handle of the shovel loose in his hand.

"She's gone."

"That's what Destry said," Trace said. "She told Gabi that Sarah came home right after our party and packed up her things."

"I don't get it," Taft said, with more compassion than he would have given his former hell-raising brother credit for. "She seemed to be enjoying herself well enough. We all thought she was great. Was it something we all said?"

Ridge took off his leather glove and rubbed at his face.

"No. I guess her conscience just caught up with her, and she was tired of the lies."

"What did she lie about?" Trace asked.

Damn, he didn't want to do this. He needed air suddenly. Air and sunlight and the pure crystalline beauty of a cold December morning on his ranch.

He grabbed his Stetson from the hook where he'd hung it, shoved it on and walked outside. After a moment the twins followed.

"What's going on?" Taft demanded.

"You know that painting she brought, the one Mom did of Caidy?"

"Yes," Trace said, his tone wary.

"Apparently, she's got plenty more where that came from. A whole storage unit full of stolen artwork from the famous Bowman Western art collection."

His brothers both stared at him, and he was aware of a horse whinnying somewhere, of the cold puffs of air they were all breathing out, of the hard knot that had lodged in his chest sometime in the past twelve hours and didn't show any sign of easing.

Taft was the first to break the silence. "Sorry. She has what?"

"She has more artwork from the collection. Dozens of items. She doesn't know if it's complete or not but it's in a storage unit somewhere belonging to her father, where it's apparently been since the murders."

"Her father—" Trace began.

"Was a Russian mafia boss whose only son was apparently killed days after the murders just a few hours from here. Sarah doesn't think it's a coincidence. For the record, neither do I."

His brothers stared.

"You're saying Sarah's father and brother were involved in the murders?" Trace finally asked. His eyes had that flinty look Ridge recognized. Sometimes he forgot what a damn good cop his brother was.

"The father, I don't know. The brother, most definitely. He was murdered in Boise a few days after the murders. Sarah's theory is, her brother fought with a partner who killed him, then her father took vengeance for his son's murder and ended up with the artwork. Why he kept it all is a mystery to her. She was estranged from the man and stumbled onto the storage unit while taking care of his affairs after his death."

He couldn't look at either of his brothers, wary at what their reaction must be. Taft had welcomed Sarah into his home. She had played with all their children, had held Trace's baby, had chatted with their wives—all while keeping this huge secret. He still couldn't quite wrap his head around it all.

"She told you all this last night before she left?" Trace asked. Some of the hardness of his features seemed to have eased.

"Yeah. Not until last night. She was here for days without saying a word. She should have told me when she first showed up at the ranch. She stayed here under false pretenses."

"The way I remember it, she stayed here because you insisted," Taft pointed out. Ridge actually formed a fist and barely refrained from letting it swing—he couldn't deny the truth of what his brother said.

"I guess that makes me the idiot, doesn't it?"

"Is that why you're mad at her?" Trace asked after a pause. "Because she didn't tell you her family might have been involved in Mom and Dad's deaths?"

Mad was a mild word for this chaos of emotions broiling under his skin. "Isn't that enough?"

"Just wondering. How old is Sarah?" Trace asked. "I'm guessing around Caidy's age, right?"

"Give or take a year or so."

"So she would have been, what, sixteen, seventeen?" He narrowed his gaze. "Yeah. And your point?"

"Do you think she had anything to do with the murders?"

He stared. "No. Of course not! She was estranged from her father most of her life. She barely knew the man, and she certainly wasn't some big art thief."

Trace shrugged. "In that case, feel free to correct me if I'm wrong, but it seems to me you're not just an idiot. You're a *stupid* idiot."

He ground his teeth and drew that fist again. "You want to put some muscle behind that, baby brother?"

"Don't be an even bigger ass," Trace said. "Tough as you are, you can't take on both of us."

"Don't drag me into this," Taft protested. "I'm just along for the ride."

What was he doing? He wasn't going to fight with his brothers, as angry as he was at the world in general. Ridge raked a hand through his hair and realized he was suddenly freaking cold.

Why the hell were they standing outside? Oh, right. He had walked out first. He felt as if he had been in a daze since the moment he had walked into the house the night before and found Sarah holding her suitcase.

"She lied to me. That's what bothers me. Or at least she neglected to mention something pretty damn important. She stayed in my house, she hung out with my daughter, she spent Christmas with all of us, for crying out loud."

She made me love her.

Trace raised an eyebrow. "So?"

"So the whole time, she knew her family had been involved in destroying ours."

"She brought us Mom's painting, though," Taft pointed out. "She didn't have to do that. She could have just stayed quiet about the whole thing, and nobody would have known. That says something about her, doesn't it?"

He sighed. "She said she's going to have her attorney work with the authorities to catalog what's there and return the whole collection to us."

His announcement was met with a long, echoing silence, and both brothers looked at him with the same astounded expression.

"Man, I hate to say this, but Trace is right," Taft finally said. "You are one stupid idiot. And an ass, to boot. So she didn't tell you the truth. Sounds to me like she's intending to do the right thing now. Or do you think she's lying about giving back the collection?"

He shook his head. "No! Of course not. If she says she'll do it, she will. I trust her word."

The brothers looked at each other. Taft was the first to snicker, but Trace wasn't far behind.

"Wait. Let me get this straight," Trace said. "You're saying you trust the word of a woman who has spent the past several days lying to you?"

Ridge closed his eyes, feeling the pale sunlight on his face as he pondered the ridiculousness of his own words. She had lied to him about her father, her brother. She hadn't told him about the paintings.

He had no reason to trust that she was telling the truth now, but somehow he couldn't make himself believe otherwise.

"Yeah. Yeah, I do. I believe she fully plans to give us back the rest of the paintings. She had no reason to lie about that part, did she?"

"So you don't think Sarah had anything to do with the murders and you believe she's going to give us back the paintings she found. You trust her word. Explain to me again the part that has you pissed off enough to take down the decorations on an eighteen-foot Christmas tree by yourself last night?"

As he listened to Trace's completely reasonable question, that hard knot in his chest seemed to jiggle a little. It didn't quite break free, but it was close.

"Because I'm an ass," he murmured.

"No," Taft said cheerfully. "You're just in love. Welcome to the club, dude. It makes you do all kinds of crazy things."

"Like jump in a river to save your ex-fiancee's children." Trace jabbed at his twin.

"Or give up a decade-long quest for justice and vengeance in order to protect a young girl's future," Taft countered.

"Looks like I made the right choice on that one," Trace said. "Thanks to Sarah, we might find all those answers anyway."

Trace was right. Ridge rubbed a hand over his eyes, exhausted all over again. She had brought them more than a painting their mother had created—even more than the dozens of stolen art pieces that might eventually find their way back to the River Bow.

She had brought them the chance to find answers to the questions that had haunted them all.

She didn't have to come in person to deliver the painting. She could have made a phone call. *Oh, by the way, I think I have something that might be yours.* Or she could have handled the whole thing through attorneys.

Or she could have kept the artwork and sold it piece by piece on the black market and made a freaking fortune.

She had done none of those things. Instead, she had taken a plane a thousand miles, had rented a car, then had driven out to the River Bow to speak with Margaret and Frank Bowman's descendants in person. She had shown amazing courage and strength of character.

He claimed he loved her but at the first bit of difficulty, he had shoved her away, said horrible things to her. He had carried her lousy suitcase out to the car, for heaven's sake.

He wanted a do-over for the entire past twelve hours.

He opened his eyes to find both of his brothers looking at him with amused, indulgent expressions.

"What the hell am I supposed to do now?"

Taft shrugged. "If it were me, I'd already be in my truck going after her."

"Same goes," Trace said.

He didn't know where she had gone, other than Jackson to stay the night then she was catching a flight out today. He didn't have the first idea how to find her and decided his best bet was to call in reinforcements.

He headed for the house. "Trace, now you've got something to work with. Go do your cop thing. You should be able to track down the brother, Josef Malikov, son of Vasily Malikov, who was some kind of mob boss. See if you can find out details of what happened to him, then look for any known associates who might have disappeared around the same time. Sarah thinks the two fought, and her brother was killed in the process. She also believes her father probably had the man offed who killed his son. Let's see what else we can discover."

"What can I do?" Taft asked.

"Keep your fingers crossed that I can find her. And that she'll find it in her heart to forgive me when I do."

Sarah sat in the café of her hotel, moving her spoon aimlessly through the oatmeal she had ordered but couldn't eat, lifting up her coffee cup then setting it back down again without a sip, leafing through a magazine without registering a single word on the pages.

She was a mess. Plain and simple.

Trying to sleep had been an abject failure. Apparently, eating wasn't something she was up to handling today, either.

The busy hotel bustled with people, families eating together or couples wearing what looked like expensive matching skiwear.

Jackson Hole was packed at Christmastime. She should have expected people would flock here to ski for the holidays. Finding a room had been a challenge, and she had ended up with one that would normally have been way out of her budget.

She could have just driven around in the rental car all night for all the sleep she ended up getting in that pricey hotel bed.

Her flight didn't leave for hours. How would she possibly fill that time? She didn't feel like shopping on this busy day-after-Christmas return day. It made no sense to pay extra for late checkout at the hotel, only to stare at a TV showing programs she didn't care about.

Since she still had the rental car, perhaps she should just take a drive through the raw wintry splendor of the Tetons. She took a sip of her coffee—an actual sip this time—trying to summon the energy to do anything.

All she really wanted to do was curl up in a ball and weep for days, but that wouldn't accomplish anything.

She felt more bruised and battered than the day she fell down the stairs at the River Bow, as if every muscle and sinew had been stretched to the breaking point.

She deserved the pain and more. A little honesty on her part would have prevented this whole thing. If she had told him that very first day why she had come to the River Bow, she never would have been in this situation. She wouldn't have fallen in love with the man and wouldn't now be consumed with the pain of losing him before she had ever really known the joy of being in love with a good man.

A laughing couple came in with a girl about Destry's age, dressed in cute brown snow pants and a pink parka that would have looked adorable on Des. She watched them interact for a moment until the pain became too much.

She had loved Destry as much as she loved the girl's father. Her heart felt shattered, knowing she had left without saying a proper goodbye to her.

She sat for a few moments more, until watching the laughing father, mother, girl became too tired for her then she signed the bill with a healthy tip and left the restaurant to return to her room.

There was no sense staying here. She would drive around for a while, perhaps make a stop at the elk refuge on the edge of Grand Teton National Park then head for the airport.

Packing the few things she had used from her suitcase overnight took her all of five minutes. When she finished, she took the elevator down to the lobby and handed her keys back to the polite desk clerks.

Just as she turned away, she caught sight of a tall man in a cowboy hat charging through the door, and her heartbeat kicked up a notch.

Settle down, she ordered herself. Tall cowboys in Jackson Hole weren't exactly an endangered species. She reached for the handle of her suitcase and started for the door when that particular cowboy shifted in her direction and she froze as if he had tossed her out into the snow.

Her heart began to pound and nerves twirled in her

stomach. How had he found her? She hadn't told him where she was staying, had she?

More importantly, *why* was he here? Had he come to fight with her more, to inform her how wrong she was to have kept the truth from him as long as she had?

Like father, like daughter.

The words were seared into her psyche. She drew in a shaky breath. She couldn't do this. Not here, in this bustling lobby. She wasn't strong enough to face him, not after she had been sobbing all night and probably looked a mess.

He hadn't seen her yet. Instead, he was heading to the front desk she had just left, probably looking for her room number—unless this was all a horrible coincidence, which she sincerely doubted.

She considered her options, none of them very appealing. The best of the lot was to avoid the situation entirely and sneak out a different way, without him spying her.

Just then, a large family carrying snowboards and skis tromped through the lobby in heavy ski boots. She slipped into step beside them, trying to blend as they all crossed the lobby together.

The strategy almost worked. Unfortunately they were heading to the front, probably catching one of the ski resort shuttles, while she needed to go to the parking lot.

Just as she turned to take different doors, she heard a deep, focused, wonderfully familiar voice. "Sarah."

Shoot.

With a few more pithy words racketing around in her brain, she forced herself to turn slowly, hating this, hating her father and Joe for leaving her this legacy of pain to deal with. Even hating Ridge a little for being so wonderful that she couldn't help but fall in love with him.

"Ridge," she said in a feigned tone of surprise. "What are you doing here?"

"You left your scarf."

He held up the soft knitted gift Destry had given her. Somehow it must have slipped off on her way out the door. The night before when she realized she didn't have it, she had sobbed more tears than she thought she possessed.

Her stomach fluttered at the sight of the sweet little scarf in his big, callused, outstretched hand.

"Thank you," she said. She reached for it, taking care that their fingers wouldn't brush, then tucked it into her pocket. "I wondered what happened to it."

"I found it on the sidewalk this morning. It must have fallen when you were on your way to the car."

"Ah. It was very nice of you to return it."

He looked so wonderful to her, all chiseled angles and hard edges, with his mouth set in an unsmiling line and those beautiful green eyes watching her with an expression she couldn't read. Why was he here? Why had he come all this way?

"How did you find me?"

Even as she asked the question, the answer seemed unimportant in light of her pounding heart. Emotions pressed in, heavy and suffocating. She loved him so much she couldn't breathe around it.

"I put Destry on it. It wasn't that tough, if you want the truth. You left the number of the hotel on a paper Destry found in your room. She did a reverse lookup on the computer, and when it came back to this hotel, I... took a chance."

Simply to return her scarf? Somehow she didn't think so.

"Thank you. It means a great deal to me. When I returned to San Diego, I would have missed it."

"What about us? Destry and me. Would you have missed us, too?"

She met his gaze. She couldn't seem to catch a breath suddenly, as if she had just jumped from the ski lift onto a black diamond run she couldn't handle.

"Don't do this, Ridge," she whispered. "Please, don't."

"Do what?"

"Make everything worse. I'm sorry again that I didn't tell you about my father and about Joe. You deserved to know, and I was wrong to keep that information from you, no matter my reasons."

"Yeah. You should have told me."

She tried not to reel all over again. Somehow she was able to keep control over her emotions.

"Well, okay. Now that we have that out of the way, I should go. I have a plane to catch."

"Not for five hours," he countered. "Destry also went online and figured out the only flight from Jackson to San Diego doesn't leave until later this afternoon."

"She's quite the clever little detective, isn't she?"

"When she has to be. She doesn't want to lose you, either."

That single word caught her heart like a butterfly net. She jerked her gaze up at him and desperately wished she could read more in that glittery green gaze.

"E-either?"

He gave her one of his slow, beautiful smiles that sent her pulse skyrocketing. "She wanted to come with me. She wasn't at all happy when I dropped her off to hang out with Gabi. I finally had to tell her there were certain things a man just has to do without any help from his eleven-year-old daughter."

She couldn't seem to swallow past the lump in her throat. "Like what?"

"Like grovel to the woman he loves."

She again caught on a single word. *Loves.* Not *loved.* Not *used to love.*

Loves.

Heedless of the busy lobby and the other guests bustling around them, she could only stare at him. Now she could read his expression—fierce, warm, tender.

She allowed herself to bask it in, only for a moment then did her best to force herself to focus on sense. This couldn't be happening. She didn't deserve for him to look at her like that.

"Ridge—"

"I took down the Christmas tree last night."

The non sequitur threw her. "You…did?"

"I couldn't look at it anymore. All those glittery ornaments, the garland, the lights. It hurt too much to see that huge symbol of joy in my house when I was feeling anything but happy."

"Oh."

"So this morning Des got freaked out when she woke up and found it like that, so she called Gabi, who enlisted Trace, who called Taft. My two brothers ambushed me this morning. They called me any number of names, not least of which was a stupid idiot for letting you go."

She frowned. "Did you tell them? About Joe and my father and the paintings?"

"Yeah. For the record, I gave them all that information *before* they told me in no uncertain terms that I needed to haul my ass here and bring you back."

"They said that, knowing everything?"

He nodded, reaching for her hand. Her heart was going to pound out of her chest. She couldn't seem to grasp a thought in her head through the mingled sorrow and joy of seeing him again.

"I love my brothers," he said simply. "They drive me absolutely crazy sometimes—what else are families for, right?—but they're generally both wise men who apparently have a much smarter perspective on this issue than I did."

"But I lied to you. I don't blame you for being furious with me."

"I was. Last night. This morning, I have a little more clarity. Trace wisely pointed out that you were just a girl when this all happened and that you barely knew your father or your brother. It's completely unfair to blame you for what happened to my parents. I certainly wouldn't want anybody blaming Destry for the poor decisions I've made in my life."

"The murder of your parents was far from just a poor decision," she protested.

"True. And it wasn't your fault, either."

He lifted her fingers to his mouth, this big, rough rancher, in an act of incredible tenderness that rocked her to the core.

"I love you, Sarah. I wasn't looking for it and sure as hell didn't expect it to show up on my doorstep one December morning, but there it is. I love you. I love your patience with my daughter, I love the comfort I find sitting beside you on a cold winter's night, I love that smile of yours that makes everything seem easier. I know we haven't known each other long, and we still have a lot to discover about each other, but I wanted you to know my feelings before you left. It only seemed right that we have no more secrets between us."

How could she believe him? Did she dare take a chance.

Yes.

She loved him. These few days had been magical, and she selfishly wanted more.

Joy burst through her like exploding Christmas bulbs, so bright and pure she couldn't contain it, and she smiled at him with all the tenderness spilling over inside her.

"In that case, I should probably tell you one more thing."

"What's that?" he asked.

"I love you, Ridge. I love the way you are with Destry, I love watching you care for your ranch, I love how you watch out for your neighbors. You're the hardest-working man I've ever met, but I love seeing you have fun with your family, too. I love you. I've never felt this way about anyone."

At her words, he grinned slowly, green eyes blazing. "That's the best Christmas gift anybody's ever given me, even if it is a day late."

He stepped forward. Right there in the lobby, he bent down and kissed her softly, sweetly, with an aching tenderness that made those tears start all over again.

She didn't know how she could swing so abruptly from despair to this bright glowing happiness in a matter of moments, but it didn't matter. The only important thing in her life was this man, this moment. And the miraculous joy she had found in the place she least expected it.

Epilogue

Ridge stood in front of the River Bow fireplace in his Western-cut tuxedo, anticipation and happiness bubbling through him like the champagne chilling in the kitchen being readied for all the toasts that would be made on his and Sarah's behalf in a little while.

"How are you holding up?" Taft asked the question from beside him, dressed in his own tuxedo.

Ridge hadn't been able to choose between the twins as best man so they had ended up drawing straws. Taft had ended up with this duty, but Trace hadn't complained, saying he definitely got the better end of the stick.

"Good. Great. It's a fabulous day, right? One I'll remember the rest of my life, I know. But to be honest, at this moment I just want it to be over."

His brother grinned. "Oh, how I remember that feeling. Just keep in mind, it won't be over. All the fun stuff is just beginning, right? That's probably what I'm supposed to say, anyway, being the best man and all that. The house looks great, by the way."

Ridge looked around at the festively decorated house. All the women he loved had outdone themselves making the place glow for the holidays. Destry and Sarah—with help from Caidy, Laura, Becca, Gabi, Ava and sweet little Maya along with Sarah's best friend from San Diego, Nicki—had been working for several days to decorate for this.

Though Thanksgiving was still a week away, his beautiful Sarah had insisted on a Christmas theme for their wedding and the result was a fairyland of lights and ornaments, ribbons and garlands.

It was a warm, welcoming place for a wedding—in no small part because of the splendid paintings that had been rehung in places of honor throughout the house.

After much discussion, he and his siblings had all picked several of their favorites from their mother's work and then had permanently lent the rest—along with the artwork of other Western artists she had collected through the years—to the small art museum in Pine Gulch, which would keep them on special rotating display so others could enjoy them, too.

It had been the right decision, though not an easy one.

Ridge shifted, as the music played softly and everyone waited for the bride to appear.

What a year this had been, filled with more happiness than he ever believed possible. Somehow he and Sarah had managed to work out the long-distance thing with video chats, lengthy phone calls that lasted long into the night and as many back-and-forth visits as they could manage with their schedules.

When her school contract ended in June, she had moved into an apartment in Pine Gulch, taking a summer job tutoring and signing a contract that started in the fall to teach at the elementary school.

The summer had been wonderful, filled with moonlit horseback rides, fishing trips with Destry, long, laughter-filled talks as Sarah helped him with chores around the ranch.

She merged perfectly into all their lives.

He had worried that Caidy, in particular, would take a long time to come around to her. His sister had suffered more than the rest of them at their parents' murder, since she had been there at the time and had seen the whole thing, and he had been worried she would never be able to accept the sister of the man who had killed their parents.

Their relationship had been strained at first. Then Trace had shown Caidy photographs of the two men they now knew had planned and carried out the heist that had turned into a murder—Sarah's brother, Joe, and an associate of her father's organization named Carl Bair.

Caidy—the only living eyewitness to the crimes—had immediately pointed to Bair's photograph and tearfully said he was the one who had killed both parents after Frank came at him with a shotgun, while Joe, Sarah's brother, had tried to stop him.

From the information Trace gleaned from Becca's mother a few years earlier, they knew the job was never supposed to have been violent. The thieves were expecting an empty house. Only unforeseen circumstances had led to Frank, Margaret and Caidy being there instead of at Caidy's choir concert.

The way Trace figured it, the two had fought after

the job went so horribly wrong, and Bair ended up killing Joe.

Just as Sarah predicted, Bair disappeared right after the murder, probably killed by someone else in Vasily's organization acting on his orders.

Caidy and Sarah had both cried in each other's arms at the family meeting where Trace strung together all the bits of evidence he had collected—and his sister and the woman he loved had been best of friends ever since.

Ridge knew it was a huge relief to Sarah to know that while her brother had certainly been an accessory to the murders, he hadn't pulled the trigger and had actually tried to call off Bair from killing their mother.

He pushed away thoughts of sorrow and loss as the small string orchestra softly played chamber music. This was his wedding day, and he wanted only happiness in his heart.

Finally, when he didn't think he could stand another moment of anticipation, the orchestra switched to "Ode to Joy," the song Sarah had chosen as her bridal song. He looked up to the top of the staircase, and there she was, stunning and delicate, ethereal as any Christmas angel.

His heart swelled in his chest until he couldn't breathe around the emotions.

She stood next to Trace, who felt he had won the place of honor by having the privilege of giving her away.

Ridge glanced at Destry, who looked up the stairs with her hands clasped to her chest and a dreamy expression on her freckled little face, as if she'd just been granted her dearest Christmas wish.

As Sarah walked down the stairs—those stairs that had started it all—past the beautiful framed art his mother had created, his stomach suddenly jumped with unexpected nerves.

He had failed at this once. What made him think he could do it right this time? He was impatient and could be inflexible. He liked things his way, as any of his siblings could have told her.

What if he was just a lousy husband and ended up making her miserable?

Suddenly, the highlighted words in that chapter of Luke came back to his memory, as if offered as a calming gift from the father he had loved and admired so much.

Fear not.

The words steadied him, and he smiled even as heavy emotion burned in his throat. This was right and perfect. He loved Sarah and considered her the most precious gift a man could have.

He wasn't afraid.

He only had room in his heart now for joy.

* * * * *

Merry Christmas
& A Happy New Year!

Thank you for a wonderful
2013...

A sneaky peek at next month…

Cherish™

ROMANCE TO MELT THE HEART EVERY TIME

My wish list for next month's titles…

In stores from 20th December 2013:

☐ The Final Falcon Says I Do – Lucy Gordon

& The Greek's Tiny Miracle – Rebecca Winters

☐ Happy New Year, Baby Fortune! – Leanne Banks

& Bound by a Baby – Kate Hardy

In stores from 3rd January 2014:

☐ The Man Behind the Mask – Barbara Wallace

& The Sheriff's Second Chance – Michelle Celmer

☐ English Girl in New York – Scarlet Wilson

& That Summer at the Shore – Callie Endicott

Available at WHSmith, Tesco, Asda, Eason, Amazon and Apple

Just can't wait?

1213/23

Special Offers

Every month we put together collections and longer reads written by your favourite authors.

Here are some of next month's highlights—and don't miss our fabulous discount online!

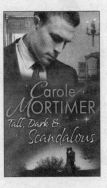

On sale 3rd January   On sale 3rd January   On sale 20th December

Save 20%
on all Special Releases

Come in from the cold this Christmas with two of our favourite authors. Whether you're jetting off to Vermont with Sarah Morgan or settling down for Christmas dinner with Fiona Harper, the smiles won't stop this festive season.

Visit:
www.millsandboon.co.uk

MILLS & BOON®
Book Club

Join the Mills & Boon Book Club

Want to read more **Cherish**™ books?
We're offering you **2 more** absolutely **FREE!**

We'll also treat you to these fabulous extras:

- Exclusive offers and much more!

- FREE home delivery

- FREE books and gifts with our special rewards scheme

Get your free books now!

visit www.millsandboon.co.uk/bookclub
or call Customer Relations on 020 8288 2888

The World of Mills & Boon®

There's a Mills & Boon® series that's perfect for you. We publish ten series and, with new titles every month, you never have to wait long for your favourite to come along.

Blaze®
Scorching hot, sexy reads
4 new stories every month

By Request
Relive the romance with the best of the best
9 new stories every month

Cherish™
Romance to melt the heart every time
12 new stories every month

Desire™
Passionate and dramatic love stories
8 new stories every month